HAWESWATER

ALSO BY SARAH HALL

The Electric Michelangelo

HAWESWATER

Sarah Hall

HARPER PERENNIAL

NEW YORK • LONDON • TORONTO • SYDNEY

HARPER ● PERENNIAL

First published in Great Britain in 2002 by Faber and Faber Ltd.
Reprinted here by arrangement with Faber and Faber Ltd.

P.S.™ is a trademark of HarperCollins Publishers.

HarperCollins books may be purchased for educational, business, or
sales promotional use. For information please write: Special Markets
Department, HarperCollins Publishers, 10 East 53rd Street,
New York, NY 10022.

FIRST HARPER PERENNIAL EDITION PUBLISHED 2006.

Library of Congress Cataloging-in-Publication Data
Hall, Sarah.
Haweswater / Sarah Hall.— 1st Harper Perennial ed.
p. cm.
ISBN-10: 0-06-081725-9 (pbk.)
ISBN-13: 978-0-06-081725-1 (pbk.)
1. Country life—Fiction. 2. Westmorland (England)—Fiction. I. Title
PR6108.A49H39 2006
813'.—dc22   2006040071

06 07 08 09 10 ❖/RRD 10 9 8 7 6 5 4 3 2 1

For my family

I'm standing in a place where I once loved.
The rain is falling. The rain is my home.
I think words of longing: a landscape
out to the very edge of what's possible.

YEHUDA AMICHAI

– Prologue –

The sound of water slipping through the wooden spokes of the cartwheels was like a slow, soft-washing hum. The vehicle breached the surface, parting the liquid as it moved, and leaving behind a temporary wake. From his position on the cart's seat the man could see that he would have to drive through over four feet of water if he wanted to pass back along the village to the high farm track on the slopes of the mountains, which would take him home. There was no other route he could take out of the head of the valley. The new concrete road was cut off by the flood, it was completely inaccessible. He peered through the water, trying to remember if the slope under it was steeper than he predicted, so that the cart would up-end and sink, sucking the horse in with it.

The man was accustomed to driving through rivers and floods in this farm vehicle, he had done so before, many times, in order to reach remote parts of the terrain where his animals needed tending or a landslide had brought down the farm walls. His horse was sure footed, an obedient creature, and the cart was sturdy. He had confidence in his working of both. He shucked the reins and the horse and cart went deeper, out into the swirling water. The shallows fell upwards behind him.

This water had once been only a gentle, tumbling river. The man thought to himself that he had never noticed the constant sush-sushing of wheels cutting liquid then, when he crossed it, as he noticed it now. But now it was an inescapable noise, it had him encircled. He listened to the sound. The rise and fall of the water's tensile voice. Its sound was unusual, a continuance of text in a land of broken fluid, of forced rock. But it was not the sound that was unusual, thought the man, it was the water itself, because there was something dangerous and slow and final about it. Something eerie and unending.

This was a monumental flood, water of epic proportions. It turned through the wooden spokes relentlessly, and as it did so it became like a music that is accidental, deeply beautiful and made only once. Somatic music that fills in space and time. A corrugated harp of orchestral rivers. Like the long end-verses of a ballad, he thought, when the key voice is joined and overcome by others. And even as the man hated this water, he could not help but find it beautiful. It stood for more than itself and it sang of its presence. But then, he was the kind of man who would have seen a mask of green fire struggling to get free from the throat of a dying bird.

Over the rippling surface of the flood he could see the uppermost skeletons of three ruptured buildings. He knew them to be a church, because he had prayed there, an old inn, where he had taken his draughts of a weekend, and a farm cottage, because he had helped a neighbour to re-hang the iron guttering after the mighty storm of two Septembers ago. In a matter of days or weeks they would be submerged, but for now they rose from the water like pieces of grey bone and he found himself divining in reverse, looking for old land. In the thick sky overhead, a dozen or so gulls were turning heavy, inhibited loops. Two or three were bobbing on the water, far out in the middle of the lake. Their calls raucous and belonging to the coastal air, to stretches of open sea, the birds seemed out of place in the dense, wooded valley.

The man pulled back on the reins and the horse and the music stopped. He called down from his seat on the cart to a sheepdog that was eeling through the liquid a foot from the cart.

– Chase, Chase. Gudgirl, close.

As if words were needed to call the animal, though a whistle, short, short and long, would have articulated his message just the same. Perhaps he had wanted to hear his own voice right then, for company, above the quiet expanse of water. And looking down to be certain, there was Chase, her slick seal's head slicing the waves, tufted ears held back, and her two bright eyes, one brown and one pale blue, looking up at her master, so that the thin moons of the white part of her eyes appeared to be cupping each iris. It made the dog look soulful. Gudog. Though it could have been the man's own soulfulness which he saw reflected in the eyes of his loyal companion. It was in everything now.

It began to rain, a fat slapping rain that ringed in the water and leapt up out of it. The air became blue with its speed. Rain hissed like soft glass coming from the sky. A cough of distant thunder in the throat of hills to the north-east. The man reached in his pocket, pulled out a flat cloth cap and put it on over his straw hair. He resumed his course, past the sinking walls of the valley's sloped fields. And there again was the soft-washing music. Water sang below and above him now. He was surrounded, held within it. The wood of the cart spotted and soon turned dark, as if sweating from labour, and its old, oily wooden scent was released easily into the dampness. The rancid, buttery fragrance of wool grease crept from the corners of the cart where some fleece had collected, it lifted and found its way up to the man's nose. Rain camouflaged the stains on the cart's wooden planks, the blood, the fluid and discharge, made during the births and deaths of many animals.

The cart was a quarter full of hay, a poor load even in the wet summer of that year, but it was all that was left to take from this place beyond the water, soon to be out of reach. So he would not come back here again. The farm which he took his load from had once been his own, managed and worked by his family, and even though the rents had been paid to the estate, he had still felt a sense of right, of possession. After the flood these would cease to exist in this valley for the man, in all but memory. He didn't want the hay, it wasn't essential to his new farm and it was spoiling quickly in the rain, but he took it like a man takes bread to eat, absently and without thought because his stomach demands it. It was simply that time of year. The cycle of the land had come back around to ripeness, sweetening the long grass, then starching it. He could have stopped the cart and pulled some tarpaulin over it but he did not. He had told his wife that this was the reason for his return to the old farm, yet, being the woman she was, she had known it to be a lie, the gentlest deceit.

The man's face and his hair melted into each other and both were the colour of red straw. Children could have landed safely in this face from a high jump off a barn rafter. He was broad set and heavy with muscle, and his tweed jacket was worn on the shoulders where his full form stretched the fabric thin. His boots were old and the laces had been replaced many times. His hands were raw over the leather reins, their nails dwarfed inside wide, swollen fingers. He was not unlike many of the other farmers of the district in appearance.

Then there was the matter of his heart. Inside his old heart a new one was growing and pushing to get out, and inside that one another one, and another, all pushing to get out. So many hearts. And that was how grief worked inside the man. Filling his chest cavity so full of hearts that it almost became sore to touch on the outside and he stooped over with the weight. So much of his life was gone. More than his home and his fields, more than the valley which contained his familiars.

Behind him was the end of his village; in front of him a swelling lake of colourless water. The cart struggled against the fluid pressure, uncertain currents jostling for a place in the filling basin, the horse now rearing up, shoulder-deep. He tightened the reins, clicking his tongue. One wheel was no longer secure on the valley floor. The cart pitched, righted itself again as it caught a solid piece of land. A slight whinny from the horse, but it moved on.

He did not look back over his worn shoulder to the place he had just left. There was a better image, an older vision, that he preferred. The grey-black cottage that had once housed his family and which he had just departed was now an imperfect ring of rubble and slate. It was a quarter of its original height, perhaps less. There was no longer a name carved on a piece of slate by the door, no children inside the cottage laughing or jumping in the corners like trapped frogs. There was no roof to speak of, only a thin web of cloud that stretched a useless tent between the shallow walls. Whelter Farm had ceased to exist on the raised land to the west side of the valley, and water was half-way up the garden, snaking at the foundations.

But underneath, the cellar was undamaged, save for a sheen of lime dust which covered the floor and a fast-dripping gable wall. On this last visit, the man had not spent long in the bowels of his old habitation. He simply removed a tatty book from his inside jacket pocket, brushed a rough palm over its cover. The man with the face of red straw put the book inside an old wooden tool box in the cellar's alcove and locked it and left. He did not say a prayer, he had become unsure of God for the second time in his life. He left the book in the cellar where he used to keep his meat cold and hang his bacon for smoking, and hang his beef until it turned black and the juices collected in its centre. Then he went up the dusty stairs and out of the front door which was now formed in part by the sky.

He walked back along the path by the side of his house, his feet scuffling and crunching on the stone debris. A piece of wire coiled round the toe of his boot but he kept on walking, with the wire scraping on the ground, and eventually it released its grasp and came loose. There were pieces of timber in the wreckage, beams from the ceiling of the house or perhaps an oak window sill. The enormous blue rock, incorporated into the corner of the dwelling rather than moved when Whelter Farm was built in 1538, was buried with rubble.

As the man approached her, Chase whined and sat up, tucking her head. She did not like her master's gait, recognizing it for despondency. But he stroked his knuckles along her sleek nose as he passed by and she settled. At the foot of the new lake he paused and then threw the key to the tool box into the water. Then the man left in his cart, which was pulled by his only horse, the scruffy, leggy mare named Spider by the man's son, named so because of the thin buckling legs which at birth had been almost unable to support the foal's own weight. He made his departure through an unmarked exit of water, with his Gudog swimming by his side. He would not return. The water would see to it.

But the book would remain behind, locked in the safe box, preserved somehow, even as the mud slid in through the cellar door, then the water, which by then was fuller and colder and the colour of indigo ink. Though the blue-blond hair that the man had found caught on his jacket button three days earlier, that he placed between the last pages of his book, did not stay. It disintegrated into dust long before water robbed the house of air, because human hair always does disintegrate when it is removed from a human head.

– PART I –

I:I

The woman on the bed was screaming bold blue murder and Jesus Bastard Christ. Curses formed like saliva in her mouth and she spat them out on to the tangled sheets of the bed, a bed which had once belonged to her grandmother and in which her own mother had been born. The cotton under her hot body was saturated with her sweat and with her swearing. The woman's body was making colours that her husband had never seen before, colours he did not know a human being could make. Soft orange on her, like human blood should never be, and white and a precise burgundy. Samuel Lightburn watched his wife struggling as internal shapes moved through her body, saw her muscles damaging themselves as she struggled. Jesus Bastard Christ. The woman screamed and slowly she came apart. He could not stand it.

– Ella. Ella.

Samuel spoke gently, uselessly, for the woman still remembered her own name. She was still in her right mind.

He swayed in the shadows, in the corner of the bedroom, his thumbs stroking the rough stone walls behind him as if looking to be soothed. The room was chilly, the walls glowing with cold. She screamed on, cursing the Lord, not caring about faith or decency or her God, in whom she had trusted her whole life, not any of the things that usually made her a tight knot of a woman, firmly wrapped, bound tight at the core. On the bed she fought with her own body, with God, with nature, unmaking herself. This was what her husband could not bear. The close threads of her were coming unwound as wave after wave of pain buckled up through her flesh and collected in her face. And her face was awful in its pain, a ripe beetroot dropped on the stone floor.

3

Women gathered in the room. Women in shawls and warm winter skirts. They told her to be calm and breathe. They placed the handle of a wooden spoon between her teeth as she raged and twisted. They instructed Ella Lightburn to control her pain. She could not. No more than she could control the snow falling fast and wet outside, smothering the valley. Joyce Carruthers had said to the company four hours ago that the Shap doctor would be needed, and word had been sent. But Dr Saul Frith was absent and, surely by now, unreachable. January in this Westmorland valley. Even the new Lakeside road was blocked by thick drifts.

Another roll like hot metal came up through Ella's stomach. The old wooden bed creaked as she pushed her legs down, arched her back, her vast stomach breaching in the cold air. She fought on, cursing, spitting, almost eight hours more that day and into the night. There were deep wet troughs in the bed, made as her limbs turned this way and that, forwards and backwards. Her eyes red with panic, she looked around the room for her husband. Had she not heard his voice a moment ago or an hour? She looked for him and was terrified.

Samuel Lightburn had been present for the birthing of many animals. He had witnessed the impossible feats of nature many times, had seen all strength from a beast draining into one part of its body, accumulating there, and using itself up. He was accustomed to intervention also, reaching inside the hot, rough canal of an animal himself with a bare greased arm, his fingers certain to find a loose ankle, a hand-hold. But never a woman before, it simply was not done. And only now his stubbornness, the direness of the situation, permitted him to stay in the room. He had never seen or heard human labour before and he stared out from the dark corner, his thumbs caressing the wall over and over. He was not prepared for this. He was not prepared for his wife's pain, or her colours, or for her terror. Nor the inversion of her faith.

There was not one household of the village which had not represented itself at Whelter Farm Cottage that day as Ella

Lightburn struggled with the passage of her first child into the world. The women came and went in the bedroom, gathering around the cursing woman, bringing water, cloths, fresh hope. They stood in twos and threes, leaving Joyce room enough to move around Ella as she needed to, taking turns in trying to usher Samuel out of the room, where he did not belong.

– Git. Git away, man. Go on with yer.

Trying to usher him downstairs into the large kitchen where the men of the village were sitting, standing, smoking. These men were mainly farmers, young and old. They listened to the woman upstairs, carefully, counting the screams and looking for meaning as a soothsayer might open up and read the intestines of a bird. They compared Ella's sounds with the torrid calls of the cattle and sheep in their herds when their time came, a stuck bellow, a panicked bleat. In this way they tried to decipher her stages of labour. But they could not, because human birth is something unnatural, something beyond animal – female pain become self-conscious. They tried to know the situation, practically, and without speaking of it, their teeth clenched over curved pipes and their fingers gripping the backs of chairs.

As Samuel passed them on his way to the front door, desperately looking out into the snow again for the doctor as he was, they placed, in turn, a simple hand on the back of his head, or on his shoulder. Thick hands, like pieces of beefsteak. There were no words. These were quiet men, economical with language, who spoke only in definites and who limited their actions to useful gestures or to work. Their individual faces wore a combination of expressions, each having many moods upon it at once, as if scowls and laughter, lines of concentration and hardship were weathered one on top of another in a single, permanent façade. Every expression set and roughened and deepened by the wind and the rain, the sun, so that one could not be accompanied without its partners. Mirth within a grimace. A frown grafted on to the bridge of lines created from squinting hard against the sun. And underneath all these encompassing masks was the suggestion, as common throughout the district, of unreachable, kept stone. Of distance.

The men were friends and colleagues. It was a small, remote district and they were joined by proximity, by community. Their wives were no different, nor their children. In the Mardale valley the bonds were strong and necessary and abundantly understood. To an outsider it might seem that the men and women of this dale were insular, as silent and self-sufficient as monks, closing ranks to off-comers, and uncommunicative and sullen with it. A joyless lot perhaps.

∾

The villagers remained at Whelter Farm for as long as they were needed, as long as uncertainty remained, leaving only to fetch new equipment, or bring food for one another, or to check on their children and put them to bed under patchwork, woollen blankets.

Again Samuel Lightburn looked out of the farm door across the village, which stood a little way off, down in the bottom of the valley. He cast his eye over the black water of the small lake to the forested hills on the horizon. Chimneys were smoking, windows were illuminated by lamps, but there were no car headlights winding down the concrete road to Mardale. No doctor. The snow was easing off. The sky's yellow lessening, and the clouds parting. A few stars were beginning to appear. Night was coming on and that in turn would bring fresh problems. It would be bitter cold and harsh without cloud cover, the snowdrifts hardening into firm barricades, a night without the doctor's instruction, for certain. This was the situation. There were no miracles in this dale.

Nathaniel Holme, an old, wiry farmer, came to the doorway and stood beside Samuel. He brought a pipe out of his

6

pocket and tapped it on the cottage wall to knock out the old, hardened tobacco. After filling it from a pouch, he lit the bowl.

– No sign ova yonder?

His voice was thick up from his lungs in the cold, and gravelly.

Samuel shook his head, took out a rolled cigarette, lit it. Nathaniel spoke again.

– Teddy's gone fer Frithy. Nowt else to dyah but wait. Thowt aboot garn misell, Sam. Twa arms better un yan, eh? Even auld bugger like misell.

The old man chuckled at the back of his throat and continued.

– Aye, til be a wunder if he gits there alive, poower bugger. But he's a gud lad, that Teddy.

Samuel's mouth moved a fraction upwards. His oldest friend had a way of lightening his spirits, even in times of trouble. Now the old man was laughing openly, deeply, his arthritic, busted hand gripping Samuel's elbow for balance as he shook.

∽

Young Teddy Hindmarsh had left at two o'clock that afternoon with his motorcycle on the new road to the east of the valley. Twice he had lost control of the Excelsior in the snow, the second time breaking two fingers on his right hand but feeling the pain in his missing left. The appendage had been lost to just below the shoulder joint during a shelling in the Great War, and he wore the sleeve of his coat flat, tucked into the pocket like a petal into a stem. He had finally abandoned the Excelsior in a drift four miles from Mardale. He bound up his fingers with a birch twig and some twine, using his teeth as best he could to tighten the splint. He began walking the next six miles on foot along the road round Naddle forest, for he dared not take the short cut up over the Swindale pass in this weather, when the snow could cling in cornices to the top of the fells and form unstable bridges suspended over nothing but air. A foot anticipating the path might go straight through, pulling the body down with it in a freefall to the crags below. He trudged along beside the lake and finally took to the trees, the entire front of him white with driven snow. The coverage of evergreen would provide him with some shelter during the trek, but Teddy would not return to Whelter Farm until the next morning with the doctor.

There was little activity in the household while he was gone. Just small episodes, a man leaving, a woman arriving with towels, a chair pulled out so that someone might sit, water boiled for more tea or to sterilize Joyce Carruthers's sewing scissors, the gathering of sweat and blood on the bed upstairs. The muffled contraction of cries.

Finally, Ella's screams stopped. A close husky silence like that found in a forest's centre settled about the house. Samuel threw his cigarette into the snow outside and strode from the kitchen doorway up the stairs. There had been so many people to help his wife, it had been a lengthy, fraught vigil. But it was Ella herself who made the last contribution to the day's efforts. The child had almost travelled through her body when she suddenly sat up on the bed and became quiet and determined, her beetroot face contorted a last time. It seemed that her eyes were filled with an unholy scorn. She reached down and pushed the baby free of herself with her palm, as if ridding herself of a heavy stone that had been placed in her lap. The women of the village drew breath and kept to themselves that they suspected from this moment on a bitter and difficult relationship between mother and child. Neither did they speak later of Ella's final whispered profanity against the Lord.

The tiny girl was blue and yellow from the cord wrapped tightly around her neck, but she needed no hand on her buttocks to start her new lungs. Blood colour quickly flooded through her, lighting the minute network of veins against her

8

skin. Her cries were fierce, like the mews of a hungry cat. Samuel came into the room and folded down on to the bed. His wife was faint against the pillows. He took the slippery child in his one giant hand and the straw turned redder in his face. A girl. A tiny, angry, malcontent girl. He turned to the women in the room and thanked them all for his daughter, overcome, and suddenly exhausted with relief. They looked away embarrassed by his sudden and unusual display of emotion, a man exhibiting such meekness, such altruism. Then Samuel turned to his wife and thanked her and he bent and kissed her wet brown hair.

But Ella was crying gently, which her husband had never before witnessed, and she was getting up from the mess of the bed, her arms lifting, tipping, to try to find her balance. She was crying for cursing Jesus, whom she loved above all, and she wanted to get away from the blood, and the baby, the scene of her crimes against Him. She wanted to limp to the church and pray for forgiveness. In those moments of guilt and regret she imagined that she felt that eternal freefall into nothingness, into isolation, and a keen desperation to be reunited with God overwhelmed her. She stood.

– No, Ella, lie back, there's more.

Joyce's words were paid no heed.

She was weak and pale and unstable as she opened the drawer of the dresser in the bedroom and took out the brass key to the church door, which she used every Saturday and Thursday when she carried out her cleaning duties. Her gown was yellow with sweat and a woman came to her and put a blanket around her shoulders. Ella steadied herself on the banister as she came down the stairs. She walked through the kitchen, past the table of empty cups, oblivious to the smoking crowd, and at the front door she paused to look back at the stunned, silent men, and at her husband, who had followed her down from the bedroom, not knowing what to say. He had their daughter in his arms. A small, screaming, blue and yellow kitten, lit up with hurried blood.

9

The church key pressed its shape into Ella's fist as she held it tight. Her feet were bare on the flagstones. She lifted the latch and opened the door and an icy gust of wind swept into the kitchen. The freezing air seemed to bring her round a little. She stepped into a pair of shoes and hung at the door frame. Ella looked at the child held by its father and again looked out into the night. Then she called out a name which was half lost under the voice of the wind, and she was gone, down to the tiny church in the heart of the village.

As she said 'Janet' for her grandmother's namesake, Samuel, half-hearing the wind, mistook her word and thought he heard 'January', for the month of her birth, and even later, when the mistake had been rectified, he always did call his daughter that, when his wife was not around to hear. And when she could, he settled for Jan, which was neither here nor there. So Ella went to the church to pray for forgiveness, and she would not curse God again for another twelve years, not until her son Isaac was born. So Samuel Lightburn grew the first of many hearts for his daughter.

∾

Before school, when she is six years old, she will accompany her father to the paddocks and the lower fields backing up on the moors. It is early morning and a green dawn light covers the valley. There are flashes of dark green behind the night clouds, which she notices, looking up, as she walks next to her father. It is as if metal has found its way into the air and is burning. They walk on, down the rocky stone path, sightless, but aware of the distance of the walls on each side of the lane, their feet scuffing up loose pebbles. She takes three steps to his every long stride, a skip in the middle to keep pace. Their eyes strain and after a while adjust to the near-dark. At this time of day unnatural, optical physicality occurs, owlish intuitions. Her father is a dim outline. When she looks at him, she sees his breath coming out in short bursts. From time to time he also looks down towards his breathing daughter. Behind and in front, two dogs slip silently along the drystone walls like ghosts swimming between their human keepers. Canine kelpies. She feels the presence of the near mountains, the pressure of them within the valley's space of air. If she were to peer into the darkness she might make out the grey rock of Nan Bield pass or the ridges of High Street. She could summon their exact position from blindness. As the girl unhooks the latch of a wooden paddock gate, the cows, with a half-remembered instinct, gather for the run up to the farm. Her father and the dogs begin moving them from the back.

Janet helps him drive the herd of cows upwards to the dairy barn each morning, slapping the hot flanks of the animals as they pass by if they rock too far out of the channel of their own traffic. Their gait is heavy and slow, their udder sacks swollen, a taut pink-white, so that the legs splay out further to avoid the underbelly. They slug towards the dyke and are smacked back by her small hand on their rumps. Tripping hooves on the uneven road and the occasional murmur of a cow are the only sounds in this dawn landscape. Not even birds sound from the hedgerows yet. The cows are huge forms compared with the thin young girl, with lolling pink tongues and soulful, black-lashed eyes that shine with a high polish in the early light. Gentle, harmless eyes, she thinks. But if she is too close to their passage the full cows may push into her, unwilling to halt the stoddering flow once they are moving, nudging her with a slow strength into the river of beasts. Or a stray hoof will cover her foot, the weight of an animal unbearable for the slow second until its next full step, her twisted ankle on fire. Her calls are similar to her father's, she has already learned his language of keeping animals.

– Cum to, cum long.

The lissom dogs weave in and out of legs, working up and down the herd. The older bitch is with pup. Samuel anticipates a fine batch, as the male breeder is a good working dog from Heltondale. He whistles and she halts and then flows to the left of the herd, slower in her condition but no less accurate. The cows press upwards on the path, hooves clattering on the shale. From the window of Whelter Farm the movement of the beasts might appear biblical. Black spines crest the tops of the walls. Shoulder bones rolling under the hide.

Gradually, light smokes into the dale as the sun comes up over the fells to the east. The cows, plodding in the thick air, are now forms filling in with detail. Mucus streams from their wide nostrils, slow heads nod with the effort of pushing up the hill, swollen and heavy with their milk stones as they are. They have the father's farm markings on the rump in a dark blue dye. This is the insignia of ownership: a cross-hatched L. Janet's hands slap across the lettering.

Pieces of colour also emerge now. Orange in the early sky. A purple foxglove towering against the verge of the path is eerie, it is capable of death, has within its tubular petals that treacherous, chemical secret. Her father's face and its beginning redness at the rear of the cows. She sees her own fingerprints coming out of darkness, under a yellow mantle of skin.

∾

A shower has passed. The rain, as if used up from its long, vertical descent, thins and finally holds off. Her father is ahead in the farmyard with the cows and she links the last gate closed behind him. The path on the way back up to Whelter is pitted and covered with miniature cairns of sheep droppings and its pebbles shine in the sudden light. As Janet approaches the farmhouse the track disintegrates into a flat, grass-tufted field. She deftly steps over the deep ruts of mud. From the chimney of the farm comes a thin trail of smoke; her mother must have just lit the fire – the damp wood spluttering to pick up flame. Whelter itself seems to stand in a damp silence, the house martins' nests under the gutters abandoned at this time of year, but as she comes closer to home there is the sound of water seeping around the house, attempting to find ground from its higher position. The walls are a murky eggshell colour, stained green-yellow from mildew under the drains of the guttering. Moss is growing on the dashing, as if the wall itself is a living thing providing nutrients. Around the back in the dairy barn she can hear the lowing of restless cows as her father begins work, and the clanking of cattle against chain. Janet walks in through the back door of the farm and a few drops of rain, mint cold, fall on to her neck from the pools collected on the roof. She is already wet enough not to notice them. She closes the door on the trickle and patter of nature dripping.

Almost immediately she becomes aware of her mother's scent. The smell of her is buried deep in the house, somewhere between the bitter rock walls and the wet grease of the dogs' coats and the dusty character of the old building. A rich odour that is just as much a presence as the woman herself, so vital, in fact, that it is as if Ella Lightburn could be summoned from that sense alone. Her human fragrance, coming from just under her skin perhaps, or from the original sacks of fat and fur lining her body, blood aroma. It is comforting and disarming also, this scent, as it contributes to and finally dominates the household. Janet thinks of the dogs outside when they have been separated a while after a run up the fell, pressing muzzles close, as if inhaling will determine the other's mood or intent. And such referencing can lead to playfulness, front legs tucked under, shoulders down and a lolling tongue, or to snarling confrontation, mostly between the female members of the group. A balance that is fine and easily swung one way or the other. The friendly tug at the collar suddenly becoming a brash of near teeth.

She pulls off her boots and leaves them on the stained boards by the door, enters the kitchen. Blue smoke curls up from the open stove door. Her mother is pulling out the drying rack.

– Lets have it, then. Tek it off.

Janet slips out of her damp wool coat and passes it to Ella.

Her mother runs a quick hand over its fibres.

– T'll not be dry fer school. Neither will you, by all looks. Yer soaked through, lass.

She gestures for her daughter to come to her and Janet pauses before crossing the room. A dog-like tension twitching between the two, mineraled water dripping from the younger's forehead on to the floor. Ella reaches for a towel hung on the sink and begins to rub at her daughter's loose hair. The sensation of it is firm against her scalp and Janet lets her head move accordingly under the pressure.

– Mam. I'll gan with Da t'put the tups out. Tom's up at Goosemire and father'll need help, eh?

– School fer you, lass. Yer father'll manage.

Her mother's voice is smoky, dispirited, like blackened stone. The brush begins to bite through the tattered strands of hair and flicks painfully past Janet's ears. She doesn't wince, but a cottony, internal itch starts in the small of her lower-left back, as it always does when her hair is brushed. A squirm of muscle. She buckles a little to one side and her mother rights her.

– Give ower, Jan. I've a dozen things niver dun yet this morning.

Ella twists the yellow mass into three separate parts and begins to braid. Her daughter does not mind this. It is like the pleasant numbness of a bee sting after butter is applied.

– Red or green?

– Red! Tup day, Mam!

Ella takes a piece of red rag out of her apron pocket and secures the end of the plait. She spins her daughter round to face her. For a moment there is an embarrassed, halting smile on her lips that starts, falters and begins again as if she is struggling in both releasing and stopping the expression.

– Daft lassie.

The administering complete, her daughter moves to the table, butters some bread and tears it in half. She scoops jam on to the larger half and folds the smaller down over it, then runs a tongue around the edges where the jam has spilled out. Ella pours out tea for herself and a cup of milk for her daughter. They drink in a willing quiet. She pours a second cup of tea.

– Tek this out to Samuel, will ya, on yer way down. Gudgirl.

Janet puts her breakfast in her pocket and picks up her satchel from a chair, slings it over her back and lifts the tea between the fingers and thumbs of both her hands. She moves to the door.

– Jan! Coat.

– Mam! Can't carry ivrything, eh?

Ella removes the wet, warm coat from the drying rack next to the stove and places it over the satchel, her actions circumventing any bickering.

– When I see you on that path back from t'shed, I want to see you wearin' it an' all.

Her dispassionate tone has returned and Janet knows that the brief interlude of lightness in her mother has departed. She is the first female of the house and as such there seems to be little room for the easy humour that her father often displays. She has within her a weightiness, as if carrying the combined stones of many riverbeds. As if gravity is the duty of a mother, not a father.

Outside, the fragrances of the farmyard and the weather and the season remove any memory of her mother's scent and she will not be able to recall and recognize it until in its presence again. She mutters to herself on the path, Sam, Sam, tea's up, Sam, her voice flexing inwards. Janet hands the cup to her father at the shed gate. His own hands are glowing from work, candid with heat. For a moment she considers asking her father if she can help with the sheep but her mother has already refused and, in fact, she does not mind attending school, far from it. Today that is the priority. She is allowed only some invasions of farm work into school time – busier periods than this, the introduction of the breeders. Lambing and dipping constitute an emergent occasion. Or an unforeseen event, the volatile weather. Her father is leaning on the gate, slurping his tea as if it is hot, which it isn't.

– Rite bonny y'look, Jan. Tek off the muck an' yer cud near pass as a lass.

She laughs uncertainly as if a joke has been made. She has never thought of herself as bonny before. It does not occur to her that her father might not be teasing. She enjoys her father's humour, though there are times when she cannot quite grasp it and meet it head on, as if reciprocation remains a little beyond her. His head is held to one side, his eyes stacked with energy.

– Gotta minute bifor class? Cum see this.

He sets the cup on the lip of a metal basin. Her father lifts her up over the dairy shed gate and sets her on to his big booted feet. Then he walks her over to the corner of the construction, through the mess of the cows, through their sweet, rank smell, which seems to solidify in the air when they are kept inside. The older dog has given birth to her litter on the straw in the corner, safely away from the heavy press of hooves. Three or four tiny, blind forms are tumbled over each other, breathing rapidly, letting out an occasional yip and crawling blindly further in towards the pink, distended stomach for warmth and milk.

– Shouldn't pick 'em up yit, eh?

Her father shakes his head in agreement.

– How long til their eyes open?

– Coupla days. Week. I'll git yer fer it. Fust thing pups'll see is bonny January with her clarty neck.

Her father flicks the tip of her nose with a balloon thumb. Janet's mother is calling from the window of Whelter for her to hurry. She steps back through the mud and vaults the gate untidily. As she passes the farm's kitchen window she has her coat pulled on backwards, over her chest, and a scowl pulled over her dry forehead.

16

As yet, she is an only child and there are just two other farmhands at Whelter, both of whom work part time at several properties in the district. There is no question that she will help her father before poring over the literature and the old atlas in the tiny classroom of the school, eager as she is for a more academic education. She has a deep love for the time spent writing or reading in the cheery, compact building with her classmates. Twenty-one pupils in all, mostly the children of farmers and labourers in the area, a substantial number for a village school and a recent increase since the closure of the Swindale institution.

On spring days the tall windows let in an abundance of sunlight and the single classroom of the school swims with brightness, trapped shafts of sun warming the back of her neck as she sits bent over the day's text, the illuminated writing. On rainy days she will gaze out of the smeared window panes to the fields and the fells beyond the school gates. The sky a deep saturated yellow, dark, greyish blue to the west where the weather comes in from rocks with layers of water. The drenched bracken and foliage on the banks of the hill find their own patterns in the wind, and at this distance look like wet blown velvet. There is mist low in the valley over the river, then mountains, the spine of High Street, and finally mist again, dissolving into nothing. She imagines her father wrestling with tarpaulin by the feed, her mother rushing washing in from the line in the garden, wooden pegs in her mouth. She knows when she goes outside that the earth will have been turned loose by water. It will smell over-ripe, too full of itself, like a matured, dropped apple. And this is the only distraction she allows herself from the school books. An eye cast slowly over the external world, so slowly that it is as if the enormous brown-red sweep of fells becomes a view that somehow belongs inside. A gentle cough from the chalk-board at front of the room. Then she returns to the page, to

17

the old wars of the continent, or a tightly woven sonnet that she will have to peel apart, weigh, then piece back together.

Her teacher is a middle-aged lady called Hazel Bowman, who drives down from Bampton each day. Her wage is not generous, though her enthusiasm for the education of the children of Mardale is not reflected in this. Textbooks and funding for the tiny school are both limited, and the teacher encourages the older members of the class to assist with reading lessons and arithmetic, sharing their knowledge within the group. A true pragmatist, she has such ways of dealing with things. Hazel Bowman brings with her newspapers for the class to read, both new and old, saved in piles in her reading room, so that the children will become familiar with history as it passes and recognize their place within it. On weekday mornings she arrives early and sweeps the floor of the classroom, lays out the books of the day, or the folded newspapers. On fairer days she will sit outside for a spell on the wall circling the small building and breakfast on bread, or a little smoked fish, watching the reflections in the lake. What she thinks of during these moments is the small number of children that will go on to college or university. This is her greatest pleasure, though she remains in touch with many who stay on in the district to farm. Hers is not solely an academic pride. Then she clasps the roped clanger of the iron bell in the porch of Mardale school and rings out the call for assembly clear across the dale. Her summons will bring boys and girls running along the streams and paths towards the lakeside building, satchels banging on the backs of their knees, sisters and brothers trying to push past each other at the gate. After an address and prayers, class will begin. History and geography. The atlas falls open with a soft thump, the leather spine cracking a fraction more. Pages rustle.

In the newspapers, the names from the old Bartholomew's atlas are brought to life, illustrated with event and nationality. Sometimes the world's place names are changed and Hazel

Bowman will mark the changes into the atlas with her small square handwriting, careful not to smudge her ink or spoil the page. Poetic, colourful names become practical, or flavoured with a different poetry, another country's mother-tongue. The shift and tussle of monopolies in this era.

Janet Lightburn approaches this volume of flat sections of the world with vague awe and wonders most of all at the pink shading of the Empire. It seems impossible that they, in their remote corner of a tiny island, should belong to such a vast expanse, such a sprawling, political colour, which includes far-off islands and archipelagos, obese, jutting land masses. It seems a wrong colour to her. It seems ineffectual, like a piece of cherry blossom, a streak of blood in water. A lurid purple would better suit, or a heavy, inching green. But such as it is, the tepid, inoffensive pink will, in her mind, always represent the impossible, a stray, romantic idea, like that of the colonial glacier.

The older yellowing newspapers describe the labour movements in the south, as well as the north, and women protesting for a younger vote, for family allowance. Cotton workers forming mass picket lines, stand-offs, the resistance to wage cuts in the textile industry. These are notable events, relevant to the north, Hazel Bowman says, effecting. Ask your parents about market prices. The Great War has been succeeded by other conflicts or schisms of the same bad spirits. There are occasional grey photographs of Flappers in bell hats with faces like flowers of war. The recent papers are bought from local towns, the *Gazette* from Kendal, the *Cumberland and Westmorland Herald* from Penrith. In the city of Carlisle they are bought from the man who stands in the market square near the citadel shouting 'Ther's nit miny lift' over the groaning stack of three hundred or more broad folded sheets. Hazel Bowman rides the mainline train up to the city to visit the library and the Roman museum, to collect news for her children. But in these papers history is less dramatic and their region seems uncomplicated. London papers shipped north are the real treasures, the ones that her class will devour and squabble over.

In them there are stories and events which fascinate and captivate the class, and so the pupils will cut out the articles, paste them into scrapbooks or on to the walls of the school building. Janet has her choices, already her mind is settling on fractures within tradition, the painful underbelly of the sick, elderly world as it rolls over in surrender to a new one growling above. In the year of her brother Isaac's birth Clyde Tombaugh discovers the ninth planet in the solar system and christens it Pluto. Such an old, extraordinary sounding name. She searches for it in the night sky, eyes blinded by the million other stars and deaths of stars in space, mouth slow over the long vowels. Pl-u-to. Twelve years old and sitting on the pointed roof of the cattle shed. Most of all she wants a telescope, like the one in the Greenwich observatory, with all its scientific precision, its ability to suck in long tunnels of the night sky, so that she can magnify location, lift out the erratic planet from the darkness and with certainty say it exists. In 1930 also, fragrant May, Amy Johnson, the pioneer aviator, arrives in Australia after twenty days of flying. Hazel Bowman smiles, compliments the girl's interests, the back of her eyes filled with sparkling grey light. In 1932 De Valera becomes president of the Irish Free State. October that same year and hunger marchers fight the police in Hyde Park, blood is spilled on the brown grass of London. And, a favourite, tragic article, almost two years later, Bonnie and Clyde are killed in an ambush in Louisiana, America. And the British press loves it, loves the simple unlikeliness and animation of it.

In the following months, close to the end of her schooling, Janet becomes aware of the dark figure emerging in Europe, across the icy North Sea, tightening the belts of his philosophy as he does so, purging his party of suspected traitors; this is 'the night of long knives', the papers announce, and the girl carefully cuts along the borders of Hitler's rise.

The changing world is illustrated on the walls of Mardale school, murder and hatred and valour and a stratum of ideals find their way into the quiet countryside of the Lakeland, like silent modern friezes set against the slow lap of the lake, the patter of rain. It is strange that the children should be familiar with the clockwork cogs and wheels of the outside world, as familiar as with their Latin verbs or Homer, Keats and Shakespeare, though their parents also are now reminded daily of the world's machinations, the airwaves lit up with news. Dislocated voices chip into their lives, issuing statements, reporting unrest, uniting the county. Bringing husbands and wives into the same room for long minutes before they move off towards the separate corners of their convenient lives.

Hazel Bowman has no husband, and though she is endeared to many in the area she has chosen a single life. She lives alone in a bungalow in Bampton Grange, with four baying otter hounds and towering bookshelves. Hers is a passionate and self-fulfilling existence. She brings the bouncing, troubled light of a new era into the remote valley, carrying it in her arms like a paper lantern, signed by a thousand men and women of the country. She brings with her a brilliant energy and liberating words, ideals belonging to the New World, perhaps, or the Antipodes. And there are off-kilter tones in her speeches, also; she has her demons. Let the class take note. Mary Shelley's husband altered the last sentence of *Frankenstein*, commanding the reader to breathe a sigh of relief where it was not intended. Never breathe a sigh of relief, she warns. In this world there is always the intrusion of one structure or another into the sacred, self-governing heart. When she leaves this valley it will be without regret, with her bright arms open towards the Spanish Civil War, late in the summer of 1936. Behind her a legacy of unique and brilliant education. The space between this bowed rack of fells having become an unprecedented arena of learning.

By then, Janet Lightburn will be grown, she will have bene-
fited from the influence of an exceptional woman. But in
these dawn hours of her own childhood and before the
school bell there are other small, hard lessons to be learned.
From her father, from the way his hands move smoothly
across an animal: superior, stewarding, so that there can be
no question of his authority. There are signs of sickness she
will be taught to recognize in beasts, fluid coming from
eyes, lumps on the flat surface of a tongue. Or a sheep
unable to get up, unable to back out of the corner of a wall,
having strayed from its heft. On the scars and lower fells she
often comes across the carcasses of dead sheep, immediately
recognizing the stench coming off the earth. At first they are
only missing eyes, the wool thinning off the face and a hurricane of flies anticipating above their bellies. With time
their bodies roll into oblique positions and open like rotting
flowers, dry flesh stretches and bones spread out over the
rough grass. She kicks them with a shoe, back into close
proximity, to create rudimentary maps of the world. She
finds India, the Sargasso Sea, Tasmania, shaped by the
ribcage of a Swaledale over heather. Eventually even the
grey bones are removed, half-buried, or grown over with
bracken. Nothing remains as a monument to death here. The
land sucks back in what it once issued.

In these early hours she learns skills without knowing
that it is an education of one form. The way to hold down a
ewe for clipping, with the upper body a brace and one leg
an anchor, the strong arm free. She will pry open the mouth
of an orphaned lamb, hold its tongue down with a finger
and thumb to introduce milk through a fake teat. The point
on the side of a head to place the rifle barrel, exact inches
from an eye, where the bullet will meet with least resistance. She will not ask if it is the same for humans. Already
she understands limits.

One morning she watches her father kill a lame cow. It is still upright in the field, but one hind hoof is rotten. It will not move and cannot be saved, must be destroyed before it destroys the herd, her father says. It sways and lets out an occasional quiet bellow. The decision is made quickly and, without remorse, her father leaves for Whelter Farm to get some cartridges and the gun. For a time she is left alone with the animal. During the wait she prays that the cow will somehow recover and move from the middle of the field where it is stuck. Even two rotten steps to the left might mean it could be saved, so that she could take her father by his cuff and say, See, see, it is still capable. Salvation. Her mother would say the word, the place, is reserved for humans, for they alone can be redeemed through God. Not the animals who have not been blessed under His Mercy. What, then, of this beast without choice or hope of mercy? Only a bullet in the brain to stop its energy and the eventual spread of its bones across the soil. And the land will borrow back that which was lent, as always. She tries not to notice the creature's gentle, living eyes, but keeps a blind company for it in these last minutes. She can see her father coming back down the lane, shotgun cracked open over his arm. He is inserting cartridge cases, looking down. And at the back of her mind she knows better than to hope for the impossible. She knows she won't beg her father not to shoot it. He would not mind her pleas, but certainly he would tell her to leave because of them. As her position as guardian it is vital that she stays, a witness to the events entire. And she does not want to disappoint him, he has no son. She wonders if she will cover her ears when he raises the gun. Her father's boots on the gravel track are louder, and she thinks, thinks hard about the motionless cow, and salvation falling away, perhaps never existing at all.

He bends down to her, the gun like a broken branch in his arm. It's such a strange and foreign object, half natural, half abhorrently man-made, cast metal. Later, she will be proficient in its handling, able to clean and load it. Later still, and her aim will be better than her father's. Crows will tumble out of the branches as she fires.

– Right? Right, lass. Gudgirl. Yer mam wants yer in. But stop here if y'like. S'up to thee.

The girl nods, barely a nod. Her father walks to the middle of the field. The cow is falling before she hears the shot.

∾

There is a smooth white scar on her forehead. It is shaped like a raised star to the right on the plateau of bone. A little too far out across the skin for a piece of loose hair to pass over it as she leans forward and so it usually remains visible. On her body there are several such masculine scars, she has spent too much time with the daily, impersonal violence of livestock and has laboured with heavy equipment too many times in poor light to come away unscathed. Her knees have been lacerated against a lifted plough and there are fingers which do not grow straight, but crook towards her palm like the bent bars of a cage. A broken rib from a frisky goat, its slight indentation in her stomach. Perpetually bruised or missing nails. Swollen ankles. These are accidents of minor proportions, unexceptional in the farming community. Even to her they are normal and acceptable. She does not consider herself unlucky or particularly broken in comparison with the rest of the valley's female population, nor is she possessed of damages out of proportion with other women of the area. As she grows, her father will gradually wean her out of farm work and instead a brother will help to move the full herd. She will begin tutoring more often at the school, write the occasional commentary for the *Cumberland and Westmorland Herald* under an assumed name, and avoid early marriage, much to the chagrin of her mother. The welts and old scars will heal and diminish, shifting position on her body as she grows.

But the star is the deepest of the collection. It sits against her head as a reminder that her life has included the sporadic brutality of her family's trade. It is the clearest mark perhaps, the key, a touchstone by which her father always finds his way back to her. He holds high regard for the scar, a reverence, the way a man might invest powerful emotion in a small icon or that ruptured portion of the past captured in a single object which he has inherited from a dear relation.

∿

She was eight years old and Samuel had already begun to suspect that there were things at work in his daughter a man should be wary of. At times, if he concentrated hard, he thought he could hear a low growl coming from her, emitted from a non-specific region of her chest, like the sound of snow about to move off a mountain in large pieces. As if she was tempered wrong. Her ways were not in keeping with her youth or her sex. She was seldom frightened as a small child will be during a new experience and she had developed a disturbing habit of staring at things, staring clear into them, so that her eyes never dropped during chastisement or argument. Her mother noticed this too, felt her face being eaten by the look as she chided her daughter for the carelessness with which she brought filth into the house. Often she bit her lip and clenched a hand at her side as if preparing to slap the stare away, though Ella had never laid an ill hand to her child. The pair butted heads like two rams on a narrow bridge as they met in conversation. Janet would not swallow God like her daily liver oil. She wanted to be shown His evidence, as if He were worms in the ground that would come up through loose soil seeking solid during the rain. She wanted her proof, a tele- scope to locate Him in the darkness. Ella warned her against false idols which she would find in such looking, and against straying too far, against fearlessness. An uneasy tension grew between them, as if they were both in themselves too charged, too magnetic to be in a room together. As if their forces would push against each other like invisible gravity from separate

25

poles and damage the delicate balance of the known world. So their time together took the form of brief intervals, both understanding this to be the only way.

That morning, of Samuel's remembering, Janet had wanted to come to move the cows as she usually did, but she was running a slight fever. Measles was spreading through the children of the adjoining Shap and Bampton valleys and her mother was worried it had now reached Mardale. Ella was acquainted with fevers of many varieties and the ones heralding trouble came with characteristics gently different from those of a simple head cold. A slight discolouration in the sweat along the temples, the eyes labouring between focus and vacancy. Influenza and child-killers made subtle alterations within the body's subtext of massive heat. But the girl was up and dressed at five o'clock and would not hear of going back to bed and riding the fever out in comfort. She would not be talked into sickness. She would not be nursed. In truth, it may have been only exasperation over her daughter's stubbornness that allowed her mother to let her go. Git out of mi sight then, lass, she said, turning from the bold gaze of the small fevered face. And the maternal anger was stored away for a later time.

It was more than just a blustery autumnal morning, her father remembers, because the wind in the leaves of the great sycamores by Measand Hall was threatening sombre repercussions in the brown darkness. There were invisible ills going on, he knew it. Slates being loosened. Fencing being rocked out of its foundation. The roses newly planted in front of the cottage must have been coming away from their crutches. He could hear foliage creaking and bending, the land of the valley itself was distressed.

Samuel held a lantern, which was flickering and threatening to blow out and would probably not last for the duration of the task. So he set it back in the shed, extinguished. Without the distraction of light, the surrounding murk became accessible to the eye. His daughter came out of the farmhouse towards him. She had on a pair of boys' breeches, which suited better the work of these early mornings. She was dressed warmly, but as he laid a hand on her head he found her hair was damp with sweat along her brow and she may have been shivering. He asked her again, would she go inside? No. She would not.

With the absence of a lantern, navigation of the path down to the paddock would be a question of relied-upon familiarity and concentrated vision. The daylight that morning was faltering, the clouds were racing across the sky. They set off down the lane. Samuel had with him a rope, wound in coils over his shoulder. Heavy wind in the valley often sent cattle and horses wild, they would take off in whatever direction the gusting force propelled them, filled with a frantic spirit. If this was the case, they would need to be bound round the neck and calmed, kept close. His daughter was walking next to him, her pace quickening as she was blown a little forward from time to time.

Samuel noticed the moving form first, a shape that was out of accord with the surrounding scenery, had movement unrelated to the wind. Then he recognized the density of withers, the curve of horn. A bullock had loosened itself from a nearby field by trampling down an old section of wall. Samuel saw it coming up the path towards them, bucking up its hind legs and cutting the rough air with its head. He gave his daughter a savage push to the side.

– Quick, lass, git up that tree.

The animal picked up its trot as it saw them, it shook its head and snorted. Janet had reached the rowan tree and climbed half-way up it within seconds, moving like a startled cat. She called for her father to join her, but he was standing his ground, removing the rope from his shoulder. He quickly fashioned a noose at the end of it. The bullock continued forward and, as it did so, Samuel tried to skirt it and come at it from the side, where there would be no horns, no hind legs to wrestle with. But the animal was twisting to face him, its

27

thick-packed muscle shifting under the skin. There was no chance of getting the rope around its neck head-on. After almost a full circle the bullock had him trapped against the rowan. It butted him twice, the horns finding his left forearm. From the low branches of the tree, his daughter saw the blood starting there, dark red through his torn shirt, snaking down his fingers. Samuel had his right hand on a horn and he was trying to pull the large animal down. His left arm hung at his side, dripping and fractured.

He tries to remember the next part of the dreamlike sequence accurately, but there is an unreal quality which is hard to clarify.

It was only a moment later that he heard the cry, a throaty half-growl, half-hiss, and then there was a flash of yellow down from the branches of the tree, on to the neck of the bullock and off, bringing enough weight against the animal for its head to drop with the shock of it. He quickly slipped the rope over the neck of the dazed beast, looped it around the tree. After a few tugs against its bindings the bullock became subdued. For a moment Samuel thought that it had been a lynx which had leapt from the tree. A rare and fantastic creature. Only the corner of his eye had caught it and the morning light was stormy at best. Until he turned and saw the cub of his daughter lying on the ground, with torn breeches and a deep puncture in her head which was beginning to spill.

By the time father and daughter had reached the Shap surgery in the Hindmarshes' old Morris, their wounds had nearly stopped bleeding, but the puncture, unlike the gash on the arm, had been too obscure a shape to stitch closed. And Dr Saul Frith had been more concerned with the girl's apparently fully developed measles than with the damage done to her head. He was less interested in tales of bravery than he was concerned with a potentially lethal epidemic, he told them.

In 1936 the village of Mardale consisted mostly of tenant farmers, as it had for a few hundred years, and the land surrounding it was devoted to the grazing of sheep, cattle and mountain ponies, a little agriculture where the soil was deep enough and rich on the slopes beneath the farmhouses. The villagers lived quietly, independently from the rest of the county, almost separate from the world, save for a weekend trip into town, to the cinema, the dancehall, a Tuesday excursion to the market. Or a visit from an adventurous explorer, a climber, the odd geological surveyor, a meteorologist, studying rainfall charts. The farmers were hard-working men, eking a hard living from the land, wholly dependent on the outcome of their husbandry. On Sundays they visited the church with their wives and in the week their children went to the small, blue-walled school, where they were taught to read and write, arithmetic and a little Latin. Although these were not a people bound by the mountains on the horizon, they were conscious of their landscape in a way that led them to live by it and from it.

The buildings of the village were squat, stout and tucked into woody enclaves, designed to withstand the ravages of the seasons, the rough, unpredictable weather common to this part of the country. There was an inn at the south end of the village called the Dun Bull which advertised in the Midland papers for boarders and occasionally received them. At the Dun Bull Inn gatherings took place, the shepherd's meet, the Mardale Hunt, evening assemblies where old men sang ballads with their rough, low voices softening like the air in spring. The inn was as much a centre for congregating as the church. And it stood almost opposite St Patrick's church on the other side of the main, mucky, wheel-rutted road.

Ella Lightburn would not set foot inside the inn; indeed, she would cross over to the other side of the street when she passed by it. Though she had delivered the placenta of Janet's birth in its snowbound doorway, there was no endearment. A place of ill intent, she called it, certainly not suitable for women, not even for men, come to it. Hers was an inflexible faith which ruled out liquor of any kind as a sin, even though she was aware that the parish vicar, Reverend Wood, himself imbibed a jar or two on Tuesday and Thursday evenings as a reward if the preparation of his Sunday sermon was going well. And sometimes as a consolation if it wasn't. It was said that Ella complained more about the grimy state of the copper pans hung over the fireplace, and the dust on the woodwork, than the moral state of the souls who frequented the Dun Bull, though how she reached these informed conclusions without first-hand experience remains a mystery. Samuel Lightburn was not so much a stickler in such matters, either divine or hygienic. He kept a tankard hung on the wall behind the bar from which he always took his ale and, as his wife visited the church often, so he propped up the bar of the Bull regularly, with his soft cap left like the wing of a bird on the counter beside his pint.

The Dun Bull Inn stood next to a small hill that was covered loosely with ash trees. It stood a little higher than the church, the tower of which was only twenty-nine and a half feet tall, excluding the spire. It was the newest of the buildings in the area, constructed in 1865 from Pennine granite and the traditional Westmorland blue slate. A tennis court had been built next to it at the turn of the century on the whim of a previous owner, the flat shale of which now provided straggling tourists with a decent car-parking facility. Tennis was a neglected sport in Mardale. Over the main entrance of the establishment hung a painted sign sporting an enormous brown bull of prize-winning proportions, and not unlike the agricultural monstrosities found depicted in the eighteenth-century wing of the National Gallery. For sixty years the Dun Bull had been host to farmers, travellers and tourists, now furnishing them with ale and spirits and terrible pies made with meat of uncertain origin. The present publican was a large and bawdy Scotsman with huge, herniated testicles, whose name was Jake McGill. He was rotund and bearded, with small, bright, brown eyes and a wicked sense of humour.

Jake, as he told the tale himself, had left his homeland in the dead of one misty spring night in 1929, to escape from an enraged wife. The reason for her rage was never fully explained, but locals guessed at unfair play on his behalf. He arrived in the quiet blue-green valley a few weeks after becoming a fugitive, with the intention of lying low for a spell in the borderlands before catching the Maryport steamer to Ireland, only to discover that the Dun Bull had been without a landlord for over a year. So he stayed on, because he felt he was needed to take care of the poor, dry unfortunates there. A calling, he said. Within three months he had imported a good quantity of ferociously rough whisky into the valley, which his cousin brought down from the last of the illegal Lowland distilleries and which proved fiery enough to strip a man's stomach lining after two fingers, taken quickly. The whisky was undisputedly revolting but rapidly acquired novelty value, as the two public houses in the adjacent villages of Bampton and Bampton Grange were licensed to sell only beer. Thus the Dun Bull, tucked into the isolated north-west English countryside, was, for a time, home to some of the most potent whisky in the whole of the British Isles.

Jake McGill was not a culinary master, but he would wake each morning at seven and rise with the discipline of a drill sergeant (indeed, it was rumoured that he had some form of loose military training) and then spend two hours in the kitchen, engaged in the surreptitious preparation of his pies, before he opened the Dun Bull's doors to the public at one.

Within two years his pies had achieved legendary status throughout Westmorland, and arguably Cumberland also, for sending cattle lame if they stepped on one, or bunging up a man for a week, should he have the misfortune to consume a whole one. Jake also created his own beer-like concoction in his spare time, outside in a shoddy greenhouse behind the inn, which he offered to his customers at the truly magnificently low price of a halfpenny a pot. It was termed, simply, 'Brew'.

The proprietor had a live-in girl called Jenny Wade, who stayed at the Bull on the pretext of cleaning for him. She helped out in the bar on busy nights and she cooked breakfast for any guests who might be staying at the inn during the warmer seasons. Dutifully, she warned them against the pies, all the while complimenting Jake as she tested their thick pastry crusts and soggy intestines herself. And when his testicles were not too painfully swollen, she encouraged Jake, in many ways, to forget about the Wretched Woman Harpy who had plagued his past life. She encouraged him to re-examine the various advantages of womankind through her plump and warm self.

The floor of the Dun Bull was uncarpeted, which was probably a blessing as it became a seabed for the tides of filth and mud brought in from the fields and farms. The odour of manure was never quite absent from its lower rooms. It had cavernous ceilings with dark wooden beams and most of its corners were lost in deep shadows. There was a variety of fox heads on the wall with fur of ranging colour, from blonde-amber to mahogany. They were the trophies of successful Mardale hunts, their jaws set in a last violent expression of defence against the hounds. A flail and a hoe were mounted above the entrance doorway, for no particular reason, and a set of huge copper pans was hung over the fireplace, spilling a dull copper light into the room when the setting sun found the right angle into the building before disappearing behind the mountains. The Dun Bull's interior was not dissimilar to many other drinking establishments of the region. Its punters, in Jake's opinion, however, were not lacking in originality, they were altogether a little rarer.

⸎

Across the road stood St Patrick's, a beautiful, ancient church, built at the end of the fifteenth century on sacred ground, where a tall, mossy Celtic cross had already stood for centuries. Upon the building of the church in 1499, the cross was incorporated into the graveyard and there it remained, older than even the two yew trees which backed up against the dry-stone wall circling the headstones within the graveyard. The building was tiny and dense, with enough room for only a handful of worshippers.

Inside, the church was cool and gave off the scent of the damp stone floor and polished wood. At the altar end was a blue and red stained-glass window, depicting Christ ascending, which let in a small amount of coloured light and which the Bishop of Carlisle had praised highly on his visit to the diocese in 1922. The hassocks were well worn and the prayer books a little tatty. The hymn board had a 3 immovably stuck in its first row, and consequently the initial hymn of any service was limited to a choice from those in the three-hundreds.

Under the front row of pews there were some elaborate and irreligious carvings. Medieval dragons, gargoyles and various other non-Christian motifs had been cut into the underside of the benches by a skilled, if renegade, atheist. They were strangely out of place in the sacrosanct setting, but could not be removed owing to their artistic merit and the age of the wooden structures themselves, and they had been mentioned at length in C. H. Simion's *Ecclesiastical Wooden Sculptures* of 1888, in which they were described as 'fascinating and not a little compelling'.

Unlike the Bull, the church was kept spotlessly clean. There were fresh flowers next to the altar from the meadows in the

33

summer, holly wreaths from the trees by the lake in winter, pussy-willow in the springtime. October saw harvest festival and the steps leading up to the altar were adorned with fruit and vegetables, plaited wheat and loaves of bread fashioned into autumnal reliefs. The children gathered mushrooms and left them in baskets around the pulpit. The pulpit itself never gathered dust for more than a day or two before it was whisked away and the eagle lectern always shone a deep brassy gold. Ella was as meticulous in her cleaning duties as she was in her faith.

Reverend Wood, a small, rodent-mouthed man, ministered the church, giving sermons on Sunday mornings and holding prayer meetings on Wednesday nights. He had been part of the community for five years and had never quite adapted to the quiet, sullen village, missing the bustle of the town, a larger, better-dressed congregation, more refined jokes. And although the catchment area for the church in Mardale was somewhat larger than the twenty-eight families of the village, including as it did the high shepherd's cottages up on the moors, along the path from the dale to Kentmere and the surrounding Naddle forest, those twenty-eight families and the remoter flock were in the habit of rather sloppy attendance, and the Reverend found that, particularly in lambing season, many of them missed the Sunday sermon for weeks on end. In truth, he found it difficult to be inspired here. Though he arrived with visions of introducing a rather more elaborate style of worship, perhaps a statue or two or even a little incense, his keenness soon departed with the rapid realization that his congregation was just as eager to preserve their 'low church', with its minimal ceremony and paraphernalia. His lectures were consequently a little subdued, a little uninventive and dull; he was known often to recycle a sermon and Ella Lightburn considered him ineffective and banal. She would rather have had her minister promising fire and damnation, pointing a crooked finger at them all and issuing warnings dire enough to make them swallow with discomfort, to flush with heat or shiver with cold, depending on disposition. A servant of God with the ability to create a shimmering congregational silence, during which many would reach for their hassock underneath the pew. Instead, she cleaned the church vigorously and listened weekly to the Mole drone on, bookishly, dispassionately, never raising his voice a decibel. She never missed a service, nor a prayer meeting, not even when infected with shingles, with bronchitis, with a crippling, inflamed bunion. She had even been known to pressure the Reverend off his own sickbed when it looked like he might be thinking of not conducting the ten o'clock service that week in February, afflicted as he was with a nasty cold.

– I trust you'll be fit fer duty by Sunday, vicar.

Reverend Wood stood shivering and wrapped in a blanket by the door of his cottage (not even a vicarage provided for him in the miserable parish!) and cradling a large brandy in one hand. It was eleven thirty in the morning. Ella was insistent.

– 'Twoud be a shame to let down yer flock, let them wander the fells in certain danger.

– Well now, Mrs Lightburn, this cold is a stinker. It could have me knocked out a week or more.

The Reverend sneezed for emphasis, thinking that he had never before met a flock more able to care for itself.

And Ella turned abruptly and strode away up the stony path to Whelter Farm, her breath frosting above her, leaving the vicar to his brandy and thoughts of a long weekend in bed with a good book. She returned an hour later, however, with a pan of foul, oily broth, tasting vaguely of chicken, as the Reverend soon found out, and with some strict instructions.

– Remember, no more brandy, vicar, it thins the blood badly in this cold, not to mention thinning the spirit! And no milk. And no bread.

Her eyes were wide, sending ripples across her forehead in their wake, they were piercing blue and unavoidable. She left with directions to heat a cup every half hour and she would return with another batch in the morning.

The Reverend Wood managed a good recovery almost overnight. By the time the morning arrived, bringing Ella with a fresh pan of stock, he was fit enough to be dressed, to refuse the pan vehemently with protestations that it must be a miracle how much better he felt, and that the soup would be wasted on him now. Yes, a full recovery he had made!

Alas, his garden fuchsias did not manage to recover quite so well after receiving a substantial dose of broth over them that February. They were sadly not forthcoming the following summer.

The vicar did not particularly appreciate such devotion. He considered the woman to be excessively fraught with the desire to be close to God, and whilst he himself did not fault a deep love for the Lord, he felt that decent limitations were needed. There was something about the woman which did not sit right with the vicar. The confidence her faith allowed her was too inflated, to his mind. He had also heard disjointed pieces of an alarming tale about the birth of the Lightburns' first child, which added to his suspicions that she may indeed be harbouring tendencies towards religious hysteria, and he often found himself picturing her wide-eyed and perspiring with a poisonous snake in each hand, in the fashion of those fervent reptile handlers in the American Appalachia about whom he had read. He had not pressed Ella herself on the issue, being slightly nervous of her reaction, but had gleaned all the missing sections of the story from other villagers over the five years of his administration, subtly, for he was not one for gossip, the majority of the tale being supplied to him by the woman who ran the local store, the village tattle-tale.

Reverend Wood would have liked to cancel Ella's cleaning duties, especially since her wage came from the money directly allocated to him for the upkeep of the parish church. He would even have taken a polishing cloth in his own hand himself if it would guarantee her safe retirement. But she had been there at the church longer than he. Her position seemed unquestionable and he did not quite know how to execute such a plan. And besides, his nerve always seemed to falter in her presence, as if he were a tiny mouse on the ground, addressing a mighty eagle perched over him, giving measly reasons as to why his existence should continue.

∾

In the centre of the village stood a row of tiny cottages, and in the last, the one with the tumbling chimney, was a tiny shop, which took up no more space than the corridor between the front door and the sitting room. It was run by a woman called Sylvia Goodman, known to all in the village as Gobby. She had converted her hallway into rows of shelves, containing provisions, shoe wax, paraffin, string, boxes of flour, tins of fish and other mixed items. She was notorious for handing out district news with every purchase of sardines or tooth powder.

– Here's yer polish, and did y'know that in Bampton three lasses are pregnant, they say sharing t'same father? I wunder, will they be sharing t'ring too? Molly Lincoln has thrown her husband out on tu t'street. Well, yer put two and two together . . . Dun't tek much gissin'.

In her yard was a hutch filled with scruffy brown chickens that sporadically produced eggs for her to sell, but were capable of laying only if she told them stories and news about the district, so she said. A well-informed hen was a happy, productive hen. She fed them bacon grease, which was no cheap meal, and dandelion leaves, muttering about affairs and deaths, local controversies, as she scattered the food, and when there were no recent shenanigans to mention she resorted to renditions of the old border myths and long-ago frictions of the area. Her rooster, she claimed, was eighteen years old, and still a fine fellow. He crowed only during the evening hours and had twice survived being shot with an air rifle, though the second pellet had blinded him in the right eye.

The shop itself half ran on a system of exchange and barter, with the swapping of produce as it was needed by each customer. Carrots for eggs, smoked ham for cigarettes or tobacco, apples for the occasional postage stamp.

∿

Measand Hall stood off at the outskirts of Mardale, as grand halls and manor houses are in the habit of separating themselves from the drudgery of village life, and it had almost as much acreage as any of the tenant farms on the slopes of the valley. There was no aristocracy living in the great hall, nobody of such lofty heritage, though it was still owned by the Earl of Langdale. Unlike much of the estate, it had not been sold off to settle the recent crippling death duties. The building itself, old and in need of much repair, had been inhabited for the past fifteen years by an artist, a landscape painter by the name of Paul Levell. Levell was from Northumberland and in another incarnation he had been a war artist, active in the fields of France, who in peacetime had retired to the quiet valley to concentrate on landscapes and remake his sanity. Several of his Great War paintings had been accepted at the National Gallery in London, with their torn scenery broken down into primary shapes and colours, abstract, despairing, as if released from an awful, nightmarish dream.

After the war he began painting with startling realism, almost photographic accuracy, an exposed clarity which seemed to resist any interpretation other than that which was most apparent, like the bones of a carcass picked clean. Where once a broken plane wing stood for a ruptured human skull, now a mountain was just a mountain. And yet his work always remained violent and unromantic, if exceptionally beautiful. There was an impossibility to the perspectives of his high mountains, breathtaking verticals, paths fractured up over cliffs, pulling at the stomach and suggesting rapid currents of air during a freefall down to the eye of a dark tarn.

He pushed the limits of Lakeland geological existence. Stony ridges disappeared into thunderous, sudden stormclouds. Edges appeared suddenly and without regard for the safe grassy flatlands in the foreground of a picture. Humans were, without exception, banished from the bleak, natural scenes, as if unable to survive or simply not welcome in the wilderness created by Levell's brush, save for a suggestive form in a rock, a woman's back surfacing in a river as a stepping stone, the curled torso of a man, moulded into the spine of a barren outcrop of granite. Figures were swallowed up by the land, subsumed. There was no harmony of man with nature or the human conquest of environment which the Lakeland artists of the day favoured. In Levell's work, life was brutal, distinct and pure.

Paul Levell himself was a tall, bearded, wild-looking man, who blinked constantly and spoke rapidly in broken sentences, with every second word seeming to be a curse. He either loped through the village on foot or wove dangerously on an ancient bicycle, his tawny hair smothered back under a fashionable French beret.

He was partial to discourse, and liked to draw his fellow villagers into political discussion, asking them to comment upon the troubles of old Europe, their feelings for Stanley Baldwin, but never made direct mention of the war, not even to Samuel or Teddy Hindmarsh, men who had shared memories of that horror, the insanity, the lost faith in leaders, and the suspicion that the present moderation was simply the country treading water. He was considered eccentric, pleasant, but better avoided unless the work for the day was complete, lest he keep a man talking for an hour or more. Mostly, Levell kept himself to himself in the old, crumbling hall, which was rented to him as a favour by Lord Langdale, who had bought several paintings from him and was something of a local patron. He ventured out early in the mornings, usually the first true tide of daylight after the herds had been moved, to run up the fells, his long legs taut with muscle, his hair a ratty, sweaty mass, always talking softly to himself as he ran, softly, desperately, as if attempting to calm the energy within him that urged him to ascend mountains rapidly, to scramble along the precarious ridges like a bolting hare.

∾

There were about twenty-five houses in the valley, most of them two or three hundred years old, that formed a dense clutch in the middle of the village and spread out as they progressed up the sides of the valley to make way for farmland. The fields undulated gently in the basin, steepening further out, where they were separated by the traditional enclosure of drystone walls. Oak and elm trees grew by the field walls, offering shelter for cattle and sheep from sun and rain.

On the low sides of the Rigg, a sharp, craggy ridge which ran up to the High Street mountain range, there was a dense covering of pine and spruce and half-way up the mountain, on the flat plateau of Castle Crag, were the foundations of an early British fort. At the end of the valley, a black, ragged-faced mountain called Harter Fell cast an enormous shadow over the head of the dale, almost to the foot of the village, and its north face was the last place to keep snow in the surrounding area, storing it in frozen black crevices until the May sun could warm it enough for it to trickle away.

On each side of the dale was a road, to the west side an old farmers' track that had been used for the passage of animals and vehicles until the building of a new, concrete road on the sharper east wall in 1926, which cut through the darkness of the Naddle forest. The two roads met up at the bottom of the valley and then led as a single tarmacked highway to the village of Bampton, then on to Penrith, eighteen miles from Mardale. The western track was still frequently used, being closer to the upper fields of the farms. Along it grew hawthorn, gorse and broom. Brambles curled out on to the road in the summer, there were wild raspberries to be picked and in June sticky, thorny roses bloomed, sweetening the air.

Further down, spanning the middle of the dale, the waves of a small lake lapped gently against the blue rock of the valley floor. The lake divided into two sections, the larger one, closer to the village, was known as High Water, and the smaller part at the bottom of the valley was Low Water. The two sections of lake were joined by a thin, deep channel known as The Straights, where fishing was always good. Four streams, Swanmere, Randale, Hopgill and Whelter becks, ran down into the lake, tumbling as waterfalls higher up in the fells on their journey. The rivulets from two tarns met up in the bow of hills at the head of the valley before they came down together in one large river, the Measand, which ran straight through the heart of the village, splitting into a tributary before joining High Water.

There was a stone, hump-backed bridge which spanned the river next to the church. In its keystone was carved a three-pronged mark, the signature of the stone mason who built it, a mark which was also found in one of the corner-stones of Measand Hall. For the last three hundred years or more there often could be seen a man or a child pausing on the bridge to look below at the water, idling in conversation with a companion, or as a solitary, watching the trout rise and flick between the reeds under the bridge. Casting an eye over the river, as if for no other reason than there was water flowing past.

I:III

One bright day at the back of the winter of 1936, a man came into the Mardale valley with the intention of changing it for ever. He came as the spokesman for a project so strange and vast that at first it was not taken seriously by the village. It was as if the man spoke to them in another tongue, or in abstracts far removed from the life of these men and women. His purpose was inconceivable.

The first that the village heard of this man was a low throaty growl, the mechanical purr of a smooth engine, as he drove up the winding east lake road in his new car. The sound rose gradually above the movement of elements, the fussing of livestock; it was an easy and toned hum, unlike the roar and splutter of the ancient iron-wheeled tractor struggling up the incline to High Bowderthwaite Farm, the clanking of chains in the dairy barn of Whelter.

The artist Levell, hearing the engine, came to the window of his studio room, once a grand dining hall, where he had been finishing an oil portrait of Blencathra mountain. On the periphery, moving glassy light caught his eye. Flashes of low red and silver flickered between the trees on the road. Almost immediately he was aware that the automobile was very new and very fine. And utterly incongruous with the environment in which it now found itself, ten miles at least from the next village. The driver not yet realizing he was lost. Hearing the sound louder, Levell left the building and walked along the walled track from Measand Hall to the village, pulling on his beret and a sheepskin coat against the cold. And all the while the vision of Blencathra's sharp saddleback edges never deserted him, but became clearer as he left his canvas.

A traveller had come astray, perhaps having taken a wrong turn at the Shap junction, meaning to go on up to Penrith, or more likely to the city of Carlisle, for such a vehicle was rare in the parochial border towns. But the car came fast and in a high gear, flashing between the trees, too fast for the conditions, for the ice blackening on the ground. The driver was not slowing or pausing to look for a widening of the road where he could turn round, nor were the gears clashing in frustration at the predicament. He drove without the use of a brake, he drove casually, comfortable with the hazardous terrain, utterly without timidity. And as the trees thinned and the Naddle forest gave way to open land, a sleek red automobile was revealed, glittering in the low sun. A sports car. A young man's dream, thought Levell.

Transfixed, Levell watched the man turn into the village and park beside the church. He got out of his vehicle, which made pinc-pinc sounds as the engine died, then finally quietened. Levell was still a fair distance from the stranger, and he heard the definite slam of the car door a moment after it had been shut, as the echo moved sharply up the valley in the frigid air. Closer over the frosty field, the artist paused within calling range but did not lift his voice. The drag of a match on the rough side of a box as a cigarette was lit. The air was clear, crisp, bringing unadulterated sound. There was the slight scuff of a heel as the man pivoted to look up at the summit of Kidstey Pike, one gloved hand sheltering his eyes from the winter glare, pausing a fraction away from his forehead. He was wearing a dark-green suit, like a forest at night, and his shoes had been polished to a high shine by a variety of street boys all over the red city of Manchester, though Levell only knew of their condition after the fact. The tight tie at his neck was yellow-gold, pinned with an opal, and there was a yellow silk handkerchief in the top pocket of his jacket. He was dressed for a dinner, or a dance, like an unusual, exotic bird, its silk and sheen foreign in the cold landscape. The artist thought to himself that the man was not lost. He had come to the valley as a man would enter a room to receive a guest – territorially, impossibly possessive, and with charm, politeness, with the tip of a hat, a warmly shaken hand. He, the stranger, assuming control.

Levell hung back behind the wall, watching the scene intently, like a tall, silent heron scanning the waters. The stranger did not appear to be in need of assistance. He twisted his neck, rolled it to the side to bend out its stiffness from the drive, but seemed at a general ease. He half-circled to observe his surroundings. A brief nod of the head. No, he was not lost. And yet he could not be in the right place, must somehow have become dislodged from his natural, metropolitan setting. Unless he was a tourist, but Levell did not think so. He had neither the attire, nor the aroused composure. The man turned again, this time to look at the village, the church. Levell cocked his head, stepping closer, the edge of the mountain now gone from his mind.

The man in the suit did not touch himself with his own hands, but kept them gracefully away from his body, his neck. As he smoked, his movements seemed perfectly to complement the action, as if he was the kind of man whose habits would always shortly become fashionable with the general public. There was poise to him, purpose and elegance. Something else too, an alarming degree of control, as if he was detached even from himself. The artist paused along the wall again, suddenly feeling unable to approach the man. All thoughts of assistance disappearing, his typical affability and garbled verbosity absent.

Levell had with him a charcoal stick and a small, porously papered notebook. He was seldom without such equipment. His hand was cold but he rested it for a moment under the collar of his sheepskin, warming it back to life. His sketch was furious, it can have taken no longer than a minute. He caught the man in abstracts, the first time his art had become broken down, deconstructed, since the war. The first time he had rendered a human being since that same troubled period, also. So the man in the suit was moving, persuasive and, in a way, terrible or beautiful, enough to bring a man out of himself for a time. Enough to set him back. In the sketch the face was dark, like the hair, and it was made up of many layers, of paper and office objects, his cigarette a stack chimney, his skin smoke. In the man's hair were the bright wings of industry.

The stranger had still not seen the artist. He checked his wristwatch, pushing his arm out so that the green jacket sleeve slipped off his wrist and crooking his hand back, without a single touch, with no self-affection. But the horizontal light in the valley told the man all he needed to know. He was standing in almost the last piece of it. It was early evening. Soon darkness would be pulling the men in from the fields.

He buttoned his suit jacket, opened the car door and pulled out a briefcase, then a hat and an overcoat, both of which he put on. Looking to the side, the stranger saw that the village was not deserted as he had thought it to be. There was a man in the field next to him. A wiry, lean character, who must have been sketching the mountains. They held eyes. For a while they did not speak, the tall, unkempt artist and the man in the suit like a forest at night. Neither felt compelled enough by the silence to break it, neither felt that an exchange was warranted. Nor did their eyes drop to the earth. Then a smile from the visitor, as if to welcome the artist forward, as if to give permission to come beyond the gate of the field and to him. His smiling mouth, like full leather, like smooth upholstery.

– Beautiful afternoon. If I could draw, I'd take it down also.

The man's accent was northern, but milder than that of the men and women of this valley to which he came. He did not turn the corners of his words so sharply. Levell lifted a long hand upwards in acknowledgement. Then he turned and loped away, his feet occasionally cracking through a shallow drift of snow blown into the corner of the field.

The suited man walked on into the heart of the village and there he stood in the frozen, rutted road, smoking another cigarette. A group of boys spilled out of the doorway of one of the cottages and began trying to scrape together enough compacted snow to form a ball worth throwing. The stranger watched them. After a while they came up to him, nervous, but their timidity overlaid with curiosity, the boldness of the very young.

– Mista, mista, yer lost in't ya, mista?

– No. I'm sure not, fellas. Boy, it is cold though.

He laid it on for them. The use of such language had the boys whispering among themselves about gangsters and guns. The man noticed their ruddy complexions, the absence of city reflections in their eyes. These children lacked the pageantry of Manchester orphans, the youngsters with their theatre of wide-eyed hunger, their articulations of distaste and misfortune. They were not any heartier, indeed some seemed more gaunt, but it was the difference between a thin working dog and a ragged stray, the man thought. They were quiet at play, their shouts few and to the point.

– Fetch us that. Gan ova bridge, will ya? Cy, Cy, gan ova bridge.

They were templated from an entirely different press. He told them to fetch their fathers, and their mothers, the rest of their families too, if they wished. He needed to call a meeting. At first the children would not go. The man was too much of a peacock, too great a spectacle for them not to observe him. Just as he studied them, so he in turn was evaluated. His polish, his pressed creases, the tight, symmetrical seams of his tailored suit, a thing from beyond the gamut of Westmorland. They found him intriguing and lingered around him, stroking the hem of his coat as if to spy a pistol kept under the garment. He handed out Saskind's peppermints from a tin to them, promising more when they returned, rattling the box in his gloved hand. He scruffed the hair of the boy nearest as he ran past him and winked, his eyelashes flickering like the dark, pollened wings of a moth.

At the cottage on the end of the row was a red post-office sign. He entered the building and encountered an old lady, with raisin-brown skin and hooded eyes, with the flesh of her face shrinking in all directions, a soaked neck. After a brief discussion he found out that there was no village hall in which to conduct a meeting, and even the church could not house all members of the village at once. It would have to be done outside. Though the woman pressed him for more information he gave her none, even as she gathered up her coat to accompany him outside. The two stood in the widest part of the village near to the church and the stranger listened to an account of one of the brawls which had occurred in the village of Shap the weekend before from the old grey gargoyle of a woman. She spoke to him casually, name-dropping and expecting him to know those individuals mentioned as if he had lived here all his life. Slowly, within half an hour, the village assembled, in the hard mud road next to the bridge over the river, in the waning light.

∾

Let them be assured that none of this was within his control, this they must understand before all else. He was simply a messenger, he said, come to tell them of their future. By the second sentence the locals had him pegged as a salesman, not the first to make it down into the valley and not a very good one, however well dressed. There was a silent pause, immaculately executed by the man. He might have been about to wheel out a marvel of the modern world from behind him. He smiled widely then, at the crowd of working men, and frowning women, as if to encourage confidence in him. Then his expression changed and was replaced by concentration, he began speaking softly, shallowly, and at the same time his accent heightened and became mannered. It was a voice for addressing others regarding serious matters, a well-oiled public-speaking voice. As he spoke, he moved his words out and away from himself, and it was as if he was speaking of another place, another land, as if this was in accordance with

47

some eventual reckoning that reaches all quiet and secluded areas in time. The modern world was just behind the man. What he was selling was the end of their valley.

∾

It began as a simple proposal. Manchester City Waterworks had been hunting in the Lakeland and the borders for a site suitable for special development. This valley had been considered among others. For the past fifteen years geologists and engineers had surveyed the area, boring holes in the rocks of the valley and testing the water. Their results, when they reported back to MCW, had been favourable. The valley had been excavated by glaciers, which melted away to leave the small lake in the basin. The rocks along the sides and floor of the valley consisted of compacted slates and grits, layers of volcanic ash and lava which became hardened by subterranean heat and pressure and could not be eroded by the passage of water, an aspect vital to the scheme. In the words of the geologists and the surveyors, it was an old, firm valley, the site was admirably suited for development of the kind that the Waterworks was considering. In fact, this valley, with its own natural shape, created as the earth's muscles cramped and pulled with ferocious sloth millennia earlier, was perfect. Six miles down, at the bottom of the dale, where the fells curved towards the ground and flattened inwards, hard volcanic rock came to the surface, and it would be possible to lay down a flat arm of cement and brick. An arm belonging to a colossal stone god, capable of holding back a full valley of water. It would be a dam unlike those built anywhere else in the country. A wonderful piece of architecture and engineering, megalithic, inspired. Yes, the site was perfect, but for one thing.

On the damp boards of the valley floor was a little village. The smallest of places.

For a moment, there was another silence, except for the trickling, cold river under the bridge. The man paused in his speech, suggesting that it would take a new turn. His face of many layers was now stacked with compassion, concern. He paused. The water trickled past, bringing finished snow from the hills. Not another sound. As he began speaking again, his forehead became overlaid with sadness, his voice was a song almost dying of it. Perhaps these pieces of language had been harder to move out and away than the rest, or perhaps the man was letting himself in on the meaning of being insignificant against the weight of a stone god. But at the same time his dark eyes were telling something else. It was magnificent, this blueprint of his words, this vision, an endeavour of capacious proportions. Moreover, it was progression, personal. It was somehow his, he had written the story. And his eyes were wholly filled with agitation and incense, amid his face of many layers, and he just could not invert their light.

∾

The country desperately needed more water supplies, the cities of the mid-north were practically drying up, rainy country or no. Manchester needed more water for its ever-expanding mouth, for its thirsty people, for its industries which had tripled in size since the start of the century. This was a city leading the way of modernity in the north, a city of new industry, a city which would roar out metals for the manufacture of cars, buildings, ships and armaments in preparation for the forthcoming war, should there be one. And there would surely be one, said the man, bigger than the first. The city would be a defender of this country. Its growth was beneficial to the country entire. It should be nurtured, with pride, with sacrifice, hard though that may be.

Here was the village. Not insignificant but it was a small

place, with no more than thirty habitations, only four or five of which were owned outright. The land suitable for cultivation within its catchment area was almost negligible. And here was a scheme to benefit the whole nation.

The original proposal had outlined a scheme to trap and transport water south from the lakes. It had been met with the perfect location. And it had already been authorized by an Act of Parliament some years before, in the spring of 1921. The Haweswater Act. So yes, a name had already been decided upon for the project. The Haweswater reservoir. The lake and the surrounding land had been acquired by Manchester City Waterworks under Parliament's backing, and the owned properties had had compulsory purchase orders placed upon them. There was no question of appeal. There was no higher authority. It was signed and sealed; a done deal, so to speak.

The proliferation of water which came down into the valley and was then lost to other, lower-lying, valleys, wasted in rivers, would soon be spilling into a bowl holding nearly twenty thousand million gallons. More. Imagine that. Water would be kept, used, driven. Water would be built. The water that presently sat in a little lake in the valley bottom was slothful, idle. Soon, it would be fattened to an enormous belly of water, it would be sucked up, and sent roaring in pipes down to the city. It was all fact, it was done and dusted. It was regrettably not within his control any more, nor theirs. This they must understand. He was simply a messenger.

∾

At the side of the crowd stood Ella Lightburn, tall, gaining inches to her height, even. Her jaw began to work involuntarily. She knew about messengers. The Bible was full of them. They came in bright armour or in rags. She knew that the messengers of the Lord came in many forms. She understood that He, in His divine ways, often gave signs which needed lengthy interpretation, that His ways could be mysterious and hard to fathom and that blind faith was sometimes required. Often as not, these prophets were thrown to the wolves. She also knew that the Devil had his messengers too. Black messengers who wrapped up their evil in beautiful words. Who were riddled with insects under their beautiful faces.

She stood to the side of the small group of villagers and listened to this man who was calling himself a messenger. Her mind worked quickly to come up with some conclusions. She sifted out the facts. He had on what was no doubt his best suit. It was not a Sunday. He was beautiful and she knew instinctively that this meant he was dangerous.

Ella closed her eyes momentarily. The man was speaking to the villagers gently, religiously, in a voice that could have calmed a storm on the Sea of Galilee. And it rose, steadily, becoming richer, fuller, spreading like a dome above them, then grew quiet. It was the voice she had waited for in the Sunday sermons which never came. As she opened her eyes she saw the man reach to the ground and pick up two objects. On the scales that he made out of his gloved hands he placed, consecutively, a small piece of blue slate and a large lump of frozen clay. He gave a speech about potential human equilibrium. He showed them with his hands that in this example there was no balance. There was spontaneity to the man, but also calculation. And something else. It was as if noise travelled at the back of the man, or he carried it ahead of him, out of sight. Noise like the wailing of inhuman voices, a loud, disparate chorus, shuddering through the air. Concentrating hard, she could almost hear it, almost feel it as the sound passed through her. Or was it only the whistle and groan of the *Hardwicke*, or the *Prince of Wales*, rattling its carriages and heaving up Shap summit, echoing from two valleys over? She reached up, touched the edge of her headscarf, close to her ear, as if to reassure herself that her hair was covered.

Ella could tell that the village was in confusion. Its members stared at the man in the green suit. Their eyes said that his idea was ridiculous, beyond reality; many looked fit to laugh out loud. And so they were unaffected by personal upset. Not so Ella. She felt her blood lift against her skin and her jaw began to work. There was a slight grind to her teeth. She kept her head up, concentrated on what the audacious stranger was telling her. The tone of the man's voice was quiet but invested with passion, like that of a prophet, and there was something about the set of his face which suggested that he knew the future. She did not speak because of it, did not interrupt him as she would dearly have liked to.

Ella knew something else. At times, the region of her birth and dwelling is covered with peculiar long shadows because the sun doesn't always throw its lines properly in the north and there can be strange interference from the water in the sky. The effect is like chiaroscuro, and under the weird, deep shadowing a human body might look spiritual, meaningful. As if Caravaggio has made a person and set it out on the world.

But Ella knew this was not one of those times. The lines of the setting sun were true. The man in the green suit was no Caravaggio Jesus. His face was beautiful in its own right. And his voice had a spirit unto itself. She felt if she were to speak out against him the strange noise on the periphery might increase, horribly, though only she would hear it and it would collect inside her head and remain there. She waited until he stopped speaking. She moved over to where her husband stood and put a hand firmly on to his shoulder, moved him forward.

∽

There was a movement within the crowd and one man took two steps away from the rest. The sound of his corduroy trouser legs rubbing as he moved forward was like the sound of sawing wood. The man in the suit smiled. The village had elected its spokesman, as he suspected it would at first, before other voices chipped in with comment and disapproval. He was one of the huge, blond-haired farmers with eyelashes so pale that they could hardly be seen, and the eyes themselves took on a sculpted, inorganic quality. He must be heard so that the village would know that it was to be a civilized invasion, the valley annexed with great sympathy, dignity. Let them show their anger and that anger will use itself up instead of breeding within itself, he supposed.

Samuel Lightburn cleared his throat. In abbreviated terms he made his stand.

– Yer tellin' us there's a dam to be built and the dale's t'be flooded. That's all well and good. But what of us? We cannot live underwater. Our children cannot swim t'class and t'church. Well, except maybe young Isaac, but that's beside point.

A little laughter came from the crowd, from the children who did not understand much of what they had heard but knew about Isaac Lightburn and his odd attraction to the Mardale rivers. The stranger used this to his advantage and he laughed also. A moderate, inclusive laugh, like apples rolling down a gentle bank towards a harvester's basket. He was a reasonable man, he said, and he did not think that they were fish. He understood that Parliament was a long way south, remote from the valleys of the north of England, and its workings were seldom this far-reaching. But its law was final. He ventured to suggest that the tenant farmers might seek compensation from the Lowther Estate, to which all rents were paid, or relocation. But, as he had come to understand it, their tenancies here would not be renewed beyond Midsummer Day of this year. He suggested that the men might stay on to work at the dam, there would be plenty of such positions for labourers. He waited for the multitude of voices which did not come, and so in some small way his expectations for the response of the crowd had been formed inaccurately. Instead of hot debate, the group was emitting absolute cold, a mossy, greenish aura hung over his audience as the air might be affected over a forest pool. He waited until the silence became uncomfortable for him, though he suspected the sombre gathering might have been able to hold out a little longer.

Then he commented on the chilly evening. He would be going to the Dun Bull for a warming brandy if anyone would care to join him, to discuss matters further. There was a slight bow of his head and upper body, as if the orchestra had finished and now, imaginary applause. A scuff of his city heel as he turned and he was gone.

The crowd broke. One man spat on the ground and left to return to his sheep.

∽

Had Janet Lightburn been present at the meeting instead of in the town of Penrith that afternoon with Hazel Bowman, there might have been a considerable amount more verbal upset expressed. Some dense and violent shades of anger would have been present in her face and, though this was the most significant news to hit the valley during her lifetime, she would not have had the same degree of astonishment and disbelief as some of the other members of the village. While not exactly anticipating such a thing, she might have considered herself ready for the blow, her whole life preparing for such an event. At the age of eighteen she had both the intellectual dexterity of an adult and the reckless tongue of any youth running to catch up with their own life as it matures, moves forward. A volatile combination.

She would return home three hours after the man's departure, only to be told by her father that she had missed a rite good show. Her mother would be muttering about the Devil's workings and it would take a little while to get the whole affair straightened out.

– Long and short of it, Jan, fella reckons to build a dam and flood valley. Sez leases are up come six month. Niver worry, mind, lass. 'Tsall a loada shite, you'll see.

– Sam! Language!

Ella sent her husband a bold look from the kitchen sink and continued with her washing, but had a blunt comment to throw across the room to him.

– You might have sed more an' all, mister. Put up a better match.

– What did you tell him, Dad?

– Nowt he didn't already ken. That it's a waste of time cummin' ower here afore Lordie's fest up t'deal, if there is yan at all. But he was a smart lookin' fella, I'll give him that, all weshed up and in slacks, like.

Janet narrowed her eyes.

– Who does he represent? What company? Was there any mention?

– Oh, Manchester summet or uther. City watter.

– Is he coming back, did he say?

– Shouldn't think so, lass. Shouldn't think we'll be seein' hide n' hair of t'bugger agin.

– Sam!

Janet left the room as her mother began to warn her father that she wouldn't stand for his foul-mouthed cursing. As she passed Ella she could see that there was true agitation in her, dampness along her upper lip, and she had a sense that the situation was not as light as her father would have it. It was too late tonight, but the following morning she would go to Measand Hall to use the telephone facilities and put in a call to the Lowther Estate. After that was done she would know what other calls to make, if any.

The next evening Whelter Farm Cottage was quiet and supper was late, the meeting in the village the previous day
seeming to have thrown everything out of kilter. The oil
lamps flickered and sent dim shafts of light across the walls.
Ella Lightburn stood at the large kitchen sink and was scraping
the back of some withered carrots with a paring knife. She
focused upon the task as though nothing existed outside of it.
A pot of stew was bubbling gently on the broad iron surface
of the range and she dropped the carrots into it, one at a time,
as she had sliced them.

By the hearth, Janet was reading and her brother Isaac
was chalking on a piece of flat slate, with his tongue caught
to one side of his mouth and held by his teeth. He was a
strange, briny-looking child, with a broad face, very pale,
and with the full straw head of his father but almost white-
blond, the colour of a newborn's hair. Though he had the
makings of a handsome lad, for now he had not grown into
his face. There was but a smudge of watery grey to his eyes.
He was wearing, as he often did, the wrinkled expression of
an old man, concentrating on a memory or the last line of a
joke, giving the impression that he was substantially older
than his six years. His mother had often commented that he
came out of the womb an old man already, the age of thirty
if a day.

Isaac sat in a pair of long underwear with his slim bare
chest glowing white in the room's half-light. Even against the
heat of the fire there seemed to be an air of dampness about
him. His feet were positioned on the hearth shelf, toes curling
now and again next to the warmth of the flames. Above him,
in the alcove of the fire, a dripping shirt and some socks were

hanging, they gave off a slight reedy smell as the pond water was driven out. It was not an uncommon scenario. He had lately been sulking after a few curt words from his mother about getting chilblains on his feet from the icy river, but had soon become engrossed by his craft. Janet looked up as the scratching sound of the chalk stopped.

– Finished? Let's see it.

Isaac held up the slate. There was a picture of a dog on it. Janet smiled.

– Show it Mam.

Her brother hopped up and patted over the flagstone floor to his mother. She wiped her hands on her apron, took the slate from her son, nodding, and spoke to him quietly. She handed it back to him and he returned to the fire.

– Mam sez it's just like Chase.

– And so it is. Cum here, little lad.

He moved over to Janet and crept in between her and the fireplace. She held the book she had been reading in front of them both, pointed her finger to a passage. Isaac began reading, faltering over the longer words and being gently corrected by his sister if he could not manage after a few attempts. After he had finished the poem she bent and kissed the top of his head and he sat back into the opposite armchair. Janet reached beneath her own chair and brought up a piece of embroidered cloth. She wrapped it around the book and tied the parcel with a piece of ribbon.

Ella finished the last carrot and dropped it into the pot. She heard the lift and click of the latch on the door and her husband and the dog came in. He bent his head under the small door frame. Fine beads of rainwater sparkled on his shoulders. Samuel took off his cap and laid it on a rocking chair in the corner of the kitchen. Its balance was fine and even the weight of the piece of cloth set it into motion, a fraction of a creaking rock.

He addressed his wife softly.

– Evening, Ella.

– Samuel.

Chase came over to where Ella had been cleaning the vegetables and she crept her nose into the back of Ella's hand, which was hanging down at her side. Ella glanced at her husband.

– Dog's spoiled.

She scolded her husband gently, but she took a small piece of raw liver from the dish next to the stove and cupped it in her palm for the dog to take in her teeth. Chase gingerly took the morsel and crept over to the fireplace, under Isaac's chair. He lifted his feet from the grate and placed them on the sleek hair of the dog's rump.

– Spoiled, but a grand worker, and that's our arrangement.

– Shall we put her out when next she cum in season to git some pups?

– Bitch is past breedin' binow, Ella.

Ella tutted. Her husband had a tendency to grow too fond of his working dogs. He lost sight of their place on the farm. In Samuel's arms was a small wrapped bundle, damp at the corners. He set it carefully down on the flagstone floor. A soft black hoof escaped from the folds.

– Fust one. Too early, eh? Niver a chance fer it. Bad day fer it an' all. Could give a man a funny turn if he were inclined towards such things.

Samuel sat at the scrubbed wooden table, a little dejectedly. Janet stood up and came over to her father. She kissed him on the cheek and wished him a happy birthday and went over to the still bundle in the shadows on the kitchen floor. She unwrapped the rag covering the lamb. Then she opened the stout door of the range and threw two logs into the ashes. Sparks flew inside and the wood began to crackle. She took the lamb by its fore and hind legs and pushed it into the furnace to incinerate, closed the range door and came to sit with her father to discuss the condition of the bred ewes.

– The others? Any signs yet?

– Yan or two. A week, mebbi less. Best git yer breeches out, lass.

Ella brought over the pot of tea and set it down on the table, pouring a cup for her husband. She herself sat and untied her brown hair, letting it fall on to her shoulders and about her handsome face for a moment, then she re-tied it.

– There's bread in t'pantry, Janet. Put some out fer us and a shirt on yer brother before he catches his death. Yer father and I have a word or two to come. Isaac, go with Janet. Go on, now. With yer sista.

Their mother was matter-of-fact and without social niceties. She had an intensity to her square gaze, a curt manner, which her family was used to and found inoffensive, though others often thought of her as abrasive, and a little too direct. Ella was a straightforward woman and had never been anything but. Her ways were a set pattern, daily, a series of restricted moves, and there was nothing indecisive either about those larger projects which she undertook. She had always been so, since a young girl under her grandmother's care. There had been no room for polite discourse and subtle gestures on the farm during that time of depression, nor through the old woman's illness and eventual death. Ella had been made aware very early on that life does not pull its punches, when she lost both parents to an influenza epidemic; neither, then, would she tiptoe around it waiting for her turn. There were two main influences in her life. God and family. Both were sacred, both were to be honoured and defended with fire if necessary. Her nature remained unchanged over the years. She was a constant.

∽

With this unalterable character, Ella Graham, as she had once been, had convinced many men to re-enter their lives in the quiet hospital in Penrith after the Great War. Men with ruined bodies and lost identities. Men brought back to the north after the fighting was over, still fighting within themselves, unable to leave the war behind and not yet knowing peace. The damage of the conflict was vast, and though she had not been witness to the front-line action, hers was a position purely at the receiving end of all its ravages. She knew it for what it really was, random and unconscionable slaughter. Many soldiers died in the months following the ceasefire, unlucky enough to suffer expansive and slow deaths rather than the quick, gasping murder of the battlefields. Many died within their living bodies, painfully aware of their fate.

Ella came to realize the technology of the war was defective enough that it failed to do its job properly. In her more pessimistic moments, she could not help but feel that the instruments of brutality were perhaps deliberately abortive, increasing their cruelty by not disposing efficiently of the victims.

The call for nurses during the war was nationally desperate and training was swift. She spent two months at the hospital in Carlisle, and though she applied for posted duty she was transferred to Penrith. She roomed in the row of hospital bungalows alongside the main building and with the other nurses took fourteen-hour shifts, changing dressings, emptying pans, injecting solutions. There were those patients who were simply waiting to die, whose bodies would never be able to repair themselves enough to sustain life. They rotted away, watching a limb dissolve or coughing up pieces of lung, eyes streaming like broken egg-white. She read them the Bible daily, and as they pleaded with her to kill what was left of them, she assured them of the Lord's open arms, in time. They pleaded mercy with some of the most eloquent lines she had ever heard, some of the most desperate and persuasive. The Lord is thy shepherd, she said, He leadeth thee to green pastures. There would be no mercy killings on her shift.

Others had missing sections of themselves, would live but only as half-men. They had to be held up to urinate or wash, strange imbalanced humans, who were unable to look at the telling space between the floor and their torso. She rubbed the stumps of limbs with peroxide solution to toughen them for the prosthetic they would eventually have strapped to them. These were tasks she did not find upsetting. She knew that they must be done. There was no call for personal distaste. Nor would she lie about the length of a life, to soften a blow. Her predictions erred on the side of pessimism.

– You have hours now. Yer mother will not mek it here on time. Steadman, tek my hand.

At the beginning of the ragged third quarter of the conflict she spent nine weeks at the Dover Memorial Hospital, the first time she had ventured south of Manchester. From the front lines the bodies poured in, pouring with liquid and bound with makeshift bandages. She was twenty-five years old and able to carry out her duties without loathing or discomfort or pliant tears. She placed a succinct finger into the rectum of a man unable to defecate, who was being filled with poison from the blockage, holding the fractured back down as he jolted up on the bed. She held amputated sections of the human body, threw away bone and thinking matter. Her hands were never oblique, her voice did not waver as she sliced into an infected wound, pulled out the hidden infestations, telling the patient exactly what was being done. Because he was being eaten. She spoke in plain tones. She investigated the worst anatomies, called by the others nurses when the doctors, few and eternally tired, were not available. After the stint she was sent back home, exhausted and saturated with images of the deceased, but she was glad to get back to the lake country, to the fresh water and the proximity of mountain ranges. Again, she began to meet the medical train at the Penrith railway station, transferring patients on stretchers, and driving them to the hospital in an ambulance van. She gave them little welcome. Changed their dressings, folded down the clean sheets of the bed and handed bibles to the ones who still had arms and eyes with which to read.

Those with torn souls screamed in another ward at the back of the hospital. Ella talked them back horizontal. She held chewed wrists closed, stitched vascular flesh quickly and without anaesthetic, scolding the attempted suicide as if it was a child that had tried to steal butterscotch from a market place. It went against God, she said, it was a high sin. They must trust in the Lord's destiny. The nightmares of the soldiers unravelled through the corridors. Each night men howled at the ceiling and spoke of eating the hearts of children, they sobbed or dissolved within themselves, their faces set in an expression of terror, of horror, arms rigid in the air. Their screams were those of madmen and villains, trying to drag her into the insanity of their continuing war. Instead, she gathered spilled fluids from their mouths and stomachs. It was a brutal landscape of the mind. In their silent moments the men watched her concentrating above them. Her face contorted with patience.

∽

Samuel Lightburn returned from France in February 1917, with feet that were digesting themselves after living in mud and water constantly for half a year. His calves contained over a quarter of a pound of shrapnel. His vision was damaged, but he would slowly be able to see again over the coming months. At first his head was lost under the gauze bandages, she could not find his face to clean it. She cut away the long blond locks that were not held within the bindings, thinking it was coarse, like a dog's. There were lice crawling in the hair. That first night she opened the dressing from his eyes. They were swollen almost closed and leaking furiously, blood and yellow saline. She removed the rest of his hair with a razor and washed his face. Inside the purple lids were pale, blue-grey eyes, moving uselessly as she touched his face.

– Do you see me?

– I don't know. Not really. Thank you fer helping me. Yer a bonny lass. I can tell.

He was a large, quiet man, easily encouraged to laughter by the other patients. At night he made no cries, did not suffer from dreaming visions, and she had no reason to pity him. He was not haunted by memories, but by his own, inexplicable survival, and he seemed to be living as if he did not quite know whether or not he should be. He would eat only half-portions of food, as if the simple act brought guilt. Once, Ella found him in the early morning sitting on the bed of a dead soldier. He had stumbled blindly in the direction of the man's gentle pleading for someone to give him company, falling once against a metal bed-rail and slicing his palms. He had not been able to find his way back to bed after the man had drifted from pain to silence, his bearings lost in the room. He had not wanted to dislodge vital tubes and equipment as he searched for the empty cot. The dressings over his eyes had slipped down, but his hands, too painful, had not been able to move them back on his head. He was speaking in a low voice to the soldier, talking of sheep and market prices, a constant deluge of mundane conversation, not realizing the man had passed away.

In the spring, Ella led Samuel around the hospital gardens by an arm. There were daffodils growing along the walls and he wanted her to gather some for him to give back to her. He had never smelled a daffodil, he said, had never fancied to. Now he thought he might quite like it. She held one to him, the fresh, light fragrance was at first not detected because of the chemical burns in his nostrils and throat. But after a while it came, and with it his confession.

His voice was raw as he began asking her the meaning of his being alive, that it must have been some crime against his fellow soldiers, he saved, and all of them gone. God had spared him, she said, he had no choice now but to live well, in His name. Samuel said the quiet behind his eyes was like a gift he could accept for such mercy, such love, and if he could not see again he would understand it to be only the residue of God's choice to keep him on the earth.

He bent to kiss her cheek, blindly, untidily. His eyes monstrous behind the gauze. She hesitated at first, then directed his kiss, her fingers finding a brass button to hold on his long military coat as she swayed against him. By the last week of April his vision was almost restored and he said that he had been right to call her bonny. His discharge papers were being completed, and she told him about the empty farm that had been tended by her grandmother until her death a year before the outbreak of war. It was remote. It was quiet, a place of recovery, a place of new life.

∾

– There's talk of another war, Samuel. *Cumberland Herald*'s full of it. Hitler's defied Treaty. It's only the start. They say he's opening fact'ries to manufacture planes. It's all cumin' again, Sam, in time.

Samuel sighed and unbuttoned his heavy tweed jacket as if he was only now coming back into his home, out of the cold. His wife was sitting opposite him, her brow furrowed. As with many women of her generation, it had taken Ella a long time to get over the war, and even now there remained a deeply unsettled part of her which clenched like a tight fist if it was touched by a memory, a suggestion of that same abhorrence. To broach the subject herself was almost unheard of. He nodded slowly, took her hand.

– I know it.

– Plenty o' lads from t'dale will be outa work if dam goes up. Not minny choices left after.

– It's all talk as yet, Ella. Nuthin's settled.

– Mind the men in t'Bull get it settled tonight. Mind it, Sam. Summet's to be dun. And mind fellas don't get thee as drunk as last year's birthday! Or you'll have a poorly head for the market tomorrow.

She stood and stirred the cooling stew with a spoon, called to her children. They came in with the bread and sat at the table, Isaac now dressed in a dry woollen shirt. Ella stood to give the grace. She did not bow her head or close her eyes, but kept them open and looked directly at her husband as she spoke. Her body held itself up, strong, like a stout pillar of oak. Her daughter's eyes remained open also, fixed on a loose point in space.

– Dear Lord, we thank Thee fer the food on the table and ask You to give strength to our community in this time when it is cast over with darkness. Keep us safe. In Your name Lord, Amen.

They ate the food quietly, without mention of the dam, though it weighed heavy on them, for it was a celebration night, after all. During the meal Janet and Isaac gave gifts to their father. He watched the pleasure in their faces as he took them, the exchange of smiles, his neck warming. Their eyes were bright, their laughter rooking. His own laughter was self-conscious and lit with enjoyment and embarrassment in equal measures. From his son, a picture. He watched the watery excited eyes of the boy as he took it and slowly turned it over. His small pudgy hands were gripping the table edge and Samuel could see he was about to explode.

– Hah! Chase, eh! Clever lad.

Isaac let out a squeal of a laugh. Samuel looked at his daughter. Her smile was almost feline, contained. The corners of her mouth upturned by only a small black part of the lips. Even her hair, blue-blonde and long and full, made him think of a lion, and in the shadows between her collarbone and the sweep of hair might have been carcasses hanging off trees in the savannah. He detected a dark mood pushing at her surface, though she tried hard to be glib.

– It's a book of poetry by Emmett Thompson. He's uncle t' Hazel Bowman and lives over in Kirby Thorpe. I think he was . . . there too. Y'might read some after supper, if y'like. Or get Zac to. He's bin practising all day. Haven't yer, Zac?

– Your father has better uses of his time just now, Janet. There's a lame calf in t'top field and I'm sure some ewes are about ready to drop. Can't afford to lose as minny as last year.

Her mother's tone was imbued with tension. But Janet had a wild cut to her. She had her father's neck between her teeth and wouldn't let it go.

– It's a first edition. There is a signature in the front cover. Mr Thompson visited the Bluebell bookshop in Kendal last month; I met him. He has a lot of interesting things to say. About what t'give up . . . and what t'keep. And why. In one poem he talks about how passing something away from you is like receiving the full weight of understanding what the object truly represented. That when you put on your own empty hands, they are about the same weight as a bird lifting from the water. I don't remember exactly. But I loved that line.

– Thanks, lass. Thanks, Jan.

At the sink, Ella banged down the empty pot with emphasis. Her daughter did not flinch.

Samuel stood up and walked round the table. He bent slowly and kissed his daughter's hair. She smelled like the rain coming on to dry earth. She smelled of the lily soap that he had been bringing her from town since her hair grew long, bought once a month, a secret expense. By the hearth, Chase pricked up her tufted ears, and a second later was by her master's feet. Samuel picked up his cap from the rocking chair and pulled it on to his head.

– Grand stew, Ella. Grand as owt. Time to sort out city fella.

As his thumb pressed the door latch down he heard his wife's voice, charged and warning.

– He's bringing ill. He's a messenger of nowt but darkness and ill. I just know it, Sam, I know it here.

She was holding a hand over her chest, her jaw working at her cheek. Then the cool damp air was sliding past Samuel's neck outside the cottage door.

As he reached the top of the steep field he found Nathaniel Holme repairing a hole in one of the drystone walls which bordered the two men's properties. By the old man's feet was a selection of good-shaped rocks for the task, some flat and short for bridging, others dense and high for volume, stones for the body of the wall. As he approached, Samuel heard the familiar, soft thwock-thwock of stone being set down against more stone, followed by a harsh scraping as it was turned into place. The old man's breathing was laboured and loud, as if the air was running on loose shale from his lungs to his mouth. He grunted as he lifted another piece of the wall.

– There's a couple spots need tending down by our barn when yer dun, if y'like.

Nathaniel turned. His voice was thick in reply.

– Git out, yer sly bugger. Watch a fella bildin' up fell en cum up en stick a stree in his hat!

Samuel hitched his trouser knees up and knelt down on the chill, recently thawed ground, next to his old friend. He picked up the biggest stone from the grass and hefted it into the uneven cavity of the wall, glancing at Nathaniel from the corner of one eye. Chase whined and bent to lick the back of Samuel's hand as he worked. Then she took off up the field, paws bounding off the ground, a streak of black and white fur. Nathaniel examined his companion's work and tutted.

– Never could wall out, thee. Look at that gap in t'middle. Fat Jake down yonder could fit through t'hole. What yer dyan up hea so late, any road, yer daft bugger.

– Same as you, yer daft bugger.

– Aye well, it's ower fuckin' late fer buggerin' about. I'm going tu t'Bull. Cumin'?

– Aye. Go on, then.

– Sam, th' knows my mind at Bull. Give ower talk of stoppin' in t'dale. Pointless, like.

Nathaniel spoke quietly, slowly, slowly, breathing hard. A

pause in the conversation left only the sharp and blunt sounds of stone on stone as Samuel continued with the walling.

Nathaniel was seventy-one, arthritic, and could not work as he once had. His body was near to seizing completely with swellings and there was a bad cough deep in him that had gathered strength over this last winter, turning heavier, taking over the old man's chest and robbing him of air as it shook itself free. Nathaniel's two sons had died in the war and his wife Angela had passed away a decade before. There was nobody left to work at Goosemire, except one part-time farmhand, a few itinerants in the busy seasons if he could afford to pay them, and Nathaniel undertook most of the farm work himself.

Samuel sighed and rubbed his hands together, brushing off shards of slate.

– Dam's not coming off. It's all in that laddie's heed.

He tapped the side of his own skull with two fingers for emphasis.

– Besides, it took years fu' t'uther dam in Thirlmere to git finish. Wilf Martin at Hinter Hall farmed up until last block went in, eh?

– Aye. But, git finish it did, Sam. Git finish it did.

Nathaniel's eyes were hazel-yellow and old and tired as he turned to look at Samuel. He was nodding as he leaned forward on to the wall, taking the weight of his wiry upper body on to his arms. Then he cleared his throat lengthily, spitting on the grass. Samuel knew the noise was a precursor, it usually meant the old man was preparing to give a speech, speak his mind. He was not mistaken.

– Sam, lad. That M'nchister fella's wearin' a suit as costs as much as thee's house, if Lordie felt like sellin' up. Fella's not up fu' t'scenery, nor buying a cottage fer lil' kiddies to grow up in. He's got some mighty weight, mighty weight. His face'll tell thee that. Next time w'see young fella, he'll niver be laffin' like t'uther day. But it suits me grand, in a way; mine are all gone. Purchase order's dun on t'farm. Notta fella more hard priss to leave t'dale than me. And thee's young enough to start ova agen. That wee un'll git gud schoolin'. Janit can teach in town. Zac's not up t'farmin'. Too much watter in t'lad's heed binow. And that bonny lassie'll not fetch up wid a complete git fer a husband if she's out of Shap's v'cinity. Betta selection in Penrith, like. Lordie's not gonna renew, Sam; bugger's not losin' out, neither. I tell thee, th'll be compensation plenty fu' t'auld bugger. Nowt fer thee.

Samuel sighed.

– Cheerful auld bugger, in't ya?

Nathaniel grinned at Samuel with a mouth of brown and missing teeth.

– I am. I am.

Then he stood up painfully, lifted off his cap and wiped his brow of sweat with a sleeve and replaced the cap in one movement. With a gnarled, arthritic hand he took a pipe out of his jacket pocket and a tin of loose tobacco. He filled the pipe and left it in his mouth, but he would not light it until he was inside, out of the wind. Nathaniel was a practical, wise old man. He was endlessly jovial, respected and admired throughout the region.

The two men walked down the fields towards the village. They walked comfortably in a silence accepted by both parties. Words, when they were exchanged, were restrained, cordial.

– Seca grand evening, like.

– Aye, grand, Nate.

The wind was getting up. It brought references to the winter within it, which bothered Nathaniel's chest. He wheezed but never slowed his pace. The two men paused by a herd of cows in the lower fields and Samuel bent to check the hooves and underbelly of one of the beasts. He stood up and sent a piercing whistle back over the darkening hill, and a minute later Chase came streaking down it with a rabbit in her jaws. She jogged lightly by the feet of the two men.

– Gudog.

They continued on towards the small clutch of houses

which was disappearing into the dusk. By the time they reached the Dun Bull, the night had almost settled down fully. From the mountains half-circling Mardale came the released scent of the earth, strong and woody from winter's concentration, and along with it came the fresh flavour of the pushing spring.

∾

Janet Lightburn had not wanted to spoil her father's birthday, nor had she been in the mood for an argument with her mother about any of the information she wanted to disclose. At the gathering in the Dun Bull Inn there was little room for her to find a clear space and deliver the news, it was crowded with men of the dale who had come to discuss the visit from the suited man and the air was yellow with smoke, making it difficult to get firm eye contact with them all in turn as she wanted to. But she stood firm among them, inhaled the collective masculinity of the place and adopted a fairly fierce tone to get their attention. It was nothing new in itself, she had been known to speak with authority on issues before, and with the confidence of a politician. Nevertheless, the men grumbled as they became quiet, begrudging her presence somewhat.

The shake to her hand was not nerves, it was not even the subconscious intimidation of being outnumbered fifty to one by men. If she trembled, it was because the issue she was discussing stirred her up and agitated her. She had put in a telephone call to the Lowther Estate, she said, that morning, and after a considerable run-around from Lordie's secretary she had managed to speak to Peter Talbot, the estate manager. They would all remember him, having helped to drag him from the lake after a disastrous fishing trip last year when he was using the Langdale boathouse. Crooked-nosedy fella, aye. He confirmed that the Mardale tenancies were under review. Relating to a private business endeavour with a

Manchester corporation. She was assured by him that they would all be informed, by letter and within a month, of the estate's decision.

Murmurs went through the crowd, a comment or two about a woman's place, very quietly. Basically, that means yer all fuckin' out, she said, and slammed a hand hard down on to a table. And if Teddy Hindmarsh was so convinced this was horse shite, and that a lassie couldn't understand grass for grain, she suggested he make a call himself and try his hand with that wan bastard who'd be better off drowned.

Behind her the tall figure of Paul Levell had entered the bar and was nodding slightly. Janet Lightburn stepped between broad unwashed bodies to the bar and ordered an ale from Jake McGill.

∽

Sometime after midnight of the following week, Janet and her father walk into the farm kitchen, which still has warm air from the glowing cinders of the range. Their hands are frozen and bloody. Janet moves to the sink and soaps her wrists in cold water. The water tank is not hot at this time of night and she has to work the blood off without the aid of dissolving heat. It sets under her nails as she scrubs, blackens. There is a numb buzzing in her head from the strong wind on the fells, where she has been braced on the ground with her father for over an hour. Her eyes are weary. Lambing season means little sleep for Westmorland farmers, but within days their bodies have adjusted to the new routine, finding a strange and fraught level of energy that comes in the wake of sleep-deficiency. It is a difficult time, when winter can sweep down into the valley just as the village is beginning to see the crests of snowdrops and crocuses budding through the earth. Snow buries and camouflages labouring sheep and only the stray sound of a bleat will indicate the hole into which the animals have headed.

71

If they can find the animals due to birth, and bring them into the safety of the farm sheds or a sheltered corner field, it is a far easier task. There is steady light from the hurricane lamps and the ewes can be positioned and helped, the sticky lambs kept warm. But predictions are seldom accurate, and it is bleak searching the fells for a twisting ewe in early labour. These births are almost impossible to assist in the black cold. The bark of the dog, frantic over a fallen animal. A wet lamb, rocking in the savage wind, often has to be shown how to live and move or it will not survive a single, tenuous night. There is precious little on the side of a farmer during this time of year.

Even later in the lambing season the spring weather brings its share of problems. Treacherous mud and constant rain churn the ground and there is no firm outside surface offering traction and stability, a table upon which to drag stillborns from their mothers. Dejected, the sheep often cry over their listless lambs, refusing to eat in the coming days, the loss double for the farm. Panicked by imminent delivery, a sheep might stumble off its heft, up into the crags where it cannot be reached. Silly season, Samuel calls it, though his daughter is all earnestness during these weeks, mirthless, and more driven than even her father.

Samuel Lightburn scuttles coal into the oven. He fills the kettle with water and places it on the hotplate. Ella has left out some biscuits and cheese on a plate, covered with a cloth. The two eat ravenously while moving about in the room, unbuttoning coats, wrenching off wet boots and setting them against the range. The house is quiet above them and a carriage clock ticks on the shelf. Two-fifteen.

Father and daughter sit at the table with their hands wrapped around mugs of hot, sweet tea. There is no point in climbing the stairs to bed at this hour. At four another shift of lambing will begin. In the kitchen only the dog sleeps by the hearth, with her nose curled under one paw, and her hind legs twitching. She works even while dreaming in her sleep.

Samuel has come to know less than ever about women through the disposition of his daughter. Where his wife is a hard, often stubborn woman, who believes in separate roles, Janet is above and beyond. She terrorizes the old notions, batters her way through and out the other side. There are no absolutes to be found in the blood on her wrists, and under her nails. She has feral qualities not belonging to either sex. But he cannot say he isn't proud of her. Because, by God, he is!

In March the running water of the valley is bitter, acid cold, as snow on the fells begins to melt and is brought down over chilled rocks and icy beds. It has in it all the breaking soul of winter, thousands of dying flakes in one long, moving water-coffin. But despite the cold, the streams and waterfalls are very clear, clearer than they have been all year, a perfect window into the living houses of the river. Sediment and detritus are bound to the ground, cauterized by ice, and are unable to dissolve into the passing liquid until the thaw takes a better hold in April, loosening the old skin of the earth, allowing it to shed.

Isaac lies half on the ground, half braced on a rock over a channel of the river. His face in the water turns purple and yellow and his lips soon numb. If he is not careful, his muscles will start to spasm uncontrollably and he will lose his balance, shocking the rest of his body into the water, electric cold. He times himself within the icy cataracts. He has perhaps no more than ten seconds before his cheeks begin to roll of their own accord, as if he is fitting, then he must surface. Knowing the direction of flow, he turns his face downstream, using his head to block its passage, protecting his eyes from the burn of the moving current. He opens their lids. There is a second when their mechanism falters, they will not adjust to the temperature, having lost the slim warmth of an eyelid covering, the lenses will not still and focus is impossible. Then, the panic subsides. Pupils retract. The world of the inside river appears, detailed and precise.

Water is white-clear. And after a while it is non-existent. There is no wetness. There is no thin element rushing past, only frigid movement, arctic winds in another planet's sky.

He sees sharply, down to the rocks on the riverbed, and a

prehistoric tail, a grey crayfish leg is tucking itself under a dolmen. He reaches down with a quiet hand and turns the rock over without so much as a particle of soil or sand lifting into the current of the river. The crayfish, a dark lobster-cat, does not move. Its whisker antennae, sensitive enough to feel a shift of life a foot away in the water, twitch, touch-sighted, its pincers gather energy. It knows the house is gone. Isaac moves a small hand through the current quick as a diving bird and pinches it on the armoured back at the point where it cannot reach a claw back to him. It kicks its tail, flicking back into the firm grip. The divisions of its shell click against each other, the sound dull underwater. He loves that sensation, the language of sound. He turns it over, examines the pale-grey underbelly, the alien anatomy riddled with legs, then drops it into the wind to watch it swim backwards under the shifted rock, to continue sleeping in the river. He puts his fingers in his mouth, sucks them, moving his tongue, as if to create a friction of heat. But his is not a fish-blood, there is no oil under his skin to keep him warm in the river's cataracts.

Ten seconds have passed. His teeth are moving against his cheek. Cold invades every pore of skin with tiny arrows. He ignores the sensation of spears a few seconds longer.

Trout gape at him. Their spots shimmering fire, locked with brown-silver and lit by the water's light. Minnows butting the current, all eyes. The black silk of a hidden eel. Crustaceans adding sections to their shells along the cratered stones of the river valley walls. It is all worthwhile.

The houses are filled with life even in winter, reptilian, marine, and the fish, sluggish in the near-zero climate. All is stark at this time of year, barren, before the sun warms reeds and algae to life from the rich beds, and grassland returns once more in the river, forestation, jungle, beating slowly in the benthic weathers. But now, life gives itself up utterly for observation.

He will stay down for as long as he can, a watery pioneer, caught between two worlds. His foreign body, learning the river's tricks. His nostrils closing, eyes in stasis, not giving away a suggestion of life, no tell-tale air bubble struggling to the surface to reveal his presence. His blood crystallizes, congeals. His lips turn blue and their cells die. But he will cut into the water again and again for the pleasure of the other world, a boy tranquillizing his face. His head smashing through the reflection of a lumbering crow in the sky. Because the March water is sparkling and icy and pure, a conductor of vision, a magnifying glass to all corners of the pools. A rare month for spying on these inhabitants, the strange and beautiful nations.

He holds his body out of the stream, better to preserve a supply of warmth, though the ground and rock under him steals at it. He allows a hand now and again into the water like a wingless bird diving for silver, keeping the other on a slippery, moss-covered stone above the river, which still has little pieces of ice tucked tight in its fur.

The crayfish is a good find, time-consuming, but he remains submerged for over fifteen seconds, unwilling to neglect other species in their tender cages.

Then the pain begins to dissolve all other sensation in his head and his eye rolls back to life. Spasms rock his flesh and he surfaces. Coming up, the air seems even colder than the water. The mountain breeze licks at his dripping ears, nips at them with quick bites, his forehead smarts. He breathes, unable to prevent a dry, clamped cough from coming up as the oxygen is taken into the halted lungs. He massages his neck and throat. The glands have tight knots. His wet collar has begun to freeze, stiffening against his neck, and chafing. He unbuttons the shirt, folds it off his skin. He puts the cold-staved fingers of his right hand under his tongue again but there is no heat left for either to borrow.

∽

At least once or twice a day Isaac will come here to do this. In the summer he will swim down to the riverbed, wholly sub-

76

merged, and in the winter he'll break ice to feel water on his forehead. Even though his mother will scold him for the damp clothing and his frozen hands. He'll tell her that God has made a botched job, that he should have been a fish, and his mother will scold him for that, too. But she knows it, really, that he cannot keep away from water. That he is mesmerized by it. Ella has set firm in her mind the notion that her son will meet his fate in the waters of the Mardale valley, though he swims well enough. That one day she will find his corpse, a pale bag locked full of water at the bottom of Hop Grumble ghyll, where the torrent meets the lake. Or that Samuel will have to wade out under the Measand bridge, grope a hand between the reeds and find a son. She has her visions, her omens. The drowned wasp suspended in a jar of honey, a silver birch leaf fallen into a puddle. She tries to explain the dangers to him, to encourage him into other habits. He will not be swayed. He is called to the river. Because there he has the freedom to fly, weightless and sighted through the currents of the valley's water. It is a better world, where life is slower and quicker at once, and there is silence except for the movement of the river's atmosphere itself.

∾

After a while Isaac stands, turns down the path, dizzy and rigid with cold. Today he has stayed down too long. There are side-effects to his devotion of the river. Bright stars of yellow light are imploding near the corners of his eyes. His peripheral vision is destroyed. The horizon is dull and its lines are separating, closing together, separating. He stumbles, sits down on a rock, rubs the last of the river out of his eyes, crushing his palms' heels into the sockets, smashing out frost and winter tears.

An impossible creature is just ahead of him, steaming on the roadside. A red dragon, maybe fourteen feet long. And beside it a man made of dark-green panels. The lines around the beast and the man chase and flex. It is a picture in a dream, an illustration from a medieval book made modern, a hallucination. As if the peculiar effects of the river have begun freezing the soft tissues inside his head. He does not trust his eyes, which are banging with light. But no, hallucinations are reserved for fevers, diseases. The river does not make him sick. He rubs his sockets, crushing yellow stars against his skull, opens his eyes, blinks. And blinks again. No, a dragon, definitely. Dragon.

∾

When the man in the suit saw Isaac he thought at first that the boy was sick. He was pale and dripping with sweat. His shirt was dark with it. He did not seem stable and was swaying on the rock where he sat, staring intently straight ahead, but without seeing what his eyes offered up, it seemed. His hair had separated into bright blond icicles.

The man took a few steps towards the boy, as if to catch him if he fell. But he jumped up from the rock.

– Don't run.

The boy stood for a moment, swaying, then sat again with a sudden jerky movement. The gesture seemed unrelated to the request. The man walked slowly up the steep path towards him, holding one hand in front of him as if to urge calmness, to dissuade flight. As if approaching a stray of some kind.

– There's no need for running. No need at all. Just stay, and I'll come to you.

Isaac squinted up one eye, bearing his teeth on that side of his face as his mouth followed upwards after the squint. There was a terrible pain behind that eye, a narrow, tunnel hole of pain going back towards his skull. An ache of bone. Ice-pain. The man sat next to him, flipping up the back of his suit jacket as he sat.

– You're soaked. Are you unwell?

– No, I'm well enuff.

There was a brief silence, during which Isaac sniffled loudly. The man wondered whether he should offer the boy a handkerchief to dry himself with, blow his nose, but decided against it. They sat for a time quietly, without talking, a damp, cold boy in a wet shirt and a man who looked as if he would be more at home in the offices of Piccadilly or Manhattan, not the lake country. Both were dressed in wholly unsuitable attire, respectively out of place in the wintry environment.

– What d'yer want?

– Well, nothing, really. I just thought you might be unwell. You looked poorly.

– I'm grand as owt.

– You're shivering.

– Aye, so'd you be, if you'd bin in t'beck.

– Did you fall in?

The boy grunted as if annoyed, as if the man had suddenly become very stupid and had asked a ridiculous question. He coughed without putting a hand over his mouth. His body was shaking.

– You mean you went in voluntarily? That's a bit irregular at this time of year, isn't it? Won't your mother be angry? Won't she scold you?

Shi'll not if she dun't know.

– Oh. Of course. Well, rest assured you can count on my complete discretion.

The man in the suit put out his hand, paused, then laid it on the boy's wrist.

– You're frozen. You feel like ice cream, you look about as pale as ice cream, too.

Then the man laughed. His laugh was full of genuine mirth and there were small, fine lines around his eyes.

– Well, what's your name?

– T's Isaac.

– Pleased to make your acquaintance, Isaac. I'm Jack.

The boy hopped off the rock and turned to face the man. He

stuck out a hand in a blunt gesture. He was still squinting one eye savagely. They shook, the older of the two charmed by the unexpected manners of the boy.

– Well Isaac, I'm a little concerned with how cold that hand is.

– Warmin' up.

– Yes. But, if it's right with you, I'll put my coat on you and escort you home in case you melt. Where do you live? One of the farms?

The boy shook his head quickly, sending a spray of icy water out from his hair like a dog shaking after retrieving a thrown stick from a lake. He pushed away the offered coat.

– Cum wid us, if y'like, but I'll not wear it. Shi'll know.

– Yes, your mother might be a problem. Tell you what, then, put it on now and take it off when we get close to the house, before she spies you. She'll be none the wiser. Do we have a deal?

Isaac considered the proposal for a moment. It seemed fair enough. The man noticed how pale his non-squinting eye was, almost clear apart from a faint bluish smudge around the pupil. He found the child a little disarming to look at. The boy took the coat and put it on, struggling with its size. The arms almost reached the ground and its shoulders drooped off his back. The man buttoned up the front, though it made little difference for a snug fit. Under his jacket the man had on a pale-yellow shirt with gold armbands on his biceps. Isaac reached out and touched the one on his left arm.

– Whatter them for?

– To stop my arms from falling off. How's the coat? Better?

– Feels like rabbuts' ears, eh?

– Rabbits' ears?

Isaac went over to the water, dropped to his knees and hunted around for a second in the grass. The man winced as the coat was knelt into the earth. Then Isaac came back over, holding out a small green and white leaf. The man took it. It was long and slightly concave, covered with downy hairs, similar in shape and texture to a rabbit's ear. The reference made sense. The boy was grinning and seemed pleased at the lesson he was giving about flora. He snatched the plant back and began to tickle a palm with it as he walked away. He walked clumsily and with tripping steps down the steep path towards the red car. The man followed.

– Yor t'fella that's gunna mek lake bigga.

– Yes, I am.

❦

A cold wind was blowing off the top of the mountain and snow from the summit was being whipped into the air. As the two made their way up the rocky track to Whelter Farm they were both shivering. The man wished he had stopped at his car to collect his overcoat and hat. It was ridiculous to be running around outside without them. Further up along the path there was a low shout, which the wind brought down to them.

– Zac? Isaac?

A young woman came round the corner of the lane by the stream. Her hair was twisted into a loose knot before it fell a good way down her back. The mass of it made her head look smaller in comparison, the face taut, leopard-like. The direction of her gaze was up towards the slope of the fell, towards the river cataracts, where she expected her brother to be. She had on a shawl and a cotton dress. Her arms were tightly crossed over her chest and clouds came from her mouth as she shouted into the fraught air. Her legs were bare from the knees down, until the beginning of two heavy, black leather boots, which looked like army surplus.

The man paused on the path to look at her. From a distance, her hair looked as if it had an almost blue sheen, but as she came closer it disappeared into dark yellow. There were sculpted angles in her face, high sheered bones, but her eyes were deep set, becoming lost within the shadow-pools of their own sockets and the man could not tell what colour they were. She lacked the combed, powdered quality of the women in the city tearooms and dancehalls, and also their stunted manner of walking. This woman strode. The hair lifted off her back in the wind. He thought to himself, she is not beautiful.

Isaac paused also and turned to face his companion.

– It's m'sista.

The young woman's head came round to face forward and she saw her brother standing with a tall stranger. His attire was fine, immaculately tailored. She knew immediately who he was. She approached them without smiling, her eyes lost, her face showing too much bone. The man addressed her politely.

– Good evening.

There was no response. She continued walking towards them, a slow walk now, careful, a prowl almost. And as she reached them, the man thought again, where are her eyes? There were dark hollows where they should have been, perhaps the edge of an eyelash, nothing more. She looked tired or blind.

– Tek it off, Isaac.

There was no malice to the words. The muscles of her voice stretched, sinewy and elastic, like a lazy yawn under a tree, and did not mirror the flagrant position of her request. She reached out and pulled some frosty water from her brother's hair with tightened fingers. He was comfortable with this gesture, his head moving slightly to one side under the strength of her hand.

– Tek it off. Get on, gaily lad.

Dutifully, he began to fumble with the jacket buttons. She bent down to him, setting one bare knee on the ground in the position of a marriage proposal, and carefully removed the coat for him, then stood. She still had not looked at the man accompanying her brother. This was disarming for him and he sensed a deliberate banishment. He spoke to gain her attention.

– Leave it on him for a while, I really don't object. He's very cold, the poor lad will probably catch pneumonia. And I'd hate to see him pass away. He's really my only ally at present. I can't afford to lose him.

The man attempted humour, found it absent from his words. Finally, the woman turned to him. Her eyes were bronze when they suggested anger to his face, an unnatural shade, somewhere between orange and grey.

– He could live under an iceberg and it wouldn't bother him. In fact, he'd prosper.

Her listless, subdued tone held, working against the bruised, shining eyes, but the accent thinned perhaps for his benefit. He guessed at her age. Not more than twenty. If that. Yet she seemed older, capable of immense control and poise. He offered her a hand.

– My name is Jack . . .

– I know perfectly well what your name is. Who y'are. And yer position at Manchester City Water. I'd congratulate you on yer timing, right on the brink o' lambing season, but then it's been done before this way, so that's not necessary. It's an old trick isn't it, get them when they're busiest? Less time to think, less time to . . . act. A good tactic. Tried and true.

Her laugh was quiet, sarcastic. She continued.

– In a week or two I might shake with you, but you'll have to come back to me when we both know more about where we stand. I'm sure you appreciate that, Mr Liggett.

He pulled the wires of his smile a little tighter and brought the hand down. His exterior was unruffled, but in truth he had not expected the first real verbal sparring on the subject of Haweswater to be with a young woman on a fell in the biting March cold. The idea had been to take care of things indoors, in a controlled environment, in his way. Her eyes glimmered. Now he could not get rid of her gaze. Her feline face, lank, raw. He thought again, she is not beautiful, and though it did not resound as clearly in him the second time, with this thought he found a little more courage and a little more certainty.

– The timing, I can assure you, bears no hidden agenda, as you imply. We simply weren't all go until recently. These things do take time, and we have known for a while, that's true, but it also takes a lot of organization before . . . well, before take off.

– That's three takes I counted. That's a lot of taking.

Isaac had not been following the conversation. He had begun walking away up the path to the thick stone house in the distance. He turned and waved to them both, though they did not see him, then he ran skittishly upwards. The man switched himself to another tone, quickly, as if he'd meant it all along. A chameleon bringing fresh colour up into his skin, regurgitating bark texture instead of rock.

– I should apologize. Here I am with your brother, a perfect stranger . . .

– No. Don't.

She would not even allow him that. Cut short, the man breathed out quickly, nodding his head a little and looking down. He almost laughed out loud at the difficulty he was having, moving with her. He continued to look down at the trickling path for a time, the measled snow. Her boots were scuffed at the toe, unpolished, the heels tipped back on the uneven ground. If he had pushed her, square on her breast-plate, her balance would surely have failed. She must have been extremely cold but was not showing it. Her arms were open, angled, hands fastened to her hips, allowing the air freedom to remove warmth from the expanses of skin. There was no protection against the cold blowing down off the mountains and circling them. She moved a leg back, as if unwilling to accept his gaze on it, as if she had read his mind and was securing her position on the ground, her boot splashing a tiny puddle of water up on to the pale, downed skin.

When he looked up again, she had his jacket next to her face, as if she was trying to find a scent kept there in its fibres.

He had not even thought to ask her for it back yet. One of the buttons was torn off with her teeth, she held it half in her mouth. He breathed in without smoothness, startled by the gesture. It might have been erotic if it had not been so unusual and brutal. He breathed in again. The air seemed lacking in something vital for use in respiration. She brought the button from her lips with finger and thumb, took the dark cotton thread into her mouth, rolled it on her tongue. He half expected her to spit it out but she did not. Then she held the button out to him.

– It was loose. You'd have lost it.

His chest was moving rapidly under his shirt, perhaps because of the cold or perhaps because of this woman's confidence, her balance, he did not know which. He took the small, moist object carefully. He had no wish to drop it. It seemed important that he did not. Then he took the coat from her.

– Thank you for yer concern for Isaac. And fer seeing him back.

Now her voice was nothing but that which it sought to convey. She bade him goodnight, saying it was late and that he would be wanting to get away. But she waited on the path for him to turn and leave, her expression absent as it had been when they first met minutes before. He wanted to offer a handshake again but thought it pointless. He simply bade her a goodnight also. As he turned to leave, the button was pressing hard into his palm, and by the time he reached his vehicle it had left the circular imprint of a quarter-pierced moon in the soft flesh on the underside of his hand.

∽

After a good amount of time Janet began to walk back up to Whelter Farm. The roar of the man's car had left the valley. It was almost fully dark. Her hands were numb with cold by now, they had lost all feeling, so much so that if someone had touched them she would have thought them alien, would not have believed them to be her own.

She had watched him walk down to his automobile, not looking back once, becoming smaller in the valley and finally climbing into his new car. She had watched his shoulders rocking under his cotton shirt, he still had not put on the suit jacket, as if she had somehow tainted it, until he was no more than a form in motion within the clothing. Then, too far away to recognize, he was a pale shell on the valley floor.

For a long time he had sat in the vehicle and there had been no gun of the engine, no squeal of tyres as he turned in the cul-de-sac of the concrete road's end. He sat within the blind cage of the car, invisible to her, as if content to be separate from the landscape and to watch it change as night came on, altering under the sinking sun, the depth of atmosphere being restored as light departed. He might have been looking up to the high buildings near the Rigg or down at the lake. He might have been looking at her across the width of the village. From her position on the path she too watched the piece of land struggle for air and light in the building shadows, watched the valley finish.

When the engine was started a rage had come to her, soft at first, but becoming more focused, like claws at the base of a neck. She twisted round behind her and picked up a stone and threw it after the man into the open valley, into the eye of her fury. As if his leaving was somehow the most insulting aspect of the meeting.

Then she had walked forward, towards the drystone wall which led down into the valley, had placed her hands on the top of it, letting the chill granite take away the last of her sensation. Her forearms grazing against the sharpness as she held on to the wall's spine. A cry of agitation into a crevice of the rock's muscle. She had not moved from there for nearly an hour. And now as she finally went home, her hands did not belong to the rest of her.

Jack Liggett was staying in the border town of Penrith, thirteen miles from the proposed dam site and nearly twenty from the village of Mardale. The road he took into the valley was slow and winding and littered with ragged-looking sheep, but he drove it almost daily, arriving in the afternoon, and leaving in darkness. He did not take the main road to Shap and then down past Swindale and Rosgill to the valley, but instead came by a more direct route through the villages of Askham, Helton and Bampton. It was more scenic, more direct as the crow flew.

On this route he encountered several gates along the way, which were chained to posts to keep livestock separate from each other and out of the neighbouring fields. He made sure to close the gates behind him, recoiling, though, from the greasy metal of the lock and the odious sheep wool snagged into its links. The bestial smears and smudges on the lattices. There were also several bent metal cattle grids on this road, which saved the effort of having to get in and out of the car to tackle gates, but were hell on the suspension and tyres of the car. There was no easy method of navigating them. Fast or slow, each one would in turn make him wince as he drove over it, each gave out a loud metal strum and the car would bounce and shake. There were always several worrying bangs and crashes from the undercarriage of the automobile, as if vital sections of the exhaust and radiator had come off.

In places, the road through these tiny, hidden villages was covered with pools of meltwater which had spilled out of the warmed veins in the hills. Other sections, in the shadow of a hill or wood, were frozen in slippery sheets. The Waterworks had assured him that access to Mardale would not prove to be a problem, that the roads of the Lowther and Bampton valleys were fair, if not in an excellent state for the lake country, and that the actual Mardale road was in very good condition, having been built only a decade earlier, a private venture of the Waterworks itself as it began to explore the region in earnest. But the new concrete road was not the marvel of modern transportation that he had been led to believe it was. The men at the Waterworks did not account for the strength and brutality of the region's weather, which, even in only ten years, had broken up the concrete and displaced middle sections of it, leaving potholes and sags, an uneven camber. Jack Liggett's car was new and reliable, but there were areas of the country where this did not matter, he realized.

Soon after his arrival in Westmorland he conveyed his disappointment on the telephone to a colleague, his concern for the automobile.

– The car's simply not up to it. She's coming to bits on me, Gordon.

The chairman of the Corporation was lacking in sympathy and seemed to find the whole matter something of an amusement.

– Consider it a challenge, Jack, you're rather partial to a good challenge are you not?

– I'm rather partial to the Sprite.

– You'll get another, Jack. Besides, I cannot understand the need for all these courtesy calls, anyway. They know their holdings are to be closed now. Langdale has assured me the letters have been sent, urging final payment of rents and evacuation. Oh! The man is so superior, he makes me feel like a bank robber, what! He's holding the bank door open, mind, the devil. But these visits, Jack, what good is rubbing their noses in it?

– It's not a question of gloating, Gordon. It's necessary for me to go, I assure you. One can't just roll in and pull out the tablecloth with all the china still sitting on the table. There are still pieces to mend, still loose ends, and you know I despise loose ends.

– Very well. Have it your way.

And so, Jack Liggett went daily to Mardale, to visit two or three of the families in the village. Though it was not an easy task, socializing with the obdurate locals, he went optimistically and with a mind to settle the matter well. It was as if he needed their compliance and good wishes, even needed them to see the beauty of his idea. They received him into their homes, obliged him with tea and currant bread, did not meet his eyes for any great length of time. He would remain cheerful, unabashed, brushing the crumbs from the creases of his suit trousers. And he spoke of the dam relentlessly, the ins and outs of it, lecturing the patients about their own diagnosed cancer.

Each evening, after making calls to a selection of houses in the village, he would drive the winding road back to the town, with the yellow-green, phosphorescent eyes of fell sheep reflecting in his car's lamps from the blackness of the moorside. Some of the animals lay in the road, sullen, ignoring the blaring horn, and finally hopping up spastically as a front wheel crept towards a hoof. At this hour the roads were less easily navigable than in daylight. Ruts became invisible, more treacherous. It would often take well over an hour to reach the dim orange glow of Penrith.

The car was a beautiful Riley Sprite, manufactured in the previous year, which had been bought from a showroom in Birmingham and delivered to his town house in Manchester. It was long and lean and sassy. Over the headlamps were thick, black spider-tapes like painted cartoon eyelashes. The running-boards were svelte as curved limbs. The interior was one of the most luxurious designs of the day, with a polished walnut finish, and brass instruments. Black Italian-leather seats still smelled of recently tanned hide. The car was a joy to drive, an enviable motor car, and Paul Levell's assumption upon seeing it had been right: it was a young man's dream, for Jack Liggett was still a young man.

Under the bonnet was a broad intestine of fitted chrome.

The car's engine was composed of four cylinders, one and a half litres of blissful, surging power. Its pedals were tight, smooth, influencing the car at the slightest touch. Jack Liggett wore black leather gloves as he drove, which were tacky on the steering wheel, and almost an extension of the car's internal décor itself. He sat upright, arms extended straight ahead to the wheel, a perfectly balanced section of the machine. The company which produced the Sprite held the slogan 'As old as the industry, as modern as the hour'. This had seemed fitting to him when he purchased the automobile, with cash in a leather zipping wallet, placed softly down on the office desk of the district manager. It had seemed fitting indeed.

∾

For six weeks Jack Liggett boarded at the George Hotel in Penrith. He would have a light dinner reserved cold for him, which he would eat late and alone, upon his return. Each evening he would telephone the chief executive of Manchester City Waterworks at home with a report of the day, including the envoy of Lord Langdale's letters issuing a discontinuance of tenancy, the arrival of four civil engineers, who had rented a vacant cottage next to Brunswick Hill in Bampton and who were pacing round the site at the bottom of the valley like excited children. His reports gauged the climate in the village, recounted what meetings were attended in the Dun Bull and by whom, there were no secret, underground collaborations going on. He made no mention of Janet Lightburn's visit to a solicitor's office in Carlisle, the fact that she boarded the 10.20 at Penrith station one Monday morning in early April and caught the 6.17 home, thinking it better not to bring up a potentially worrisome event without anything else to go on. He supposed she had been told that any resistance was futile, that the position of the tenants was not a litigious upper hand, that they had no ground to stand upon, so to speak. He would reassure the chief executive that the situation was tolerable, there were rumblings, yes, but the locals were adjusting to the idea of modernity, the prospect of change.

He anticipated that the evacuation would be smooth, he said. The word protest did not enter the discourse once. Occasionally, if the man on the other end of the line seemed agitated, he would suggest a plaque, bearing the name of the chief executive, to be erected near the dam wall on the road-side, in honour of his role as primary overseer of the project. He would give his kindest regards to the chief executive's wife and he would hang up the receiver with an upbeat cheerio.

Then he would pour himself a large French brandy from the bottle he kept in his suitcase and smoke cigarettes out of the high window of the hotel, watching the town's nocturnal character unwind.

In the street below there were nightly trysts. Stray cats hissed and spat on the walls, their bald, shredded ears twitching, their songs mournful on the black roofs. A fox came stealing from the crates in the kitchen alley of the hotel, silent as it blazed down the middle of the road, grey theft in its mouth. There was the racket of the Board and Elbow, ejecting its punters after midnight, their loud protests.

– Fucking cunt. A lot more's come in nor goes back. Yer fucker.

And, in the old, bitten-at language of the area, with its sluggish, ugly vowels, there were words which he did not understand, which sounded brutal, and he could not guess their English equivalent. A brawl until a jaw broke, or the bully left to vomit himself sober against the town's red bricks. He watched a man kicking blood from his wife's stomach. Maybe for a wrong look given to a friend, or nothing at all. She crawled to his feet and he lifted her on to his back, carried her home like spilling coal. Occasionally there would be lovers in the alley also, not truly lovers, but passing, drunken exchanges, nothing more than a quick grunt of lust, shoes slipping for grip on the ground as the woman was pushed back against the wall. The awful scene of three men holding a young girl down once to take turns on her. Perhaps money being passed, he could not be sure. And after they had gone, her crying was like laughter, disbelieving. He threw a cigarette down towards her weeping laughter, and a box of matches with the gold crest of the hotel's arms.

Towards three, when the streets cleared, and all human heat evaporated, the sky would begin to bruise with thunder. And between the long rumbles, sometimes he thought he could hear the muffled, unshod hooves of the wild fell ponies on the road as they came down from the scrubland on Beacon Hill, though he never saw them, moving slowly, single file through town, as if on a pilgrimage. He would close the window and retire to bed. Or, if the two daughters of the hotel manager were available, Marion and Dorothy, he might stay up for a while, turning them to meet his body as the moment's fancy took him, a hand over the mouth of one, fingers clenching indentations into her cheeks, bringing her to his groin. The other moving above him, stepping away, the glow from a streetlight on her spine. He would sleep for about five hours usually, not needing more than this, sitting against the pillows, his right arm crooked over his chest, his hand holding his left shoulder. In his suitcase, next to the brandy, the corrugated glimmer of a revolver. Though he had spent much time in rooms similar to this one, Jack Liggett was not a man comfortable in hotels.

⌒

Here in the George Hotel, there are nights of unending rain when he dreams of the blue-green valley that he will destroy. The hotel groans in the downpour, its foundations settling. His arm lifts off his chest and touches the cotton pillow, his fingers curling around the iron flowers of the headboard. He is somewhere between death and the beating drum of his subconscious. The dreams recall his youth, they return his

92

first visions to him, the libation of frontiers, new elevations. As a boy he was an avid walker and climber, scaling the sharp-side of peaks and ridges in the Langdale Pikes, the Kentmere valley. And the black crevices of Harter Fell, above Mardale. In his dreams he is there again, high up in the vein of a ghyll. Below, the valley edges are wet, like the sides of a green china cup, and there is only enough of a lake to take one sip. He finds miniature holds in the cornices of overhanging granite, weighing his body in the air for a swing to the next level, the summit. His nail ripping out as he pulls up the fractured crag towards a circular cave, a button in the mouth of the cliff. There are no ropes to secure him to the mountain face. He does not yet believe in immortality.

∽

An hour after he had taken the room upstairs in the Dun Bull Inn at Mardale head, and hung up his suits in the dusty wardrobe, Jack Liggett stood in front of the bar, sipping ale from a cracked tankard. It could have been concern for his car that led him to quit his quarters at the George Hotel in Penrith, though the motor was in no genuine danger of wreckage, making the forty-mile round trip each day. Now it was parked rather prominently on the tennis court at the back of the building, in the rain, instead of under a roofed garage as it had been at the George.

Jack stood opposite a group of farmers who did not look at him, uncertain about his more permanent presence in their pub. Neither did they speak amongst themselves at first, or remove their wet caps from their heads. They moved lengthily, arms and bodies shifting quickly, rearing up and moving back, like a herd of upset cows. Outside, the rain hushed, a constant finger held to the lips, bidding quiet. An artificial humidity stifled the air inside the pub, grown from a combination of damp clothing and warmth from the fire, which only seemed to add to the heavy atmosphere.

The barman of the Dun Bull was less hostile towards him and so they conversed sporadically about the Scottish Highlands, favourite whisky. He kept his voice low, leaving the conversation now and again to attend to a new pint for a man, resuming it only when he was certain he could not be overheard by his regulars, hopelessly strung between local loyalty and the level of courtesy required for his new customer and guest of the establishment. It had been difficult to accept money from the man, more difficult still to allow room and board, considering his notoriety and what he represented, but Jake McGill was loath to refuse a customer. He considered himself to be reasonable and lacking discrimination. Furthermore, as the man himself had neatly stated, at this point in time it would be futile either to deny himself financial benefit or to make a political statement by putting out the lodger.

Jake watched the man's easy movements. There seemed to be a substantial degree of impersonality towards the whole affair as far as Mr Liggett was concerned, though it did not manifest itself as brassiness, nor the cocky manner of a victor entering a defeated port. Jack Liggett was an emissary, by all means, yet he was not here to drive out a lingering foe. He did not consider it improper or insensitive to submerge himself in the village biography. But could this not have been done for a reason? There were now no clear borders drawn from which the two sides could hurl insults and offence at each other, having neither the protection of distance nor rigid standpoints. Jake considered it a most ingenious tactic, if indeed it was strategy. Almost gentlemanly.

After a while, unable to cope with the hung atmosphere, he switched on the wireless radio, housed in a robust leather box which sat behind the bar. It took a short while to warm up at the mains, finally tracking some crackling symphony music. The concert ended and a recorded programme of popular, contemporary songs began.

– As you can see, sir, we are not without contact to the outside world.

94

The man smiled at him. Jake refilled his own glass, relaxing somewhat. It was difficult to find a sharper tone or take a harder line. He was a likeable enough chap and, if it weren't for the situation, Jake would be pleased for the new company. Liggett's manner was exceptionally pleasant and genial. And he was well turned-out. His hair was a blue-black that was almost Eastern, with a slight greying at its sides. Not enough to suggest senescence. He kept it combed to the slight right, never touching it with his hands, as men are prone to ruffle and ruin themselves within a drinking establishment. There were several sagging lines around his eyes, indicating their track to middle age, but none towards his mouth, which was upturned, sensuous and full, seeming not unlike the Herculean mouths of the latest batch of Californian actors in favour presently, with faces six feet high on the billboards of the New Picture House in Penrith. Jake supposed that ladies might find him handsome, the lower half of his face warranted such a judgement. But his forehead was perhaps too low, and his eyebrows were too fine, too shaped, a little feminine. His eyes, a tepid brown, were too large, too assuming, backed-up and overlaid with what Jake could only suppose were issues. It might, of course, simply have been intellect. But certainly the eyes complicated matters. Overall, the upper part of his head was more pretty than it was handsome.

The man had removed his suit and was dressed more casually, in a thick Aran jumper and corduroy breeches. His walking boots were not the new, unbroken leather which locals found so worrisome. That was something of a relief, thought Jake. Rather, they appeared well used and well oiled. Even without his city garb, the refined vestiges, Mr Liggett still cut a distinguished figure. Jake observed him lengthily. He was shaking his head.

– Indeed not, Mr McGill. Do you get enough reception for the Light programme here, with the hills?

– Aye. Comes and goes.

– Tomorrow there will be a broadcast of Victor Sylvester

95

and his ballroom orchestra, if you're interested. Nine o'clock, I believe.

– Oh. Yes, that would be good. Another pint, sir?

The room filled with crackling songs. The man at the bar looked towards the open fire, humming slightly. 'I've got you under my skin, I've got you . . .' He tapped a finger against his tankard. The heat of the flames reached him from the other side of the room, glowing along the low ceiling and filling the hung copper pans with burnished orange light. There was now a strong smell of pipe smoke in the air, most of the regulars had curved vessels clenched between their teeth, one or two preferring rolled cigarettes. A farmer was staring at him from the corner. His face was blown red and he had familiar pale eyes, dry coarse hair. His tweed jacket was substantially worn at the arms. The gaze lacked confrontation, but not intensity, that too was familiar somehow. Jack Liggett lifted his glass to the man, recognizing him then as the spokesman of the initial meeting, and head of one of the families he had not yet called upon. The farmer nodded, one or two of the other men turning now to acknowledge him by raising a forefinger off a beer glass, then turning away to resume their game of darts.

– I suppose this is rather a man's club? Ladies not allowed in the bar?

– You could say that, sir. Nothing formal, mind, they choose it that way in the week, except one or two. Saturdays are a little livelier. But only local lassies. We don't run any parades here.

– And do most of them come? Even from the higher cottages?

– Occasionally. Not as often as the rest, it's more trouble getting back up the scar. It will be hard for them to move, when the time comes. Houses don't come down fells all that easily. Neither do old shepherds, for that matter.

Jack Liggett studied the man behind the bar counter. He did not mind his indirect comments, the light chastisements. His thoughts were elsewhere. He was a little distracted when next he spoke, looking around the group of farmers.

– Yes, it's unfortunate. They might have stayed, but raising the lake's level will in all likelihood displace the water table upwards and undermine the foundations of even those dwellings not being submerged, those on the higher levels. Plus, with the heavy rains here, the reservoir could flood right through the houses. So you see, they must move. It can't be helped, I'm afraid. Is that Mr Lightburn?

– That's Sam Lightburn, yes. Yes, it's all very unfortunate. All very regrettable. Sam's house will be submerged, of course. And that gentleman there, sir, is Nathaniel Holme, whose family has been in Mardale for nigh on three hundred years. He's something of royalty around these parts.

Suddenly Jack Liggett frowned and returned his gaze to Jake.

– But you own this hotel?

– Aye. I do, sir, in part.

– And the Corporation has outlined your compensation?

– It has. Generously. I won't say I'll not miss my home, though.

– Good. Good. What'll you do?

Jake cleared his throat and stroked his beard. He glanced around the man to the group of farmers.

– I was thinking Canada. I've not mentioned it yet. I'll ask you not to.

Of course. No, no.

Jenny Wade popped her ginger, curled head round the corner of the kitchen door, asking that Jake come and assist her with some lifting in the cellar. Jake excused himself and broke away, went through to the kitchen behind the bar.

Jack Liggett swallowed the last amber inch of his ale. He set the tankard on the counter and approached the group of farmers. They had halted their game and were in conversation with Jamie Brent, a poacher from the Naddle forest, who had entered the Bull and was showing off the loose body of a tawny owl. A wing was splayed out between his stunted, gloved hands, the serrated feathers white and yellow and reddish-brown. They looked up as he arrived, eyes empty of welcome and concern.

– She's a beauty. For sale?

– Mebbi. Mebbi not.

– How much?

The poacher smiled drily. He had a sarcastic mouth, small bright eyes and a virile, mannish stance, even for a character of his moderate height, or perhaps all the more so because of it.

– Don't reckon thee's got much call forra dead birdie. Norra live one, come to it. Cept mebbi a report to Lordie about all t'fuckin' poachin' as goes on round dale where thee happens to be stoppin.

– Oh, I'm sure Lord Langdale has far more pressing matters to attend to than a few lost woodland inhabitants. Besides, I'm positive I saw that very bird dead on the roadside not an hour ago as I drove in. It must have been a fox that got it. You probably just found it, am I right?

One of the farmers let out a loud bellow of laughter and a few of the others chuckled. The poacher grinned, revealing perfect rows of pink gums.

– Aye, one of them flyin' fuckin' foxes from ova yonder in Kendal. Twa pund fu' t'woll.

– A ridiculous price, of course. You'll get me a golden eagle for two pounds, I think.

The group quietened down, realizing after a second or two that the man in their midst was not bluffing. Jack Liggett held the gaze of the poacher, looking down a little at the smaller man dressed in moleskin breeches and a suede coat. He was smiling casually, as always. The poacher carefully folded the owl into a tatty leather satchel strung over his shoulder. He wiped his nose with the back of a gloved hand.

– Golden eagles wud be mor'less gone, gone or illegal these days, like, notta funni bizniz t'be gittin' mixed up in, eh? What kinda daft bugger d'yer take mi for?

– Bluff! Deer and owls and merlins would probably be illegal also, on an estate, would they not? If I'm not mistaken, that's a merlin's feather in your cap and an antler sticking out of your bag. Legal? Depends on where you lifted them from. Now. As I'm sure you know, there is one nest up on the Rigg and possibly another over on the crags of the Pike, and it's not common knowledge, but don't try to deny it. Get an adult. No juveniles. And no eggs, I don't want my time wasted. A female, if you can. And I don't want her as ragged and tatty as you made that owl, you understand?

He reached into his trouser pocket and took out a pound. He held it up, showed it to the man. The group of men watched with interest. Astoundingly, the gesture had not been tawdry or flamboyant, Jack Liggett had learned the various ways of handling money, depending on circumstance and who was involved. Rather, it had appeared subdued, almost sage.

– The rest when it's done. Yes?

The poacher considered the money being offered. His face was twisted a fraction at the edges. He would have liked nothing better than to make a refusal. There was an expression of obvious dislike about his mouth, but his eyes did not leave the pound, and finally he took it.

Jack Liggett turned as if to leave the group of men. But the poacher called out to him again, his tone bitter and his words quick.

– 'T'll be a shame when all t'bonny birdies git drown by watter.

And Jack Liggett did not turn back to defend himself or his industry, but continued walking out of the room. As he left the bar, he said a small, curious thing, if anyone had been close enough to overhear.

– This is the wettest valley in the country. It's designed to hold water. That is what it was meant for.

It was customary for the members of the Mardale Women's Institute to meet in each other's homes every other week, with both host and guests providing refreshments for the duration of the meeting in the fashion of a co-operative supper or tea. Janet Lightburn was sometimes present, though her mother disapproved of many of her comments during these afternoon and evening sessions. She often made mention of the Freedom League and other such organizations, and Ella would scowl at her across the table, or cut her off if the younger girls present began to ask too many questions, their curiosity piqued. Being in the chair, she did not consider the WI a suitable occasion for political discussion and canvassing, or an opportunity to blether on about the wage structure, the allocation of benefits, but thought that rather more pressing matters should be considered: poultry management, preserving, vegetable growing and other rural endeavours. Things relevant to day-to-day living.

The WI had been operating since shortly after the war ended. In the past, speakers had come from as far afield as Newcastle to instruct on dancing and dressmaking, and Hazel Bowman was regularly invited to speak on literature, though it was dangerous to have the teacher and Jan in the room together for too long as they became wound up in weighty conversation. The ladies often sewed to collect money for charitable events or organized village fairs, Christmas pageants. Lately, handicrafts had dwindled and the discussion had been directed at the presence of the Waterworks man in their village, the impact of the dam and what was to be done, gossip and speculation about both.

– But if we just stay put, thez notta lot they can do, eh?

– Except flood us out, Agnes. What are y'talking about, woman! I don't want my smalls floating down to Bampton for all an' sundry t'look at!

In the corner of the room, Janet Lightburn lit a cigarette and blew smoke out into the chimney. The group made a few high-pitched remarks in agreement with the last comment. Ella coughed. Although she was at the opposite end of the room to her daughter, it was as if the smoke bothered her. She did not approve of the habit and wished Janet would not indulge, especially in public. The meeting was descending into the clucks and squawks of indignant women without the focus of a definite goal. She quickly regained order, speaking clearly.

– Did y'all receive a letter from the estate?

There were murmured ayes. A few rustles as several women reached into their coats and bags to produce the documents.

– Never thought it'd cum, Ella, and that's the truth. But it did. It did.

– No, me an' all.

– Well. That's it then, in't it?

– Buck up now, Nancy lass.

There was a break to a few of the voices, the suggestion of tears about to be shed, one woman setting off another. Janet stood, threw the cigarette into the fire grate and reached for her shawl. Her mother turned to her. Dry-eyed, they exchanged a brief glance across the room.

– You've bin very quiet all along, miss. Nowt t'say this evenin'?

The others turned also, a few muttering Aye, go on, Jan, expecting some kind of wisdom, or at least proud resolution. But her daughter shook her head slowly, as if fatigued.

– Where y'off to?

– The Bull.

– Oh, Janet!

She closed the door on her mother's disapproval, her tutting.

101

She had been swimming between the groups for days, weeks, it seemed. Sitting in the domestic arena of the women of the valley as they bickered about the situation, complaining that it was unfair, unreasonable, and visiting the bar later at night to push in past the sullen, awkward men, and attempt to budge their stagnant dispositions with some rousing discourse. Avoiding Jack Liggett was high on her agenda, when he was there also, because she was still not yet prepared to acknowledge him. There had been evenings spent at Measand Hall with Paul Levell, which had not amounted to much. He was keen to help, but assured her he had no influence over Lord Langdale, even if a good number of his paintings did adorn Askham Hall's dining room. His ideas were confused, if well intentioned, and he seemed to have an outdated notion of the law, believing that much could be accomplished by a blind charge or rhetoric. Even Hazel Bowman could come up with little in the way of a practical remedy, though she did pass on the name of a reputed solicitors' office in the city. But again, a dead end. Janet had been advised that the position of the tenants was grim.

The valley had no united front. And overall opinion was splintered, at best. Some wanted a fight, some wanted a quiet exit. There seemed to be precious few threads to be tied together. She felt that any space to move inside the boxed future that they had all been handed was tightening, becoming more restricted. And her energy was fast ebbing away.

As she walked down to the centre of the village, she resolved to try harder when she got to the jerry, not to be drawn into an argument about any of the usual upsets, the petty remarks, but rather to remain clear-headed, in the hope that some kind of solution could be unearthed.

The swell of voices outside the Dun Bull Inn assured her that the Waterworks man was not present that night. She could hear the aggrieved tones of Teddy Hindmarsh, laying it on thick.

– . . . bloody girt truck parked in t'roadway. I had to cum six mile back and tek t'uther path. Wi' not even left yit and they've got buggers in ready. Well, it's a fuckin' cheek if y'ask me, like.

Following news of the dam, more evidence that the project was in fact going ahead had appeared in the valley: trucks, engineers, timber. This rant from Teddy was merely a response to the latest. The meetings in the Dun Bull of the village men had become strange and fraught occasions, and, because there were seldom evenings when Jack Liggett wasn't present, where they could speak freely, if he was absent all hell seemed to break loose. The old bantering atmosphere of the Bull had long departed. Where once there had been foolery and merriment, simple contentment, now a dull sense of vapidity overtook the men, or they were quick to anger. The singing and the ken John Peels dried up, there were no tales told about past hunts or bets won at the races, and even Jake's wireless could do little to lift their spirits.

She pushed open the door. Immediately quiet fell on the room.

– Give ower, lads. If y'can't say it t' t'fella's face, what's use in iver sayin' it?

A collective sigh went through the bar and sporadic conversation resumed. She made her way up to her father, who was standing at the bar with Nathaniel Holme.

– Evenin', Jan. Buggers are fleart of him, lass, that's all.

– Aye, well, at least it gives them more t' fret about than grizzlin' coz a lass is in t'bar, eh?

Samuel and Nathaniel chuckled.

– Where's Liggett? His car's not gone. If he's upstairs he's probably heard every word of this racket, anyway.

– Up fell, sez Jake.

– At this hour! We'll be stretchering him down.

Her brow was furrowed with concern. The two men spoke quietly for a time, discussing the outbreak of scrapie in the sheep population at Heltondale, and that they would not be walked to market in Penrith that August if it had not cleared by then. Around them conversation was stilted, ragged. There was a general inertia in the bar. Even Paul Levell, usually verbose, sat in the corner staring quietly into his ale. Voices rose and quickly subsided.

A squabble broke out at the back of the room. The mention of rustled livestock, the half-hearted accusation of a disappearance in the night. The deep voices of Jonathan Carruthers and William Noble and Lanty Farrow mounting, inflammatory remarks multiplying. Tom Metcalfe looked about ready to take a swing. Nathaniel Holme stepped forward, wiped the palms of his hands on his shirt front and held them aloft. He was not noticed. He turned and picked up his shepherd's crook from an alcove in the bar and banged it on the stone floor. The sound cracked like a gunshot.

– There's nowt to be dun, lads. M'nchister fella's not one fer sharp'nin' saw without cuttin' wood. No point in grousin' and talk of theft, well, it's a false git-up, any road. Won't do a scrap o' gud fer t'dam. Y'all know better. Now give ower while I sup me pop in peace, eh?

He stared them down and then walked over to the fireplace to throw another log on the grate and sparks blew up into the hood. The room was simmering with discontent. Nobody would speak out against the old man, though.

Samuel rubbed his eyes with the balls of his big fists. They smelled faintly sweet from the sweat of his horse that he had been tending an hour before and the yellow straw of the barn. It was a good smell, rich and pleasant, reassuring. He looked at his daughter. She was leaning back on the bar counter with her eyes closed, as if asleep standing up. The dark marks under her eyes were fading, now that lambing was finished, but another sort of weariness had descended on her.

The room was restored to a temporary lull in aggression, but it was not to be long-lived.

In the quiet, the Reverend Wood addressed the Bull's regulars from his vantage point of a corner table.

– Gentlemen. Might we not consider this a blessing in disguise? A change is often good for the soul. Besides, many more people will benefit from this endeavour than would benefit from the lack of it. Christian doctrine encourages us to make sacrifices for others. Even those outside our realm of acquaintance. Remember the Samaritan on the road, offering a helping hand to a complete stranger. Or John . . .

– With all due respect vicar, I'll ask you not to sermonize in my establishment. The men don't come here for moral supervision. And you might remember that you've been in the parish only five years, have you not? Your attachments here are, oh, how shall I put it, vicar, a wee bit inconsequential. And I don't think we'll be seeing you at Penrith hiring fair in the coming months.

There were a few gentle ayes in agreement from the men. Jake's right eye twitched, his cheek spasmed, which was a bad sign, and the Reverend, highly irritated by the contradiction, coughed, and, after a moment taken to recover from the attack, gave a disgusted glance at his ale. He swilled it in the glass and set it back on the table untouched.

– Oh, aye. What was that look all about? Something amiss with your beverage, vicar?

– Nothing more amiss than usual, Mr McGill. No. I wouldn't expect a man of your standing to comprehend the principles of such a matter as sacrifice. Not a man who tries to pass off such filth as this ale as worthy of sale to the public, while other Christians do not have clean water to drink.

– Filth. Oh, filth, is it?

– Yes, sir, it is exactly that.

And the vicar stood up as Jake McGill barred him permanently from the premises. The gentle tension which had existed quite comfortably between the two men for a number of years, and which had led to sparring and sporting debate, finally spoiled. Nathaniel muttered under his breath, something about the bizniz getting outa hand, and he put his cap on his head and left the Bull. Samuel and Janet followed shortly after. She paused at the door of the Bull, as if about to return inside, then thought better of it. She had had enough.

∾

Jack Liggett's first visitors to the large room over the hotel's bar were two or three small children from the village. They peered in through the grimy window pane, waited until Jake McGill was bending under the bar and then slipped through the side door and stole up the stairs, knocked loudly on the door and scampered away amid a chorus of uncontrollable giggles. The man was confused to find the doorway empty as he answered the knock, he had been sleeping late and deeply for once, and he wondered if the noise had simply slipped out from a dream during his slumber. Hearing the patter of small feet on the bottom of the stairway, Jake stuck his head out of the hotel door in time to see several children running between the lilac bushes in the garden and trampling down the rhubarb patch next to the greenhouse. He called after them to stay away, or he'd bake them into a pie, so he would, and he picked up an oversized shoe lost by one of the boys and tossed it after them.

The second caller was Janet Lightburn, and she was not about to turn tail and run anywhere. She strode through the bar without so much as a nod to the proprietor and took the guest stairs to Jack Liggett's room. Jake began to wonder at his lack of authority in his own establishment that people abused the premises so casually. He could not help but detect something of her mother in the straight back of the girl's gait, so he decided to let the matter drop and get on with the morning's baking.

Expecting only a ghost this time as he answered the sharp rapping on his door, Jack Liggett was surprised to find flesh and blood and a face of all protruding bone in the dim hallway. His lower stomach turned, as he remembered his coat next to her face, the cotton she had kept inside the cave of her mouth. The two had exchanged glances in the hotel's bar since, but had never spoken after the meeting on the fell almost two months ago.

On this occasion they shook hands like civil colleagues, or reasonable acquaintances. Her hair was knotted at the nape of her neck, tidily, and he was only partly shaven, his visage halved, a white and dark, theatrical mask. He invited her in, and continued attending to his face in the mirror over the sink.

– I miss my barber. Somehow I do not feel it would be in my best interest to have a haircut locally. I might find my throat cut instead, yes? It's not the same, administering to my own face. I'm no good at it, would you believe that?

He put his silver comb under the tap and ran water through his hair, watching her in the mirror. She made as if to leave.

– Perhaps another time . . .

– No! Stay. I'm done. Will you sit? You'd rather not?

She shook her head, cleared her throat. He began making the bed, smoothing the rumpled covers.

– I understand Manchester City Waterworks will own the farm property in the valley after this quarter's rents are paid. Is that correct, Mr Liggett?

– It is.

And, as a rough estimation, how much time until the properties are no longer viable?

He smiled at her. He sensed an impending negotiation. Similar to the calm facilities she displayed during their previous encounter, involving her brother, she did not seem unsettled by this meeting. Rather she was clear and direct, a tactic seldom employed by the men of the city he was used to dealing with, who were characters altogether more slippery and furtive. In the artificial light of the room he was aware of her skin's detail. The shattered-disc scar on her forehead, the small curls over her ears and frontal scalp, and flecks of orange within the imperfect grey irises.

– Why ask?

– Might not the Waterworks benefit from a few extra rents until such time as the buildings are no longer safe?

She looked to the side, out of the window. In profile, her face became less severe.

– I suppose it might. However, I don't think we're hurting in any way.

– Let me be plain. There has been a national depression. You might be enjoying a little more comfort in the city, but here there is not much recovery yet. Tenancies do not fall from trees in this part of the country, especially not now. Wool cheques are down by a large percentage, it's barely worth clipping. Twelve months of a year is about what it takes to break even, all told. If the people here had a little more time to find alternative accommodation, it would be helpful.

– Helpful?

The rough edge of her accent had been kept in check up to this point, subdued, as if she had been conscious of not wanting to sound colloquial or compromise her position. Now it came back with fury.

– Yeh. I tek it yer dam won't go up in t'blink of an eye. How long?

Jack Liggett laughed out loud. His dam! A personal note buried under her emotionless façade. It was a cracked exterior, after all. But don't we all have these false surfaces, he thought, imperfect, with tiny fractures? If force is applied to those fractures the whole thing splits, falls off like shell, and inside, a genuine, delicate piece of flesh, too raw for untruth. He gestured for her to sit on the bed and again she shook her head. He sat himself, leaning back on the plastered wall, wishing to prolong the exchange. In truth, he was enjoying it considerably. His head moved into a beam of sunlight which lit the grey hairs at his temple. She was looking at his neck, the flick of a pulse.

– A year. Maybe less. Maybe more. There are several factors to consider. Weather permitting a speedy construction, for example, and all the damned things going on abroad have to be taken into account. I have others, if you're interested. You'd be the only one who is.

– And if some want to remain until then, you'll accept rent? Same rates as present.

– It's only a year. One year only. No point in burying in . . .

– A year is a year, it can mean all the difference. A month's notice fer severance should work, both parties. It's mutually beneficial, there is no argument against that I can see. Well?

Jack knew full well that this would bother the chief executive, who wanted a definite clearance of villagers as soon as humanly possible. But there was little that Jack Liggett could not convince his colleagues of when it came to business. He sat forward on the bed and took her hand. They shook for a second time and then she released from his grip, which had been of the strength of a handshake given to another man, an equal. As if he knew gentleness would, for her, be an insult, would be perceived as humouring her, trivializing her efforts. Within the handshake there was a margin of agitation, a touch of static.

– Honestly, I thought someone might have ventured this before now. I'm quite surprised they didn't.

He was aware she would not thank him for his acceptance, nor did he wish that she would. Sure enough, she left without another word. His door closed softly. There were no audible footfalls on the wooden steps of the hotel, but he knew she had gone.

❧

Soft, breezy May of this land-altering year in Mardale. Samuel and Ella Lightburn walk to the church in the village on Sunday morning as they have done many times before, though now they know it is finite, that somewhere just out of sight on the horizon is the sharp, sudden edge of the world. Along the sides of the verges are primroses and the first bluebells of the year.

From the hedges along the path comes a quick chittering, and small birds dart in and out of their nests, stealing at unripe berries from within the briar. On the path in front of husband and wife three scruffy sparrows brawl and peck at each other, scuffling in the dry, dusty earth and lifting off as the couple approach, only to land hopping and scrapping again a few more feet in front of them. As if it's all for show.

As the two walk, their shoulders knock against each other a little, the path is uneven, throwing the weight of a body slightly into its centre. It is Ella that breaks the twittering quiet and her words are unhesitant, perhaps louder than they need to be with her husband so close by.

– Eileen Ferguson says she has room for a secretary in a month or so.

– Oh?

– Penrith Agricultural Committee. They cud tek Janet, eh? It's a gud wage. She's enough experience typing to git by. The rest'll pick up.

– She'll niver go. Not now.

– The's nowt to stop fer.

They walk on in silence for a while under the pale-blue sky, the sparrows still scrapping on the path. The bell begins to ring from the church and Ella steps up her pace a little, frightening the birds off once and for all.

– Yer might try persuading her fer a change, Sam. Shi's stubborn, that lass. And if it cums from me, it's got t'be a poor idea from t'start t' finish.

– Mebbi, after dam an' all.

– Place'll be gone by then, Sam!

– Lassie should git ter college. She's a rite gud heed on her. Minny's a lass gone ter college in this day an' age, eh? Nowt unusual. Not like in our day.

Ella stops and swings round to face her husband.

– Pardon me, Mista Lightburn, but am I not alive on God's green earth yet? This is still my day, then! And as t'money? You tellin' me we've enough to send a daughter off fer study?

A daughter! It's niver a wonder she's not gotta fella, not with yer handlin' of her. Never comes t' worship.

– Besides, Ella, shi's grand as owt at balin' cum a coupla weeks. I'll be glad o' t'help. And she loves helpin' Hazel wi' kiddies. Let her a while bifor the school shuts.

Ella takes her husband's hand in hers. Her eyes have in them both anger and gentleness, a battle which is often fought in her. Samuel bends and kisses her forehead, he puts his arm round her. She reaches over and straightens his old brown tie against his collar.

– And what about us, Sam lad? What of us after dam?

– Give it a while, Ella. Summet'll cum.

They walk on in silence for a while, with the ringing church bell in the distance. At a fork in the path, they meet with the Hindmarsh family, on the way down from High Bowderthwaite, father, mother, two young daughters, all dressed in their best, and a son, who wears a suit with only one filled sleeve. As old friends, they greet each other with warmth, the women walking ahead and talking in low tones, the men quiet at the back. This fine May morning, as on many Sundays, the valley's paths become a stage for well-dressed villagers on their way to church, for the kings and queens of Mardale.

I:VIII

For almost two decades Janet Lightburn has walked the roads and fells of the Mardale valley. She has lived every day solvent. Her knowledge of the place is as unconscious and simple as the mechanisms of breathing. The seasons of the farming community have structured her knowledge so that a margin of fell or common land does not exist without agricultural references. She is surrounded by an intricate union. There are deaths that have made more sense than lives here. But nothing hangs in the balance. She has been pressed between two vast mountain ranges without claustrophobia or repression; each year she is re-forged. She accepts the weather and the ability of the rain to overwhelm all else. It's inconsequential. This is a sacred place. It is a holy land. She has picked up its old habits. Her body chemistry alters as the terrain decomposes, turns, begins again. She would have her ashes scattered to the open face of the scar. She has given herself over to this saturated strip of Westmorland.

What she begins to see now is the shadow of her own ideals, simplicity overwhelmed by its old adversary. Many faults and errors have entered the orthodoxy of her system. She has sculpted the corners of their existence herself, in a way, with all her mundane, extreme acceptances of land, of liquid soil, of time and continuance and balance, which leave a void for something else, a blemish in the mirror image, invaded space. Hazel Bowman had warned her in her youth of the structures that always enter the self-governed heart and the words were lost on her, cast aside as not being relevant. She was in a place too remote to fall prey to political or industrial dissembling. Now the horizon pulls in. Now she has to alter her vision. She must look with new eyes. In the mornings, the grey mass of

Harter Fell faces her from the window of Whelter Farm, no longer in stasis. It flexes new limbs and its base is temporary. Filling the valley, there are subjective angles, rushed states of existence. A rock is not dimensional until it is lifted or turned. Neither is her heart useful without first being averted.

∾

There must have been encounters which kindled emotion, some kind of internal, controversial passion. A visit from Jack Liggett to Whelter Farm with a new contract to be signed by her father, where she had been sleeveless from working in the garden, discouraged by the swift compliance of her proposal, secretly wanting contention, a conflict which she might feel gratified in undertaking. But instead she received decency and did not know what to do with it. So she handed him a clump of soil-stringed onions from the vegetable patch, wordlessly, seriously, as if fulfilling her end of a treaty. A stray glance across the felt-capped vista of the Dun Bull on weekends, after accidentally coming to know some of his subtle domestic habits, what his face was like clean and unshaved, how he tucked the corners of the sheets under his bed as if sealing an envelope. Her eyes able to convey honesty at last, in which dislike and desire are not exclusive states. The fact that the tellurian pull between two people is often an inexplicable, belligerent thing, not manufactured willingly by the parties involved, but arriving like a tumour along a piece of body. Of it and yet deformed, damaging.

There were those days when she observed her brother in the man's company, the two chatting civilly, spiritually almost, like men of the cloth, or Isaac handing the tall man a plant or a trinket for him to look at, which he always did patiently, and she was softened. Or it could have been that there was no avenue of flight for the anger building, the force of frustration over the new world that was beginning to stack upwards. And when the structure became too tall for itself, it tipped over in an oblique direction, scattering into a section of herself where there was less rigid government of the heart.

It could have been sheer mischance. For there are times when passion can describe a random passage of its own accord, like electrical energy in the atmosphere which will strike out in any direction, seeking a high object to ground itself on. This, then, could have been the reason for their affair. Though it has never been fully understood in the following years, by the later generations of that family. Even now it might be written as a smudged signature, a blurred identity of non-specific proportions. In language which does little more than crawl below the underbelly of love.

Perhaps, though, there is a simpler explanation. Those unguarded moments when Janet caught sight of Jack Liggett's gracious side, that which she would have as non-existent, more in keeping with his perceived role in the village. A good-humoured, self-damning joke for the benefit of the men of the valley, who did laugh; they granted him some credit, some humanity. His lifting of a stubborn lamb out of the road when it would not shift as he drove up to it in the red car. Picking the thing up like a hanging child. The look of confusion and slight embarrassment on his face as the creature bleated and skipped back towards him, naïve and too young yet to be skittish around humans. He was not wholly a bad man, for all his blunt infiltration, and it was becoming apparent as he spent more time in the village. He had his lighter folds and creases.

Or she passed by his hotel window, on the way to the cottage store, looking up to see a glimmer of bare skin as his shirtless back moved past. A fraction of a second's sexual exhibition. An accidental flirtation, that's all, and unintended, but enough of a sighting to startle her, and she lost a breath. His back had been like marble through the square frame, pure and aesthetic, masculine. A classical sculpture. This intimate glimpse of a man who had already aroused a volatile state of emotion in her, could have helped to carry those affections and agitations into another context. It could have been the tiniest and most direct of arrows.

Nor could she have avoided him in the village, with its small confines. There were words exchanged between them which might have moved her, even though she took care never to match his level of warmth and amiability. There were his eyes, forged from compressed sable. Was he playing for her? This able and ponderous man. His peacock feathers now blanched and gone. A beige, quail-like normality finding him. Was he more plausible now, simply a possibility of flesh? Were his eyes suggestive, giving something away, his nocturnal visions that included her treacherous mouth?

He stopped her once at the gate of the hotel in the second week of his residency at the Bull.

– Hello. Tell me something. How does that woman in the cottage with the shelves of perished sardines ever come by all her information? I've never seen her leave the village. That old wagon of hers looks as if it wouldn't make it five feet.

– Her name is Sylvia. She makes half of it up. Take care not to believe all you hear in these parts.

– Oh, I think I'm learning to separate the whey from the chaff, as they say.

The moderate weight of his words held her momentarily. Was his tone imbued with references? Or a turn in the flow of colour at the back of his eyes, past their pupils, like a piece of water suddenly shifting around a stone in a riverbed. But she hurried past, barely pausing to fulfil her end of the conversation, and leaving him to wonder at her ability to be frugal, to separate herself from her voice.

Or could it not have been her dreams that eventually turned her? Alluding to remote possibilities. As Jack Liggett's body was filled with longing in sleep, so too hers lifted towards him in those amorphous hours. Hours when the pent-up, raging ghosts of the subconscious are released into the body's fluid. To swim slickly though the water of limbs and influence cells, to touch, to caress, morphing into imaginary solids, hands,

115

fingertips. So that when she woke, a papery spasm fluttering internally, she slowly remembered the figure who had moved through her dreams, and, try as she might, she could not discard the memory in daylight. So when the torch finally lit, it burned savagely, and the air surrounding it went roaring inwards, towards the mouth of flame.

∽

Inside the enclosure, there was tar up to her elbows and on her shirt. Her long hair was wound up and tucked under a flat cap to keep it from the thick, black treatment. Though several strands had fallen free, had gathered black on their ends like paintbrushes. As Jack Liggett strode down the slope of the fell he observed her with her father and another farmhand working in the corner pen of one of Whelter's fields. The two men were pushing sheep through the narrow enclosure, holding each one for Janet to coat their tails with the solution, which would make it impossible for maggot infestations to take hold in the softer flesh there. They had recently been dipped in a solution of whale-oil and arsenic to kill any residual lice and ticks, and the sweet-bitter stench from the dipping-basin wafted out across the field. The sheep were coughing and hacking, bleating, avoiding each other, pushing against the fences.

Since Jack Liggett had entered polite society, he had not seen a more unusual or subversive scene concerning a grown woman. He was fascinated by it and slowed his pace, imagining the faces of those from the upper strata of the Corporation if they could see such a thing. The combination of agricultural odour and her attire was as disconcerting as it was intriguing. She painted the rear of the animals and kicked them on the rump to send them on. Her movements were liberal and generous, unrefined. There was a dark patch of sweat on the shirt from the small of her back. Her forearms were soiled, a filthy, sooty, bitumen colour.

He opened the hook on the gate of the field and came through on his way down to the village. There was pitch on the wood of the frame and as he re-hooked the gate he looked at his hands. They were both smeared with the sticky, burnt-smelling tar. Janet saw him staring at his hands, as did the two farmers. He looked up and smiled at them, slightly whimsically, holding up his hands. The men nodded curtly at him and Samuel Lightburn spoke a few quiet words to his daughter. She walked towards Jack Liggett with a rag in her black hands. There was a streak of oily-looking pitch on her chin. She gave him the cloth. He could not be sure, but he thought her smile, for once, was without derision. Though there still seemed to be something of a struggle about it, as if the expression was against her will. For a moment, he leaned in towards her, towards the smile, careful to keep enough of a respectful distance in her father's presence, though the two men were concentrating on the tarring once more. She did not step back. He was close enough to have moved a painted strand of hair with his breath as he exhaled. When he was done cleaning his palms she took back the rag, careful to leave a soft, black fingerprint against his wrist as she did so.

~

June. The rain comes as if out of nowhere. Suddenly it is fat and fast, warm in the air. A strong breeze the only warning of the impending torrent. Then the sky is gone above cloud, and a fractured column of water rests between the hills. Anything living in the valley heads for the nearest place of shelter. Sheep into wall corners, rabbits back into the maze of warrens within ground, and the villagers, if they are out, find the cover of trees or neighbours' houses. The summer cuckoo at the far end of the dale lets up. Everything sentient is moving, except for the half-wild fell ponies, which stand absolutely still in the rain. Pure to it. They stand in the meadow's long grass, afraid to move, or perhaps contented in the downpour.

Six or seven black and white animals, static, steaming with heat, the sweet odour of their rough coats trapped in the mist of water now filling the valley. A small swish of a coarse tail. Nothing more. Beads of water collecting in their beards, and on their backs, shining.

So sudden is the rain, and heavy, that the two do not realize they are sharing the same shelter, a vast sycamore tree. They have run blindly, with rivers on their foreheads, stumbling for dryness. Until he comes around the trunk shaking his untucked shirt, the shelf of his ribcage dripping, to face her, and both gasp at the shock of proximity. Neither can breathe or speak. This moment has been imagined to death, never expected, and the coincidence of it is like a poor joke. The valley is alive with water. It roars down, drums, patters, splashes over the webbed-handed sycamore leaves, trickles on the ground.

He looks away. He cannot tell her she is not beautiful, here in this sudden rain, the rain half soaking her hair and clothes against her skin. He knows only that he wants to cut it off, bury her hair under the roots of the tree, so that her head will be bare and will not provide him with ropes to wind round his fists. He wants to lift her up into the branches, let them catch and tear her dress away so that he will not have to use his hands. And there will be an aftermath of blame. He knows that.

For now, there is only the ceremony of rain, the swell of blood, a pulsing sound of water in the meadow as the long grass is flattened. The temperature of a body. She exists like light grown in water, slightly ahead of him.

At first she will not let him touch her. She bangs her head back off the bark of the tree trunk when his hand reaches for her waist. Her scalp is cut on the sharp wood, as if she is demented, trapped in an asylum with walls of precipitation. The sobs leave her, torn and long. Her banging head damaging the seduction that she cannot otherwise articulate no to. He waits for her. Rigid with anticipation as she calms. Then

118

her mouth's violet against his neck, taking soft rain from the skin. His head falls to the side, his long fingers are at her throat. The damp skin along the collarbone is one deep bite away from stopping his lung, though that organ is useless, he is not breathing. His hand presses on the tree for balance, she is small between the two structures, her arms, her hair, fluid. Then, a man she is required to hate above all others is quietly begging love as he holds her to him, head held back, please, please, and she, trying not to break him, enters his open clothing.

It is rain, running within the space of one valley only, which ends as suddenly as it begins.

∾

She would never agree to meet him. She would not listen to his invitations, the places he wanted to arrange for their encounters. It would only ever be chance, in the dark woods next to the new road, the cave by the tarn, which would bring them together and allow that, so she could keep a tiny piece of resistant anger by her side. Unwilling to admit it was within her control, that she was complicit. She preserved her warring state of mind as best she could, would not let him smooth away her resentment with a simple hand on her cheek. There would never be a public appearance as far as she was concerned, never courtship on an open bench, of lovers linking fingers. So he kept watch on her house from his car with its window open. Rain splashed inside and the seat's leather perfumed, became a strong, acrid odour. Even this aroused him, reminded him of what was to come. He did not know that she was more aware of his movements within the valley than he was of hers. That the direction of her walks was dependent on first pinpointing his location or hearing word of where he had been.

He saw her leaving the school, bidding goodbye to Hazel Bowman one last time, because her mentor was leaving

Mardale for the war in Spain, one of only a handful of women who would go. The two exchanged a rough, desperate kiss and he watched the scene like a silent picture. The words passed between them were a mystery, but he felt sure that Janet had made a confession of the affair, to the only person she felt she could without serious repercussions. Her head fell to the woman's shoulder, a rare and unexpected tear, he could not be sure. Her teacher took her chin, lifted her face. The advice or blessing was given with love. It must have been a meaningful culmination to all the philosophies and lessons of the past. Words injected with pride and an abundance of mortal strength. Hazel Bowman handed over her heart's marrow and Jack Liggett was moved in a way he could not have anticipated.

He followed like a star in the distance, with an umbrella at his side, ineffective in the sudden Lakeland storms.

She would take long walks, as if his coming to her would be accidental, his fault, his responsibility. The obtrusive car was parked on the roadside like a red rag on a door, but the village had become used to its conspicuous presence in the corners of the dale. In the woods, she smeared pine sap into his dark hair, telling him it would never wash out, that he would forever carry a piece of her ruined home with him. She told him she would have him branded if she could, that she still hated him. He laughed at her and threw her to the soft, pine-needled floor, pinning her down with his foot. He wanted any tactile response from her he could provoke. Even force. A struggle, combat. And she flung a fist sideways into the cap of his knee, making him fall perfectly straight as though his strings had been severed.

There were always injuries. Bruises as she struggled to leave him, again and again, a ring of blue fingers round her wrist, her ankles. Pieces of her hair torn out when she demanded he leave, feigning indifference, pushing him back. He grasped her anywhere he could, a handful of hair. She would scream, demand he release her.

– I can't.

– Go back to your wife. Go back to the city. You don't belong. I don't want you.

He crawled up behind her, over her, put an arm around her neck, whispering.

– I know that.

His torn lip, as she struck out, furious with herself for letting him come inside her, for asking him to. Fuck sobriety, she had said. Her quiet lectures to the village schoolgirls in the blue-walled classroom about birth control forgotten, or abandoned at the back of her thoughts that afternoon on the moorland climbing up to the tarns. She sat facing him with her chin on her knees, her skirts about her waist, dry grass scratching their flesh. See what we've done? He himself badly shaken from such lucid lack of restraint. Then she stood and began to gather bracken for animal bedding, saying it was needed at the farm. He watched her ripping at the ground, blood starting on her hands.

– It's not enough. I can't carry enough.

He began pulling up the plants too, his palms becoming raw from the thick, knotted stems. They carried it down and left it in a heap by the gate next to Whelter's upper fields. She turned him away from her and kissed a spot between his shoulder blades. Later that day, she found herself staring at the abortive bottle of vinegar in her mother's cupboard. An old wives' tale clucking at the back of her mind.

Each time, at the start, everything was done to him. He let her fists hit his body, covering only his head for protection, sometimes laughing, because she still needed to attack him before she could love. And calmer, she would kiss him, delicate and without apology. His body was a sallow heart, the walls moved easily when touched, she massaged emotions through him. He was unable to keep his voice in check, vocalizing low, every move she made. As if he could not help but cry out after so many nights of restraint, where he was unable to let himself be touched, having to position a woman away from him like a chair under a window. As if it was all an adolescent game now, how long he could hold back, her exquisite mouth slowly moving over his stomach, down. Finally, reaching for her, for the soft bones in her shoulders, which he felt he could almost break with the force of his grip.

She stood and left without saying anything. He called after her, unable to stand yet from weakness, his legs shot from orgasm, stumbling to button his trousers, fasten his belt.

– Come back. Please. I want to talk to you. Don't go into the woods.

But she would always leave him, breathless and with her glass body smashing past trees and low branches. She followed shortcuts that she knew he could not find, would not be able to track her down, hiding behind walls if she heard his voice calling near by. Slapping at her own face from the frustration, the absurdity of it all. There were times when she carried her father's bowing knife across the slip of her underskirt, thinking she would slit his throat if they met that day and leave his beautiful form out for the rooks and the vermin to strip clean. Or herself, a quick, open vein. A solution she desperately sought, and easier that way than murdering another. She would empty herself out, endure her own failing resolve no longer. She would not keep the magnetic blood that tormented her, that spun its compass-pin north when he came, bending underneath a wire fence, coming towards her in the wet field with the look of a man walking dead. As if he would devour her heart. And time after time she whispered into the gully of his bare back.

– Can't stop. Can't keep away. This must end.

∾

After she leaves him he reaches into his sticky hair. He smells like the character of the forest.

– Come back to town with me. Spend the night. I'll get a room in a hotel. I want to see you sleep, that's all. And we can go dancing. Don't you get tired of wading in mud and filth?

– No. I can't do that. Y'know it. Especially this coming week, there's too much to do. I've already been away too much.

– One night, then we can decide how to find you a flat in the city. You can't move around this valley as if nothing has changed. Make your peace with it, it will be better. I won't have to behave like a sick dog whenever we meet. You know I adore you. God, I can't spend a day without you, Janet!

– Don't ask me again. And don't look for me for a few days. I'll be working.

She sat up from the argument, pulling the dress over her head and tying up her hair.

– Leave it down, you look less sabotaged. I'll have to leave soon, the Waterworks won't always need me here. Hell, they don't need me now. Has your father found another tenancy yet? If he wants to buy I have money . . .

A hard slap on the left side of his face. His eye stung, broke water. She was suddenly weary of her own violence.

In July and August the farmers in the valley sweltered under the dry sun as they worked, rolling and collecting hay, and transporting it in carts to barns and out-sheds, tying the bales down under tarpaulin for storage. Chaff and pollen-dust filled the warm air and floated around on the summer currents, and the smell of dry scorching grass was heavy and sweet in their nostrils. It was a good time of year. The men worked together on each other's properties and their families joined with them, for there were usually only a few days of good weather before the next rains would come. A fast shower to disrupt the work, saturate the hay bales and set in a rot. It was more practical to form a skilled group rather than undertake the hay timing as individuals, which would take twice as long. They watched the morning and evening skies to predict a spell of dryness. Sniffed the breeze for a pure gap of summer. The older farmers observed the behaviour of birds, and the shoots of plants. There were always indications, narcotic references within the biology of the wildlife in the valley that a continued period of dryness was coming. These men could read nature, could navigate its warm signs. The limp head of a bullfinch, drowsy in the warmth. Stray feathers. A retracted stem of elderflower. The farmers consulted the shepherds on the higher stretches of land, were told if the marshes were firming, if the springs were thickening with moss and weed.

Around dawn the air was fresh and soft, the temperature rose during the day with the sun's ascension and passage between the fells. The men took off their shirts and their backs reddened, skin peeled and finally became tanned. Their forearms were burned a deep brown, masking the veins which had previously been seen easily, bluely, under their pale, northern-English skin. They hung their shirts over fences and walls, left them on the handles of pitchforks piercing the ground.

Freckled children, broken from school for the summer, had written cards and letters to their departing teacher and promised to continue studying when they resumed school in Bampton. They climbed the bales and slid down the undulating sides of the mounds. They leapt from the rafters of the barns into the new, fragrant hay, built tunnels and passages through it, in which a secret kiss was traditionally stolen if boy and girl met head-on. Kiss or dare. They brought their fathers water and bread when the two o'clock heat became too heavy to move in, and the men sat in the shade of a tree, unstopped the bottles and gratefully drank. They slapped clegs off their bare arms as the insects came drilling in towards the sweet smell of human sweat, seduced away from the dry mounds of horse-dirt. Butterflies and bluebottles lumbered about over the fields, admirals flitting between the starched blades, and the cuckoo called from the trees at the bottom of the valley without interruption.

After lunch the men unhooked their horses from the carts and led them to the river to drink, standing in the water up to their knees, their boots skidding on the loose, slippery pebbles, the sucking clay, as the animals shook their noses in the flow. The farmers cupped their hands in the water and poured it over their brown necks. Back in the fields, one man held a bale while another tied it with twine. More men cutting a new section of field. The slow, hand-driven harvester turning. The horses steady, linear in the haze of the valley floor. It was an old dance, the members of the village were used to these movements, though they knew that this would probably be the last haying season in the dale. The last summer.

Later in the day the women joined their husbands, their hair tied back with coloured scarves, bending with forks to lift loose hay up into a cart, the hem of their skirts tucked up into the waistband, ankles scratched by the sharp, cut grass. The drips of blood on their skin firmed into tiny red domes in the heat. Recognizing the potential of the scene, Paul Levell broke with tradition and set his easel up in the field, caught the women and the stacked haycocks with a stroke or two of a brush. He said that posterity favoured life over war, as far as humans were concerned, and so too would he. They were among the last scenes of Mardale ever to be painted, and in that brilliant season they came away glowing with colour, aesthetic rural compositions. The artist himself wondered at his bucolic creations, mystified by his own visiting serenity.

Jack Liggett also watched the summer carnival of haymakers on his walks through Mardale. They nodded to him if he passed by, politely, but did not break with their labour as the publican and the artist did if he encountered them in the village. He sat on the crossed-wood stiles and squinted over the farmland. The smell of the hay left him lethargic and contented, the sun was a warm anaesthetic on his shoulders. He was slipping under.

With their hair lost under scarves, he could not tell at first which woman was Janet Lightburn. The faces were in shadow when facing the ground and masks of white when upturned to the blinding sun. They were a group of bobbing heads and lifting hands. It was only at rest, when they sat on the carts, tipping back liquid, that he could distinguish individuals. She sat with her mother, slightly apart from her, close enough for the two to pass a canteen of water between them, leaning over to swing the leather strap. The strong, handsome face of Ella Lightburn emerged from a moon of shallow planes, and next to her the daughter, with deep shadows and hollow eyes under a scarlet headscarf.

As he watched her, he saw her former life brought alive, the old actions of her limbs were suddenly reinforced. She had helped out with haytiming since she was a child, just as she had helped with lambing season in April. For her, these were seasons as natural as winter and spring, locked into the year's calendar. So she had stepped back into her past. He could now believe almost any story she told him. Her sarcasm of the previous week, when she had mocked his spare time and leisurely existence, compared his flexible work with the constant effort of agriculture, began to seem less harsh, less unfair. He wanted to approach her, his mind filled with ideas not of who she suddenly was but who she had always been.

He had not seen or touched her for five days. She had told him to stay away during this busy time, making him swear to remain in the background. Inanimate, like a piece of dead wood left at the river's edge. But it is she that composes the background, he thought. Without her presence any meaning the terrain once possessed had become superficial, had gone. For the first time in his memory the region had become invested with a human element. On the tip of his forefinger he held up a ladybird, bringing it in line with Janet's red head, two bright spots of colour in the yellow fields.

∽

In the early evening the haymakers finished their work, and laughter was heard alongside the rattle of the cartwheels and the snorting of Clydesdales. Jugs of cold beer came splashing down in the hands of the children. Sometimes the group sat in the fields they had been tending until the sun lost its heat and the tree shadows lengthened and dispersed. And the cooling air brought sage notes, fragrances released at a different temperature. Then the group would wander home with aching backs and sore palms to wash up for supper, before everyone made their way to the garden benches of the Dun Bull Inn. Even on the periphery of it all there was pleasure enough for Jack Liggett, as he watched the ground become satisfyingly shorn, heard the slow laughter in the dusk.

∽

The next time the lovers meet, after the week of haying, it is in darkness. She has gone to the hotel and is standing under the window, silent and waiting. He has told her of his tendency to prowl round the village in the early hours, if he can't sleep, which is often. Or, if a bold spirit comes to him, he will go night climbing on the crags, his sense of touch the only means of traverse, eyes almost useless in their sockets, secondary. She has heard of certain individuals who tackle the peaks in this manner, the extremeness and legend of such sport baffles and irks the local population, who consider it utter recklessness and somehow disrespectful. Though in some circles, among young men who have not yet had the thrill of a war to explode the myth of human invincibility there are coveted prizes for 'night-bagging', underground wagers, and the entitlement to rarest bravado.

Jack Liggett claimed that he once climbed Helvellyn this way, at night, tightroping the knife edge after months of daylight practice, and as she heard the story she believed him capable of it, foolish enough, lacking respect for the terrain. There are evenings when he does not return from High Street until ten o'clock, later. In the darkness, he has trained himself to listen, noctambulist-perfect, to a mountain, to detect the passage of wind across open chasms or immutable rock, and aim at its face as if aiming at volatile levels of an imaginary human body with a knife, a fist. He spins between crevices, punching shadows in the solar plexus, as if he wants to outmanoeuvre and overwhelm the nerve system of the mountain as he would an enemy. It is a strange skill, this blind murder of landscape. There are chemicals that the body releases to tighten the concentration, he said to her. The feeling is pure, fluid exhilaration. It is better than love, sex, power, morphine, all these things. She laughed, dismissing his theory. Is there anything better than this, she had said, reaching for him, and the argument fell away. Afterwards she told him about the man who was found face-down in a peat gully under Harter Fell a year after he went missing. His body had decomposed, but the face was preserved by the bog and still wore an expression of freefalling terror.

Now she wants to summon that spirit of restlessness upon him. At the window of the Dun Bull, her fingertips leave mist along the glass. She passes the silk of petals from the flower planters outside the hotel.

This is a warm night towards the end of the summer in 1936. The stars are brilliant above the fells, many still unmapped, unnamed, though the solar system is being completed. She uncovers her shoulders and waits, hopeful of his insomnia. A new tenderness has led her here, coming from their short separation. During the long days of haying she missed him, sorry for her demands that he keep away. The fatigue of her limbs dissolving as she imagined his hands on them.

After a time there is movement by the hotel's door. The sound of a body, cautious in the black. She follows the noise, with her hands held in front of her and her heart thumping madly in case it is not the man she wants but a stranger that she will inevitably touch. She can hear the slight scuff of boots on the gravel car park, the fizz of bootlaces being tightened, retied. Her blood pulls and she trusts it. Her fingers brush past his face. The figure recoils, startled, as if a large moth has alighted on his shoulder, releasing a stifled cry. He hears someone inhale, the growl of energy gathering somewhere in a near portion of darkness. He is being attacked. Then her hands touch again, more certain this time, and he knows it is a friend.

– Lord! I didn't dare breathe!

They tangle arms, laughing, his face in her hair, and make their way out of the hotel grounds, messily, tripping on flowerbeds and over an abandoned bicycle. He is unused to an extra body on his back when he navigates the darkness. He is trained only to move his own body, as a solo hollow. But he finds her breast with ease in his practised medium, his hand slipping between two buttons of the loose shirt.

– You sleep in this? I sleep in my skin.

She laughs, moves away, but he has found her again and has her close. He gloats, showing off his ability to kiss precise bones across her shoulders, her ribcage, whilst she is clumsy in working buttons loose, naïve in tracing his anatomy. But he is overjoyed at her broken habit of denial, and she knows it. It gives him a new determination, fearlessness is pouring out of him. On the moors they move with speed, half-running over the springy ground, falling over peat gullies, the distance seeming further, the movement faster, when it is invisible.

On the ground next to the river he brings her legs up over his shoulders and she cries out without fear of being heard, her cry just another kill in the night landscape. Darkness camouflages noises as it masks vision, the ear will not recognize a sound without the balance of light, so the lovers are unbetrayed. He is brutal with her, selfish, superior within his knowledge of the turbid atmosphere, the pitch black, aroused by her sudden vulnerability, her nakedness under the old shirt. He is able to wrestle her arms back, she does not know the direction of his coming to her. Then tenderness, it is fascinating to guess her emotion and pleasure against him. From nothingness, the sudden shock of his lips at her navel.

There is more peace in this night than at any other time they are together. The absence of light is liberating, both agreeing to go without themselves. He has no guilt, and for her there is only a body under the stars.

– You think I hate this place, that I've taken it, carelessly. I have always loved it, even as a boy. I used to ride the six o'clock train from the city without paying, standing outside the car when the inspector came through, not knowing if a structure inside a tunnel would swipe me clean off and kill me. At Shap summit the engine always slowed and it was possible to jump down if you were inclined to. If I came away with no sprain, I'd walk across Swindale to here, or someone would give me a ride to Borrowdale. My grandmother lived there, you see. She was good at keeping secrets and glad to have me, hated her daughter's husband, said he was responsible for her death. But a terribly kind lady. My father worked weekends and didn't know I was gone. He worked on the ship canal, on these endless weekend shifts. He was a mechanic, a fixer, always being called to one faulty mechanism or another. The canal was never a masterpiece, even in its day, whatever they might say. It was floating with junk. But he made it seem so impossible, keeping water. Always a losing battle, a fallible endeavour, and constant. There were no successes, just resisted failures, I hated that idea. I went with him to get out of our house sometimes. You can't know the filth of Manchester back then. To breathe was a waste of time! Children shitting in the streets. This was another world for me, up here, away from the city, all the little wet slate towns between the mountains. God, it was clean! I stole some boots from the Keswick Arnison's, walked right out of the double doors wearing them, and carrying my shoes. They were the best thing that I had ever owned.

– How did y'mother die?

– It doesn't matter. My father found the boots and guessed that I had stolen them. He broke my wrist and nose. Just like that. No warning, no indication of what was coming. That was his skill. The ability to throw a punch from a complete standstill. Afterwards, he said I had no sense of fair earnings. He earned less in a month than the boots cost, poor bastard. I didn't hate him. I just had to make sure there was no lasting residue of my being his son.

She turns in the dark, an imaginary imprint of her buttocks on the cool grass. The moorland coarse behind them with its nocturnal noises and smell. He takes her hand and kisses the back of it, a strangely formal gesture after their intimacy.

– Everyone thought you were very wealthy. That y'stepped down into the valley from someplace soft where you were made. You have that smell, like you've always had finery, and time for the midday forecast.

– I imagine you don't get time when you're rich. It's probably

131

a vacuum. Suddenly that sense of dragging hours disappears, there aren't any factory clocks. Just a pleasant tick on the mantelpiece that means nothing except when dinner will be called. People would call it an achievement, I suppose. They think being poor and educated is an utter miracle, but it was easy. A scholarship, a bit of politeness, it really made all those concerned with my education feel good to think they were improving one of society's wrecks. They like to make room for an occasional new member, in that way assuring themselves that the structure remains intact and operating, that we're still a staggered lot. I didn't even work my way up. I walked into the Corporation building like I had shoes hanging off my arm. And people don't ask your name, of course, it's too bloody rude.

He sighs and sits up. The moon's reflection in the river is skimming the current to remain in the same position. Janet is quiet beside him and he knows she has been allowed sudden access to him. He smacks an insect on his arm, lifts his body above hers.

– I'm being eaten alive! It's your turn, I think.

– You're building a dam so y'can sink your childhood. Is that it? But you're right, you haven't been careful enough in abstracting the damage. You're sinking ours too, mine, and Isaac, who hasn't even finished his, and we never wanted rid of it. We never did.

∾

Jack Liggett holds the warm, dry body on the dark lunar banks of the river. He is remembering the importance of money, has devoted much of his life to it, and remembering the smell of rotten vegetables in the kitchen of his father's stack-house, the interruption of fists against human matter. The delivery of unrelated anger. And swinging his own small fists at effervescent corners of space, kicking his feet wildly in the slop on the kitchen floor, the blackness finally congealing.

The past unfurls. His hand between Janet's breasts tracks the minimal double-tick of her heart as it lifts outwards, shudders in. Above it her sternum dulls the echo of the movement of manufactured blood. His forefinger slopes upwards, pointing towards the back of her neck. If a bullet were released there it would travel through everything vital, bringing in its wake a river of red.

In his arms, Janet turns, restless in the summer humidity. The river also moves past, sounding out rocks and inclines. She interprets a blunt, introspective mood stirring in her lover. His limbs have tightened a fraction across her. She places a hand behind his head, moves her face down to his.

– I think you understand yourself too well. It should be more of a quarrel. You need to leave room for a portion of uncertainty, space to get away from yourself now and then.

– Yes. You speak so . . . never mind. I want you to know that if there was any way . . . this valley. It's too late now. And I am sorry.

– Don't. It's better to just keep ahead. Because I can't stand the thought of being as I was before you came. There is only one way it can be between us. I believe that.

A hand on the base of his skull dragging him up. The smell of decay in the kitchen. And sounds like those of an animal being dragged to the roadside, awful, coming from his own mouth. He closes the memory, as if putting away a book.

∽

In the morning the light was terracotta, a burnt orange lapping over the eastern fells. The road to Swindale was still eerie and unlit, twisting through trees on the steep valley side, soaked by shadow. Jack Liggett drove as he always did, with speed, exhilarated, as if there had been an agreement made upon purchase of the vehicle that excess caution would not be used in any circumstance. At the head of the valley he parked the car and the two walked up into the bow of hills towards the waterfalls. She did not want to go back home yet, she had said to him on the banks of the river as the night began to thin. So they had gathered up their clothes and left Mardale, stealthy like criminals. She wanted them to visit a place that they both knew, had both been to before, separately. Half-way up the fell the waterfall became audible before it was seen, a hidden rushing noise. She moved ahead of him, finding footholds in the broken rock, between the wiry clumps of grass. Once she held out a hand to him and he smiled wryly, but did not take it. Instead he moved her fingers lightly across his lips. She shrugged and moved on.

Higher up, the waterfall poured into deep pools and dark narrow troughs, increasingly inaccessible. At almost the top of the fell they scrambled their way down a steep incline to the rocks and water below. The pool was brown and floorless and frothy under the waterfall where the surface was churned. Janet unbuttoned her shirt and removed the rest of her clothing. He watched her movements with anticipation, but she undressed naturally, as if preparing to wash at an enamel sink, and without flirtation. She stepped to the edge of the water and dived in, swimming cleanly through the liquid, up to the sheet of the waterfall, pulled herself half out of the water, her hair dark blue down her back. She called to him.

– I have something for you, but you'll have to come here.

Jack moved to the edge of the pool, ran a hand through the water and shook it. It was icy cold.

– Cum round, if y'have to! You'll manage. It's not Scawfell.

He removed his boots and shirt and crossed the flat boulders at the bridge of the pool where it was shallowest. There were ledges along the cliff face, which became slippery as the spray reached them, and ferns grew in the small pockets, glimmering with water as it pulsed past. Her face looked bluish in the pool as he moved skilfully along the edge to her.

– If I fall, I shall no doubt die. That water is not going to sustain my life for long. Look at you, you're as inhuman and waterproof as your brother! You're making me feel very ill.

The spot where she had lifted herself out was secluded, difficult to reach, but he twisted down to her, green moss smudging along his chest, his fingers aching as he clung on. She was braced on her hands.

On the ledges below him were four or five slender orchids, tenacious, hardy, bruised by the spray of the falls. They were almost colourless, only slightly blushed with mauve, as if deprived of light, and utterly delicate. A faint shiver of a stem.

– Northern marsh. Remember that, if you want to.

– Christ! I didn't know. How remarkable.

– The Wildlife Society has been informed about them, they aren't uncommon, but it's a fairly well-kept secret. There aren't many so adventurous as these. In general I think they prefer mires or beeches, you know, flat reedy soil. You can understand that I preferred not t'pick one for you, Jack.

She emerged more fully from the cold water, glistening and white and chilled. Made as if to come up to him above.

– Would you believe me if I told you it was warmer in than out?

– No! Hell!

She dipped herself into the water again. He turned his face so that the other cheek pressed on the cold, damp cliff. As he made his way slowly back round, she followed him in the pool. He glanced down and smiled at her. She was suspended in the thick liquid, her pale skin rippling in the brown murk. He could not see the bottom and he asked how deep it was. She swam down towards the basin floor, surfaced moments later and laughed. It was a laugh he had seldom heard from her, uninhibited, lacking any opposing tension, and it fitted with her white body, and came from it without protocol, suddenly convincing him that she was much younger. Then she rolled in the water and swam back to the bank. As he inched along, he wondered at the contents of the pool, strange prehistoric fish with fat lower jaws, jagged spines, and the inevitable decomposing carcass of a sheep. Now that she was gone from the water, above the surface of the pool there seemed to be an abundance of dragonflies. They churred in the air, making furious sudden loops and stalling down on to the ferns. There was one just at his elbow, flickering double-winged on the rock. It looked like a blue vein, flown from the arm of a child. Another by his right foot, a smashed tube of amber. Then both shot into the air, released from the wall to follow their invisible strings through September and into October.

The cliff flattened out in front of him, becoming less slick and overhanging. But he closed his eyes, lifted his hands from the cliff face and, after a moment leaning back, his body was swallowed by burning cold water. Its shock on his skin was electrifying. He gasped air, sawing it down into his chest, and struggled to the shallows. Ahead of him, Janet was standing naked, still, except for the water running from her body. She looked like a statue of rain.

∼

Her mother must have sensed that a change had come over Janet. Perhaps it was in her skin, an altered fragrance, the telltale sign that her body was being moved towards maturity, nightly. There was a soft lustre to her. Where once her face had been kinetic and lean, now it was often sleek, at rest and her eyes quiet. A lift of the forehead to smooth an expression. She had new moments of abandoned peace that were uncommon for her. Her mouth resting against an upper arm, her gaze off at the horizon. Everything stilled about her. And yet she was not entirely reduced to placid relaxation. After these moments of contentment in her daughter's face came anxiety and agitation, seemingly arising from nothing, no good cause. Then the two extremes ran neck and neck, vying for precedence.

Ella carefully observed her spells of restlessness too.

Occasionally, she found her daughter engaged in frantic activity, washing her hands continuously at the sink, forgetting she had just completed the task. She would brush down the coat of the horse incessantly, the same section of stomach over and over with the metal brush. At these moments she could not be approached, would come out roaring from herself, suddenly livid. Even her father and brother would shrink back, but they seemed not to realize that Janet's state was anything other than an extension of her torrid, choleric temperament, her typical self. When pressed on the subject, Samuel put it down to the loss of her home. Her dwelling on the future, as indeed they had all been. Not Ella. To her mind there was something else. Something to do with love, or loathing, she was wound up within a consummate situation. In addition, there were the missing hours. Janet had always been keen on time spent outdoors and alone, but there were endless days when Ella could not account for her daughter, her food was left cold on the table. And the farmhands could not report on her whereabouts. She harboured suspicions that it might be a man. While this did not sit badly with her in principle, she did worry that there was no formal courting going on, which suggested a poor match. Ella wanted to broach the subject, hoping to offer advice, but she found she could not. As with so many other issues, there was no way to reach her daughter, no obvious bridge. She did not guess that the stranger in their midst was largely responsible for her daughter's moodiness, though in retrospect she could not believe she had failed to miss it for as long as she did.

∽

She steps out of the cottage door, walks past the drying flowers in the garden, the farm gate, and the dog follows her a little way down the path before turning back. In her hands, a large china platter, which her mother wants returned to the woman to whom it belongs in the village. A strange request; her mother does not ask small, irrelevant things of her such as this. And her face too was strange when she asked it, passing between curiosity and hardness, as if an accusation lay behind it somewhere, or a question. As if this duty was a test, though neither knew of what, or how exactly it should be undertaken.

A fresh breeze is coming down from the Rigg, stirring the hedgerows. Above, a flock of small, dark birds reshapes itself effortlessly in the sky, perhaps heading away from the cooling climate. The season is close to its end. Soon there will be the inevitable break in weather and one morning she will wake and know that it will not be warm that day or the next, that the rain and storms and an occasional hurricane tail whipped in from the Atlantic, the Irish Sea, will shortly perform surgery on the landscape. Pulling at its flesh and taking off skin. Filling in the dry holes, bringing back streams that have not existed for months. And finding a piece of land on which to lie with him will become more difficult. And finding ways not to know him will become more difficult.

If he stays. He says he is staying.

She passes the church and the hotel. On the bridge, two men are in conversation. A brief exchange with them, her mind not able to engage further, though they require no more from her than cursory acknowledgement. When she has moved by, they resume their intermittent discourse. A backward glance at the hotel across her right shoulder. Hopeful. Affected. And as her head is coming round, the sky is rolling strangely, grey and white, empty of wings. And then a flush of trees. And stone.

As she falls to the side, the village walls move past her vision, so the sky seems to harden. For a moment she feels like she is spineless, without an internal frame to support her, and it is sickening. Then the earth reminds her that there is a composition of bone within, banging hard against it, mapping each joint as it hits. There is a noiseless shattering. The itch in her palms tells her she is cut, perhaps badly.

There is blood and dust on her forearms, and broken pieces of green china embedded in her hands. When she looks down she is holding half the smashed platter. As if she might still use it to carry air. As if it isn't destroyed. There is nothing in the road to indicate a reason for the fall. No obstruction, stray timber, cow-shit. No new rut that she has stepped into while her eyes were engaged elsewhere, not conscious of the path.

The men on the bridge come over to assist her as she stands and to investigate the damage. If she bends her fingers to pull out the shards in one hand others will go in deeper. One of the farmers takes her by the wrist, and the rest of the bowl drops to the ground, this time sounding accurately like something delicate blowing into fragments. The man looks for signs of an alarmingly fast leap of blood and, seeing none, begins to pull out the pieces, starting with the largest cusp at the base of her thumb. The sensation of it is like he is pushing dead glass in further. Her face is ambivalent to pain, aware then detached, as it has been all morning. Behind them Jack Liggett says not to do it. Says to stop doing what they are doing. He says that the best way to get glass out from a person is to wash it out. To let the water remove it softly, water will get behind the glass and lift it from the skin, he says. His hand is pushing down on an invisible object before him. He does not move in and the man lets go of her wrist.

The river does not begin to sting until the china has come out and the cuts are exposed. In front of her two men from the village who have known her as a child watch her palms being scoured of debris by the current. Behind them a man they do not know, whose birth-markings she could point to blind-folded, waits for an obscure indication that he should move forward. That he should leave. His face is flushed and abrupt, as if alcohol has suddenly made its way through his flesh to there. Her own face suffering the carved distance to him. And surely everything is apparent. Everybody's position revealed, their simple motives identified and hovering about like loud insects. Her eyes strip between the men deployed on the river bank. And she realizes how invisible massive human conditions are. How secret in status the largest portions of life can be.

Jack Liggett had tasted coconut before. He was one of only a few people in the country to have enjoyed that privilege. A few were being imported without sanctions from the Indies on Liverpool-bound trade ships and, in turn, they found their way on to the crowded market tables of Manchester and London. Under the creaking awnings of Old Shambles market place he had picked up the object and examined it. There were three sensual dips in its shell, a beard of hair at its head which reminded him of a dark female. Back at his Manchester townhouse he had broken into it with a carpentry tool, bitten into the flesh. The taste of it was unlike any other he had encountered. It was sweet, unique, and he thought never to find its equivalent.

He had not ever found the flavour of coconut rich in the air as he did now, after descending a steep, loosely shaled mountain. He was standing on the common scrub moors of Mardale Ill Bell – a half-mountain tucked behind the crags of the Rigg. At first he could not locate the source of the fragrance. He realized he was surrounded by flowering gorse bushes that were exploding perfume from their yellow flowers into the air. Nothing else was flowering yet on the high moors, except a stray flock of heather.

In his wildest imaginings he had never expected to come across a little Westmorland oasis where foliage assumed a tropical identity. After scrambling down the last of the scree into the rough half-valley, shrieked at by a lapwing guarding a hidden nest, he came close to a brilliant yellow bush, bent close and waited for the slow, itching bee to finish in the hollow yellow flower and lumber off before he inhaled. His nose entered the prickly, silky domain and was overcome with scent only like that of a coconut. It was fresher than roses, somehow heavier, stickier, but without the sugar. It was a steamed-island, oily sweetness, nutty and bringing to mind the humid air of the Indies that lies on the skin like a damp, hot shirt. And he stood back, laughing, looking around the mountain, across the brown grass for someone to mention his find to, though he knew he would not find a soul. He laughed at the strange and marvellous world, surprising him with its simple, divulging gifts.

He did not know that the gorse would emit the fragrance for only a few short weeks, for a brief, very un-English season. But he knew that in this dale he alone could find a mirror for the scent in an exotic fruit from thousands of miles away. There was a quick reconciliation within him. Suddenly he felt validated, the reasons for his presence, old and new, fused, and the position of his boots' soles against granite and heather became absolute.

~

For a few sacred months that summer and autumn, Jack Liggett renavigated the mountains of the Lake District. He journeyed out to the ragged peaks in the centre of the area, ascending the lower slopes and climbing rocky veins thousands of feet high. He stood up against the wind on the narrow paths of the Helvellyn and Blencathra ridges, balanced marionette-like on the razor edges of the Langdale Pikes, with gravity heaving at him from all sides. Wast Water, a sucking black hole beneath him, deepest of all the Lakeland pools. There were vertical pillars of rock in Kentmere and Coniston that provided him with peripheral splendour, needles shafting out of the moist valleys. Or the ordinary brown vastness of Skiddaw brought him up into the fast weather, the eerie realm of shifting mist.

What could he say of this land, with its influence over his body and his mind? Though he had heard of that certain healing quality of the region before, from acquaintances who had been seduced by the beauty of the area, even from the infamous poetry which people absorbed as if it were a travel guide, he had never believed it reasonable, judging those protestations as sentimental and verbose. Only now did he begin to reconsider, to trace a marginal accuracy in the accounts, however loquacious and fanciful they might have been.

The Riley Sprite became covered with mud as he drove down the most inaccessible lanes to reach the base of a pike. Dirt firmed within the wheel arches, dropping off in dried chunks as he parked back in the driveway of the Dun Bull. It was not a suitable car to be navigating the Lakeland in, with the region's conspiracy of water and landslides, the perpetually leaking solids, but he worried less and less for its pristine condition. He felt a youthful strength returning to him, knew that the invincibility of his boyhood was close at hand, and if he just reached another summit, crossed another ridge, he would have it again – that freedom of having stolen away from the city, that entrepreneurial spirit, adventure. He left stones at the summit cairns to be smoothed by the winds and the rain, broke off portions of mint cake and let it chill sweetly against his inner cheek as he caught his breath, surveying the world below that he had pushed upwards away from. And this was satisfaction, peace.

∼

There were still his duties at the bottom of the valley. He would spend no more than an hour in the company of the engineers each morning, minimal contact, then the rest of the day was his own, and he was untroubled with the practicalities of the project. Telephone calls to the Corporation headquarters were rare, the excuse being the lack of such utilities to hand. He knew that the chief executive was displeased with the developments in Mardale, the lenient extension of tenancies and such, the absence of his right-hand man, his most trusted counsel, but Jack Liggett also knew his position to be secure. His Lakeland sabbatical was something which would go unchallenged, it would be viewed as a reward for a job well done. He was something of a favourite amongst the directors, a conductor for pride, this young man of intense ambition and insightful business acumen, who had sown the seeds for treatment plantations and underground systems throughout the north-west, and seen them blossom. A practical, agreeable man, he rested as a jewel in the crown of the Waterworks.

Known for his gallant manner, and his foresight, he also demonstrated a reliability in bringing both ideas and schemes to fruition with a minimum of fuss, with an aura of serenity and without being in the least phlegmatic. Nor did he bow under pressure, or negotiate lightly. He seemed to have a gift for besting, without encouraging enemies. Manchester City Corporation's take-overs in that decade were refined affairs, with Jack Liggett the driving force. It was as if he was simply born for his position, though few knew the circumstances of his upbringing.

So well did he play the role of upper manager that his colleagues never had cause to suspect foul play. He could have carried a safe out past their noses and they would have presumed he was making way for more light at his office table. Had any of them attempted to glean his past or question him too closely about family or connections, he would simply have stepped up his attitude a notch, convinced them of a history glittering with fine wine, college alumni and private wealth. Sufficient evasion of topic to suggest a charming modesty, not so much as to draw attention to the desire to elude interrogators. He knew how to enter a room of applause without seeming relieved, was wasteful enough with pâté and champagne at social gatherings not to seem unaccustomed. The only fault in the performance was perhaps its perfection, though textbook class was seldom disagreeable, and, in these times of threatened social disorder, was more likely to be welcomed and protected than it was challenged. Jack Liggett was a man who commanded his own life, worked hard and gave away little. The Haweswater project was his, a product of mental stretch and insight and his longest commitment at MCW. It had been nurtured from conception, through a bureaucratic maze and the corridors of Westminster, through the development of the drawing office, to its physical realization, the metamorphosis of linear thought into the final weight of construction. There was nobody the Corporation would rather have on site.

As the summer progressed, there came to be more traffic in the Mardale valley. Machinery and equipment were brought in for the clearing and levelling of the dam site and the first of the workers, the machine operators, began to straggle in. The new road was often blocked with heavy machinery and the locals, who had grown accustomed to using it since its construction, once again began to favour the old western track down to Bampton.

The four engineers, who had made a quiet presence for months, became more animated and increased the volume of their discussions. They pored over plans and debated positioning, indignant to rebuttals of their suggestions. There was, for a time, stalemate between them. A divide of two versus two, as the group fought between plans for a slightly curved dam wall, allowing for irregularities in the strata of rock, and a straight-walled design, which would require a lesser amount of land alteration for its foundations. When the latter was eventually chosen, the issue of facing arose and created a problem of equal contention. The grey dolomite, originally intended to face the dam wall, was proving too difficult to work with. An entire section of planning had to be abandoned, opening the door to fresh argument. Jack Liggett often felt like a parent calming a squabble among children when the engineers started bickering. He would be curt and plain of manner, allowing little room for the stand-offs, sulks and ultimatums of the four to invade his private schedule. And, in a way, it became inconsequential to him. He was contented in these months, another life was opening up to him, and love, and now that the scheme was well under way, he happily took a step or two back, camouflaging himself within the valley. From this position he could curse at the wagon driver who brought down sixteen yards of valley wall with his careless reversing, as if the damage done was somehow personal. The violence of his swearing coming from an unchecked portion of himself, with which he had little prior association.

～

There were long days when he was content to skirt the mountain ranges which surrounded the Mardale village, and as the machine operators began to arrive and set up the dam site, he sat in the long grass on the slopes and watched from afar. The season was turning bitter, the short, hot summer had all but bled out. There was a fresh, woody smell in the air and the red bracken was wild over the sheep paths, twisting its stems together in firm, mature knots so that his boots had to rip through it as he walked. Warm rain from the summer was gone. Now, when the first drops came they were cool and refreshing on the back of his neck, the water was exhilarating on his gasping face.

His muscles became hard and the skin on the back of his neck burned a deep brown. The taut wires running through his stomach came to the surface. And he felt comfortable within his body, energized. He went unshaven, a stubble darkening his full mouth, the start of a soft beard. Lifting his hands to his face, he would rub his jawline, marvel at the new texture. Breeches and a woollen shirt were all he now wore, a uniform of comfort and flexibility. He carried with him a tall wooden staff for the purpose of steadying himself on the descent from a ridge, but, more than this, he enjoyed the firmness of it within his palm, growing accustomed to the smoothness of the surface against his fingers, the groove for his thumb. He knew he was throwing off his old façade, but it was irrelevant. All that existed now were those mountain steps, one after the other, lifting him above the horizon.

He begged Janet to accompany him on his hikes, but she would seldom leave the quiet school during the mornings, determined that the establishment would not miss out for the sake of her own pleasure. Hazel Bowman had left the valley a few months earlier and Janet was now charged with the establishment's future, which would hang in the balance unless a new building was erected beyond the reservoir. The pupils of Mardale were being merged with the children of Bampton endowed school, which was an excellent institution in its own right. She was heartened by its reputation for turning out both intellects and undefeatable wrestlers, and she knew the headmaster, Andrew Jackson, to be a decent man of high principles, yet there was a part of her desperate to preserve an aspect of the old Mardale establishment. Her nostalgia was shared by many in the dale and they gave her their blessings to organize a fund. She was busy writing letters, enquiring about aid for a new school building, from charitable organizations, endowments and alumni, and would not be swayed from her task.

Jack Liggett would have to be content with her evenings, or an early-morning encounter, when the scent of her skin was like honey. The two had developed a discreet system for their affair, a paradoxical union of spontaneity and caution, excess care. He urged her to allow him public courtship, but she insisted on the affair remaining private, and he was obliged to grant her wishes. Though it irked him, the taste of her in his life was all he desired, and so he complied.

He was aware that a meshing of his pleasures was probably the key. The fulfilment of a high climb and the sensuality of release as he flooded into her body, each brought a level of contentment above any he had reached in the past. The two at once seemed to offer a spiritual answer. As he thought of it, he lay back into a quiet cave within himself.

Naked, the two of them wrapped in a blanket against the dew of those early-autumn dawns, there was more pleasure than there was discomfort, and he could not manage to summon a severe degree of objection to their subterfuge. Images of her in the Swindale waterfall haunted him. And her frozen body slowly warming after, under the friction of his own. With this joint gratification in mind, he continued to ask for her presence on his outings to the mountain ranges, imagining her limbs angling against a high plateau of rippling grass, the final strands of her hair before an edge of cliff fell away. Moving with her under only the weight of sky. As he had dreamed of it in the George Hotel in Penrith, so he wanted the reality. Pulling up to the cave of her mouth. In that place, he felt he could once and for all explain to her that a truer section of himself had come into being, he felt the infection of it in his blood. That through a metamorphosis in this wild, saturated, palatial land, he was becoming abridged, and finished. A new and better piece. But she would not come. She would not. As she sat in the old classroom next to the lake, he set out into one range of fells after another.

Occasionally Isaac would walk with him to the tarns. He was glad of the company and fond of the odd, dauntless child who was put off by neither climate nor association. The boy loved to submerge his hands and face in the freezing water, searching for life, of which there seemed very little. Jack explained to him that here the water was more acidic, poor in nutrients and fairly inhospitable to all but the most specialized of creatures. And Isaac grinned at him, pleased with such knowledge. When the reservoir comes, there will be fish such as the rest of the country has never seen, Jack said.

∾

During those days of hiking he seldom felt lonely. The traffic on the fells of the Lakeland was constant, if sparse. For centuries the area had been a favourite for sporting activity and leisure. Walkers traversed the ridges and met one another at summits or on chicaned passes. A few civil words passed between them like a secular prayer. This was enough human contact for the entire day, the sixteen miles of solitary passage, where the wind and a mind full of thoughts were the only other company. A brief encounter with an ancient, buckled-looking shepherd on the peaty wasteland above Mardale, the man's face rippled like over-sewn leather. Jack Liggett sat with the character against a flock of grass. Here was a man of infinite patience, of quietude, and overwhelming calm. Who might not see another human for weeks, or for months in winter, who was willingly separated, and owned by his work.

Jack Liggett was included in a conversation regarding the unusual weather, about the late rains and the streams low with water, so that next year's spawn would be affected. And how the mist over the Mardale beck was often like dry skin that the water had shrugged off.

– Yes, yes, that's right. I hadn't thought of it before.

The shepherd did not ask him to justify his business, though he surely knew the circumstances. He was required to show no papers on this afternoon, but allowed free passage. As if he, too, now belonged in part to the region.

❧

He watched the early workers preparing for construction of the dam during the first weeks of September, watching from the tops of the hills, on the old Roman route from Galva to Brocavum, which encompassed the fort on Castle Crag. There was, flowing from the green and brown depths, no longer a sense of emptiness of the kind he had felt as a boy all those years ago. Back in 1915, when the country was getting bare of men, when he was learning to step out of the life that had been prepared for him. He knew himself to be entering a new era of reflection and concession. There was a small part of him which felt at home, living as he had been for the past months within the confines of the village, forging connections with its residents, he allowed himself that. Hostility was ebbing away, now that his initial incarnation had been revoked. There was still time, another year, perhaps slightly more, to stay. The village would not be disassembled until construction of the dam wall was almost complete and the valley was ready for its rebirth.

He was sensitive to the fact that the coming months would prove difficult and irregular for the locals, living as they would be alongside developing evidence of the valley's new role. He would lessen the blow in any way he could, another pair of arms for lifting as a family moved out, keeping his ear to the ground for new tenancies or work. He would remain there until the end, he was convinced of this, governing, helping with the exodus. For the respect of the woman he loved. For himself, also. He did not like loose ends, not when they included people with whom he had developed some kind of relationship, or in a place where he had some kind of forgotten jurisdiction. He would witness that almighty flood up the slopes of the mountains, the filling cup, would be witness to his own vast influence, because she would want this too, he was certain. She would want him to see it done. And, in truth, yes, he would miss the tiny village he was now so fond of, so settled within. Perhaps a twinge of regret now and again, as he lay within Janet's arms, his head against her stomach, enough to make him choke. So, his life here would be on borrowed time, with each day another drip of blood out of the heart of the village, as a family secured another tenancy here or there, the contents of a house being transported to a new dale, another town. But treading water did not matter to him. There was still time.

∽

He walked daily on the lower ridges of the mountains surrounding the village, skirting under the knife peak of Kidstey

Pike. The wild bracken crunching and snapping around him, whistling on the side of his oilskin when he sat and moved slightly this way or that. Everything was red and damp underfoot. He sat on the same brow of hill each time, gazing down. Through the waxy mist in the valley he could hear the voices of the men working. The strange acoustics were carried in slick waves through the thick, porous air. Their shouted words were unidentifiable, just tones that were brought to him in spasms, lapping bursts. And when they began clearing trees and topsoil, the sounds of the machines grinding and scraping echoed only very softly around the damp fells. Even when the excavation for the foundations started up three hundred yards from the existing lake, these noises, ear-shattering at close range, were not distracting or overwhelming to Jack Liggett, two thousand feet up in the Westmorland hills. Not the gelignite blasting and the clanking of the caterpillar-tracked crane, the removal of overburden and rock via rumbling cableways and tip-wagons to spoil-banks further down the valley. Not the constant hum from the centrifugal pumps, used for water-displacement and testing the bore holes for watertight pressure greater than that of the estimated, static head of the reservoir. It was cinematic. Sound overlaying a picture and missing slightly.

One autumn day a new self-conscious thought came to him as he looked down on the area below through the low, shifting clouds, seeing only patches of life and movement. Slightly to the left of him was a white blur in the red bracken. He turned his head to identify the interruption of peripheral colour. It was a fell sheep, with its wool ragging down towards the ground and snagging in the ferns beneath. It had been shorn poorly, and on the rump of its hind leg was painted a thick blue H, like a terribly botched tattoo. The tail was clumped with infestation. He imagined its underbelly, riddled with ticks and permanently swollen from probably the full four pregnancies. It must have been lost for some time, unable to fend for itself and close to death.

The sheep looked at him haughtily for a moment, with pale eyes, and in the dampness he could faintly detect the odour of grease lifting from its coat. After a while the animal flipped awkwardly around and limped away. He saw that one of its fore hooves was broken and split wide open. It had been pulled forward on the end of the animal's leg, tipping upwards, so that it gave the impression of a shoe only half stepped into. He felt vague nausea as he watched the animal's painful descent of the slopes, which remained a while after the sheep was lost from his sight.

Then, looking back towards the valley bottom, he saw that the mist had lifted somewhat and he noticed that the voices of the workers were becoming quiet without the clouds to conduct noise. It was grand theatre down there, becoming clear but silent. There was a wide foundation along the ground, with two deep chambers at the position of the dam's future buttresses. It seemed they had suddenly been created, though he knew that they must have been finished for quite some time. The river had been redirected out of the lake and was now flowing within a man-made channel away from the heart of the building arena. Workers swarmed around the construction site. They were ready for the building of the colossal stone arm, the arm of a god, as he had once described it to the villagers. At that moment, Jack Liggett understood that dreams are pinned through with iron and that art might be no more than the materials which line its sides.

– PART II –

II:I

Between the spruce trees rocking lanterns throw stray beams
of light. The men carrying the lanterns cannot be seen in the
morning dusk, only their hands on the staffs are visible, like
white-skinned wings high on the birch. They each carry
enough water for the day's work, in canisters strapped over
their backs, and a ration of corned beef and bread. In the
pockets of their heavy jackets are numerous pairs of gloves,
perhaps a cigarette or two left over from the weekend, saved
with discipline for Monday morning as an anticipated comfort. They walk in this early hour without life, as if moving
from a grave, merely following the ghoulish form in front to
create a procession of spectres, lost into the dark, undulating
through the rips of trees. Occasionally a man at the back of
the line hums, funeral-slow. The ground is soft and giving, a
sponge-bed of fallen needles which collects sound, muffles it,
though any listener coming closer to the group would hear
the minuscule bending and cracking of dead needles underfoot, the squeak of many boots on the spicule-leaf tapestry of
the woodland floor. But from a distance, only the flickering
lanterns among the trees signal the presence in the pre-dawn
murk of four hundred men in silent, wordless convoy.

Other than the man in front and the rocking luminescence,
they do not see. As if they have been buried in the darkness
underground, eyes removed from sockets and the spaces filled
in with leaves, with fur. They are chained by the glow of the
swinging lanterns. Already the short distance walked in the
hard, steel-toed boots is proving uncomfortable, an uneven
rubbing of leather and metal on the soles of their often sockless
feet, their toes curling into hard callused balls, with split nails
beginning to grow inwards. Old injuries returning, unhealed.

Yesterday's sweat odour arises from the fibres of their rough shirts as their bodies warm with motion. In this way, they find evidence of their past commitment to the project, the amnesia of sleep falls away and the scent reminds them of who they are, what they must accomplish. As they near the clearing in the forest, nostrils inhale lime-dust, unsettled and still present in the air from its disturbance the previous day. The fresh smell of the pine disappears, a clue to their location. Shallow light from the lanterns reveals a thick coating of white on the spruce trees now, as if Christmas has found its way into the forest early, powdering the branches with festive snow.

Then the trees are suddenly gone and the dark thins, becomes only branchless air. A last star or cut of moon lingers in the dark-blue sky between nocturnal clouds. No chance to determine the coming weather yet, though poor weather seldom halts the work, now that the foundations do not have to dry. At the dam site, a mile and a half away from where the men began their rote and listless trail, they break formation into an untidy mass. They select a space in the rubble, on low-walled platforms, and drive their lanterns into the ground or between rocks, close to where they have been working over the past weeks. The handle of a pickaxe tucks into a palm, a stiff shoulder lifts. Three diesel engines driving DC generators, which supply electrical energy to the site, are started up. Machinery begins to wake, the slush and grind of mixers, metal resounds off stone, and sections of scaffolding scrape and groan as they are assembled. The air-compressor drones; another hums further down the valley at the quarry, when the group of men separated from the labourers' wake reaches it. Soon an orchestral racket of industrial noise is swelling between the black valley walls.

This is the best energy of the day. The human hands are precise, even without light. No exposure to air has left wet cracks along their knuckles. Under the gloves the skin congeals, splits, digits macerate, but the hand in question does not stop its movement and will not for six hours. By then fingers and arms are without sensation, knocked numb from gestures against solid material. They could be skinned or sliced open without their owners realizing it, and often are.

If there has been rain in the night the ground becomes as soft as clay and the men lay new boards over the mud where they will need to walk, carry ladders, where they will wheel slopping barrows of concrete and mortar. Perversely, overnight frost is welcomed: trenches harden and the mud forms frozen peaks; movement is made easier on the rigid ground, though ice on the scaffolding boards is dangerous for the men working on the upper wall itself.

These high-wire workers have already peeled away from the main group and have climbed the slopes on either side of the site, parallel to the as-yet invisible structure. They begin work in the darkness also, strapping themselves into harnesses that will let a man fall a hundred feet down into the valley from the skeleton of a buttress. The internal beams are positioned with the aid of flares, so that at places in the middle of the valley it appears that a fire is burning in mid-air, that a falling star has arrested to prolong its end in stasis above the inky pool of the lower valley. White fire burns out and a crucified man hung somewhere in the darkness strikes another star alight. Like a stellar factory. At the corners of the framework, bolts are blindly driven into another piece of scaffolding before the sun issues a complete illumination.

Within the mammoth ribcage of the embankment, foremen look upwards, knowing another portion of sky will be lost that day, ahead or behind schedule. They bark commands, search the site for faults as human bodies flow around them.

The men riddling the ground are stonebreakers, welders, fitters, joiners, construction workers of every kind, and gaffers, who will never have any liberties on the site but will have to fetch and carry ladders, pass and lift timber and rock, undertake the most menial and mundane tasks for the duration of their time on the project, receiving almost half the pay

157

of other men. They move the most and at the whim of a call or a gesture, swimming through clouds of debris, leaving mud tracks on the boards, whores to the skilled labourers. They are the youngest men, barely men, a boys' anti-network, almost, used to the sudden rush against each other for a piece of equipment, a bag of sand.

Within an hour of arriving on-site, the men's lungs are dry with dust from the broken rock, their throats choked with it. Angle-grinders roar and buzz through static, compressed lava a million times faster than glaciers undertook the task of folding it together millennia earlier. The Lower Silurian strata melt under a spinning blade. But the hard volcanic rock leaves a thick wake above the cut, it will not be displaced without first soaking up oxygen and sparkling like planetary rain in the aura of a lantern. The men remove cloths from their pockets and tie them over their mouths, spitting into them to keep them airtight, to prevent the mist of dust from creeping up inside. Saliva forms bloody-looking patches of wetness at the oval of bandage covering a mouth. The men cock heads, squint into the unknown to conjure reality in the singing terrain. They are dependent on sound to know which machine is operating, and at what distance, from the small pool of light in which they work.

As daylight comes up over the hills, the skeleton of the dam is revealed, towering above the workers. The dream of an imaginary construction thaws along with the silver points of the mud, dissolves into reality. Now falling timber can be seen and a dropped hammer avoided as it clatters down through the scaffolding. A fast rope which has come loose from a pulley buzzes by the men attached to the dam; they swing upwards, outwards, and their legs remain free of trenched rope burns. Tea kettles whistle simultaneously at eight points over the site, as if only now in daylight is it acceptable to imbibe the thin brown liquid, though some men will drink from the tin cups through their bandaged mouths to filter sediment. The work buildings erected on the dam site, a fitting shop, smithy, joiner's shop, saw mill and the storage yards, begin to emerge out of the greyness, as do the tracks which carry the small diesel locomotives. Three-ton girders are winched into the giant ribcage, now definite visions.

And all around them is paradise. It is the most beautiful vista many have ever seen. A damp, shining valley hangs before them. Used to smoky towns and reshaped ports, the Westmorland countryside is a glorious backdrop for the construction. Screens of foliage fold alongside the mountains. The density of landscape draws their eyes away from rusting apparatus and their mongrel patches of the site. But these distractions of beauty are rare and short lived. Muscles ache with fatigue to remind the crew that the physical world requires them to give up their bodies for premature or eventual ruin, for the sake of a living wage, or less. Still, high up above the site, those who work in rafters of the sky cannot help but dwell on the view. It opens before them, a world of rivers and the quilt of foliage, brown mountains, hills they can easily see over, and beyond that, a land of discreet, unfolding water.

∾

A man calls sideways. The canister of water swings back between the beams and the ropes of the pulley for him to drink thirstily. Far below him the ground is blanketed by dust and he is thankful not to be choking in it. But high on the structure there are other dangers. Heavy showers might give a short reprieve from work, but rain turns the boards into slick walkways, rotting at the joints, and the tubular piping streams with water. It is better to stay tucked into the enclave of the buttress until it passes, rather than risk moving under the tarpaulin at the corner of the scaffold. Wind is the most feared element on the outer reaches of the dam. Rushing up the valley from nowhere, perhaps from the gathered, unpredictable energy of the north, it can easily lift a man out of his foothold. Or a sudden whirlwind comes down from the top of the mountains, spun into the bottom of the dale as if casually thrown from the gods into a world where they are pawns, expendable. There is no place for the careless, the atheistic. Safety lines and harnesses are, without question, essential measures, attached to the solid dinosaur skeleton itself, which can be relied on for stability. The trapeze artists at the top of the building understand this vulnerability, keeping their superstitions as acutely as they are meticulous with the screws of their heddles. Often a man has walked the distance back to the village to collect a lucky charm, a brass key, a coin bent on train tracks, forgoing half a day's pay for the sake of the talisman which has hitherto kept him safe.

They move out in air to check drying mortar and rivets and true spirit levels, as to the side of them the wind moans past, a section of scaffolding collapses and crashes, splintering and buckling into the clouds at the valley's bottom. The two Henderson cableways, luckily, are unscathed by the collapse. From the cabins placed directly over the winding gear the men lean out and signal with flags, an old-fashioned gesture to convey their messages. No harm. Continue. Each Henderson's lifting capability is vast, as is its span, a commanding reach from the fixed-head mast. Ballast boxes filled with rock provide the machines with stability against overturning. The two Hendersons are responsible for the majority of the dam's construction and any damage sustained to the apparatus would prove disastrous, not to mention expensive, slowing work down to the organic creep of mere humans.

During lunch, machinery is temporarily switched off to save power. The pieces of meat and bread are unwrapped, consumed without enjoyment. It is bland sustenance. On the ground, food and dust mix in the mouths of the stone-cutters. They eat quickly and rub their hands back to life.

The men strapped to the top of the wall sit back against a

metal pillar and watch over the woods. The valley flows away from them, becoming flatter and then only river on the blue horizon. Small birds flit past, encouraged by the brief quiet, often landing on the metal scaffolding rail, their precise claws ticking against the tubes as they sidestep closer, eyes blinking and heads tilting. They have become beggars, scavengers. The men throw crumbs for them to share and the birds dart inwards. The workers begin to recognize species, breeds. Sparrow, siskin, wren, a raven. They can even differentiate between similar members of the same species. Brambling, almost identical to the chaffinch apart from its white belly. As if they were middle-class retirees, birdwatchers luxuriating in the private aviary of a town-house garden. A glance to the west might reveal a golden eagle climbing the ladders of air pressure or, if they are very lucky, they might spy one piercing the low cloud, if the noise of the machinery hasn't driven them over to Ullswater to hunt for rabbits. So many times an excited shout from one of the men has led to the minor disappointment of a mere buzzard, dispatched ahead of a group of three as they surround the hillside warrens.

Now that they are not moving about on the scaffold the structure seems to sway slightly in the moving atmosphere, and if they were to sit all day, a slight sea-sickness would eventually overcome the men. Standing up to resume work, the startled birds fall away into nothing. The men urinate against the vast, coming wall, signing a name with piss which will evaporate or freeze, depending on the season. A blast from a foreman's whistle after thirty minutes of rest and construction is resumed, men limping back to their heavy instruments. But their limbs have already begun seizing from half an hour of sitting and the second part of the day's work is like swimming through treacle. Arms pour out with inexorable slowness. At a point somewhere too far away from a body's torso limbs begin to shake spastically, spasming as the lactic acid, built up tightly in cells, refuses to budge or be reabsorbed. The afternoon drags by.

And at night, on the slow, painful walk home, the white dust-ridden faces are as expressionless and fixed as the faces of the morning. They are caught somewhere between the living and the dead. Lanterns remain extinguished, it is not yet dark at six. After the fake Christmas trees the men remove their handkerchiefs, it is now safe to breathe. Mouths are strangely pink, or clown-red against the powder-caked eyes and foreheads. They might be fools but for their persistence, solemn, withdrawn, and the final product of such an alarming endeavour, a captured lake.

∾

Industry lit up the quiet blue-green valley and overwhelmed it with noise. From West Cumberland labourers were bussed into the narrow dale to begin on the body of the construction. In the west of the country at that time sea ports were closing, the dockers laid off with little warning, and unemployment was high after the Depression. Jobless men seeking work from all quarters began to arrive in the valley, from Workington and Barrow, from Halifax and even Lancaster.

They caught the company buses in the market places of their towns, which were free and had the orange logo of Manchester City Waterworks painted in tall letters on the side of the vehicle. During the journey they signed their names on a list which was passed round, or asked a man next to them to do so if they were not literate. They were informed on the buses that the weekly wage was to be two pounds, four shillings and eightpence, and that accommodation would be provided for them, the rent deducted automatically from their pay. The labour would be varied and in shifts of twelve hours. A prior health check was not necessary, but any man failing to meet the requirements of his job would have to make his own way home. For the manual labourers, it was pressed that families were not allowed to accompany the men, as housing was limited. The buses rattled their way into the quiet corner of the country, one after another, spilling out men.

Others arrived in droves on foot, startling the valley's pop-ulation, which joked that there had not been such an influx of foreigners since the Border Raids. Often a farmer's cart had to swerve wide around a corner to avoid a walk-in, a half-wave of apology from the man in the road. They arrived often in only the clothes they stood up in, a few possessions perhaps tucked into a handkerchief, or a deep pocket. They walked into the valley like a disparate army of discharged soldiers, searching for discipline and orders, routine.

Many of the walk-ins were navvies, an odd, dying breed of labourer that led a semi-nomadic existence. These tramped in silently and were not turned away from the site as there was much of their type of basic work. They stood before the fore-men like emancipated slaves, brought back of their own accord, stood absolutely still, with pale-blue eyes keenly set on a point in space in front, until direction and wage were issued. Men seldom breathing so much as a word, let alone a name for contract. And such unquiet, intense blue eyes!

The arms of these men were dark and sinewy, their boots were always cracked and worn. Oil on their skin formed a sheen over the sun-opened pores on their faces. Dirt and the sun's work were often indistinguishable. They moved from job to job, without fuss and with little forethought, beautiful, ugly men, who wore heavy jackets and moleskin trousers tied at the knees. They were silent, secret characters, aloof and enigmatic, who rarely spoke, either to passers-by or among themselves, but were always polite when questioned. The navvies had great strength, their bodies were enormous, or wire-thin. But broad or svelte, each was a tight drum from the hard end of lift-ing and dissembling. To watch them work was to witness a ballet of fine, constant movement, incredible stamina, a pace which never faltered. The men ran on one speed only, that which was of their own choosing, and they were quieter than the other labourers, more keenly introverted. They did not learn the names of their colleagues to shout across for equipment, as the ex-dockers and factory workers did. Ah, George! A hammer if y'please! Instead they moved like graceful birds to collect a tool, like proud, independent stags.

Speculation about their identities was always rife. They were a cauldron for rumour. Some recognized photographs of wanted murderers among them, others murmured that they must be released convicts, dead now to society for their past crimes, the rapes, the arson, the robberies of previous years, and saved from hanging only by a loose feather of justice, no doubt. So, they were moving to be free of their own guilt's shackles, just as the country would no longer accept them back, and here they were as good as nobodies anyway. Condemned to pick up the worst, back-breaking employment. Common gossip had them down as ex-gypsies, Hungarians or Russians that had slipped into the country via the coal-bowels of supply ships in the Scottish ports. With only enough language to get by, they remained outsiders, solitaries. Or perhaps they were the residue of the closing fairgrounds, the carnival spirit having melted away to leave hollow, masculine vessels, seeking fill. Once bold spirits, now without tongues or traditions.

There was some cryptic quality about the navvies which intrigued and unsettled those who came into contact with them, though the farmers appreciatively acknowledged the manner in which they stood humbly back on the verges as cattle and vehicles passed, unlike their colleagues. The foremen held deep-rooted suspicions about their lifestyle and were, in truth, afraid of these men. They could not be dominated as the other workers could. There was no assumed authority. And they ghosted away as quietly as they came, at any point in the work which they saw fit.

～

MCW began construction of a new sub-village in the thick spruce trees near the site of the dam in the autumn of 1936, and in a month it was complete. By late October over four hundred men were housed in cheap, prefabricated bungalow-huts erected in the woodland a mile and a half from where they would toil daily. These new dwellings were largely for the unskilled labourers responsible for building the hundreds of metres of dam wall. They were basic in comfort, would prove to be hot in the swelter of warmer months and freezing in winter, when the bitter north-westerlies howled through the boards. Eight, ten men or more shared a sleeping room, packed in tight. There were bunk-beds nailed to the walls, and drying racks for work clothes. Washing facilities were shared.

The bungalows smelled of lime-dust and sweat, which clung to the wooden walls at night, mixing with the scents of oil-smoke and human secretions. On the colder nights in the huts the men warmed their hands in the back fold of a bent knee, drawing the issued blankets up over their bitten ears. At five in the morning a siren sounded in the village for the men to wake. Six in the morning was when they began work, and it was a twenty-minute walk to the site. The canteen hall served oatmeal for those with an early stomach and prepared the lunches for the workers to take to the site. Then they trudged out and began the day.

From the mountains on each side of the valley, the swarms of workers looked like insects, undulating in lines, patterns of lifting and digging and climbing ants. The machinery was as a child's toys. In winter, they toiled until the light died and they could not see the rock wall in front of them, then walked back to the huts hidden in the wood, the square ants' nests, with lanterns lit to guide them through the trees as the days grew shorter.

The new shanty-village was called Burnbanks, though the *Herald* and *Gazette* reports of the settlement preferred the nickname 'Aquaville'. It was largely self-sufficient, made up of fifty bungalows, including a concrete mission room, where all denominations of Christianity could worship on Sunday morning or in the evening, a large canteen, in which a sandwich supper cost a shilling, a recreation hall, a shop and a dispensary, which had a resident nurse and was visited by the district doctor bi-weekly. Badly injured workmen were stretchered back from the dam through the woods and driven to the hospital in Penrith, bleeding on to the floor, a limb bent back on itself. In the first four months two bodies were lost down into the hollow embankment walls, the first recovered by a team of workers with ropes, the second too difficult to reach in a narrow trough between the east buttress and the valve system, so it was left, broken-necked and cemented over, inside what had become an enormous mausoleum. There were also many near-fatal accidents. Blades from the angle grinders used without guards so that an untidy arm would be half-severed, arteries split, nerves luckily cauterized by the heat of the blade. The excruciating pain would take an hour to materialize, but when it came it was like hot steel inserted every second into the arm. Two men broke their backs falling from scaffolding. Another four lost sight in an eye from flying debris and metal. The hundreds of men working on the project suffered thousands of fingers broken, re-broken, toes fractured. An Achilles tendon was sliced cleanly through by a falling beam and recoiled up the back of the man's leg like elastic, nails were torn out and became infected under permanently damp gloves. Once a navvy was impaled through his gut by a piece of piping which had been left too close to an area of gelignite blasting. He walked back to the village holding it protruding from his stomach, an inch away from his spleen. The injuries were listed in a file kept by Manchester City Waterworks, any major operations necessary were initialled by the doctor, otherwise the nurse was left to minister treatment. The men came back from work each day with bruised and broken bodies, open wounds, infected sores. They might have been returning from the front lines of trench warfare for their so-often sorry states.

So it was that hundreds of men lived in the woods for a year. In the blink of an eye the population of the valley had increased over tenfold, and a whole village materialized with startling speed in the slow wet district. The buildings came up quickly and discreetly, like mushrooms growing stealthily in the night. They were made from redwood timber, some with a concrete facing, these being favoured as they proved warmer in winter, and they were roofed with asbestos and tile. Most were lit by hurricane oil lamps, although the larger buildings, those provided for the foremen and their families, the accountant and the hut keepers, had electricity, generated by water power, three sets of Ryston and Hornsby diesel engines and dynamos. There was a good water supply for the village from Blea Water, a tarn with an inconspicuous weir, a wet pocket in the High Street fells which was swiftly harnessed.

The village was served by Bedford motor vans from Penrith. There were Saturday bus excursions to the town where workers and their wives and children would go to the market, or to an afternoon matinee at the New Picture House, to watch Joan Crawford and the other modern working girls, or to be terrified by Bela Lugosi's Count Dracula, his back-lit eyes and Renfield's awful, slow, madman's laugh. They watched newsreels and re-runs of *All Quiet on the Western Front*. Members from Burnbanks came back to the Westmorland hideaway quoting Hollywood scripts. Happy times, boy. Happy times. From the town dancehalls they came back singing 'I Get a Kick Out of You' and 'Let's Face the Music and Dance', as aware of new music as any city dweller.

On Saturday mornings the men played football and, having a good selection of athletes, soon set up a team, which travelled the district and won several trophies. They played on a sloping field beside the river, calling themselves the Haweswater Boys, and MCW sponsored their kit of Company orange. They were renowned for their second-half stamina, perhaps due to the vigorous training routine of hard labour, perhaps having the advantage at home games of being used to uphill play, or exploiting the downhill slope against a toiling opposition. The children of the engineers, foremen and accountants in Burnbanks walked to the school in Bampton, swelling the numbers considerably, rather than going to the tiny school in Mardale, which would soon be demolished. It was a round trip of eight miles, often made in rain and snow.

Burnbanks was an odd village, hashed together out of practicality. By those with an interest in American history it was said to have been, at first, compared with one of the Western gold-rush towns of the previous mid-century, born as it was suddenly, out of the desire for profit, born without the evolution of character and history, a bizarre, ill-fitting encampment. A place of newness, emptiness, inconsistent with its ancient neighbours.

∿

On weekends the workers drink heavily, using up a large portion of whatever pay they have made that week. They live like the newly wealthy, buying rounds for each other with abandon. During the first few months of construction they walk down into Mardale, to the Dun Bull Inn, which has a good selection of ales and is also licensed for spirits. They drink side by side with the locals, bragging about pay and eyeing up the young women of the village. But they do not fit in here and are not wanted. They come for hard enjoyment, not slow communication, and witness themselves standing out, like the scent of busy yeast beside racks of baked bread, but they are thick-skinned and do not care. The atmosphere is too tense and the villagers are too sullen for it to be a good watering hole. The women are without a sense of humour and cannot be engaged in flirtation. There is no banter. There is no life! The Scotsman behind the bar will not free pour, he measures their units in brass cups and speaks only when spoken to, even as they line his pockets. It is a strange and paradoxical time for his establishment. Immediate prosperity brought by those men who are the heralds of a future collapse. In the room, the new punters buzz arrogantly round each other like wasps in a shaken jar.

The navvies are the first to leave the establishment, reading the mood of the place astutely, and within two weeks they are gone. They begrudge no one and will not court trouble on any front. They have sat quietly in small groups, enjoying uninterrupted drinking, uncommunicative, and now they are leaving for a last time, all of them together as if of one mind. They put on their coats, blue eyes averted from human contact, giving nothing away, but nodding their bare heads to a farmer by the door. They might be leaving for a murder, for all anyone can tell.

Soon, even against the dulling of alcohol, the rest of the workers begin to comprehend the atmosphere. They tire of the frigid tension in the Dun Bull. They do not know that even the bearded man sitting at the end of the bar, who is, in a way, one of their employers, does not wish to drink with them either, does not wish to be in their presence. He disclaims them, preferring anonymity. He has become a man disinherited from his profession, though he still works for MCW, he moves through duty and obligation like a militant guerrilla through the trees of a conflicted jungle, or as if he is now spying for the other side. For the workers, the crowd is dull and he is amongst it.

The catalyst for leaving is a sudden brawl. One of the young farmhands, a man with only one arm what's more, has had enough of the loose comments about the dam, and the glinting eyes at his sister as she sits with him by the fire, lifting her skirt off her ankles to dry her wet shoes. He is next to the owner of the eyes and comments in a flash, three good right-hand punches into the bones of the face. But the worker is hardened with alcohol. He shakes off the pain and, though one eye is smarting, swelling, he throws himself on top of the farmer, head butting into his lip and splitting it down to his gum so it will take seven stitches to join together again. In his inebriated state he does not even realize he has a two-armed advantage over the man below him. As her brother is, so the sister is also quick to anger. Had she seen the stare, the lewd gesture, the original offence, she would have been the one laying out punches. She kicks the man attacking her brother in the temple with a swift, unrepentant wet shoe. He slouches backwards, out cold. The fight is over.

In the aftermath there is little to be said. A few choice words from Jake McGill, not exactly an ultimatum but enough to convey his wishes. The workers leave, carrying their unconscious comrade over their shoulders. Later they will tease him about being beaten by a woman and another brawl will break out, one involving several of the dam workers, friends in fact, and the damage will be much worse as there will be nobody to break it up.

For now, a small amount of peace is restored to the Dun Bull. There is mild jubilation even, a temporary victory has been won. It has been a while since tension departed and merriment entered through its doors. Nathaniel Holme laughs.

– He's a gud lad that Teddy, he says.

∽

For the dam workers there are other public houses in the district to frequent. St Patrick's Well and the Crown and Mitre in Bampton, where the welcome is warmer and the climate less personal, less hostile. If they fancy going that far, the food at the Helton Jerry is excellent and reasonably priced. They will spend their money freely, because at the weekend they are rich men indeed. Not even the pay for the navvies is mean, though it is slightly less than that of their counterparts.

The off-comers from West Cumberland are happier than they have been in a long while, as there has been no consistent work in their home towns for a good decade or more. They flirt with the Bampton village girls during these hours of freedom at the weekend, having scrubbed themselves almost clean in the steamy, communal bath-houses, offering the girls a fun time if they would come back to the woods. So, on the luckier nights, the Burnbanks shanty huts are sometimes filled with inexpensive female scents too, Lily of the valley and rosewater. Lavender, borrowed without permission from their mothers' dressing tables. The lucky workers' hutmates will promise to stay outside for an hour if they are granted, in return, a couple of pints the following weekend. Besides, they can listen to the muffled cries through the boards of the door if they are so inclined, or perhaps win some money at cards in a neighbouring hut. The arrangement works nicely.

But for the Bampton girls, often there is that belated regret, two weeks of tense waiting, barely daring to think of what might be happening inside their bodies. And the walk home from Burnbanks is lonely, dark, the trees twist up into gargoyle faces, the branches follow them down the road like lecherous arms. They have to run, run fast without looking back, or the whole wood will crackle from its roots after them, damp skirts knotting round their legs as they run. And the moon is a bleak, faceless disc, unsympathetic above them, above the dark haunted road.

Some workers will marry local girls, because love, even under barbaric or temporary conditions, will always prevail. It is a beautiful area to settle down in, to raise a family. Others will simply promise marriage as a way to reap the early rewards from girls willing to forgo pre-nuptial celibacy. A promise is a promise, after all. Then the men will return to their west-coast towns and to the wives they have already, who will be none the wiser, glad, in a way, to have their menfolk home. Perhaps now they can stop gutting fish in the processing rooms or get off the canning-factory belt, surrender their identity as Miss Lowis, Miss Spence, Miss Jefferson, once and for all, and with the money their husbands have earned, buy a new frock or some heeled shoes.

But, aside from all this secreted heartache here in the Westmorland dales, there is contentment. The owners of the Bampton pubs have never had so much trade, even though the establishments are already popular with hunters, walkers and sheepdog competitors. Laughter booms out of the low doorways. So, while herniated Jake McGill is winding down his garden distillery and buying his ticket for Canada, St Patrick's and the Crown are ordering double shipments of ale to cater for the large crowd of thirsty workers. The establishments are booming. And yes, it's a pity about the village and the dam and such, but the register here is overflowing on Saturday nights!

Though, should anyone note it, the Mardale locals are enjoying their quiet pub again. Leave us alone to our last romps and tears, leave us alone to our demise, they had wanted to scream, each and every villager at the full stretch of lung and cord, to the rowdy, leering workers. And they have been left alone. Gone too are the squabbles between them, the pressurized anxieties, the bursting hearts. The man in the green suit, who now wears a pilled old jumper and helps dip sheep or move furniture from bedroom to cart, once said something about the end of a life becoming amazingly bright, that the valley would never look more brilliant than the time when it was finishing. Because even a retreating army will come to love the red fields that it is leaving. He does not speak in this way any more, and his words were more an argument than they were poetry when he uttered them. But they must agree that never has the fiery whisky warmed them so well on a cold evening, nor the Brew tasted so fine, so sweet, as it does in these years of 1936 and 1937.

Samuel Lightburn reaches around the man's leg to pin him to the ground and the crowd cheers. He locks his wrist into the grip of his big right hand. The held man is flipping like a drowning fish, trying to get loose before the pin is signalled good by the referee. Samuel transfers more weight from his body on to the man, careful not to lose pressure. Sweat jumps out of his red face, gathers in the dark, yellow straw of the hair at his temples. He puffs loudly. The count seems eternal. Amid the cheering he can hear the rip and ping of stitching on his long johns coming loose. The man on the grass is slapping at the bare flesh of Samuel's chest now in a last effort to break the press, but he is unable to gather enough strength to counter or twist free. On the side of the bale-marked ring, Isaac is shouting madly for his father to hold down. His daughter, next to the hopping boy, has a wild grin on her face.

For the last two years Samuel Lightburn has lost the Cumberland and Westmorland wrestling trophy at the High Street Meet. Previous to that he held it for sixteen years unbroken, and his reign might have begun even earlier but for the Great War. The wrestling is one of the highlights of the gathering. Reputations are made and broken in the space of seven long minutes. A man might become heroic. Samuel Lightburn is a legend but for the past two years. This year he is determined, it might be his last chance of fame as a local of the district. His challenging competitor in the last round is a strong lad of about twenty with small, narrow eyes and a thin mouth. His name is Edwin Morrison. He is the strongest of the five Morrison brothers, who live at home in Culgaith with their father Henry, a bullock herdsman by profession. Edwin approached the ring and stripped down to his underwear in front of the crowd to reveal a tight wiry form, banded muscles along his back. Saying cheekily that he was fancying his chances against an old man, he stepped into the ring.

But Samuel understands balance and the youngster is too hasty, too eager, his energy can be converted to Samuel's advantage, redirected. Keeping low, the lad came at him quickly, several times, imagining speed and surprise might overturn his opponent, sheer force, but on his third attempt he was swung and flipped over. Now Samuel has him in a full pin. A second or two more. The referee shouts good and the crowd erupts into whistles and cheers. The two men stagger up, shaking hands.

– Ne'r mind, lad. Gud try.

– Aye. Nobad fer en old fella.

The beaten youth is a dignified loser. He takes Samuel's great, hairy blond arm and lifts it in a gesture of acknowledged victory. Isaac hurls himself at his father's leg and tries to tackle him to the ground, but the big man reaches down and hefts his son on to his shoulders. The engraver begins adding Samuel's name to the silver trophy base, joking that he could just use initials as the name was getting repetitive and folk were bound to realize who S. M. L. was, were they not? Janet blows her father a kiss and disappears into the crowd. From across the moor, Ella approaches the wrestling ring and sees her husband's gaping attire.

– Sam, yer hanging right out! Yer not decent, man!

She ties a shirt around her husband's waist, hands him a towel to dry the sweat on his chest. The wind picks up a little, blowing dry leaves and some loose straw along the ground. A few grey clouds are scudding along in the sky, but other than this the weak sun is bright. It is late November, the traditional time for the Meet. On the gentle slope of the fell-top near Helton, stalls have been set up and their sides flap in the strong breeze. Horse tackle tinkles and clangs as it sways on leather strapping. Women make a grab at items about to blow off the stall tables – cakes, tarts, sloe gin, gooseberry and damson wine, pies and winter vegetables, kitchenware – which rock dangerously in the breeze, clatter into each other and spill down the tablecloths. Their skirts lift, revealing heavy slips and winter petticoats. Doilies take off into the air like white-lace kites.

– Me sponge cake! Wind'll wreck it!

Ella runs back over to the stalls to rescue her entry for the competition, which is a fierce one and can often result in two women breaking friends for a year or longer. Accusations of published recipes being used have resulted in bitter arguments and even the occasional hurled tart.

In a wooden horse-trailer next to the stalls, Jake is serving hot soup and pies from a billy cooker, dressed up in drag as a buxom woman. Behind him, Jenny stirs the soup pans, seemingly untroubled by Jake's attire. He has a printed scarf tied around his head, sporting a repetitive field of flowers, and a skirt falls just below his thick, lumpy knees. Into the brassiere under his blouse he has stuffed a substantial number of socks, to give himself an imposing shelf of a bosom. Red lipstick and rouge are smudged across his face as if applied in the dark. The men laugh and whistle as they pass by the trailer and Jake, in good humour, winks and blows kisses. He calls to them in a false soprano brogue.

– Gentlemen. Come taste ma lovely wares. Penny a pote!

Nathaniel Holme tramps up the metal ramp into the trailer, his boots covered with mud and bristled with straw. There is a flagon of ale in his hand. He laughs a high-pitched, thick, brown laugh.

– By! Thee meks a grand lass, Jek.

– Ah, Nathaniel, why thank you. Listen, you couldn't do me a wee favour, could you? A small bet on the pig bowling, number six. A shilling ought to do it. I can't leave my post with Jenny here.

– Aye, nummer six.

Nathaniel takes the shilling, bends over in the trailer and

coughs deeply, struggling for air. He clears his throat, spits out over the ramp. But he is still wheezing and is visibly weakened by the coughing fit. He wipes his mouth on his sleeve. Jenny leans over the counter and places her hand on his jacket shoulder.

– Are y'all right Mr Holme?

Nathaniel is still wheezing but he blinks at her. His eyes are alight with mischief and animation.

– Oh, I'll not mek it to another grass, I shouldn't think, bonny lassie.

The old man turns and tramps back down the ramp towards the pig bowling.

ᔡ

Later that day the racing begins. Between the ancient standing stones of the circle, each now leaning over almost completely to the ground owing to the ravages of time, a racetrack has been set up for the horses and the hare coursing. The thunder of hooves echoes thickly into the turf. A hare is let loose and the hounds streak along the ground, their shoulders pumping, eyes red with excitement and tongues held to one side in their jaws. Money is exchanged and the gamblers split off into groups of winners and grumbling losers, bringing hip flasks out of their coat pockets to drink to it either way. The fell runners begin to straggle in after completing a ten-mile course, with Paul Levell leading the group, his thighs rigid with muscle. The afternoon light is pewter over the yellow grass of the fell. Brooding clouds stack up above and below the horizon, but the rain looks to be holding off for the Meet. Faces blush in the fresh winds and the short grass ripples, stroked and swept into ruffled designs. The smell of pastry and potato soup drifts across the field, and the locals head into the trailer now and again for a warming mug before lining up to watch the shooting competition.

Samuel Lightburn and Kenneth Jeffries, an elderly farmer from Dale Head Farm over the mountain in Patterdale, manage the arena of the stray-sheep exchange. Any lost sheep found in the district are brought into the pen to be returned to their rightful owners. If the animals are not claimed, the farmer responsible for their recovery will keep them for a year, so that the owner might have a chance at a late claim, and after a year the animal may be sold to pay for its upkeep, or kept. The two men converse as their dogs work the sheep into neat groups

– Dam's cumin' on, is it?

– Aye, it is at that, Ken. Big bugger an' all. Red T and whoal't. Sarge Thompson's yow?

– Aye, Sarge's. Sarge! Sarge! Git ova, stop yer yakkin'. Crupper, Herdwick, belongs to Les Kitching, eh? 'Swhat happens when heafeds get selt on. Cum right back ower t' t'fell it's birthed on. Slump at fleece market's got to lift or w'll be swapping til kingdom cum nex year, what wi' sellin' off herds and shiftin' buggers on!

Samuel leans down and pushes the sheep with a semi-circular smear on its rump past, down in to the end pen. He whistles for Chase to round up the stragglers from the back of the wagons.

– Found owt else fer work yit, Sam?

– Not yit. Mebbi Staingarth. Property's bin empty since Carl Atkinson passed. Land's a bit rough, like.

– They're lookin' fer fellas at Cropper's paper mill in Kendal. Drivers, eh? Fancy fetchin' a wagon aboot?

– Oh aye? Mebbi. I'll kep it in mind, Ken. Pop smit. Park Mounsey. He's settin' hounds; leave it in t'pen til fella gits dun.

A fight breaks out among the hounds. There are the sounds of yelping and growling and the sheep exchange is halted so that the men can go and break it up, placing bare hands into the dripping jaws and pinching at pressure points to unlock them, releasing the animals from each other. There is blood and saliva on the ground and the eyes of the dogs are red again, as if to scrap is as good as to race for the hare or the fox.

～

Jack Liggett approaches Janet Lightburn at the creaking stalls. He has a full beard now, with flecks of grey in it, and is wearing a long leather coat that flaps against his legs. In his head, he calculates his own age and does not feel slighted for the years it has taken him to get here. He's not yet forty. She is standing with her mother and her brother, holding his small hand. Though she has similar colouring, against them she is as a photographic negative, darkness to their light, inverse, the deep corners of her face casting shadow. It is as if she has been born the wrong way, inside out. She might well have been. Today she passes condiments between women, tomorrow she will be out with the Mardale Hunt. Looking at her now, he could fall to her feet, tell her she is beauty, that which he has always known existed. But he does not.

She is unaffected by the cold. She gives her woollen scarf to her brother and the cliffs of her neck and shoulders receive the exposure without complaint, as if hurricanes and squalls could not harm her. In the wind, her hair is blown in every direction, like a basket of rearing snakes, and she tries to smother it with a free hand, catching only a few stray sections, the tamest vipers. There have been young men approaching her all day, as if they can smell the residue of sex on her. They stand in lusty groups and try, one after the other, as if she is a Western rodeo bull, and whoever remains in her difficult company the longest will be the victor. The bravest man. As if one day she will suddenly be broken, the notorious force dropping out of her. Jack Liggett sees them return to the group, one at a time, an imaginary harness in hand, shaking a head. She vexes them. There is no inherent respect for their gender and they disapprove of that, always have. They despise her intellect, the manly language, her autonomy.

She's a bad breed, a eunuch, a malcontent, for all her striking looks. Not worth it, but still they try . . .

As she turns, she sees him coming towards her. His face is rocking in the wind. It is giving away every put-aside emotion. He is tired of secrecy. He is tired of her hands only in the darkness and the constant borders of their love. His rocking face is calling it love, simple, above all the schisms in the landscape that surrounds them. His face is weary with it, with agreeing to do without her today, as on so many days. The public spontaneity is long in coming and now it has within it an exhausted quality. As if there is nothing left over to stop him. So he removes the decision of disclosure from her.

In front of two hundred locals and her fearless mother, he offers himself to her, gaze held only on her bright living hair. As if this is their first meeting and permission is required for courting. As if this is another insignificant minute in time. Her moving hair is hypnotic.

– Walk with me? To the river?

The leather coat flaps against his legs in the strong wind. Her mother is all astonishment, of course, and burnt-metal faced. She will rip out his heart for the audacity, given a chance. She will howl at the wind for his ruthless, tender entreaty. This makes sense! Now her daughter's behaviour is clear. It has been brought on by this turncoat of a man, who has come up from the city to pretend another existence. It could only have been such a man, such a dark, handsome devil, to create her daughter's assortment of moods and emotions. She will curse him with her worst scowl but that he is not looking anywhere except at her daughter. Those are his only eyes.

Janet cannot quite believe her brother is letting go of her hand and this beautiful, hateful, loved man is now taking it. Because the warmth of it feels no different, no different at all.

∾

That evening Jack Liggett drives Janet into town, proudly, in his red rag of a motor. There is a tired smile firm on his lips, as if he has finished a long walk up a steep mountain. Under his shirt his chest fills slowly with air, releases it, with the gradual pace of a sleeper. In the car there is a short, one-sided argument about his revelation.

– Look at all the things I was taught to hate. You were one of them. They think of you as a person without basis. One of those classless types who believes that this place is about scenery and escape, and gettin' something out that hasn't bin put in! You have done this for reasons none else will see. It looks like spite, Jack. Don't you understand that?

He is all smiles, unashamed, unrepentant. She curses him. He's a fool. He does not realize the battle he has started within her family. A mother, who at first was too furious to speak, then who smashed dishes and ranted about sin for two hours. A father who is still quiet with confusion.

– And Isaac, well, you've completely spun that boy! I left him getting the worst of it because he admires you. Because he thinks yer some sort of disciple. God knows what the lad thinks! What anyone thinks!

– I just couldn't manage our game any more. That's all. They'll see it's right. They'll see it like we do.

He moves a hand on her thigh as he drives, meaning nothing but reassurance by it. Her fingers stroking the glass window, petulant. Then she pulls his hand away, bites his fingers. He yelps. The sore finger inside her mouth now. Her anger converts itself. She unbuttons his trousers, leans over to him. The car swerves a fraction before he lines it back up on the road, drawing in breath erratically.

༄

The dancehalls of Penrith are always crowded and warm and charged with palpable tension. Inside the old William Tarrant building, he sweeps her out into the middle of the floor. They spin. Heels turning on the worn, dimpled maple floorboards. The band plays one number after another, without a break, the musicians perspiring against their starched collars, flipping music sheets over. The flare of a clarinet, muffled tin of a trumpet, snares. Old jazz numbers and twenties favourites. And more recent tunes, fuller, as they head towards the big-band era. Jack mouths the words as they slide out on the floor. He is a handsome, able dancer, and now that he finally has her in such an arena he displays his skill, showing off, spinning her on a half-beat. His body moves like a tight river, sensually against her lower torso. He sings along, keeping her eyes to his. Her hair wound up off the nape of her neck, tendons like sculpted marble.

– I need water. I'll be back.

His grip tightens on her waist, the beginning of another bruise.

– I'll be back, I said!

She pulls away, grimacing, moves through the reeling crowd to the hallway of the building. At the water fountain, she sips slowly. She is surrounded by soft-hatted men, smoking, laughing, parting for her. She smiles at them, turns to find her partner on the dance floor. The space is a mass of shining heads and flaring skirts, dipping shoulders. Jack Liggett steps on the periphery, in a dark corner. Dorothy from the George Hotel is in his arms. Her short, dark hair bobbing to his shoulder. She whispers something in his ear and he laughs, shakes his head. She pouts, puts a finger to his new beard. The two continue to move, jauntily, at the edge of the dancers.

Janet moves back, stunned, her stomach hot and her throat clenching. Her eyes sting. Her skin is tingling, the tiny blonde hairs on her arm lifting. Only a dance, she tells herself, but it is weak reassurance. There is half a year's worth of rage and surrender and trust to support her anger now. She steps backwards on to the heel of a man's shoe. His hands rest just above her buttocks, on the small of her back as he stops her.

– Excuse me.

The jealousy hardens, becomes a rigid incentive. Only a dance. She removes the stranger's hat, tosses it to a table and takes his hand. He likes that. Likes the signal, the encouraging gesture. On the way to the dance floor he removes a pin from her hair and it sinks on to her shoulders. The two begin to move, the man's hand under her hair, between her shoulders. She does not search the room, instead, her eyes blaze at her new partner's neck. She holds her breath. A feeling of rocking beginning within her, easily, as if this is a man with whom she has already danced and moved through back rooms.

Within minutes Jack Liggett is at their side, Dorothy abandoned in the dim corner. He cuts in, his old courtesy and civility barely catching up with him.

– I'll take her off your hands, if you don't mind.

– In a minute.

– I'll take her. Now.

The man halts his movement and holds Jack Liggett's eye, both of them playing out a brawl in their minds, quickly, a series of pictures, like cinema projectors tracking the same scene from different angles. The man cut-in on steps aside with his hand held out to Janet. Before leaving, he brushes a kiss across her cheek, to her ear. Then back to Jack Liggett.

– Pleasure's all yours. If I were you, I'd not be gone s'long next time. I'm an impatient man.

Janet is moved out into the floor once again, this time with gentle hands, his head held to her yellow hair. But his voice is unsteady, low.

– Put your hair up. The way it was.

– I can't, he still has the pin.

– Please do not do that again.

– Don't you. You fucker, she whispers.

He has become accustomed to such language, from her. His lips find the base of her neck. It is too indiscreet a kiss, too sexual for the public dancehall, too damp.

– What did he make you feel like? Like this, Janet?

– Yes.

Jack Liggett is not a man given to sharing any more, in theory or otherwise. She moves across the floor with him to the doorway, he stiffens against her, the stitched hem over her shoulders in his fist, bunched tight. Behind the Tarrant building she pushes him down against the stucco wall, sits across him, ignoring the couple that staggers past them with a bottle of wine. The indentation of stone in his back chafes the sallow skin. She moves above him, her upper body bare to his mouth in the cold November night, his arms cradling up her back so that his hands rest on the base of her neck, holding her hair. The small restraint of the dancehall now gone.

II:III

When Samuel found Nathaniel's body it was purely by accident. His eyes might even have happened across the old man
twice, three times or more, there on the mountain, before recognizing his camouflaged form. It is said that when great and
wise animals die they instinctually leave their homes and
herds for sanctuary. They hunt for old, spiritual places to give
their bodies over to, somehow knowing the route to be taken
even if it has never been travelled before by the herd, the
pack. Elephants sway to jungle graveyards, to the overgrown
fortress cages of ivory. Cats disappear in the night, finding
that surfaced root of a rowan tree to wrap themselves around,
serene, slack-jawed, and eagles come in from flight, step
claws into a remote, dark crag, an arrow-slit fissure in the
rock, where they lock away their wingtips, bringing a head
down on to the soft feathers of a breast.

In December, nine days before Christmas Eve, Samuel and
two other men took the winding path up to Blea Water and
Smallwater in search of a neighbour's missing pony, which
had come untethered and left hoofprints out of the village
towards High Street. At the base of the fells the hoofprints
were joined by others, a herd of wild ponies had come in for
shelter, and several tracks led away, indistinctly in the night's
fresh snow. The three men split up in different directions
around Harter, Samuel following the mountain stream to the
remote pools. At a higher altitude, the earth was frozen several
inches down and the water was creaking to a halt around the
lip of the first tarn. Up over Nan Bield pass he walked, circling
round the blackness of Smallwater on the chilled path, his
breath frosting above him. His boots rucked precisely against
the stone and sharp granite, a sound-sensation so satisfying

and clean that it will seduce walkers and climbers up a pike or ridge in even the most frigid and prehistoric winter temperatures, even without the excuse of a lost farm animal. The air was so clear that he could faintly hear the workers down at the dam, almost eight miles away. It was over the ridge next at Blea Water, the larger of the two tarns, that he found Nathaniel Holme and the missing horse.

The Lakeland paintings of Paul Levell are key to the enigma. There are hidden riddles. They reveal rocks in the shape of people, and bury bodies in the environment with formal accuracy. Humans are jigsawed into a cliff or river, or hewn out of the landscape, a man's torso kept in a cairn of rock, a child in the womb of a mountain wall, vast amalgams of environment and humanity. People of kept stone. They are almost always secondary, hardly existing at all against the background. These images speak a certain amount of truth for those who live with the land.

Samuel's eye was first caught by the colt moving at the tarn's edge. Across the water, the pony was grazing at some short moor grass under the snow.

But then something within the range of his peripheral vision emerged. Nathaniel was sitting on an outcrop of rock overlooking the unmoving steely water. He was not leaning against a supporting stone. Instead, his spine had settled into a position of natural balance, curved and holding the body's weight exactly. Only fifteen feet from him. Samuel's eyes adjusted, pulling out the form. The rock became a man, an old friend, grey with the cold and death, as grey as the background of scree. The place must have been chosen with care, with instinct, perhaps. He had loved the view from the tarns and the sense that the high-altitude pools were vascular, open grey wells collapsing deep into the earth's core. To its heart's source. There had been enough air left in the old man's chest for the painful climb up out of the valley. Samuel smiled with sadness, with admiration. He turned his collar up against a flurry of snow, pulled down his cap.

His friend had been sitting there long enough that the wind had egged him safely into the hillside.

༄

There is a track that begins at the head of the Haweswater valley which travels up the sheer sides of Mardale common, up over the Naddle mountain, and it weaves across the black ridges and peaty moors, past Swindale, until it falls back down into another plush green hollow several miles away. It ends at an old sandstone abbey, which, customary to many such monastic sites, until 1965, and especially in the 1930s in Westmorland, was inaccessible by motorized vehicle of any kind. The name of this path is the Old Corpse Road. Previous to 1729, the date when burial rights were granted for the church in Mardale, it had been used for centuries by the rural community of the area for passage of their dead to a final resting place.

In the iron-hard winter beginning December of 1936, Samuel Lightburn and Lanty Farrow bore the body of Nathaniel Holme over the pass to the monastery near Shap for burial. The corpse was wrapped in lint-mesh and tarpaulin, then placed in a small, rough coffin, which was strapped to the back of a squat, sturdy pony from the Farrows's farm. The path was icy and tricky to negotiate in places, the men having to guide the horse into making several attempts at a high step as the grade steepened. A bray or two in protest and then a final push up. The horse kicked through drifts of snow at the summit of the lugubrious, arctic passage, leaving behind long hoofprints in the white terrain. But above, the sky remained blue and clear, sparkling light reflected in the icy streams. As had been the burial rite of many before, Nathaniel was accepted into the remote monastic gardens for burial.

Nathaniel Holme had several members of his family in the cemetery of Mardale, including his wife, Angela, and war memorials for his two sons, but he would not be buried there. The following spring, the bodies were to be exhumed. In the thaw from the particularly harsh winter the inhabitants still residing in the village would dig up the remains of their families and move them to another graveyard. The decomposed flesh of the oldest corpses would always remain part of the land, supplying it with nutrients. The crumbling headstones, and even the pitted, lichen-mottled Celtic cross that had been the solitary presence in an uninhabited field long ago, would be uprooted and removed. The cemetery would be combed clean, and the rank, coppery odour of old blood and wood mixing would find its way into the air, as coffins were lifted from the red-black earth. Funds for exhumation and transport and new burial costs would be provided by the Waterworks, but the locals would have to make the necessary arrangements themselves. It is not often that a family must bury its dead twice.

∽

After Nathaniel's funeral, Samuel sat by the hearth, warming life back into his feet at the fire. He was reconciled with the loss of his oldest friend, had catered for the remains of the man and lifted him down into the ground himself and covered the coffin with sods of cut earth. The loss was not unexpected. Nathaniel's health had been deteriorating for months, and his farm with it. The valley had lost a man who had been fundamental to its population and to its character, who had accumulated more intimate knowledge of the area than the rest of the village combined, could spin its history into threads and weave them together, births, marriages, deaths, nature's cycle and its distortions, the amalgamation of the community and the external world through which it survived. He had been a man who knew that, essentially, he had not succeeded as a possessor, but rather he himself had been heritage, passed down to that which had also received his ancestors. He was the last of his people, surviving his offspring, solely inheriting the pride of the family's lengthy settlement, and he had died well, just as he had lived, immersed, with genetic comprehension of the landscape. Nathaniel had been a stitch in its very fabric, a true spirit, and in mourning that loop undone Samuel must also grieve for the unravelling valley. Yet how to? It was too large a thing. Too colossal a death to know what acknowledgement suited it best or how to show appropriate respect. So much was yet to be stopped and lost.

He turned to his wife, as if to communicate this failing, to find a sympathetic nod, an equal in the situation. Ella was carding wool opposite him. Her fingers worked quickly and the corners of her mouth were downturned. A cheek moving as if she were chewing the inside of her mouth. Her mannerisms suggested irreconcilable thoughts. Samuel turned back to the flames, knowing then that for each of them the mourning would be private, personal and endlessly varied. Like the grain and structure of an antler, he thought, each would grow with its own inherent pattern.

Outside, in the fresh snow, Isaac was playing with Chase, he could hear the barks of both, and upstairs their daughter was reading, perhaps, or trying to settle her own thoughts shifting relentlessly against each other. She had kept to herself lately, and had not been forthcoming when her mother questioned her about Jack Liggett, the apparent affair. She would turn away and murmur harshly under her breath.

– Mam! Leave it be, fer once in yer life.

But her mother would not let it alone, she could not help but persist with her inquiries, even though she tried to hold back, knowing it would lead to argument. She heard herself hissing. Why had she been late in for her supper? Had she been seeing that man? The one who was responsible for wrecking their lives. What did she think she was doing? What kind of a useless girl was she to tarry to such a man? Did she not appreciate the damage he had wrought? Was she so unmoved that she had no remorse for the loss of her home?

The questions came and were unanswerable. And tension gathered about the house, seeping into its pores and skulking in corners. Their daughter collected her coat and left without nourishment, again and again, slipping out into the wet, falling snow, past their waiting faces, past the anticipation flooding from them that there would be some kind of explanation soon, a bright epiphany for them all in this strange matter. Her brother looking as if she had taken something away that he could not understand. It had come to this, a ravine of silence over which she would not travel. Her bitter energy dormant. And, secretly, her mother worried at the loss of fire, the dwindling anger, which had always been amply witnessed before, surface deep and writhing in her daughter, because it was not unlike her own and so she could understand it, if not navigate it. But more than this. It meant ruddy health, equilibrium in the Lightburn women.

In the upstairs room Janet moved from wall to wall, a hand resting on the back of her neck, the book abandoned. She would have dearly loved to find the words to explain this obsession, this split in her own psyche, the venom which sent her again and again down into the village, to the side door of the Dun Bull. Gathering the antidote from his hands. She would have desperately liked to be able to find those oblique words which would come close to representing the widening gulf in herself, the senseless, driving desire, perhaps more satisfying for the groping hands in her own mind than for her mother's anguished questions. Their clashes had become perfected, the quickest route taken in, an immediate blockage of reason, pivotal stalemate, the inevitable ill-parting of mother and daughter. The arguments now took only moments to mature, their velocity incredible. The house shuddering in the squall of tempers.

– You've been t' town with the man agin.

– Jack had to go to the bank . . .

– Jack! Oh, Jack, is it? I'll be jiggered if I take the name to my mouth.

189

– It's not your business, not your concern. There's more to it than . . .

– Get out of my sight! I'll not allow it in my home, niver, do y'hear my girl?

Sometimes her father tried to defend her lover, perhaps unaware of the extent and history of the relationship. It was soul-destroying for Janet. She would rather he stride up to Jack and strike him full across his face. For all the taking he had done. Better than his blind, diffident vindication born out of an unconditional loyalty to his daughter, and going against his wife. She had blown a gale in between the members of her family with her indulgence, with the bellows of her obsession.

– He's not a bad sort, Ella. Just doin' his job. See how he tries with folk here. Fella nearly fell in t'dip t'uther month. Fumes got him, poor lad, didn'e know when t' breathe and when not te. And dam's his proper job, Ella. Can't blame fella fer owt else.

But the words were lost on Ella. She had gone too far the way of her fury to be turned back.

At the fireplace she looked up at her husband. The flames blowing red against his face. He was a good and honest man, who had lived simply, his whole life an arrangement of natural actions, of gentle, moderate behaviour which was set against the harshness of his profession. The lifting of a lame calf, his hand squeezing in the sides of a loaf as he cut it, the way he left a wet cap in the sink next to the crockery. These were gestures which belonged without explicit motive. The way he pressed his boot down on a clump of daffodil bulbs, pushed them back into the soft soil, was simply a matter of seeing them out of place and responding. It was merely retaining what had gone before. His songs in front of the men and women of the valley, standing in their midst on days of celebration, were without shyness and hesitation, just as they were without conceit. His were un-selfconscious, natural duties. They were extensions of himself which had never become the spokes of a wheel turning the opposite direction from a man, as so often happens, thought Ella. He assumed a position of least resistance, walking behind walls when the wind raged down from the fells, or refuting controversy by abandoning the quarrel. He was by nature a preserver. His visions of the future were unspectacular. She could not call Samuel's defence of the Waterworks man weak or brittle, nor was there an agenda. He wanted nothing more than his children's continued existence, contentment as they themselves envisaged it. As for his daughter, he had never had the strength, nor the desire, to nullify, to contain her. It would have been an insipid achievement in his eyes. He simply walked behind a wall when she raged.

Ella left her carding and moved to the window. On the other side of the house the front door closed discreetly. She had not heard it open. As she watched her daughter stride away down the fell, Ella saw something of her own nature in the girl, not for the first time, but now without the control which usually accompanied their brooding hearts, which made them both women to be feared in the district, having a high degree of self-mastery accompanying their tempers. The potency was unchecked, worrisome. The girl was too full. She was spilling at the edges. Ella climbed the stairs to the landing window, and watched until Janet moved out of sight behind the grey stone wall.

There was nothing to do but rely on her own inhibited behaviour, her touchstones, the checks and balances of her life – God, decency, her own zeal and puritanical government of matters – to handle this situation, as if, by having enough propriety for both, she would somehow override her daughter's lack of restraint, and her sinning. She knelt to pray on behalf of her daughter, in the dark alcove window where so often lately she watched for the girl's comings and goings, a black pagan bird of fear lifting its wings against her chest.

– Forgive us our trespasses.

But the black seemed to grow in her, reaching her throat. She could not go on. She re-laced her fingers for prayer. Her husband placed a hand on her tense shoulder, and for a brief, lit second, Ella imagined it was Janet, come to relieve her.

– She loves him. She's given ova to it, Ella. Can it not be that in all this upset, there might not be sum consolation? Dusn't it mek up fer it all? Can't it do that?

His wife turned. A slight tear along her bottom lip where she had bitten into it. Such a good, simple man her husband, so settled into his life and detached from anything unordinary.

There was a vast black bird in her heart, she said to him, foreboding. It warned her of sickness and ill change, lifting its morbid wings. And with the dark man in their midst there was danger, she knew it. But Samuel could not understand. And how could he see fear taking shape or feel its feathery wingtips along her ribcage?

∽

Light leaves the sky. But the ground is all white, a carpet of illumination. It has stolen the day's radiance to keep locked in its cells, throwing it up now against the darkening fells, and the landscape is backlit. Isaac rolls with the dog in the powdery snow through the gates of the garden and down, down on to the land skirting his father's property. And, laughing, comes to rest against a spring of heather. He had meant to check the river again before night, perhaps catch a lethargic trout if he could. Now it is too dark and the fish will be balanced on an invisible axis of current, sleeping. He stands up and brushes snow off his breeches. His gloves are sticky with packed snow. Isaac climbs higher on the scar, looks down into the ground-bright valley. Smoke rises from the chimneys in the snowy village. It is a pretty, winter scene, like a Christmas card, he thinks.

Two days more waiting for Christmas. His stomach flips over with excitement. What he adores most of all is the tiny orange left in the toe of his stocking over the fireplace, tied with a red ribbon, pinned with crystallized fruit. It is always there, bulbous underneath the sack of nuts, the string bag of marbles or the wooden toy, every year, a colourful delight, and sweet, juicy, when he peels and eats it.

Whelter Farm Cottage smells of cloves and mincemeat and pine sap from the tree. A holly wreath is hung on the front door and the lamps are turned up in the windows in festive welcome. But there is little in the way of merriment within. He will delay going inside, so that the eventual overwhelming of warmth and fragrances will be all the more pleasurable and the lack of spirit will not be so hard to bear. Things will be better soon. His sister and his mother will make peace. And Isaac knows, despite his mother's slander, that Jack Liggett is a good man, who respects water in a way that not many others understand. Besides, it is, after all, his favourite time of year, not only for the evergreen and the treats, but the songs and stories also, and this fact alone should make things right. He loves it when the carollers come to the house, their voices faint like angels, until the door is opened and song swells through the hallway, then they come inside for warming spiced soup. There are stories told to him only at this time of year. Fantastic, magical stories, the old Hollier in the woods finding only three red berries, which peel back in the night to reveal gifts of frankincense, gold and myrrh, Christmas in hot deserts, dust-blown countries, the necklace of tears and the story of the robin. There is an old, leather book from which his sister reads to him in the dark evenings. The season peels back, allows for diverse brilliance, and dreamlike enchantments. He loves his mother's hands, rubbing oil into the wooden back of the baby Jesus, Joseph's staff, so that the figures of the Nativity are imbued with a dull, unearthly shine. Set up, usually in the church, but this year by their cottage hearth, the hewn forms have within them a viscous, textured life. Mary's arm links to Joseph's. They are of the same, carefully carved piece of oak.

With his head full of the coming wonder, Isaac walks over the moor. At first he can't quite make out the strange symmetrical markers forming a line in the snow. He comes closer. Yellow wooden pegs have been driven into the ground about twenty or thirty feet apart. They skirt along the side of the valley as if left like a trail or a signposted pathway. He cannot see what they are for, these strange, mysterious man-made objects. Then an idea occurs to him. Into the yuletide-filled head of a child comes a reason for their presence, so pure of innocence and so far removed from their original purpose that those who drove them into the earth might hang their heads in shame. Isaac gasps. These are the guides for Saint Nick to find him. A runway for his flying deer. But they are placed all wrong! Too far away from Whelter Farm, high above it. His house will never be found and there will be no filled stocking!

And how could he guess that these are the markers of the new waterline, the estimated shore of the full reservoir? That afternoon they were driven in by the engineers and their crew, who ghosted around the periphery of the village, encompassing it with the psychic yellow border of a murder, as if tracing a dead body, outlining the scene of a crime that has not yet been committed.

Isaac bends down and kicks at a marker, rocks it free out of the ground. He sees his sister walking down into the village and he shouts to her, but she seems not to hear him and disappears from view. Then he moves to another peg and pulls it out. He has some work to do if he is going to get that orange.

∽

On Christmas Day the men do not have to work at the dam. They are free of machinery and welding rods, the sounds and smells of metal efficiency, endless compositions in stone. A morning carol service is held in the worship room and four hundred men squeeze in, their hair combed straight, slicked down under water and oil. Their voices boom in the confined space, rich and lifting at the roof: 'O come, all ye faithful, joyful and triumphant'. It is magnificent noise, the singing throat of the woods. After the service, a roasted turkey dinner is served in the canteen, in two shifts so that half the men must wait in their bungalows, having lost the draw, sent almost mad by the drifting aroma of savoury meat and spice. They flip over cards with growling stomachs, unable to concentrate on the game. Then it is their turn for a feast of a meal, with potatoes and mashed swede, Cumberland sausage – the butcher and his boy at Shap have worked late through two nights to prepare the hundreds of meat and spice-filled tubes – bread sauce, followed by brandy pudding and a sixpence inside one of the portions for the lucky man who taps his tooth on it. The first half of the group of workers sways out past their hungry colleagues, they haven't eaten so well since they began work six months ago. Inside the warm canteen, the second batch of men hold the puddings in their mouths, trying not to chew too fast, letting the softness and flavour melt on their tongues. There is a quart of ale each, crackers with folded paper hats. After the meal the men put on gloves and scarves and go out into the snow to play football, kicking drifts at each other when the ball is at the other end of the field. The game is chaotic, hundreds of men trying for a shot at goal.

In the afternoon the workers walk into the village of Bampton. The landlord at St Patrick's Well has promised to open at two and, sure to his word, the doors are unlocked, the fire is blazing with logs and dried peat, which he bought specially at the market for a festive aroma.

In the Dun Bull that evening there is also a small celebration. Jake has baked mince pies and dusted them with sugar. There is whisky or brandy for a first drink on the house. The village has dwindled in numbers. The artist Paul Levell is gone now, back to Northumberland to paint the horizontal coastline, as are a few of the farmers, and the Reverend Wood has secured another parish over in Kendal, though he has promised to come back to give a last service in the spring at the Mardale church, along with the Bishop of Carlisle himself.

For the first time in its existence the church in Mardale is empty and locked on Christmas Day and the Hindmarshes, the Lightburns and the Farrows have to drive through the snow to the chapel in Keld for the morning service. Ella still has a key to the church and, even though her cleaning duties are now over, she cannot bear to give it up. Once in a while she will take brass polish, broom and dusters and unlock the musty door. The muscle in her arm burning as she shines the fixtures. The key remains in the Book of Common Prayer in the top drawer of her dresser. She has not been able to post it away to the diocesan secretary. Besides, somebody needs to let in the Carlisle Cathedral wardens when they come for the lectern and the font. And when they do, will that eagle not shine as if it had never been left to the settling dust! On this Christmas night she walks with her husband to the Dun Bull's doors, kisses him and crosses the road. She lets herself inside the tiny, creaking building opposite, kneels at the altar and, in the corner of her eye, a faint unshed tear glimmers. She will keep it back yet, against her eye, as if this place will always have a nest of liquid sorrow within her.

Jake McGill pours out brandy and Samuel lifts his glass in toast. To Nathaniel Holme, God rest him well, and to all the noble men and women ever of this dale.

∽

In his room above the Dun Bull, Jack Liggett hands Janet a box wrapped in silver paper. She is embarrassed by the gift, not wanting to open it in his presence and suspecting that it contains some kind of hard glittering extravagance. But he is insistent. As she pulls the silver ribbon from the top of the box he leans in and kisses her hard, bruising her lip with his teeth. It is too intense an embrace and she smiles, her brow lowered with confusion.

– Open it. Open and see.

She carefully folds off the shiny paper. Inside the box, a tiny, crafted village rests against a green valley and is held inside a half-bubble, in a womb of clear liquid. There is a tiny church with a weather vane and a blue shining river snakes down from the moulded hills. She shakes the glass. Flurries of snow swirl and descend slowly over the village.

And what of her gift to him? It is a new life, she says. Not ways of living, but a new life.

~

1937. A new and last year for the village of Mardale. The dale seizes with cold, creaking to a halt in the bitter winter. A tearful auld lang syne is sung on New Year's Eve and the villagers embrace one another. Jack Liggett steals a public kiss in the corner of the Bull, annexing the woman he loves, and surprising no one. In this coming year the villagers will begin a fuller exodus, packing up their belongings for the evacuation. Crockery and furniture and books and even a piano, stacked up in the back of carts and vans. In preparation for the migration of farmers to new stretches of land, cattle and sheep will be taken to auction and released for prices well below their true value, the market has not recovered sufficiently to make sales worthwhile. They will be bought back at a later date for twice the price. Little by little the houses will empty, stripped bare of fixtures, and even wallpaper will be peeled away in torn shreds, paper roses ripped in half, only to be stuck together again in different cottages. Bulbs will be lifted out of the gardens of the farmhouses, redcurrant bushes transplanted. Nothing is wasted in the valley if it can be saved. These are practical times.

Late in the spring a final service will be held at the Mardale

197

church. Three hundred people will stand in the wet fields around the monument, dressed in suits and hats, unable to be housed in the limited capacity of the building for the ceremony. Automobiles will be backed up and bottle-necked along the new lake road. The Bishop of Carlisle will take the service, and will solemnly bless the sacred ground on which they stand. Hymns will lift over the mountains. By then the ancient yew trees from the graveyard will have been cut down and fashioned into altar candlesticks. They will be presented to the purple-robed bishop after the service. Then the church bell will be brought down from the tower and the life of St Patrick's church will be over.

In this coming year, the villagers will be able to buy frozen produce for the first time from Renkin's in Penrith, a packet of garden peas, but many will not be able to store such luxuries and will have to bury them in the cold ground. Sylvia Goodman will scatter hers for the chickens and will tell tales of her poultry laying frozen eggs. On the BBC they will hear that the Duke of Windsor, the abdicated king, will marry Wallis Simpson in France. The old systems crack up, amorphous modernity emerges. It will be a year of upheaval abroad also, to be discussed in the Bampton Jerry over warm ale. In April, new German planes are to bomb the Basque city of Guernica, the loss of civilian life will be horrific, bringing many European men and women into their churches where they will fall to their knees and weep, and Ella Lightburn will clutch the altar rail of a different parish church and pray desperately for history not to repeat, dear God, not to repeat. Similarly, Shanghai will smoulder in ruins under Japanese bombers. A handshake between Hitler and Mussolini. Now the British government cannot keep its eyes averted. Edgy and cornered, Parliament votes on a course of action. Air-raid shelters are put up in the nation's largest cities, York and Manchester in the north, and the country waits.

Jack Liggett had wanted the trophy bird because it was the largest to be found in that region, indeed, the largest in the country. He had wanted it stuffed by the best taxidermist, given amber glass eyes and mounted in a glass case in his Palatine Road residence. He had wanted it as an effrontery, a snub to the class he had successfully bluffed his way up to, which would consider it gauche, irregular and in poor taste. The golden eagle was no Indian tiger, no polished ivory tusk, it was not another country usurped, or the spoils of exotic adventure. It was indigenous, a symbol of the beauty of the islands, the hub of the empire. It would be considered by many as similar to scoffing at the new king. But, best of all, Jack Liggett had known that he would not care, rather, he would relish it, he would know he had become high enough up in the chain for his eccentricities to be unimpeachable. He would know he had made it.

He'd imagined its lifeless yellow stare disturbing the guests in his fine home. The comments, the uncertain, adulterated compliments over his prize. He had played it all out in his mind. He would keep it covered with a cloth, then unveil it dramatically to the crowd. Women would fidget nervously or emit startled little cries, as if a rude hand had been placed too near their backsides. There would be awkward silences among the men, he would be considered tasteless, a rouge – brutal, even.

The man in the dark-green suit with its gold adornments, who first came to the village like a conquering prince, had anticipated this exact style of controversy and the inability of others to judge him. It would have meant he had finally advanced to a standstill, and was mocking his equals for allowing him that. He had played them at their English game of class and was now waving a proletarian prize. But that was then. The Palatine house was gathering dust and had not hosted human life for the best part of a year, even the weekly maid had been dismissed. Jack Liggett now was in another incarnation. He was a turncoat, or a better piece.

Jamie Brent, the poacher, came to the hotel door and asked for the Manchester fella to come outside. He had not been seen in the village for months until that day, in the third week after Christmas. Jack Liggett stooped under the door frame and walked over to the scruffy little man. The poacher noted his casual attire, the weathering of his skin. He walked as if his shoulders were no longer holding up the pressed granite of the city. Like a fine wire had come loose and was curling in his spine. He nodded to the tall man, then jerked his head backwards.

– She's in t'sack.

– Oh? Who is? Your wife?

The poacher pulled the hessian bag off his shoulder. He held it out to the gentleman without opening it. There was an uncertainty in the taller man's face, as if he had forgotten the arrangement, as if it had been a deal struck in another life-time. The poacher scowled at the hesitation, he did not wish to be left hanging.

– Twa pund. Eh? Yan more ootstandin'.

Jack Liggett stared at him, recalling their last meeting. His humour evaporated. The desire not to honour the contract was overwhelming, though he still carried with him the sense of a businessman's notion of settlement and knew he must see it through. After a time he reached out and took the bag and he was about to open it when the poacher clicked his tongue.

– Settle! Git yasil' inside fust. It's jus a chicken I'm givin' yer, unnerstan'?

– How? I mean, how did you . . .?

– 'Twasn't easy, al tell y'that fer nowt. Nearly got misel kill.

He pulled his lips back off his gums, shook his head and continued.

– They cum in closer in t'winter, less prey fer 'em on t'scar. Jus' had t' bide me time. Knew ad get 'er eventually.

The poacher held up an imaginary shotgun towards Jack Liggett, aimed and pulled the trigger. He laughed nervously, his mannish face becoming puerile.

– Clean like. Right thru t'neck. So you'll ne' be disappointed. But ad a helluva job climbin' out t' where shi lay. Helluva job. Should charge double, like.

– Oh, I see. Wait here, I'll . . . I'll see about your money.

He entered the hotel by the side door to avoid the bar room, where Janet and her father were propping up the bar, and climbed the stairs to his room. He laid the sack on the bed and went through his suitcase until he found a rolled-up bundle of notes. His heart was loud in his chest and sweat broke on his forehead. He felt a sick-panic rising within. The warm, watery dizziness which overcomes the body when a wrong that has been done is self-acknowledged and begins damaging the perpetrator internally. He faltered, dropped the money and went to the bed, sat down and took the bird from the bag. The weight of the eagle was shocking. This alone made him catch his breath. That so heavy a creature was capable of soaring, turning great arcs in the sky, precise loops and plummeting down to an unerring kill. The weight of what had been done shook in his arms.

Even in death, the bird of prey was magnificent. He put her gently across his knees. She was like a silk gourd, the neck gentle and loose. The head fell to one side, rolling against his thigh. The eagle's talons were curling inwards, joints broken in relaxation, but their strength and power could still be interpreted. Her wingspan must have been close to six feet, he guessed. She was perversely beautiful, fallen. He bent and touched the short downy feathers of the eagle's underbelly. Remorse flooded through him.

– Oh, God. So foolish . . .

Quickly, he made his way outside to the poacher, who was drinking a pint in the open air, ambivalent to the cold. He thrust a note into his hand, took the man's collar in one balled fist. The ale slopped from the glass.

– Where did you get her from? Which nest? Which, man?

∿

The Rigg was quiet and black that night as he made his way up. It formed a steep saddleback up to the triangular point of Kidstey Pike's summit, where the land became fuller and eventually flattened off as High Street. He understood the eyrie to be about half-way down on the north-facing crags, which were deeper and longer than those on the south side, a gentle fall down to the first of the tarns. It was a starless night, the darkness unremitting, but patches of snow and ice gave off a moderate glow. Details were reduced to unified forms. Using his hands and feet for guidance, he navigated the winding path up. At the start of the ridge, after the path up the slope ended, he strapped on crampons.

On his back he carried the hessian sack with the eagle, but was confident of his climbing abilities even with the added weight. At the middle crest of the Rigg he would work his way parallel and down until he reached the rocky shelves where there should be, at some point, a loose pile of sticks and moss. He doubted whether he would be attacked for intruding, more likely the birds would sheer off, circling high to avoid contact. That was as far as his thoughts took him. He trusted that his hands would be competent at their task, he had on thin gloves for extra sensitivity, to detect changes in texture along the crags. He trusted that his feet would brace him securely into the schisms and fissures of rock.

And yet he knew that he was not filled with that eager spirit, nor the adrenaline which had led him on his night excursions many times before, and he had not spent a month mapping the route by day, as he had Helvellyn. He had neither the right balance of taut muscle and slack carriage, nor the mental arrogance, the undaunted mind-set to navigate the mountains in these conditions. He had not walked the ridge for two months. More. A hollow under his lungs left him airy and light, yet he could feel the definite weight of his own organs within his body. Liver, heart, spleen, suspended in air and swaying in him as if on pendulums. And there were no cognitive specifics for the returning of the prey, it was an unexacting plan, sheer emotive distortion of the mind.

In his room above the Dun Bull Inn Janet was waiting for him, knowing nothing of this night-climb, expecting him soon. Her hair probably blue-yellow in the candlelight, her temper flaring a little as she thought of his absence in the late hour. Then she would leave and wait for him to come to her. Of all the challenges he had ever made within himself to be worthy of her, the woman at the back of this beautiful valley, torn into his back as she slept and relentless as she lived, this was his simplest, the most sincere and human.

The snowline became densely frozen ice before he expected it would. Digging in with his crampons he stepped widely along the wall of the ridge. He tried humming to focus his concentration. 'I've got you under my skin . . .' After a while the route became inaccessible this way, a slick sheet of ice. The interior of the crags was locked up tight. He would need to skirt upwards and along where the black rock came to the surface of the snow and it would be easier to grip, then down again. He started back. But in front of him it was all ice, a highlighted mass of shining ice. Had he come this impossible way in? He struck a spiked foot at it, and it scudded off, hardly breaking a chip or splinter with it. And he laughed, a self-damning, gentle laugh, as if amused by the predicament or surrendering good-naturedly to it, his eyes suddenly bright with water. Then he sang again. 'I've got you, deep in the heart of me . . .'

The bag slipped a fraction off his shoulder, and he reached back for it, his hand lifting off the wall.

Janet sits at the kitchen table within an edgeless pool of light. At its centre the illumination is strong, becoming weaker as it unfolds, and at a place somewhere further out, a point which cannot be verified, it disappears altogether. The oil lamp on the table emits a greasy odour which has come to be part of the house after years of slinking over its walls. It has joined with the aroma of rock and wood and paint, with the smell of her mother, her father and brother, and her own scent too, which is coming to her tonight as she breathes, a faint under-fume, though she doesn't feel she should be able to detect it, by all rights, as if she isn't supposed to. Today she is aware of herself in the room. Her scent. She has been waiting all night for her life's marrow to return. Now it is morning, wintry, still dark within the light. Her mother is already up, dressed and gone to the shop in the village for the last of the baking soda on the shelves, and her father is out with the dogs. Tiredness burns in her eyes, but she has a second wind, her body clock is signalling a new day, overriding the druggish stupor. In her hand is a single piece of old-fashioned yellow paper, which arrived in the post the previous day. It is stamped with a London borough postmark. Ruislip and South Harrow. She turns up the lamp's wick and reads the letter again, breathing deeply as she reads. It is typewritten and there is no signature. A private well-wisher has made a generous donation towards the re-establishment of the Mardale school.

The genderless benefactor would seek to have no mention or credit for the aid. Simply, he, or she, would be satisfied with the knowledge of the establishment's continued existence. It is requested, though, that the original building not be destroyed. Rather, the bricks and slates should be dismantled and transported to a suitable location where the school might be rebuilt, according to its previous structure. No larger, no smaller. This is the only obligation. A practical, if unusual, request, covered by the sum of the donation which will be sent in a banker's draft to the branch in Penrith for collection.

The letter is brief and lacking in perfunctory language, formalities. It is as if the author were swallowing back words when it was composed.

Janet folds the letter and puts it away into the yellow envelope. She had wanted to tell Jack last night, of the fortune, the reward for all her hard work. A small shiver travels the length of her spine. Blood speeds up in her veins and for a moment her heart clamours, missing beats, rushing others. A raw and painful thought, she puts it aside. She focuses her eyes. The lamp on the table with its wick turned high hardens its edges. Abruptly the table finishes and uninhabited space begins.

She considers all the children who must have travelled through the school over the years, some surely finding wealth and success later in life, all the visitors who happened upon the quiet lakeside building and were enchanted or moved by its unobtrusive, monastic character. Its unique display of modern history, walls made of printed words. The benefactor is somebody perhaps responsible for a piece of news which has been cut out and pasted to those pale-green painted walls. An influential sort, willing to get things done.

With only months left until its anticipated demise, the building has finally been saved. Janet breathes out, tension flooding away. For her, the mission to preserve a separate learning centre for the children of Mardale, rather than have them amalgamated into other schools permanently, has been of the utmost importance. It has seemed essential to the memory of the village. To Hazel Bowman and the teachers before her, the children themselves, to the efforts of so many. A tribute to the fact that learning has been such a loved and brilliant thing in Mardale. And essential for her own sense of achievement, for winning a small battle in this vast, already-won war. For future hope. Another shiver, flowing along the streamway of the first. Her own scent in the room.

The door latch lifts and her mother enters the kitchen. She has not worn the face she has on now for almost two decades. It is flat with the countering of agony. She moves swiftly to her daughter and clasps her shoulders firmly, gently, and from this rare, maternal gesture her daughter knows already that Jack Liggett is dead. Suddenly there is silence, over-whelming all else and blanketing the voice of her mother. She cannot hear her own screams until Ella tells her to stop them. And until her body stops breaking open an hour later her mother holds her, with arms that once held so many rupturing bodies, remembering how it is done, exactly, effortlessly. As if she has never stopped doing it. But this time it is her own issue, broken and dying.

In the shimmering calm, Ella takes her scissors from the dresser drawer and cuts off her daughter's hair, without ceremony. As if she knows instinctively that it must be done.

∾

There are some people who are born containing a residue of sorrow, blackbrae, the dark slope, this disposition is called in the north, as if in a past life they have been party to tremen-dous suffering, or because they are fated to endure the slip down into some kind of torment. As a child, she often dreamed of drowning in darkness, like the Swindale pools, and she woke holding her breath, with something awful at the back of her mind, her heart struggling to move blood. As if she had always known that sorrow was coming, sometime in the future, that it would be incorporated into her life. So now it is familiar to her, horribly known, and she meets it head-on and accepts it. She closes her eyes, opens them again. Sleep is evasive when she wants it, times like this unbearable, sunny afternoon, though at points it engulfs her in an exhausting, narcoleptic tide and she lies down wherever she is, surrendering to its wishes. Loss of consciousness is perhaps her worst enemy. It will trick her with its powers of neglect, its forsaking of memory. It will bury the knowledge of loss until that quick awakening hours or minutes later restores the taste of death again, fresher than ever. For a second, he might still be living. Then the truth, rushing above like the rain when they first touched. Jack Liggett is dead. Each new day, he is dead, rawly and again. She cannot bear the multiple imparting of ill tidings that come on the brink of no-man's-land, between waking and dreaming. The mind locked into a repetitive nightmare of having to realize truth. It is better not to sleep if she can, to remain faithful to the pain of now, to the one, all-consuming sorrow.

She shudders on the bed, turns to face the ceiling. The sore on her shoulder tingles. She has been in one position too long. Her stomach begins to heave from lack of protein, from the long absence of substantial quantities of food, from days of sub-standard nourishment. Saliva rushes in her throat, agitated by the acid in her gullet. Then her belly finally relaxes. It seems massive now under her dress, in comparison with her limbs, which are thoroughly wasted.

There is blood in one of her eyes, and its pupil is dilated to fill the iris, an eclipsed planet. The corners of her mouth are torn from the pressure of the instrument which has been forced there, from the extension of her cries. On the bed there is a wooden spoon with deep marks in the handle, from where her mother has inserted it between her teeth, forcing her head back. To save her tongue, to allow her the ability of language in the future, if she can ever crawl her way back to civilization. On the ceiling a crawling fly, the noise of it moving to the locked window is deafening. A precise roar. Her good eye tracks it, loses sight of it as it comes to land on her forehead. To drink from the pools on her face.

Her mother keeps her away from the village, a mile from their new cottage. She is an aberration, after all, a creature of singular horror, with splitting skin and a face like a bruise. Not only the madness of brain-fever, but she is with child. A sick, insipid breeder, lunatic mother. Ella Lightburn stands her ground in public, her reputation allows her some dignity, and in return discretion. Nothing is said to her face.

There will be no asylum, no madhouse sanatorium for Janet Lightburn. Her mother will not have her sent to the workhouse for unmarried mothers in Penrith. Delinquency, if that is what it is, and immorality will be kept within the family walls, though it is whispered about in Bampton, over the tops of the garden walls and on the slow, rattling bus to town. The gossips and tattle-tales in the rural suburbs are still feeding off the carcass of her love for the Waterworks man. It is not an auspicious start for the Lightburn family in the village of Bampton.

But she is quiet on the bed now. Her fits have subsided, and in the aftermath, her tongue traces her mouth's walls. There are splinters deep inside her cheeks from the spoon. There is the sound of running water in the room next door, where her mother is preparing a basin to clean her daughter's fresh wounds and the old ones.

The fly roars off her face. She turns again, faces the window, away from the bare room, the broken red eye spinning backwards and forwards. The bedroom has been emptied of furniture and fixtures, now having the appearance of a cell rather than a cottage dwelling. This is her mother's doing. There are no tools with which to wreak havoc on Janet's body. Her fingers are tied together with pieces of cotton, three fingers broken. She has no energy left to strip them off with her teeth, though later, when the grief becomes too much again, pitching her upwards, her ungodly moan intensifying into a wail, she will chew them away and the smallest fingernail on her left hand with them. Her feet and hands have been tied to the bedposts over the last few days with cord. If she remains quiet, she will be released to use the washroom. If not, her mother clears away the drenched sheets from under her. So, of sorts, it is as if she has already been condemned to a hospital, to the relentless care of Ella

Lightburn, and consumed by dementia, though her writhing and cries are the most accurate and natural expression of her sane grieving, if only her family could know it. If only it could be understood that way.

The punishments are of her own worst volition. She leaves her mother little choice, attempting to gouge out an eye from its socket or cut away her throat with saved metal. The injuries are a testament only to her sorrow, the bindings simply an outcome of her misconduct. A desperate attempt to preserve the life of an unborn child and the bonny exterior of a daughter.

A twist in her belly, this time of another kind. A gentle, insistent kick. A ripple. In the liquid of her womb. Through the window the sun is bright and warm on her face. It refuses to indulge such things as grief and torment, human sorrow. It is the worst of all castigations. A blinding reward. Anti-sympathy. A brilliant orb that will not desert the sky in solidarity, as she wishes it would. Though this will be the last of her own blinding energy.

~

Had she not been pregnant, Janet Lightburn might have taken her own life in the first months after the death of Jack Liggett. The grief she suffered from left her mute and self-harming. She beat her own face and breasts constantly to create another type of pain, one which would override her internal anguish. She broke bones in her fingers, externalized her despair. But the bleeding inside would not stop. Her heart haemorrhaged itself empty, filled again with love and hate and longing for Jack Liggett. Her mother met the fierce end of her mourning with compassion and practical care. It was a rare time when the two women met truthfully and naturally, balancing each other in some respects. Ella felt a purpose and an unconditional role in Janet's life. But there was a hole in her daughter and through it poured despair. Its flow could not be stopped. And, in truth, Ella was not able to grasp the core of that despair, to turn it over in her hands and understand its existence. Though she never spoke ill of Jack Liggett again – that much she knew to be essential.

Janet had given herself up to the man, without fully realizing the consequences of it, without knowing or understanding the route she had taken to get there, so that she could not return. The struggle to reach him had been intense and had left yawning blue voids in its wake, the valley, her family, the past. It was political and personal suicide, where meaning had shifted form. Because he was the meaning of it all, in that remote point far out from herself, far out from all she had known and been or stood for. All that she had given up was eclipsed by his face. In his death, there was nothing to show for the long battle, nothing except herself, given up and remote. Purposelessness and impossibility rushing past. No resolution to the troubled affair. She had not been able to live it solvent as she had with the other days of her life, each and every one. Her sacrifice was null and void. And so, she was left alone, stranded, a solitary in that distant place where they had once struggled and fucked and vaulted against the walls together and it had not mattered that they were lost. It was a place where only their being together made sense. In his absence there was no reason to that place, the terra nullius, and yet she remained there, severed, pounding against the void to get out. There was no way back. She screamed and wept for him until vomit jerked from her open mouth.

In the long weeks after his death, sorrow finally destroyed itself, until even the last shards of misery deserted her and she sat back, took her nails out from under her skin and let her hand stop banging down. She began to implode. She went unwashed, functioned without care. She refused food and gradually the bones jumped out of her face. She became all skull, her cropped hair shattered over her scalp.

She had made no mention of her pregnancy to the family, but her mother felt it. As she held her daughter in those first raveling moments at Whelter Farm, her mother, the green-winged angel of death, she knew it. A gentle swelling against her. A hidden bump, perhaps no more than four months of development then. She placed her hand on Janet's belly as she rocked with her, asked for no confirmation. As the hair fell away from her daughter's head and the shears worked in her hands, Ella began her prayers for the unborn child.

In the initial days of Janet's mourning, the most violent period, Ella became afraid her daughter would strike her own stomach during the fits, induce miscarriage, either purposefully or not – though she did not dwell on it, could not afford to dwell on it. But Janet did not smash at the foetus. She cut and broke and harmed the outer reaches of her body, her face and hands, kicking her feet at windows, rocks, but leaving the vital section of herself alone.

As she wasted, her mother held food to her mouth. She must think of the life of her unborn child. She slapped her daughter, forced morsels of milk-soaked bread into her mouth, she held her close. But her daughter was gone. Samuel and Isaac stood by, in the doorway, unable to summon the strength for such bloody-minded exhibits of love and care. They watched Ella nurse her, checking her stomach daily for marks, combing the short clumps of blue-blonde hair which came out in her hands from her daughter's tearing.

When the baby arrived a month early, in late April, Ella thought her daughter might turn back towards them. But she did not. She nursed the child with her eyes averted and would not name her. Samuel and Ella called the girl Miriam, registered the surname of Lightburn, and sealed the infant tight within the family. She would have been the last child to be born in Mardale, would have held that sad, saturated honour, if the family had not moved to the next valley. A month after Jack's death, the Lightburns left the village and moved to a sprawling farm at the edge of the Bampton commons. The Shap doctor called by regularly to see the infant, pronounced it healthy on each visit, but did not know of any treatment for its mother, other than incarceration. He confessed that he had always suspected such a proclivity in the girl, his brow furrowing, remembering in particular details of the incident which had left her head severely scarred. But he supposed that now they were away from the scene of the tragedy, things might improve in their own time. Yes, in time. If they did not, he would prepare the papers, regretfully, of course, but he would do it. And Ella curled her hands into fists at her side to prevent herself from throwing the doctor through the door.

Samuel bent to his knees in front of Janet and begged her just to take his hand while Ella held the newborn in her arms. He searched the fells for his daughter when she slipped away from the house and found her rocking by the river or sleeping too close to the current. He watched the star ending, a little more light melting away each day. It was as if the rage, her energy, so bright in her youth, had been too much, had come too quick and fully, life had used her up, so when fate dealt the most reeling blow, she had no characteristic fury left with which to hurl herself headlong and screaming back at it. Or pull through. She had burnt away. He wept openly against her skirt with his big hands in the earth, and the river rocking past.

Isaac brought her flowers from the meadow, stroked the velvet petals on her neck and cheeks, he became garrulous, reading to her, stumbling over uncorrected words, long poems. He found smooth stones in the mosaic of the riverbed and gave them to her, explained patiently that they would not shine best until placed in water. It was their secret, he said, they must be where they belonged in order to come to life. She regarded him with air-focused eyes, perhaps then a faint smile, too slight to say for certain.

The weeks passed and the veins came to the surface of her hands.

Then, as spring gave way to summer, for a time it did seem she was getting better. Her mother would find her dressed in the morning, standing by the crib, though never holding

Miriam, the dark-haired baby. Instead, an extreme masculine spirit descended on Janet, as in the hub of her youth. She began helping with tasks on the farm, herding cows and even birthing the last of the lambs. She changed wheels on the farm vehicles, oiled the chains in the dairy. From a distance, thin and with her short hair tucked under an old cap, she might have been mistaken for a young boy. In the kitchen, if asked, she would cut vegetables, though her mother watched the knives closely, the black bird filling up the cavity of her chest. Because she saw something. Because the air around her daughter stayed bent as she moved through it, like she had not made peace with the passage of her life yet. And Ella sensed a violent composition somewhere in the air in front of her.

II:V

The man who replaced Jack Liggett at MCW had never been to
Mardale. He had never been to Cumberland or to
Westmorland. As a boy, he had holidayed with his family not
in the Lake country, where one could never be sure of fair
weather or a downpour, but on the south coast of France,
where he built moats for castles in the sand, waiting to see if
they would withstand the tide. He had never jumped a train
to escape brutality or city, had never climbed any of
England's brown peaks, and he had never selected a character for himself that was several leaps away from his upbringing. Then renounced it. Thomas Wright was not a man given
to leniency or sentimentality where profession was concerned, and his knowledge of the tiny village was not viscer-
al, not personal. Though he could sketch out a plan of the dale
with exact measurements, mapping the distance from the
Dun Bull to the shore of Low Water in inches, he could not
have told that the upper fields were ploughed lengthwise like
rice fields for better drainage. That nine of the slates around
Goosemire's chimney were missing, that Whelter Farm was
built purely from sight with not a single true right angle existing. Or that if the wind changed and moved east to west
across the valley, the weather vane on the church twisted
backwards to create a shadow on the roof which appeared
like that of a rampant lion.

What Thomas Wright was aware of was that his title and
role as overseer to the Haweswater project was nominal. He
was a shadow minister. He might as well have been a portrait
of himself. He was the silent undertaker who would tend to
the body of Jack Liggett's work, laying it like a giant sarcoph-
agus to rest. He had graduated within the company to an

empty seat, where the tasks were already fulfilled. Some days in the new office, Jack Liggett's seat did not even feel vacated, rather there was a ghostly presence, the legacy of a man imbued with inordinate opinion and respect. He had become a corporate legend, his recent abstraction from the company seemingly forgotten. Neither glory nor fame would belong to Thomas Wright in such imposing circumstances. As such, his position was clear. There would be no unnecessary preservation or delay with matters. The project was to be completed, it was to be closed, it was to be put aside. Then, and only then, would he have the opportunity to pry open a few oysters of his own and hold aloft a pearl or two. First, a little catharsis, a little devastation, a little washing away of sandcastles was in order. An exorcism.

In the smoky, silent Waterworks boardroom, Thomas Wright gave a convincing speech. In it, he maintained that the Waterworks had always prided itself on a certain code of conduct that was the essence of good taste and safety. Jack Liggett, he said, with all due respect, had let things slip a fraction, through no fault of his own, doubtless, for what man could maintain stamina throughout such an immense and lengthy project whilst also tending to local matters. His memory should be celebrated by a proper culmination of the scheme. There was the question of what was to be done to the village next. Mardale would be drowned by the new reservoir, yes, but for the existing structures a plan was needed. There were over thirty buildings. To leave them standing would be both hazardous and unsettling. A village underwater and perfect? There was something sinister about it, was there not? It would look like slaughter, or like murder, like martyrdom, certainly incriminating. Something was to be done. And, if he might so venture, he himself had a solution. He outlined it, simply, persuasively. The executive board took a vote on the proposed course of action. And it was decided that the village would be razed.

By June of 1937, Mardale had been almost completely abandoned, except for the Hindmarsh family in High
Bowderthwaite Farm, who had the advantage of a little extra
time as theirs was the highest inhabited point of the valley.
They continued to farm the steep fields and the fallow paddocks, herding sheep alongside the near-vertical drystone
walls, crooks in hand, dogs working with heads tucked down
and forward. They would continue to work their land until
finally evicted three months later, when the Waterworks
revoked the last of the hill-farm tenancies.

Aside from the Hindmarshes there were, quite often, a
few other folk about in the deserted village. Locals returned,
lingered, surveyed their old homes, especially on days when
there was activity from official quarters. It was as if they
could not bear to allow intruders into the lives they had left
behind. Samuel Lightburn was one of these stragglers. He
was drawn back often, even though he had secured another
farm tenancy on the high land between Bampton and
Butterwick, the Staingarth property, a five-hundred-year-old,
ramshackle dwelling with tumbling barns and stony fields.
When he came back to Mardale he wandered through the village, kicking at loose stones, or stood on the hump-backed
bridge watching the river flow past. It appeared as if he was
looking for something, some forgotten piece of his family that
had been left behind, his daughter's spirit, perhaps, for it
seemed she was soulless now. Or he was simply waiting, bent
over on the bridge with his elbows resting on the parapet, waiting for a time when he would be able to leave completely, a
dismissal, which for now was not forthcoming.

Isaac accompanied his father on these nostalgic excursions.
He was a persistent child, wound within his own beliefs,
maintaining a relationship with Measand beck whenever he
could, and the inhabitants of the cold, plunging streams. He
wallowed in the rocky pools with a piece of piping that he

used as a makeshift snorkel, so that he could remain submerged until his father was ready to leave, or until the crest of a current splashed over the tube and he came up spluttering. They were a strange pair, the father on the bridge tracking ghosts in the land, the son a spirit swimming among the underwater territories. Both biding time.

The valley received other visitors. An occasional photographer, a tourist, those with a morbid curiosity who had heard of the fate of Mardale and wanted to see the condemned place before it perished.

The final chapter in the history of the valley was not long in coming, for Thomas Wright was indeed keen to move ahead with the project, then move on. When the wrecking began the relief among the villagers was almost palpable, and though such an abrupt, emphatic end to the village was deeply disturbing, it brought with it a sense of closure, a sense that now they could in earnest begin again.

∿

No local explosives expert was hired and brought in from Carlisle. The dynamite blasters of the region's quarries were out of luck and a decent wage. Thomas Wright had other ideas with regard to MCW's plan for the demolition. Ideas altogether more grand and demonstrative. Instead, the assembling British Army was sent for, forty territorial officers of the Royal Engineers, members of the 42nd East Lancashire Division. They arrived in green canvassed wagons and set up a temporary camp in a field just on the outskirts of the village. Borrowing barns or squatting in the empty farm buildings was strictly against orders. There were to be no temporary attachments. The officers set up tents, dug holes in the thick Westmorland soil for latrines and observed the village from without, as if studying the enemy's habits.

These were cheerful, polite men who went about their business slickly, as if each man were running on rails, and able smoothly to turn corners. The men whistled popular tunes. They snapped their fingers as they walked, hummed songs as they banged signs into the ground surrounding the village, stating that passers-by did so at their own risk. Their uniforms were new, not yet faded by north European rain or south European sun, not yet darkened by blood or torn by wire. It was a smart, enthusiastic group that had the pre-war optimism of the young. The soldiers kept a fire going for the entire sixty hours that they were present in the valley, and there always seemed to be tea brewing in a kettle and men drinking from tin cups, day or night, leaving old, swollen tea leaves spattered on the ground.

Witnessing the sudden appearance of the men, the Hindmarsh family strolled down the fell to chat with members of the odd encampment. Teddy saluted the superior officers, shook hands with one or two of the other men and was delighted to relate the grisly details of his missing appendage, though conversation between them was cropped, un-abutting, and Teddy's hopes for an insight into the contemporary military remained hindered. The weather was mentioned, the roads, the dam. The weapons factory that had been set up within the pink-turreted hangar of Lowther Castle. The Army denied all knowledge of the base.

But gradually the mysterious presence of the forty officers became apparent.

The Army had been given permission by the Waterworks to test new plastic explosives on the abandoned buildings as training for a forthcoming war. Another war seemed inevitable and understood, as the political powers of Europe gathered aggression. New explosive devices were already being manufactured in Germany, and subsequently in the factories of Britain, the arms race was under way. Before they could be used in the field, the British military wanted them to be given a fair trial. Any home testing-ground was useful in the present, fraught climate. The Waterworks had been only too happy to oblige and a stout little village had been offered up for target practice.

Teddy grimaced at the news, put his sleeve back into his pocket. After serving his country well, his country appeared not to be reciprocating. This was nothing less than an insult to his home, to the church where he had been christened, the pub where he had drunk ale and thrown darts. Had they any idea of the age of this place, he asked. There was no reply. A shrug or two. He said nothing more, saluted again, and led away his blushing sisters, who were unhappy to have been removed from the company of the charming young officers, back up to High Bowderthwaite. Soon the rumble of the ancient tractor could be heard as it ground up and down the incline. Teddy was taking his disapproval out on the landscape. The two sisters hooked up the horse and dray and trotted off into Bampton with fresh butter for sale and news of the recent development.

The Army continued with its initial organization. Everything was done in true military fashion over the weekend, from beginning to end. On Friday afternoon the camp was set up and by Monday morning it had been struck and was gone, as if the appearance had been ghostly, like a phantom sighting of Roman legionnaires, marching south from Hadrian's Wall. Equipment and supplies were checked a dozen times. There was over 600 pounds of explosive to be unloaded from the wagons and transferred to a secure location, a plot of land free of quartz and flint, which was covered with hefty tarpaulin. A local policeman, stationed in the village of Bampton, was deployed to the valley during the day to help guard the explosive material, kept in a tent on the very outskirts of camp. The precise, volatile nature of the new substance was as yet untested and unrecorded, so it was considered prudent to keep it at a safe distance from the men and the spitting camp-fire.

The first building subjected to the bombing was Measand Hall, a building so old and run-down that it appeared already to have been the target of some heavy shelling. As it stood a little away from the rest of the village, it had been selected first, thus the predicted shudder and radius of the tremors would not affect any of the other buildings, rendering them perilously unstable. The roof of the Hall had been pulled down and transported away, as had the old oak panelling inside it. Carpets and chaise longue were gone, valuables auctioned-off at the town hall in Penrith. It had been gutted. Only the thick walls remained, and an unfinished painting, which was leaning against a wall in the long hallway.

On Saturday morning a handful of villagers gathered to watch the proceedings, among them Samuel and his family, the Nobles and Lanty Farrow, the Hindmarshes, Joyce Carruthers. Sylvia Goodman brought a wicker chair from which to observe the proceedings and had with her four lace handkerchiefs for the purpose of mopping her rheumy, grief-filled eyes, which she did in the manner of a righteous old dame who might be prone to sniffles at the opera. There was also a reporter from the *Cumberland and Westmorland Herald* newspaper, who slouched at the side of the group, holding a pad of paper with a pencil attached to it by string, seeming utterly bored by the whole situation.

The work of laying charges began at nine thirty in the morning. The crowd was asked not to smoke during the proceedings, if they wished to do so they must retreat to the concrete road at the east side of the valley. Immediately several pipes appeared from pockets.

It was a dry day, with a pale, warm sun, and the men were glad not to have the complication of torrential Lakeland rain to deal with. Nobody much fancied messing with a dripping, effervescent explosive. Two young officers drilled holes in the stout walls of Measand Hall with pneumatic equipment. After the boring had been done, the officers' superior examined the holes and nodded his approval for stage two. Another soldier marched in with the plastic explosive, which was placed into the walls as carefully as if it were a sleeping kitten. The children in the group strained forward for a better look. It resembled a small ball of odd-looking clay fixed to the ends of TNT. The officer handling the explosive wore gloves, which were consigned to an airtight steel box after the material was inserted. Then he checked the seams of his sleeves for lethal detritus. Connecting-wires were fitted and the soldier checked and re-checked the fixtures, the detonation device. The latter was considered faulty and it was exchanged for another. Then he barked a few curt instructions to the gathering.

– Few hundred feet back, if you please. Over by the hill.

Sylvia Goodman fussed over her chair, struggled with it to the new location, re-sat and drew a blanket over her stout, bready legs, though it was not a cold day. She delicately lifted a tissue from her unsnapped purse and waited. The rest of the spectators did as they were told also. They shifted uneasily. They looked at the noble old building. They fixed a picture of it in their heads. It was 11.56 a.m.

At midday, a one-minute signal was given. Then there were three ragged bangs like shotgun blasts, the echoes of which ricocheted about the valley. Tiny clouds of dust rose from the building and floated upwards, settled downwards. The thick Westmorland stone walls of the Hall remained perfectly intact, except for a slight widening of the bored holes in the centre of one gable. The crowd cheered spontaneously and the reporter scribbled in his notebook. An officer coughed loudly and walked towards the group.

– We were just checking to see if the connecting wires and detonator were in order. Just a test run. Next one should do it. Minimal amount of explosive, you see. More next time. Don't come any closer.

He spoke cheerfully, matter-of-factly, but his cheeks were a little flushed and there was an almost apologetic smile in his eyes and about his crooked moustache. He walked away, back to the group of officers, exchanged a few words with them and began the job of hastily recharging the holes in the walls, which had deepened and widened and could easily take more explosive. Again the clay-like substance was inserted, again the gloves discarded.

Samuel turned to Teddy Hindmarsh.

– Fellas've gotta fair bit more munny fer t'clobber these days, eh?

– Aye. Five paira gloves each bugger.

The men chuckled and Samuel offered Teddy a cigarette. Sylvia's buttocks squeaked against her wicker chair. She tutted and muttered to herself, and took out a flask from her handbag, from which she took a sip.

After another thirty minutes or so there was a terrific explosion, much louder than the first, which reverberated around the valley. Clouds of smoke and dust filled the air, and when it cleared everyone could see that Measand Hall was not, in fact, a pile of debris and rubble, but simply a decrepit old building, now a little worse for wear, with beams of sunlight spilling through the gable, but still mostly intact.

By now there was much discussion going on among the group of Territorial officers. Clipped voices were raised. A radio call was hastily put in to the military base at Orton, and within two hours a truck arrived carrying another 400 pounds of explosive and extra supplies, by which time the villagers had picnicked on the grass banks of the dale and the Army had gone through several batches of tea and a ration of sardine sandwiches. The new equipment was unloaded quickly and stacked in the supply tent.

One final blast in the afternoon successfully demolished the Hall. It was not blown sky high, nor did it explode in a mushroom of shattered rock and stone. Instead, it folded heavily outwards, wall by wall, almost gracefully as it scattered bricks. It lay open like an enormous stone flower in bloom. Sylvia Goodman let loose her sobs, covering her eyes with the lacy rag. The moustached officer came back over to the villagers. The locals were quiet, but for the weeping woman, standing very still. There was an atmosphere of ill-content and mild disapproval around them. The officer did not quite understand why they were there in the first place, unless it was because there was nothing better to do of a weekend around these parts, which wouldn't have surprised him.

– That's all for today, ladies and gents. The rest will be done tomorrow. Oh-nine-hundred hours, sharp. If you want to be present.

On Sunday, almost exactly the same crowd was present as the previous day, give or take a few extra children, who were keen to miss Sunday school under the watchful eye of the Bampton vicar's wife, and a few less women, including Ella Lighthurn, who were not about to miss church for the spectacle. This time the charges were greatly increased, the amount of explosive multiplied sixfold and more. There was less discussion among the officers and less cheerful belligerence among the spectators. The Army had moved within the confines of the village, and was working around what had once been the graveyard, stepping over fresh rectangles of exhumed earth. The next building to be demolished would be the tiny church.

∾

It was Private William Garry who railed from corner to corner with wires and explosive. He was from Tadcaster, first child of Mr and Mrs Harold Garry, the pride of his family. Gloved-up and bright-eyed, he fitted the charges between the slabs of the building, whistling all the while, though somewhat nervously. He let it be known to the rest of his division that he was amazed by the resilience of these village walls, which had been witnessed the day before, and after the church failed to shatter on the first attempt, he also let them know that he was not just a little worried that the explosive being used was perhaps too weak for the purpose of blowing off enemy legs and arms. After wiring up the church a second time he mentioned his fears to his superior. The old hall had been snared three times, he said, before falling. Perhaps the tacky was dud, not in working order. And it didn't feel right, sir, wiring-up a church again that wouldn't drop. Perhaps He Himself didn't like it. He was told not to be simple, that the Almighty had better things to do than keep this church upright. And then Garry confided in his superior that he'd heard about a bomb the Germans had that landed first and exploded later, taking out half a city after you though it was dead. A bomb that no one could defuse. Private Garry, his superior almost shouted, less lip and get on with it lad, the nearest farm if he was so damn worried for the church.

As it was, Private William Garry did not have long to contemplate the quality of British arsenal once the Army was mobilized and deployed. He lasted a month in the violent tides of the Second World War before receiving eleven high-calibre bullets from an enemy machine-gun. His suspicions about delayed-reaction bombs were right, however. The country would be digging them up and defusing them for almost the remainder of the century. From under cathedrals, the sand dunes of beaches, wells and mines. Children would swing round them and jump off them decades later without the benefit of historical knowledge to identify the funny cylindrical drums.

But on that day in Mardale, at least, his fears were somewhat assuaged, as the plastic explosive was used more liberally and gradually, one by one, the old walls of the buildings collapsed. The Army recorded the damage with each increase of volatile material. After a while they became heavy-handed with its use, and it was quite a show for the spectators. The sound of the explosions grew louder, and the crowd flinched and covered their ears for each detonation. Odd fragments of debris landed hundreds of yards away from the sites of the bombings. The officers ducked behind sandbags, with rocks clattering off their hard, round helmets. The Bampton policeman moved the crowd back, and further back still, leaving his position at the explosive tent to ensure public safety. A shard of rock landed on the windshield of his motorcycle and he ran over to find it shattered and hanging loose from the Norton.

This duty was more than he had bargained for.

At one o'clock that day the Hindmarsh family retreated indoors for their traditional Sunday lunch. From their high vantage point they could still see the damage being done, the smoke rising in blue-grey clouds above the trees and hedges, and they could hear the blasts as they grew louder. Outside the cottage the dog was barking furiously and throwing itself against its chain. But the family was determined that their Sunday roast would be consumed, come hell or high water, and they would not leave their home even when a young officer knocked on the door of High Bowderthwaite, issuing a polite order to leave for an hour and have the lunch cold later, and making the sisters blush. He was chased off by the one-armed Teddy with a carving knife and the ferocious barking of the ratty terrier in the kennel outside the farm. The family sat eating their roast lamb and mint sauce, blocking their ears from the booms and crashes down the hill. The cottage walls shook and glass cracked and tinkled from the window panes. Teddy's younger sister, Sandra, took her hand away from her ear and looked at it. There was a small patch of blood on her palm. A trickle of blood ran from her ear.

❧

By Sunday afternoon the damage was done. Everything was razed within the village and on its periphery the rubble spread outwards, scattered up grassland. Riggindale Farm, the Dun Bull, Whelter Farm Cottage. All the houses were blasted to ruin except for the school house, which had been dismantled in the previous March and rebuilt exactly as it had once stood in the next valley over, and the church, which held on, gaping and groaning. Dust began to settle over the wreckage of Mardale and it was only the battered tower of St Patrick's that remained at any substantial height. It shook and crumbled with each bomb detonation but withstood the shocks, and though by the end of the day it appeared that only one ounce of explosive would have brought it crashing down, there was no explosive left in the guarded tent to be used. So, finally, the Army left the church be. It was gradually knocked down with sledgehammers and pickaxes over the next few months by MCW labourers, reduced to a pile of brick and stone and stained glass. It was said throughout Westmorland that the noise of the bombing could be heard in a twenty-mile, corrugated-mountain radius, but that sheep and cattle across the fells continued to graze silently, oblivious and unconcerned.

After the bombing, the village lay in a smouldering heap for a few days before the dust finally blew to the earth and the last bricks toppled. If Britain had happened to look in on the valley for a moment, it might have found some way in which to prepare itself for a sight destined to become common over the next few years. Cities and towns decayed by the fury of explosives, bombs rained down from carrier planes and enemy aircraft. It might have seen a vision of the Blitz.

Years later, in 1979, when a severe drought would take the water levels down further than they had been since the flooding, and would turn the lakebed into dry, parched skin, the shallow skeleton of the old village would rise again, crumbling, out of the desert-looking earth. The bridge in the village would be almost perfect, even after a vast, inverse river had been flowing over and above it for almost fifty years, though the mason's mark on its keystone would be eroded to nothing. It would be discovered that the cellars of some of the buildings were still insolently intact, despite the British Army's vigour, and items within had been preserved. They were collecting mud quietly after all the years of separation from their upper structures. Like forgotten war veterans. Or skeletal prisoners left in a concentration camp.

By the time of the arrival of troops into the Haweswater valley Janet had regained much of her strength, and would
exchange words with her family if she was spoken to. Her
child had developed the ability to smile and Jack Liggett had
been dead for half a year. Her mother took her to the village
of Bampton when she went to get the groceries and she
walked as a pillar among the sane, cancelling rumours of
wrathful delirium, though she was not the same wildcat she
had been in her day, they agreed. She was not at all what she
had once been.

When she learned of the impending devastation of the old
village, Janet insisted that she accompany her father to
Mardale to witness the spectacle of the bombing. She had not
returned at all since her family had moved, when she had
been wrapped in a blanket, growling softly like an injured
fox. She told her parents that to go now would give her the
peace they so desperately wanted for her. That she wanted
herself. But Ella noticed her daughter's fingers touching her
lips as she spoke. There was enough animation in her to convey the lie. And Ella Lightburn was a library of lies, of collected, stored, macabre signs from her patients. The licking of
a tongue at the corner of a mouth. A wrongly timed blink.
The direction of an eye, up-cast. Tell-tale mannerisms which
suggested hidden motives. The overspill of ill-thought, of
premeditation.

Men with hypodermic needles hidden under their hospital
pillows had searched out their faces with the stumps of their
arms, phantom fingers playing over lips and eyebrows,
accompanied by sudden conciliatory conversation. Ella saw
the missing digits, blue flames roaring out of their wrists and

burning at their mouths. Then, in the morning, they would be swimming against a pillow of viscous red, a precise puncture to the throat, needle pressed in by the jawbone under a chin. The downward nod, the aye to suicide. Or a razor tucked into the broad artery at the back of a knee. Kerosene swallowed from a lamp. Ella knew that to anyone but a nurse there is little argument for an increase in life and calm as being an adverse occurrence in a patient. In the circumstances of improvement, it appears touched with a tainted concern, or with unwholesome intention. But she was a master of noticing behaviour that went against the grain of what a person wanted her to see. All Ella could do was lift the baby into her daughter's arms and with silence accuse her of orphaning the child. But Janet passed the child back, went outside and hooked up the horse to the cart. She drove her father and brother to the valley, her conversation sparse, her fingerprints leaving furtive tracks across her mouth.

∾

Janet watched the bombing alone, from the gentle hill next to her old home. Sitting on the dry ground hidden between the gorse and holding her knees, close enough to the soldiers to watch them work. Her father wondered where she was but knew better than to search her out and approach her. He believed her to be making her own private peace, and, in a way, she was. The sky moved its pieces of white. Above her were the towering shadowy crags of the Rigg. A circling eagle, stretched on the gale in the upper atmosphere as it left the valley for silence. She thought of Jack Liggett, who felt close by. He was in the air, where his sallow chest had breathed out, the ground, where he had spilled out of her as she lay next to him, a hand on his wet stomach. Once she had found herself in the elements, felt the pull of nitrates and molecules in her body as the land changed within its existence. Now he was living in the old territory. A man who had torn his roots out of the city for her and transplanted the best of himself. He was here, within reach. The landscape had him enfolded, safe, like bark holding back the spreading rings of a tree. She put her face in the grass and her tears swept down concave blades and soaked into the dry earth, into the fossils and claws and muscles of rock from thousands of years ago. And her mouth was open and rigid like a paralysed flower, letting out fluid. The scar on her forehead raised as her face contorted with grief. It seemed he was shouting through the soil to her, faintly. A ghost in the elements. She swore then that she would make her life worthy of his death and gradually the tears bled away.

She kept away from the crowd that included her father, remained concealed from the group of army officers as they marched to and from their camp. Explosions tore through the grass. She inched closer to the volcanic axis. Pieces of rock landed around her as she sat, they nicked her face and caught in her hair. She did not move. Even as she felt the sharpness of stone on her cheeks, she would not leave the surroundings where Jack Liggett spoke through the land. Her mind faltered across past meetings. It had been here in the corner of this field that she had cut out from under his skin a piece of shale that had become lodged in his back after they rolled and fought on the ground. His eyes watery and laughing with the pain.

– You're enjoying this.

– I'm not.

– Then why is it taking so long. Is that blade sterile?

– I want to be sure the scar is worth having.

She reached for a small stone lodged in the grass, put it into her mouth, and its wet minerals lined up along her tongue. She put two more in the sockets of her closed eyes and lay back as if to sleep. After a time the explosions became so loud she thought they were right next to her. And still she did not retreat.

The bombs continued to detonate, bragging through the village, to where she was sitting, alone. She caught pieces of the old village in her new locks of hair, in her lap, in her skin.

Above, the sky moved pieces of grey and white, meaning a change of season was coming, exactly as it had a year ago. When she had fallen on the bridge for no reason and the battle had been about stealth, about who could find the next hidden channel in the other, and she still had one foot solid in her old life.

She did not move until she saw the Bampton policeman leave the tent where the military equipment was kept, to shift the crowd having rocks rained down on them, and then to survey the damage to his motorcycle as it was hit by a large shard of slate. Her fingers came to her mouth, brushed past. There was a splinter in the cushion of her upper lip. When the man was gone she stood, walked low and silent around the village, down through the dust and debris to the outer tent, without taking her grey eyes from it. Within a few steps her body became feline, remembering how it had moved before the energy had left her. A rough flap of canvas brushed against her forehead and she was inside, surrounded by a bitter smell of clay in the semi-darkness, hands groping for wire, a loose detonator and the tightly wrapped bundles of explosive.

❧

Isaac climbs back into the cart, where his sister is already sitting holding the reins. The fireworks are over. The village is gone and his collar is dripping with river water. Under his sister's feet is a hemp sack, held tight between her ankles. Big enough to contain a dead lamb or a large bird, small enough to be overlooked amid the clutter of the cart. Her face is dry, lined with fur on the bridge of her nose. His boots are wet and his shirt is dripping. A last swim in the Measand river before it is consumed by unrelated water. A salutation to the trout and the water boatmen and the mystery of the riverbed as it washes itself clean and smooth. He has said his goodbyes now, will conquer the rivers of another place. He is seven years old. A boy with a head full of strange ideas and notions, a belief system already too resolute for his youth. He sees that the spirit which has evaporated from his sister is back, flickering under the fur of her skin. It is not gone yet. Will never be gone. Energy can only be displaced, never destroyed, he had once heard it said.

For a moment he is not sure that she is silent, the closed statue on the wooden seat. There is a voice in his head that is speaking to him, telling him that this is who they are, she and he, people from this carnal realm of water and earth, full of the atoms of this old, dying, re-living place. The blood in his hands will tell him where he belongs, where it will be brightest. Seven years old. An old-before-he-was-young boy, who came out of the womb that way. In this valley, his heart is a beating stone that will carry him down to the depths. Where life is slower and faster at once. And better. The voice in his head tells him that he will come back. One day you will surrender your heart of stone to the place that has made you infinite.

Isaac moves to his sister's side. She raises her arm to make room for him. She is saying her goodbyes as he has said his, in the silence, with the voice in his head. And he, no more than a child in years but ancient still, having more understanding than he will ever have in his life again, lets her go.

– PART III –

III:I

Looking up, there are stars. The plough, Orion's belt.
Constellations only seen from this northern hemisphere. In
Australia and New Zealand there are different stars, Hazel
Bowman had told them in school, other points of reference
that the warrior nations navigated their boats by, waged war
under, and the moon is bigger there, too. Somewhere at the
back of the sky is Pluto, discovered in the year of her brother's birth, but dying for millions of years before. Janet feels a
little warmth coming off the northern moon. Enough to warm
the backs of her hands as she works, gathering wood. It is late
summer and the season has been cooling, slowly, on the black
roof of the Swindale pools where dragonflies are in abundance. In these past few days summer has flared up again, as
if striving for temporary renewal, and for now the air remains
humid, close. The dam is almost complete, only the last facing
remaining absent from the structure. Water is not yet building behind it, and the divided river takes it through what will
be the sluice gates of the reservoir. There is not water enough
to create a disaster of biblical proportions, should it be
released.

She arrives at the site a little after one in the morning,
builds a small fire from brittle pine cones and sticks on the
forest floor, and she walks around it, east west, west east,
trying to dissuade or convince herself about that task for
which she has walked seven miles this night to undertake.
Though perhaps the walking is only for summoning a spirit, and she already knows the course of her life. She keeps
the old satchel which she has carried a good distance from
the flames. For all her uninhabited body, she is still able to
bring to mind rationale, techniques which she will need,

reasons for her presence on the edge of the wooden site buildings, technicalities. She knows that her life had been pared down to this. She knows that she had dissolved already, in part, and that there is only a body remaining, a few thoughts, purpose, enough. She is a single, disparate cell. There are small recollections, shards of memory scattered above the grey mass of her disposition, not enough to prevent a journey towards release. A slight, warm wind coming off the moon, whispering along the wall of the dam. She reaches out hands towards it, presses smooth rock. Looks up, up.

The stars begin at the flat platform of the embankment's edge, as if it is holding them in place. Jack Liggett's monument envelopes the valley, it roars stone upwards above her. A vast monument to a man who has remade the world, sucking up earth and space and moulding it into the urban rib of Adam. It is a perfect colossus, the Waterworks' obituary read in the *Manchester Observer* a week after his death, an emblem of the man who suffered that first magnificent vision, who had thought to regurgitate nature through the serpentine mouth of industry. It honours him more than anything else can.

But in this valley of broken water, of constant remaking and living earth, there are no monuments to death. Nor should there be. The land sucks back in what once it helped to produce. And the dam is a false idol, the hollow arm of God. Her hands on the wall lift, as if she will fall backwards and be swallowed by the landscape.

It takes her three hours to scratch and chip holes into the joints of the vast slabs, using an old chisel belonging to her father and, when that breaks, the iron hook used for removing stones from horses' hooves. The facing is not so difficult to work with and the under-wall is almost beautiful, perfect and dense like marble as she tunnels in. She did not know it before, the cold beauty of this foreign piece, had never wanted to come with Jack Liggett and place her hands on its cold flanks while he lived. She deepens the holes as well as she can with the instrument, unhurried, her fingers still damaged from old wounds and stiff. At the base of the structure she digs away the sods of earth, creating tunnels towards the foundations. She lights two candles to see better by, stands them at the foot of the mighty wall so that their auras meet, as if at an altar. They do not even flicker in the still night. She must always have known that there would be this sacrifice, her life has been in readiness for it, that her hands would prepare for it, quietly, writing herself into the blackness.

She slows all her movements further, is precise about them and focuses on her slender thoughts as she works, setting the charges in the trickery of the moon's light. There is not much wire, only what her dreaming hand had stolen in darkness, and now it slips through her fingers like ink, like quick liquid. She prepares the detonator exactly as she had seen the young officer attach the instrument.

Later, a long way past midnight, it hits very dark. Dawn is only an hour or so away now. Above, the sky is gathering cloud, stacking it up in towering columns. The moon begins slipping away behind the obscure mass. She smells the coming rain, only a morning away. And still the candles do not flicker, are utterly without movement.

She allows herself only a few moments to prepare her own body, perhaps finding a reasonable blue cage within herself that she turns and walks into. Locking herself away from the torn hills outside, the bright, living water of the valley, her father herding cattle and her mother praying or kneading her knuckles down through dough. The beloved face of her brother. His pure dislocated, swimming form. Or a step forward, out away from captivity and the tight drum of the present, out towards the disparate shape of her love, his presence in the mountains. She closes or opens, renouncing all but the last aspect of herself.

∾

On this night of gathering storm there is no regret. There is only the energy of the half-hidden moon that reaches her, dying over her hands on the detonator, and even the air, littered with the lost breath of the dam's god, does not move. She is at the edge of a vast universe, where old elements are fused. Like a healed wound.

Then a flashing second, and her too close, too close to the wall, but she had known that all along.

She is caught up into the beauty of white light and noise, rock singing, and the speed of the air as the mouth of the explosion inhales once, deeply, then blows out fury. Trees leap into the sky. The elements combine. She pivots within the meld, brought up into the nucleus of a white dream.

And then she is struggling to sit up, her limbs not wanting to appreciate her brain's flickering message, not willing to recover. She cannot even reach for her face, which is gone. She remembers at last that there will be no water rushing in a tidal wave over her, no lashing cataract, breaking loose and washing down the valley, destroying rivers in its wake. The uterus of liquid does not yet exist. But, even so, she feels it coming over her, a great pressure, a sea of red darkness, swallowing air.

❧

The navvy does not hear the explosion but he feels its tremors, travelling through the wooden bunk-bed and into his body. He wakes from the periphery of sleep. He is aware of the direction of the seismic event, without having to see the bursting light over the tops of the spruce trees. History has picked up its pace and is speeding past him. The windowless cabin is unnaturally dark, a thick liquid black that offends the eyes, drips inside, makes a man dizzy and nauseous. But he has become accustomed to it, as the other men have also, they are able to move about inside the black hut even with this disability, until the door is opened, a column of unforgiving,

238

morning light blinds them, makes them double over and cover their aching faces. The hurricane lamp lies under the last bunk on the wall, for emergencies only, its oil too expensive to buy in the shanty village for everyday use. Other than a lasting affection for the local jerries, wherever money is concerned they have adjusted the capabilities of their bodies to avoid letting go of what little wages they have.

He hears the heavy breathing of the other men in the bunks below him. No one else has been woken. Their exhaling is in unison, with the occasional bark of a man as air catches in his throat, tongue on the roof of mouth. Their heads are like lead against a crooked arm, a bundled shirt. It is more like fine death than sleep. In their pure exhaustion, they possess no dreams, these men for whom only dreams might bring pleasure and release from the daily drudgery. They mention their own names so rarely to others that they are never called to in slumber, as if having forgotten an identity, the subconscious wary of vanity. But this man in particular is a light sleeper, has slept under trees and the rose bushes of lawns with his senses tuned to the slightest sound or shuffle along the earth, the rolling of automobile headlamps across his borrowed patch. He is aware of the movements of land and water around him, the slow-rolling obelisk of time. He knows it is early, and that something near by has been destroyed. That history for a few uncharacteristic moments tore through the valley.

He lowers himself down from the bed, hanging in midair for a second, then his bare feet, coming softly on to the carpetless boards of the floor, are as exacting as the ballet. He reaches back for his trousers, his boots, hooked to the bunk, but will not dress inside, where the lifted buckle of a belt might wake the sleepers, give the false impression that the day's work is at hand. It is concern born of complete empathy, paternal almost. Then he hangs the boots back up again. He will not wear them until it is necessary for work. The greatest pleasure for the men away from the dam site is the absence of restrictive leather and choked laces against the roof of a foot. They walk like children, barefoot in the grass, to the canteen.

As he moves, his gestures are perfectly mapped in the blind room. Seven steps to the cabin wall. The turning handle of the cabin door. A small finger muffling the latch as it sits back down.

Outside, new air floods him. The sky clearing its throat a long way away. And at the back of it are the last echoes of the tremors he felt at the edge of his sleep. He does not question their reality, he could not ever have dreamed such nebulous sound. He leans on the hewn wood of the hut, urinates, and then pulls on the moleskins. He lifts a lantern from under the lip of the hut and lights it, moving like a honey badger in the darkness, his muscles dense and stocky. On his shoulder a tattoo ignites, indigo blue. Old enough, weathered enough, that it is beginning to spread through the skin, letting out colour past its own borders. The shoulder lifts ink as it pushes up the lantern. In this opaque, oily glow, the light from the moon might be wasted, but still it drifts from behind the full clouds. Enough for the man to see the outlines in the distance, trees, mountains, the motionless road. He cocks a head, as if to gather more sound, and turns into the woods, pine needles bristling under the soles of his feet. Free of the line of men he moves fast, swinging between the columns of fragrant pine and spruce. The path almost doubles back at one point where the wood pinches in. He cuts through the twist of fairytale branches to join it ahead. Past the split tree three-quarters of the way in, where a man has tucked a small bottle of Rot under the bark for his workmate to collect as he passes. Such narcotics and poteens are illegal in the encampment, and cannot be risked passing within the huts. Sky up ahead. The trees fall away.

The halo of light from the lantern finds the body before the man does, at the edge of the wood, next to the dam site. There is bitter smoke. A fire has been left to die, streaking into the earth as the blast pushed past. Dry grass has been scorched.

In the yellow light over her she is a terrible mess of flesh and bone. Around her there is also prolific destruction. The smoking, ragged-black wall of the outer dam. Burnt grass. The trees have been unearthed, blasted full of rock. And against an untouched piece of wall is one impossibly lit candle, to the right of the yawning hole. The explosion, blanketed and dampened by the thick woods, flung back on itself, has brought down most of the smaller buildings on the site, and upended the boards set over the mud. His eye plots the incident.

He looks into the pool of light again. It is as if the man has been privy to the worst kind of killing in his lifetime and has within him a source of power to look at her. Though his eyes remain quick, a brevity of assessment. There is still beauty to her, the shapes she has made. The dress is purple with blood. She has no face. Though blue-blonde hair has disguised the damage to one side, masking it. The arms scarcely belong to the rest of her. Fuse wire has become part of her stomach, snaring into her ribcage. She is a broken marionette. Eight feet away from her a broken detonator lies on its side. Ticking bubbles of liquid leave her chest, but it is simply the spirit-levelling of fluids in her body. She is dead.

He bends down and places her boneless arms over her body, gathers her up, lifting with extreme care. Through the woods he carries her, the two joined like an awful and subverted walking pietà. As they reach the cluster of prefabricated houses and huts he sets her down into the grass, careful to gather the flags flying from her body and bring her together as best he can. With difficulty, the dawn is coming, above the forest, inhibited by rain clouds.

The navvy walks to the large building at the end of the row of huts and opens the door. He ghosts through the house, past the milky kitchen, along the living-room corridor to the back of the dwelling, where there is soft breathing, searching until he finds the master bedroom.

∾

Gregory Barber turns in sleep, for a last minute contented, then gradually he senses a presence near by, outside the realm of warm slumber, and he wakes under the heavy stare. His vision struggles with the absence of background light. Pupils spill outwards, pour back in. A figure emerges. At the foot of his bed is a gargoyle, a leering monster. The eyes of the intruder are white in the dimness, luminous. A frame of skull. Throwing off sleep he starts back against the headboard. The mattress creaks under his legs. Vision restores itself after unconsciousness. The ghoul is a man, a sub-human, no, one of the crew, a navvy, he can tell by the swell of the shadow, its stance, the unblinking, lurid eyes. The naked upper body, primitive, its gleaming skin.

At once the foreman is certain of his death, his fears and suspicions confirmed about this strange breed of labourer. Since their arrival at the work site he has never been sure of their capabilities, the scope of their dark souls. Now the diffuse foreboding becomes an accurate arrowhead of criminal motive. It hits him it the middle gut and his spleen haemorrhages fear. Beneath the covers he reaches for the body of his wife. She is warm, living. He turns his face to her. Her mouth is open, sucking air, her hair tied in rag-curlers under the headscarf. She will witness his death first then, his body cut open by the navvy, for it will be a deep and unerring murder, or perhaps a precisely timed swinging fist, bludgeoning his head to the beat of that cold internal song which moves them all.

He emits a startled cry in the darkness, his own imagination now governing his panic. And this is what Gregory Barber reduces himself to: pure, inebriated fear. There are no quick thoughts of bribery for life, reason leaves him and instincts of survival ebb away. Panic flicks at his temples.

The silent worker at the foot of the bed leans in. He gestures with his thick neck for the man to follow him, a jerk over one shoulder, and he disappears, white eyes suddenly leaving space. Gregory Barber is delirious with relief. His bowels spasm as if he needs to void himself urgently. He collects a dressing gown and slippers, careful not to wake his wife as he leaves the room, shaking.

Outside the house, Barber can see the back of the silent man moving away, down the path in front of the row of huts. He catches up with him, careful to hang back a little. In the premature light he can see blood on the bare foot lifting in front of him. Under the man's arms, on his naked flanks, dark smears are also visible. Murder might not then be out of the question. He says nothing, marginal fear returning, but continues after the navvy. At the patch of grass at the end of the village the man leading stops and moves aside. An animal carcass is curled on the ground. The navvy has killed a stray lynx, or a rabid dog. The foreman leans in to make sure the creature is dead. He is about to kick at the underbelly but the shape of a girl emerges.

– Holy mother, no . . . no . . . Oh, sweet Jesus.

The foreman clutches at lurid air. He leans away, vomits thickly. He heaves in oxygen, waits until the rising bile subsides. Then, spitting the taste away, composing himself, he searches the ground for the bloody feet and a way to restore manliness, to shrug off his embarrassment. They are gone. Barber looks up and around, but the navvy has disappeared.

∾

Unknown to Gregory Barber, the man had gone back to the dam site, moving steadily through the trees, to gather evidence. He paused at the cabin hut to gather his boots, a shirt, a few belongings, and as silently as he last exited he closed the door on the sleepers. In ten minutes he reached the dam site again. He took his broad handkerchief and spread it on the ground before collecting pieces of sodden dress, a candle, the ruptured detonation device. These he placed on the handkerchief and wrapped the corners up tight, a precise, four-pointed knot to secure her witchcraft leavings. He picked up the girl's leather satchel, slung it over his back, under his shirt where it would not be seen. Then the navvy took to the Naddle forest above the concrete byway. Within an hour he had reached the Shap road, and three miles outside the village itself he paused along the quiet wayside.

At a bend in the road was an ancient-looking oak. It had two heavy branches which thrust out from the trunk horizontally before thinning and growing upwards. A three-pronged tree that sat like a buried wooden fork at the bend in the road. The man dug a hole between its earth-receding roots and buried the bundle of objects and the satchel, placing moss over the shifted sods of earth. As if the ground had never been opened or disturbed at all. Then he continued on through the village, an ugly beautiful man whose face had been damaged by years in the sun and whom history had torn through for a few brief moments. In half a day he would be in Langwathby, another two and he would be gone from the county, crossing the border into Scotland, where law and language blur and at some point separate as different smoky elements under the same crown. Nothing remained in the shanty village to suggest that he was ever there, except for a deck of old cards and the impression of his head in the slim pillow of the bunk. His bloody feet that Gregory Barber swore once existed.

III:II

Word of the dead girl spread quickly through the village of Burnbanks. The men came out of the huts at five o'clock expecting breakfast from the canteen, the usual routine. But the mechanisms of the village had ground to a halt. The two cooks had deserted, leaving congealing vats of oatmeal, unsteeped tea, and gibbering about murder and curses, encouraged on by each other's hysteria. The men gathered around the body on the grass. Gregory Barber sat next to the girl, smoking cigarettes, unable to suggest order, unable to leave it to anyone else. The taste of sickness would not leave under the hard cut of tobacco on his tongue. Unwillingly, he had taken charge of the corpse. His eyes skipped to and from her form, constantly pulled back as if he was not able to avoid the terrible sight. Greenish sweat gathered on his brow. His screaming wife had been sent to the infirmary to telephone for the Shap doctor and the Bampton policeman, though there was little hope that either could restore what had been brutally ripped from the girl. It was not known to her then, but Mrs Barber was the first person in the village to use the national emergency number which had come into operation only several weeks before, although, had she been so informed, her screams would not have ceased. The men goggled at the bloody mass, smaller than a human should be, they removed work caps, and searched for a framework of appropriate action, or inaction.

After the initial shock they began to murmur, curious and stepping neatly into the role of gossiping onlookers. Who was she? Who was the dead girl in the grass? What had killed her? Coming round to the babble of voices, Barber stood shakily, began to interrogate the workers. He was met with a wall of ignorance. Nobody could answer his questions. Soon he became frantic, holding their collars with clenched hands.

– Where is that man? The man who found her. Have you seen him, one of yours? Who is she? Who was fucking her? Who is responsible for her?

A shaken head. Men avoiding Barber's hysterical touch, his violent eyes. Descriptions of the navvy were useless. Tall, graceful, dark. Eerie blue eyes. Bloody feet like a man who has traversed a battlefield after the slaughter. Barber could not offer them more than a mirror in which they saw themselves. But his only link to the dead girl had slipped out, into the grasping hands of the onlookers, and theories began to multiply, solidify. So at that point the workers began grinding the rumours which would sit in the valley like cats in the grass for years to come, similar, and breeding. She had been killed by a navvy, her partner, who had disappeared, abandoning her to the injuries. Or a rape and murder, random, without personal vendetta, without previous carnal involvement. At the back of the crowd, several men moved off like quiet stags.

A search party returned from the dam site with word of the damage, seemingly a large explosion of some kind. The destruction was extensive, but only on the superficial outer wall and the work area itself. There was no vital structural damage. The massive dam was internally secure. But there was no sighting of the man in question either, the man with the answers, perhaps, to the mystery of her death. Quickly, Barber ran to the site. Nothing but the wreckage and a small patch of blood being lost into the ground gave any indication of a crime. There was no equipment, no clues. He returned to find that the policeman had arrived, and there followed a short, painful dialogue between the men.

– Who is the dead girl in the grass, sir?

– I'm not sure, it's hard to say. Perhaps one of the farmers' daughters. No, no. I don't know.

– You found the body. Has it been moved or otherwise tampered with?

– Yes. No, I didn't find her. A man carried her here, I think.

– What man?

– I don't know. He's . . . vanished. One of the workers here.

– Vanished, sir?

Barber, fearing arrest, broke into a constant, suspicious sweat. He was conscious that his position was riddled with damning interpretations. The Bampton policeman called for reinforcements from Penrith. By eight o'clock the doctor had arrived. Uselessly pronouncing the young woman dead, he gave an estimated time of death and covered her over with a coarse blanket. Immediately it began to soak against her face and body, as if she was weeping beneath it, weeping so hard that her reddish tears were streaming through the wool. The doctor placed another blanket over her. Still she cried blood. The sight haunted the workers, marched widely through the sub-region of their minds. It was supernatural, they told each other. She was possessed by a spirit, her blood was still living, still being made in her body. It was necromancy, they said, black art. And the rumours became seamed with sorcery. Thunder broke the sky, added to the tension, to the mood of the crowd.

Nobody would go to work that day. It was the first halted work day mid-week since Christmas. They lingered and were lined up for individual interview, four hundred men with nothing to say, no information to give. Barber's hands were shaking, by now he was poisoned by nicotine. He sat, stood, twitching around the body. He wanted desperately to leave it in the grass, to get far away. He wanted to bring in the dogs to consume the remains, pour petrol over it and flick in a match. Again the police questioned him, this time a chief inspector from the town. Again he sweated and clutched at half-clues left by the navvy, and the bombing of the dam. He was edgy and quick to anger, paranoid in his role as secondary overseer to the tragedy.

– How did it happen?

– An explosion by the dam, I think. I wasn't there. Fuck's sake . . .

– Has it breached?

– No. We're not flooded, are we? I'm sorry. It's just distressing. The reservoir isn't viable yet. All this talk of her bleeding is . . . well it's thrown me.

– Do you suspect sabotage? Have any devices been found?

– No. She must have been there . . . by accident, I suppose. Oh, God. Just a girl. Has her family been found yet? Do you want to move her, only I can't stand the sight you see. I can't . . .

Barber brought prayer-shaped hands to his mouth and swallowed. The chief inspector narrowed eyes at him, turned a page in his notebook.

– And the man you say brought her here, can you give a description of him? Would he have wanted to sabotage the building? Has he a grudge? Was there some kind of political agenda here? Are any of the men union members?

Barber shrugged. The contusions in the sky finally issued water. Rain pattered over the dirt and the grass, pinged off the drains on the hut roofs. The workers were herded into the canteen and worship room to continue being interviewed. Gingerly, the body was carried inside and laid out under the stained blankets. Gregory Barber remained out in the dampness, his cigarette spotted with drips of water, the orange tip singeing in the rain.

∾

Samuel Lightburn had been awake since early that morning, since the first rumbles of thunder along Helton Fell as the weather moved over from Ullswater, east across the region. He had been working since six. Three of his sheep were missing, a ewe and two of her lambs, they were not fully hefted yet, he was trying to introduce them to the scar, but for now they could not be relied on for faithfulness to a piece of moorland. This was only the third night they had been left out on the fell instead of brought back down to the farm sheds. He had taken his cart and driven down to the Bampton commons, where livestock usually wandered off to, in search of the animals with his dog. He stopped the cart intermittently and whistled for Chase to run up and check sections of the lower moors. At the stone weir over the stream she began barking excitedly, and Samuel followed her ruckus. By now it was raining. A blue, surrounding rain that seemed as if it would go on and on without stopping. A pure Westmorland rain, which would stop, effortlessly, gently, as if it had intended to all along.

The ewe had drowned in a deep pool next to the concrete structure. It lay afloat against the banks of the weir, tipped on its side. The lambs were nowhere to be seen. There was an iron ladder leading down into the pool. Samuel climbed down it to the water and pulled the bloated creature over to him with a boot. He stepped down further into the cold liquid, up to his thigh, fastened a rope twice around its belly. Then he climbed back out and began to haul it upwards, bracing his feet against the rim of the concrete pool. The sheep was weighted down with water and it took much of his strength to haul it out. Hand over hand he drew it up. When it was positioned at the lip he reached over and yanked the ewe to him. Holding it by the rope, he threw the sodden body on to the back of his cart.

Samuel was driving back along the rutted moor path when he noticed company on the rough grass. A group of men was walking towards him up the fell. He had never seen them before, except for one man. With them was Ian Marshall, another farmer from the Bampton village. As they drew close to the cart, Ian held up his hand and Samuel pulled back on the reins to stop the horse. The man approached him.

– Bin an accident, Sam. A bad un.

– Oh, aye.

– Up at dam. Fellas want yer t' go identify body, Sam, in ces' it's a local lassie. Me an' all. They say summet about an explosion at the works.

– Git up then, lads.

The four men climbed into the cart, Ian at the front, and Samuel flicked the reins. Chase ran alongside the cart and leapt up into the back. All five men remained quiet for a time, braced against the rain, but Samuel's stomach was burning. He was suddenly thinking of his family. Of his wife, with her tightly bound core, her uncompromising love, and of Isaac, with his briny skin that always looked damp, and his sudden maturity. He was thinking of his sick and grieving daughter, sleepless in her bed, or sleeping by the river. How her collar-bones had deep shadows, and in them hung the carcasses of animals in the savannah. He was thinking how much her hair had grown back since the winter of Jack Liggett's death, and that he would buy her some lily soap from Penrith the next visit he made to town. Just as he used to. And her hair would smell of it when he bent and kissed her.

– Lassie, y'say, eh? Owt else, Ian? Owt else known of her?

– Not a drop Sam. Not a drop.

∽

When they reached the Burnbanks settlement Samuel stopped the cart next to the crowd of men and jumped down. The rain was letting up again and the workers, with nothing to do, had emerged from the shelter inside. The site of the dam was still under inspection and work could not resume anyway, but the labourers had been asked not to leave Burnbanks village. Not until some kind of accident report had been pieced together.

Chase wove a path through the legs of the workers standing outside the infirmary doors, as if following a secret scent trail. She began to whine. Samuel and Ian Marshall followed and the crowd parted to let them pass. Multiple pairs of eyes slithered over the two men but the farmers did not meet any one gaze. Their faces were the single masks which contained many expressions at once, weathered one over the other, unreadable. As was common of men throughout the region. The doors swung closed as the men passed through. The crowd waited silently outside, eager for any indication that the body might be recognized, and given a name. That the girl who cried blood would be identified, and, with her, her family.

Inside, Samuel moved to the covered form. He moved without hesitation, knowing that he had little choice. He bent and pulled off the blankets and witnessed the body, emotionless, as he had been with the dead sheep not two hours previously. A ruined girl lay beneath. She had fronds of green grass caught on her red skin, from lying on the field outside. Ian Marshall hung back, waiting for a nod, or a shaken head. Neither came. Nothing came.

Then Samuel bent and wrapped the blanket around the girl. He lifted the pelt of his dead daughter into his arms and he walked out through the doors of the infirmary with her, his face an expressionless, expression-filled mask as he passed through the swarming assembly of men. Under his feet trickling rivers of water ran, altering direction around simple stones and around the heels of his boots. Samuel walked like a man towards certain death, when nothing can be achieved except that final trip to the firing-squad wall, to the gallows, to the gates. At his cart he set down the body, next to the drowned, sodden sheep. Still enough free blood in her body to mark the wooden surface. And the river water and the blood mixed.

Gregory Barber had followed the farmer through the crowd. He strode forward, shouldering past the men, angry that, after his dutiful watch over the girl for hours, this farmer would steward her so wrongly, so mercilessly. His protestation was vicious, hissed out under his breath.

– Not next to this animal, man, it isn't right or respectful! She needs proper transport, her family . . .

But the farmer turned to him, and he opened his face a little. Just enough for Gregory Barber to see inside, to see the howling eyes and the saliva cobwebbing in the corners of his ragged, open mouth. And the kept stone at the back of his face was breaking. It was the face of mortal love, of a father's worst imagining made real. There was more horror in it than there had been in the destroyed body of the girl. He saw inside the face just long enough for him to wish he had never seen, and to know that he would never lose sight of it from his memory, that it would visit his own dreams nightly, from that moment on.

III:III

In secure, rural places, small villages and insular hamlets, where grand events and theatrical schemes rarely take place, enormous human episodes, when they finally do rip apart the fabric of normal life, sometimes come away lacking clarity. Where you would imagine there should be absolute and utter adherence to the facts of the incident, that uncommon thing which has taken place, because nothing much else goes on in the sticks and this sits up from that nothing, the opposite will occur. Instead, a peculiar, quiet abstinence comes over the local storytellers, and the truth will seldom out, can never be agreed upon if people are pressed on it. Or they veer far away from the event with their tales, like children will elaborate and invent when caught doing something they feel bad about. So, the borders between fact and myth have a tendency to blur in these regions. History fogs, or becomes loose and watery. Bizarre mythologies arise. Half-lives. Half-truths. Events are built up or deconstructed. Leaps of faith are made, often for the strangest of sakes. The past becomes indistinct and subplots continue, subversions. It is not clear why this should be so.

The explosion at the Haweswater dam in 1937 was never fully explained. It remains largely unrecorded in the history of the reservoir. The little museum in the pumping station at Burnbanks makes no mention of it, except for a short police report, which barely describes the one fatality of the accident, and an engineer's report stating that the damage to the dam took two months to repair. The two offer no collusion. They are separate branches on a wide tree. Nor was the role of Janet Lightburn ever understood within the events. Locals speculated in the coming months and years. Had she been involved at all? Had hers been an unfortunate but accidental presence there that night? Had insanity sent her wandering randomly in the darkness? And what of the navvy, who must surely have been a bad sort, an uncaught, faceless criminal? Was the attempt on Haweswater his failed Jericho? Did he go on to other black deeds across the region? The slaughter of innocents, high sabotage, eerie disappearances. The girl strangled in Keswick eight months later, the Greystoke robberies. Local unsolved crimes were endowed with his reputation, and it was even suspected for a time that he was the Croglin Vampire.

The notion of a kind of loose and accidental tragedy was spread over the end of Janet's life. She passed swiftly into folklore. But for reasons no one could comprehend, and she was moved inside other tales, old wives' gossip, whispers of witchcraft and haunting. Politics and love and that odd union of two opposites seemed all but forgotten. It became irrelevant. People pecked at her corpse like a flock of marauding crows, pulling at the flesh to feed to their bits of stories. Of her mindset to wreak actual and deliberate damage, to commit an act considered heinous and abhorrent in its day and in an era of such moderation, perhaps no one can be sure. But for Ella Lightburn's convictions, perhaps no one ever will be. Nor can anyone know for sure the details of her troubled affair with Jack Liggett. On this, Ella was always far more guarded, would entertain no questioning, even at the end of her life. Miriam Lightburn, the daughter of Jack and Janet, had to do without their united presence, corporeal or otherwise, as she grew. When her grandmother was dying, and history was finally handed to her, amorphous and streaming from her hand which tried to keep it, only then did she begin to dream and imagine, and speculate about the sort of romance that shakes up history and devastates valleys. People used to say of Ella that she was a fierce woman, cut out from granite by the north wind itself. And so she was. Her soul had a weightiness to it and she was steadfast. And that lent itself to making her difficult, immovable. Too subjective, perhaps. But even so, the accuracy of her account as she told it does not matter, and the blank sections might not be so empty. There was something else passed along the edges of it to Miriam. Later she realized that her grandmother's story about belonging to the land was also a story about longing for those who have lived upon it.

There is a photograph of Janet in the Haweswater museum. A photograph taken without her consent or knowledge, it seems. In it, she is sitting on a wall by Whelter Farm Cottage with her young brother. Isaac is standing in front, holding one of her thin knees. She has on breeches which are grey in the photograph. Her arms are defined, masculine, thin like her legs, but her body and shoulders are thicker, powerful. Her brother has on a boy's tweed jacket, and for once his white hair is dry. There are deep shadows under the marble angles of Janet's face and a sharp groove splits her forehead in two. She is not beautiful. And yet there is something else to her, even reproduced, spilled into the pores of the old photograph. Energy. As if there is something within that by all means belongs out. It appears as if she is scowling at her brother, as if a deep anger is splitting her head in half. She might be thought querulous for this expression, with a mangling personality, perhaps. But what can a static picture reveal? And how does the moment's light influence a face that is poured permanently on to paper? It is northern, interfered-with light that often has to make its way down through the saturated sky, after all.

The identity of the photographer remains a mystery. A tourist? A reporter from the *Cumberland and Westmorland Herald*? Her father did not own a camera until his seventieth birthday, by which point she had been dead many years. And Samuel only took pictures of birds in his garden. Now the photograph of Janet forms part of a display in the informal museum in the pumping station that stands not far away from the high, smooth wall of the dam itself. There are pictures of the navvies also, working on the half-built embankment as it flexes out of the ground like a taut bicep, or walking in sombre lines like a wake, back to their draughty huts. Their eerie ballet of work. The boys of the 42nd East Lancashire Division are there also, chipper, grinning, immortalized by the lens. Not a one of them surviving the Second World War. And there are pictures of Jack Liggett, standing against his long car with that slight smile of sagacity bridled on his face. It is early on in his involvement with Mardale. He is still very much a product of the city, before the land up here, steeped too full of itself and capable of radical influence, pulled at his blood, and he let go. He was not the first man to come under its spell. And won't be the last. Though for him the outcome was fatal, for all the liberation. The camera does him many favours. He is a handsome man, in a well-cut suit. The best of the post-First World War generation, some might say. Others might consider this not so, but that he turned out all right in the end. His hair is black, and the dark eyes, they are cast somewhere in the distance. To the high buildings by the Rigg or the crags under Kidstey Pike.

∾

For all the determination of Jack Liggett's successor, the Haweswater project could not be completed within the decade. External factors of hugely mitigating proportions interrupted that and most other private industrial endeavours, and the country switched its attention to the next monumental catastrophe of the century. During the Second World War building on the dam ceased, just as many other blueprints and architectural plans were locked in safes or left on office drawing boards. So Thomas Wright had to wait, impatient and aggrieved, for the moment when he could shrug off his inherited millstones. It was only after the country began to reshape itself in the next two decades that the aqueduct plans were completed, the draw-off tower came into operation, and soon after water found its gurgling way down to the grimy city of Manchester, to be held in clean glasses, boiled in aluminium pans. Pipes with a diameter the height of a six-foot man were sunk into the hillsides to catch the flow of water from the largest of the fell becks, and were led down to the foot of the reservoir where they are, to this day, churning the water white into the still, reflected sky. A hundred chisel marks were left in the upper concrete walls of the dam as the illegible, artless signatures of a hundred men who had toiled in all weathers and had slowly bolted together the skeleton and then walled in the anatomy of a huge stone dream. The river channel was arrested and backed up. The valley was sealed. And then the water began to rise, unstoppable, a flood unlike any other. Mardale slowly drowned, and Jack's green cup filled.

The last villager left not long after this, with his cart of hay taken from the overgrowing fields of his old abandoned farm. A book was left in a locked tool box in the cellar, which spoke of the weight of empty hands, and which would not be found until the lake dried up in the strong grip of the drought of 1979. By then the blue-blonde hair between the pages was dust, and the heart that had grown other hearts inside it, as if one was not sufficient vessel for a man's grief, had stopped. When he left the devastated valley with his heavy chest, the new lake was rising. As Samuel drove through the village, the sound of water spilling through the wheel-spokes of his cart was like a soft-washing hum. His horse cut through the swirling lake, and his sheepdog swam along next to the cart, fighting the new current.

About that time, in the valleys of Westmorland, strange fables and legends began to be told.

෴

The story of Janet Tree has an uncertain origin. For almost a century the myth of the witch which inhabits the old oak tree at the edge of the Shap road has troubled and intrigued inhabitants of the valley. It is the only oak tree on that road, and though it is so old that the branches sag almost to the ground, obese with bark, the local council has never reinforced it, or cut it down. You have only to ask around and dozens of sightings come to light.

Marion Benning, who runs the petrol station in the village of Bampton, swears that she sees her every time she drives that road, reflected in the rear-view mirror, sitting in the back seat of her car, knitting. She is a young, blue witch. Bonny, in a way. Her face is that of a cat's. For others she is old and gnarled, a hag, wearing scarlet lipstick, her hair a bright, wild white and her eyes bloodshot from liquor. She is bad-behaving, always drunk, some say, hanging from the oak's branches, exposing herself to all and sundry, and she is surrounded by animals that are not found in this country. Leopards asleep in the uppermost reaches of the tree. Impala. Alligators in the bark. She is unlike any other Westmorland ghost, has something exotic to her. Others agree that drink plays a part in the sightings, though not on the part of Janet Tree.

It is also uncertain what kind of luck Janet Tree brings. Some swear ill, having seen her only hours before they receive news of an awful event. Some even regard her as the death-bringer herself, coming like a screaming banshee from the trunk of the tree and chasing alongside their cars, clawing at the window, leaving trails of blood on the glass. She is often said to bleed. From the eyes, the mouth. Her belly. Day or night, she startles the driver of the car so badly that he swerves along the road into a stone wall, into the path of another vehicle, into a hiker on the verge. And it's knock-for-knock in these treacherous parts, where blame is seldom attributed to an individual motorist, to one protagonist alone. So who can prove her?

Janet is blamed for accidents throughout the valley, but especially on the twisting Shap road. The man from the wrecked car speaks of newly serviced brakes that suddenly fail. But it does not help that, by the oak, there is a nasty curve in the road which tourists tend always to assume their cars will manage at fifty miles per hour, so deadly a curve that it has been the scene of numerous accidents, many near-misses, several fatalities. Warning signs have been put up in the road to advise people of the sharp corner, but visitors who have been on their way to or from Haweswater tell of having overshot the corner, seeing no such sign, or that a woman was standing in front of it obscuring it from view. A woman who disappeared when the driver of the car walked back around the curve in need of an eyewitness. Nor does it help that the road is usually slippery, wet from intermittent showers, from the rain that gathers energy in the north and west and unleashes itself over the mountains on the roof of England. Or helpful it is not that the view is beautiful from this road, there is a distracting absence of urban hysteria and concrete, the light over the waterlogged fields, the trees, yellow, red, red and shining, a burnt copper sunset, and if you glance to the left you can just make out the Haweswater dam in the distance.

The less irrational, less suggestive, believe that Janet Tree means no harm. That she has resided tragically in the bark since her untimely death, the details of which have long been forgotten by most, and are only half-remembered by a dwindling few. Marion is content to share her car with Janet Tree, her hands tensing on the steering wheel when she appears, but never being pulled by a mysterious force too sharply one way or the other. Though she does not like it when Janet appears, let that be made clear. No. She does not like it one bit.

How long the tree has been haunted by the witch, nobody is willing to guess. But older villagers in Bampton will not even speak of her, as if the name itself is full of potency, and dangerous. As if in their living memory they recall a time when the tree was just a tree and Janet was just a girl. Their faces when you ask are slightly sad, their eyes sitting back a long way from you, behind kept stone.

259

– Epilogue –

The Haweswater dam is salmon orange on the side next to the water and lichen-mottled grey on the other side, where the sun is mostly absent and the trees are thick, sheltering. It stretches a third of a mile across a slim artery in the fat, wet heart of what is now the united county of Cumbria, what was once one of the last corners of old Westmorland. Its walls are metres thick at the bottom, and slope inwards as they proceed upwards. It is a bizarrely elongated, Egyptian-looking triangle, a structure well out of place in its surroundings, but of no wonder to the modern generation inhabiting the area, who are used to it. They have always lived with it and do not appreciate that in its day it was a unique blueprint, a master-piece of modern design. Visionary.

Usually the lake is full. This is, after all, an old divining dis-trict, with ample water supplies. It takes care of the thirsty fur-ther south. In the centre of the dam, between the two buttresses, is a lowered piece of wall. When the reservoir laps over the top of this line, full to its meniscus brim with rainwater and debris, a man from the pumping station, five hundred metres away in the shadow of the dam wall, will open the sluice gates. There are two pipes that travel through the bottom of the dam, belling out into the lake at one end, and at the other spilling into a small pool. This is the source of a small river leading as a tributary to the main river of the next valley, through Bampton and Knipe and Askham. If the pipes are not running water through them from the full reservoir, they lie empty and dripping, like two giant dinosaur nostrils, holding back the weight of the lake with a series of man-made valves.

As the sluice gates open, a miniature tidal wave sweeps up the river of the next valley and threatens its banks with sheer vertical volume. When this happens Bamptonians will watch patiently out of the window for a recession in the water and then go out to collect driftwood left on the broken banks of the river as a residue from the purged lake. They collect wood like squirrels collects nuts. Storing it for winter. Old women go out sticking with baskets and aprons and young men drive farm vehicles down to the water's edge and saw through logs and throw them into tractor trailers. They look forward to the autumn, when the sluice gates come back into frequent use. The newly collected rains are released then, gathering momentum as they come down the valley, shouldering past streams and sitting down heavily between villages. During the summer, green-brown algae collect and congeal on the surface of the river, around the banks. The smell is putrid, that stagnant odour of low water, of rotting reeds, and of bitter, toxic chemicals that have crept into the liquid from the sprayed fields. Locals look forward to the cleansing rain, to movement.

∾

Half-way through the century, before the sluice gates were ever used, two divers went down into the thick water to check the mechanism for blockage. Self-contained underwater breathing apparatus had improved substantially within the last decade, and the subaqueous world was no longer a domain reserved for the gilled, for the lucky who had not been born into the wrong world. It meant freedom for God's botched jobs.

Isaac Lightburn could at last spend long minutes underwater, as he had wanted to so desperately as a child.

By the time the dam was ready for operation, he had spent many hours cataloguing sea- and freshwater-life in the Scottish Marine Centre at St Andrews, and was an experienced diver, even at the age of twenty-two. From the valleys of Westmorland he had gone to the tall, old city of Edinburgh, not being the type to remain and farm the harsh fell land as his father had, and being yet another good mind put out by the local schools, and from the city he had moved up the coast to the broad beaches and lively rock pools, where there was work for biologist's assistants, if you didn't mind standing waist-deep in the freezing-cold currents of the North Sea.

Isaac was amazed at the variety of odd and gory life under the waves, sketching each find into his notebooks. Helping with dissections. He was a willing and eager assistant. He was also the guinea pig for many of the early dives, having a unique ability to hold his breath and recover from accidents and failures of equipment in the deep pools of the sea. In the salty water he wore a glass mask, teasing urchins from crevices in the rocks, pressurizing his body in accordance with the stresses imposed by the water.

He became a full-figured young man – like his father he had a broad back which would wear out coats a little at the shoulders. And similar to his father also was his quiet yet unabashed disposition. He would read passages of poetry to his colleagues at the marine centre in the evenings, relaxed, as if reading to himself, or to a familiar audience, walk out over the wet sands watching the lift of a fin on the horizon, the turn of a porpoise. He became a man who would see a phoenix of red fire struggling to get free from the throat of a dying gull. His eyes never did find more colour, remained quite disturbing, in fact, for their clear opacity, though his hair darkened from white to dirty blond. After his sister's death he seemed to grow up quickly, reaching a gentle, welcomed level of maturity. Growing into himself, his mother might have said. There was a shadow against one shoulder which never shifted or left him, though, one that could not be dispelled by friends or family. He wore it close, like material on unexposed skin. His grief was a strange one, of a kind that expanded over the years so that he came to live comfortably and in agreement with it. As if her death made more sense than her life. He did not shed tears for her, nor did he display any hostility towards the circumstances of her passing. In truth, under that shadow, he managed to preserve a luminous connection with his sister, so deep-rooted that it seemed untouchable, irrefutable, inextinguishable.

At times he would wake in the night believing that he had heard someone calling to him, the woman by his side stroking his hair to calm the panic in his voice. Had he heard the voice again, she would ask. But already he had stifled any emotion, was sleeping once more.

During the day he was at ease, swimming with a tank of air on his back, twenty-five to fifty feet beneath the fishing boats and surface flotsam, seeing a gull cutting white into the ocean to steal a fish, becoming fluid like the sea itself. On weekends he might venture inland, where the hills became more pronounced and there was freshwater which ran quickly through deep channels, tasted of minerals and relaxed ice and reminded him of the lake country.

It was common practice for the marine centre to accept freelance work to bolster its lagging funding. The divers there were skilled and worked in many of the country's lakes and off the coast, retrieving bodies and lost valuables, repairing vessels, or checking mechanisms, bridge structures. When Isaac heard of the request for divers at the Haweswater reservoir he insisted that he be selected for the task. He wanted to visit home, he said. Reacquaint himself with the crayfish and the minnows of the Lowther valleys. Perhaps catalogue the life of such an unusual body of water, which he believed would be home to rare fish. And his local knowledge would benefit the team. He could tell them where a shelf of land gave way to what was once air but would now be water. There was no question that he would not go. So he came back to the district a young man, had left it ten years after his sister's death a wise, introspective student. Though he had written, visits home had been few, Miriam's confirmation, his mother's sixtieth birthday, Christmas, now and again. He did not send word to his parents that he would be coming this time, he would surprise them after his work was complete at the dam, striding in to Staingarth farm with four trout strung in his hand. Or maybe five.

∽

The divers prepared their tanks, checked their instruments, the pressure gauges, and took a giant step from the small boat at the end of the reservoir into the water. Silt and mud had dissolved into the new lake and the water was murky, but they kept close as their weighted bodies sank, going down in stages, equalizing the pressure in their ears with every breath. Above, rain circled the water's surface, like a ceiling of glass eyes. They reached the valley floor ten minutes after leaving the surface, swam heavily across it to the murky wall. There were no pieces of wood at the base of the sluice pipes, nothing to get sucked into the vast mechanical intestine. Nothing but cloudy water, mud hanging like gas in the liquid and the underwater structure itself like a temple wall in Atlantis. So, they began an ascent.

Before they reached the surface, one of the divers took out his mouthpiece and it flared a stream of bubbles into the water. At fifty feet he removed his mask and tried to blink back the weight of the lake with his eyes, just as he had tried to see through the valley's water years before. As if he thought he might be able to see down the six miles of inky liquid to the drowned village that had once been his home. Or perhaps a voice had called to him, telling him to remember who he was, where he was, remember it with his heart of stone. He stripped away the apparatus. Unclipped the safety line.

Water pushed his eyes closed and snaked into his mouth and lungs. It relaxed its weight upon him as a cave might come crashing down on a thin, single beam trying to hold up its ceiling. The mighty reservoir breathed out into Isaac's chest, and overcame him.

There was that notorious, silent part to his drowning, no doubt. The body defeated by sleep. The spirit becoming dormant. And perhaps Ella felt it in her heart then at that moment, the tug of wings, a black bird, lifting itself again in her, though she thought her son was far away. There would be no comfort for her, she who had seen omens all her life, predicted her son's death in such a fashion. Not even the knowledge that in his drowning there was a beautiful state of peace which he reached, nothing like her imagined violent passing of him, would furnish her with any consolation. And for a moment in her life not even God would lay light hands on her shoulders, or help her up from the cottage floor as a generation of the family was lost.

The diver's partner saw no thumb jerking upwards in an airless sign language, and by the time he caught sight of Isaac the body was sinking slowly, twenty feet beneath him and limp. He went down and took hold of his friend. He took his own mouthpiece and placed it in the mouth of the sleeping diver. But Isaac did not taste the familiar texture of rubber on his tongue from his saviour's mouth plug. Nor did he taste the intimate flavour of the man's wife, which he had kept secretly in his mouth until then after their loving each other that morning. The rubber mouthpiece slipped from the cage of Isaac's mouth. And by the time the two reached the surface moments later, pulled up swiftly by the one remaining safety line, Isaac would never taste or see or breathe again. His body did not have the chance to bubble and fizz inside or send red needles through his skin from coming up too fast, as his friend's did. He was already dead. He was home.

Acknowledgements

I'd like to express gratitude to R. J. Cooke for allowing me access to his research on Mardale and the building of the Haweswater dam. Thanks also to the following people for help with general and local historical research: Pat Garside, Ben Walsh, Anthony and Elizabeth Hall, Helen and Peter Farrow, Chris Holme, Carl Walters, Adam Ferguson and many others from the Bampton area. Thanks also to EMR for dauntless optimism. And a special thank you to Lee Brackstone.

While inspired by the building of the Haweswater dam in the early part of the twentieth century, this story is fictional and is not intended to depict actual individuals, companies or situations, nor are the dates historically accurate relating to the original Haweswater project. None of the characters are representational of any persons living or dead.

P.S.

Insights,
Interviews
& More...

About the author

About the book

Read on

A Conversation with Sarah Hall

Courtesy of the author

Where were you born, Sarah?

I was born in a tiny little hamlet with a few farming settlements and cottages in Cumbria in the Northwest of England. We were near a small village with a couple of pubs about eight miles from a wee market town called Penrith. It's pretty close to the Scottish border. And very close to the Haweswater Reservoir.

Where were you raised?

I lived in this same place until I was eighteen and then went off to college. To give you a fuller picture, the area is very rural and remote, mountainous, wet, and beautiful.

What events from your childhood stand out?

What I think stand out from my childhood are the big natural occurrences—floods where the river threatened to come right up the garden and into the cottage, storms that took down old apple trees and ravaged the fells, and droughts that exposed the ruins of Mardale

Village underneath the reservoir one valley over from home. They stood out because I was keenly aware of the environment around me, as was everyone; in a way it was the most familiar and important thing. I seem to remember illness vividly too, not a lot of it because I was quite a healthy and active child, but I hated it when I was feeling poorly; it was a despicable interruption of life. I do remember being very sick inside the Haweswater dam. I have no doubt this led to a lasting sense of the monument being a colossal and dark and sinister thing. I came down with measles during a school outing and my temperature went up far enough for me to get a little delirious. At this point we were inside the structure itself. All around were metal walkways and the walls were dripping and all the vaults were echoing. I remember a terrible pressure in my head and a sense of terrible pressure on the dam walls from the water held in the valley.

What is your earliest memory of reading and being influenced by a book?

I think it must have been *The Story of Ferdinand* by Munro Leaf. I guess the illustrations (by Robert Lawson) have stayed with me as well as the words. For many young children the visual and the verbal coexist inseparably in memories of their first books. But those gorgeous, detailed, black-and-white line drawings of Ferdinand the bull really stuck with me. And it's such a simple, humbling, resonating tale. Pacifism is always triumphant, even if at first it does not seem to be so. I also like the idea of character behavior that goes against the expected. Other books that resonated for me at a young age were: *To Kill a Mockingbird* by Harper Lee; *The Handmaid's Tale* by Margaret Atwood; and *Z for Zachariah,* by Robert O' Brien. I liked Steinbeck too.

What do your parents do?

My dad works in a local paper mill, as he has for more than thirty years. My mum has retired, but used to teach English and sport; she also taught adults with severe learning difficulties.

Did having an English teacher for a mother encourage your literary tendencies? Did you ever feel the urge to rebel and throw yourself into physics or herpetology or something?

I have no doubt my mum's encouragement helped me to better enjoy literature. My dad has a love of books too; the cottage was, and is, full of reading material. I think parents watch for natural proclivities in their ▶

A Conversation with Sarah Hall *(continued)*

children and then try to steer them a little. So if I was destined for science they would have aided that impulse instead—I wasn't, of course; I seemed to be able to break every piece of equipment I came into contact with in the school biology lab, but that's another story. Politics was my other big interest earlier in life; I was an opinionated, aggrieved wee madam, and probably still am. It doesn't really count as rebellion though, does it?

What is the strangest experience you've ever had?

I was struck by lightning during my undergraduate years at Aberystwyth University in Wales. And I do mean literally, not literarily.

Wow. What did that feel like? Has that experience changed your life in any meaningful way?

Painful. Heart-stopping. It's kind of like the feeling you have in your stomach the second before a glass you've dropped smashes—that anticipatory internal explosion. Defibrillation, only magnified by a million. I was in no real danger—the current hit the building I was on and blew me off, so it wasn't a direct strike to my noggin or anything. I don't think it was life-altering, though it's taught me never to be on the roof of a building in a storm with my arm stuck out like a conductor. . . . I was nearly hit again in Washington State a few years ago. I was in an empty paddock and some bad weather rolled over. Lightning kept striking the dirt nearby as I ran inside. A church tower was also hit very close to where I was staying in Devon last summer. Maybe I should start worrying about this a bit more.

What kind of work have you done other than writing?

Oh dear, it's a bit of a mishmash. Jobs include: waitress; barmaid; fly-fishing mail-order packer (I was eternally sending out the wrong size lures and flies and having them returned by irate fishermen); receptionist and spectacle adjuster for an optometrist; sausage factory packer (a job which consisted of a twelve-hour shift in Wellington boots and overalls packing frozen meat, hauling boxes onto carts, and trying not to weep); creative writing tutor; bookseller; wine seller; and dog walker.

Were you already thinking about your second novel, The Electric
Michelangelo, *when you were writing* Haweswater? *Do you see
thematic connections between the two books?*

I began writing *Michelangelo* almost as soon as I finished editing
Haweswater, well before its UK release. This was partly because I figured
it was officially my new job to write, now that I was getting published. I
probably gave up the other work I was doing a bit prematurely, so there
was also a pretty strong financial imperative to sell another book. And
there was a slight sense of terror too   peripheral thoughts of what
now? what next? this is a precarious game and I'm in it—so I tried to
concentrate, stay calm, and forge straight ahead. If you're going to leap,
don't look down. At that point I was flying by the seat of my pants, didn't
have an agent, and didn't really have a clue—I just figured that so long as I
was writing away everything would be okay. Somehow. And I already had
the idea for a tattooing novel. For me there is a huge amount of comfort
in ideas, no matter how rudimentary or consigned to fulfillment in the
future they may be. It is truly amazing what can develop when you choose
to focus on a simple idea.

There are definite thematic connections between the first two novels.
Perhaps their having been written in close proximity has something to do
with it, though the settings and subject matter are very different and the
themes are vast, renewable, and multifaceted. They include: place and
identity; the decline of old Western industry; loss; tragic love; challenges
facing the human spirit; female resilience, strength, intellect, and capability.

Do you have any writerly quirks?

I write in the mornings and afternoons on a little white Mac. I'm really
not much of a night owl. I'm sure I do things that are bonkers while
working. But the peculiarity of quirks and compulsions is that they
eventually become normalized and, after a time, seem like ordinary
habitual behavior. At least they seem that way. It's perfectly reasonable to
count all the nails in the floorboards, spin round three times, and adorn
yourself with a feather boa before starting to write, isn't it? I've recently
developed a grim paranoia about the occasional demonic appearance of
the multicolored Mac spinning beach ball, which suspends all computer
operations upon arrival. I'm sure it's sentient and knows exactly when
optimum chaos and loss of work can be achieved. ▶

A Conversation with Sarah Hall *(continued)*

You've been highly praised for your precise and beautiful prose. Do you agonize over every sentence as you're composing or do you defer concerns about language until revision?

Why, thank you. Probably a bit of both really. I can't leave a sentence if it seems too clunky or dull. It has to achieve a basic level of literary success. Then again, if I'm after something good and it's not happening I may leave a blank, move ahead a little, but still be pondering. I scroll back and forth—kind of multitasking, I suppose. I don't scrutinize my work too heavily in the initial drafting process, as I think it would be prohibitively slow and disruptive. There's got to be a balance between big motion and small detail. I think writers have to forgive themselves for imperfection at the early stage. But a good eye is essential for editing, the process of looking at your own work and adjusting it, adding to it, or discarding it. And there has to be ongoing flexibility. Every time I polish something to what I think is its highest gleaming standard I quickly become aware that it could stand another buffing—mostly thanks to my editor!

Do you read fiction to inspire you as you write? If so, whom do you read in particular?

I don't use literature as a tool to enable or improve my own work, at least not consciously, though I'm sure there is a certain amount of subliminal fertilization if what I'm reading is very good. The artistic mind is such a complex, mulchy region, composed of such richly nourished soil. I know some writers read a lot or don't read at all when they are producing their own work. You can be subject to the dangers of overinfluence or the benefits and communion of language; writers may feel they must block out the work of others or give themselves license to connect with it. I'm a sporadic reader at best and have an odd relationship with books. I both revere and have trouble with them. Novels are such strongly contained, independent worlds. No matter how much I warm to them, enjoy them, and appreciate their creation, they always seem to be somehow other. I think writing is more about harvesting inspiration, tone, plot, and images from your own imagination than it is about snipping off buds from over the fence. Although who knows, maybe smelling someone else's roses makes you a better gardener (sorry, I'll stop with the nature analogies now). And I do believe that in order to sustain a large work (or any work) there has to be something compulsively and inherently personal going on—the most insistent voice, the ultimate growth, is your own. If I've actively gone looking for inspiration it's in mediums other than my own: music, poetry, and art. And of course in people.

What are some of your other passions and hobbies?

I love fell walking, and try to do it as much as possible in my home county of Cumbria. I'm a little bit afraid of heights though, which is odd for someone who enjoys trekking up mountains! I'm also a bit of an art lover, so I tend to visit galleries quite often. I think this interest in art tends to bleed over into my writing—it certainly did with *The Electric Michelangelo.* I have a couple of friends who are artists and my favorite thing is to go round to their studios and see what they are doing. The intriguing thing may be the strange materials found there: tubes of paint, cloths, easels—from these things amazing works are created; it all seems like alchemy. It's a very inspiring thing. I've also become interested in natural foraging. Last year was a fantastic year for sloes and blackberries in the UK, so I've been experimenting with baking (not my strength at all, unless grit in muffins is a good thing) and home brewing. At the moment there is a demijohn full of murky, purplish sloe gin sitting on the hearth waiting to be filtered. It looks worryingly potent. ❧

Land of Natural (and Supernatural) Wonders Sarah Hall on Her Beloved Cumbria

I THINK THE VALLEY where I was brought up in Cumbria is one of the most gorgeous and redolent places in the whole of England. It lies in the eastern part of the Lake District, an area remoter but more utilized than the rest of the national park with an ongoing tradition of hill farming and animal breeding. The district is wild, wet, and earthy. It is atmospheric; a place of sweeping rains and cloud-obscured mountains, where there is a sense of geological and liquid partnership. Everywhere there are rivers, lakes, and waterfalls running over the withers and under the massive bodies of the fells. The landscape is rugged, powerful, and firm, but includes compliant, movable elements.

The people of the area have always seemed to be somehow comprised of these similar yet bipolar atoms. There's a hardiness and a quality of endurance found in them—not surprising for those who live and work with the land, so close to the once-turbulent Scottish border. And yet they are earnest, companionable, and softhearted. They have a fondness for quietude. Often little is said on any subject, but those words that are spoken or sung or committed to ballads and poetry seem carefully chosen. There was never much talk on the matter of the lost Village of Mardale and the Haweswater Reservoir when I was growing up. If a great loss had at one time been felt it was carried deeply and

66 The district is wild, wet, and earthy. It is atmospheric; a place of sweeping rains and cloud-obscured mountains, where there is a sense of geological and liquid partnership. 99

silently. All I knew was that I lived close to a lake which was not truly a lake, with ruins sunk below its waves, and that was that. There was an absence of dramatic nostalgia. Perhaps because of that I never imagined that one day I would write a novel about my home territory, its people, and the story of what had occurred within living memory to our community.

I can't remember the moment I conceived of this project, and I can't recall much of the writing of it. It has always simply felt like something lifted out of me. I can say, though, that speaking on behalf of a proud, reserved, and self-sufficient people is risky. What right have I to do so? My hope is that *Haweswater* conveys the fondness I have for them and for the land of my upbringing, that it is written with local spirit and communion, and with humility. My strongest desire is that, rather than having simply produced a portrait of Cumbria's terrain (which has frequently been a romanticized subject for art over the years), something of these remarkable individuals has also been captured in this book.

It is an unquestionably lush region to draw upon for literary inspiration, as Wordsworth knew well. Perhaps not surprisingly in this evocative environment, a rich culture of folklore and myth has developed. There are legends, fables, ghosts, and superstitions tucked into all the rocky nooks and crannies and submerged beneath the networks of water. In my small patch there were haunted woods, haunted cottages, tragic and heroic figures, and mysterious specters. There was a subrealm of imagined dimensions and alternate histories to the land, which allowed for curious energies and fantastic and brutal events, and which was undoubtedly the ▶

> ❝ My strongest desire is that, rather than having simply produced only a portrait of Cumbria's terrain (which has frequently been the subject for art and has been romanticized over the years) something of these remarkable individuals has also been captured in this book. ❞

9

product of a very creative population. One of my first memories of school was our "story hour," that time of afternoon when we sat cross-legged on the library floor and the headmaster kept us enthralled with folktales about wraithlike ferrymen on the misty mere or ogres who had lost their toes in gardens not too far away.

But the most sinister and compelling local character in the supernatural inventory, at least for me when a child, was a woman known only as Janet Tree. Her origin was unknown; nobody was quite sure how her legend arose, whether she was perhaps a victim of a crime, a banshee, or just a witch. But she was frequently mentioned and frequently seen. Her objectives were neither obviously good nor bad. She was meddlesome and manipulative, a watcher, a guardian, and both protective and a harbinger of death. An old oak on one of the wending link roads between villages was her usual place of apparition. People would arrive back in the settlements pale and shaken; they would say they had caught sight of her in the rearview mirror of the car, swear she had appeared before them as they traveled, or whisper that she had suddenly joined them at their side. I used to drive the darkened road at 5:00 A.M. to get to work in a local factory, wondering if I would come across Janet Tree. It was an invariably unsettling journey. She was a shape-shifter: old, young, hideous, beautiful, bloody, lascivious. She was gentle and she was terrible. She had all the contradictory rudiments of the region.

And so I have taken the liberty of

> 66 The most sinister and compelling local character in the supernatural inventory, at least for me when a child, was a woman known only as Janet Tree. 99

borrowing her. She has become a character in the novel, a real girl, a ghost, and a motif of the area in which she still walks. Janet, the novel's central protagonist, is full of her own land—she stewards it with her father, conducts a turbulent love affair outdoors in secret, and enables her lover Jack to view the valley he has helped to condemn in a new light. Like the land itself, she is capable of both violence and tenderness. Her intuitive brother Isaac also has this proclivity; at one point in the narrative he describes a premonition of his fate: "The blood in his hands will tell him where he belongs, where it will be brightest. . . . His heart is a beating stone, that will carry him down to the depths."

Cumbria is an old, old county—not in name, but in essence. The towns, stone cottages, and tracks look today much as they have for hundreds of years. The sheep are still herded up mountains by shepherds; wild ponies graze by the rivers. The fells are saturated in summer and snowbound in winter. And water from our ample supply is piped to cities in the south. People still farm, despite the difficulties facing the industry. They still choose their words carefully and sing when they feel so inclined. The county was once part of the ancient province of Rheged, which included Wales, and was also once part of Scotland. It even used to have its own language, though only a few expressions are still remembered and spoken. If I am lucky, there is a Welsh word, *hiraeth,* that might be appropriately applied to these pages. It is defined as a longing or yearning ▶

> " Cumbria is an old, old county—not in name, but in essence. . . . The sheep are still herded up mountains by shepherds; wild ponies graze by the rivers. "

Land of Natural (and Supernatural) Wonders *(continued)*

for one's native territory. It is not patriotism. It is simply love.

Haweswater, perhaps not surprisingly, is my first novel. I thought the story in it was worth telling, even if the tongues that could have told it better never have. It's a story in equal measures about place and people. Above all else it is a salutation to my home. ◠

An Excerpt from *The Electric Michelangelo*
Finalist for the 2004 Man Booker Prize

Chapter One: "Bloodlights"

IF THE EYES COULD LIE, his troubles might all be over. If the eyes were not such well-behaving creatures, that spent their time trying their best to convey the world and all its gore to him, good portions of life might not be so abysmal. This very moment, for instance, as he stood by the hotel window with a bucket in his hands listening to Mrs Baxter coughing her lungs up, was about to deteriorate into something nasty, he just knew it, thanks to the eyes and all their petty, nit-picking honesty. The trick of course was to not look down. The trick was to concentrate and pretend to be observing the view or counting seagulls on the sill outside. If he kept his eyes away from what he was carrying they would not go about their indiscriminating business, he would be spared the indelicacy of truth, and he would not get that nauseous feeling, his hands would not turn cold and clammy and the back of his tongue would not begin to pitch and roll.

He looked up and out to the horizon. The large, smeary bay window revealed a desolate summer scene. The tide was a long way out, further than he could see, so as far as anyone knew it was just gone for good and had left the town permanently inland. It took a lot of trust to believe the water would ever come back each day, all that distance, it seemed like an awful amount of labour for no good reason. ▶

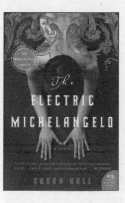

An Excerpt from *The Electric Michelangelo*
(continued)

The whole dirty, grey-shingled beach was now bare, except for one or two souls out for a stroll, and one or two hardy sunbathers, in their two-shilling-hire deck-chairs, determined to make the most of their annual holiday week away from the mills, the mines and the foundries of the north. A week to take in the bracing salty air and perhaps, if they were blessed, the sun would make a cheerful appearance and rid them of their pallor. A week to remove all the coal and metal dust and chaff and smoke from their lungs and to be a consolation for their perpetual poor health, the chest diseases they would eventually inherit and often die from, the shoddy eyesight, swollen arthritic fingers, allergies, calluses, deafness, all the squalid cousins of their trade. One way to tell you were in this town, should you ever forget where you were, should you ever go mad and begin not to recognize the obvious scenery, the hotels, the choppy water, the cheap tea rooms, pie and pea restaurants, fish and chip kiosks, the amusement arcades, and the dancehalls on the piers, one way to verify your location was to watch the way visitors breathed. There was method to it. Deliberation. They put effort into it. Their chests rose and fell like furnace bellows. So as to make the most of whatever they could snort down into them.

There was a wet cough to the left of him, prolonged, meaty, ploughing through phlegm, he felt the enamel basin being tugged from his hands and then there was the sound of spitting and throat clearing. And then another cough, not as busy as the last, but thorough. His eyes flickered, involuntarily.

66 The large, smeary bay window revealed a desolate summer scene. The tide was a long way out, further than he could see, so as far as anyone knew it was just gone for good and had left the town permanently inland. 99

Do not look down, he thought. He sighed and stared outside. The trick was to concentrate and pretend he was looking out to sea for herring boats and trawlers returning from their 150-mile search, pretend his father might come in on one of them, seven years late and not dead after all, wouldn't that be a jolly thing, even though the sea was empty of boats and ebbing just now. The vessels were presently trapped outside the great bay until the tide came back in. Odd patches of dull shining water rested on the sand and shingle, barely enough to paddle through, let alone return an absent father.

Outside the sky was solidifying, he noticed, as if the windowpane had someone's breath on it. A white horse was heading west across the sands with three small figures next to her, the guide had taken the blanket off the mare, the better that she be seen. As if she was a beacon. Coniston Old Man was slipping behind low cloud across the bay as the first trails of mist moved in off the Irish Sea, always the first of the Lake District fells to lose its summit to the weather. So the guide was right to uncover the horse, something was moving in fast and soon would blanket the beach and make it impossible to take direction, unless you knew the route, which few did in those thick conditions. Then you'd be stranded and at the mercy of the notorious tide.

—Grey old day, isnt it, luvvie? Not very pleasant for June.

—It is, Mrs Baxter. There's a haar coming in. Shall I be taking this now or will you need it again shortly do you think?

—No, I feel a bit better, now I'm cleared ▶

> 66 The trick was to concentrate and pretend he was looking out to sea for herring boats and trawlers returning from their 150-mile search, pretend his father might come in on one of them, seven years late and not dead after all. 99

> **❝** The woman
> watched him
> from her chair.
> She resembled
> a piece of boiled
> pork, or blanched
> cloth, with all
> her color
> removed. **❞**

out, you shan't be depriving me. And if I need to go again I'll try to make it to the washroom. You're a very good boy, Cyril Parks, your mammy should be proud to have a pet like you helping her around here. Well spoken and the manners of a prince. Is it a little chilly to have the sash open today, luvvie?

The woman watched him from her chair. She resembled a piece of boiled pork, or blanched cloth, with all her color removed. Just her mouth remained vivid, saturated by brightness, garish against her skin, and like the inside of a fruit when she spoke, red-ruined, glistening and damp.

—Yes, Mrs Baxter, I'm afraid it is. Would you like some potted shrimp? Mam made it fresh today.

—Oh yes. That would be lovely. I do so enjoy her potted shrimp, just a touch of nutmeg, not too heavy. . . .